THE SHOLTIE FLYER

By the same author

THREE GIRLS
LOST TIME
THE SHOLTIE BURN
MAEVE'S DAUGHTER
THE DISTAFF SIDE
MEN WHO MARCH AWAY

THE SHOLTIE FLYER

Frances Paige

SOUVENIR PRESS

First published 1990 by Souvenir Press Ltd,
43 Great Russell Street, London WC1B 3PA
and simultaneously in Canada

ISBN 0 285 62992 1

Photoset by Rowland Phototypesetting Ltd
Bury St Edmunds, Suffolk
Printed in Great Britain by
Mackays of Chatham plc, Chatham, Kent

1

Ginny McGrath, sitting behind the reception desk of the Sholton Hydropathic Hotel, or the Hydro as it was known in the village (as well as to hundreds of satisfied customers all over Scotland), flattered herself this particular morning that she gave the right impression for such a reputable establishment.

Most people knew it had been a Red Cross Hospital during the War, but not so many that it had been her cousin Lizzie's home, Sholton Hall, the ancestral home of Lizzie's first husband, the Honourable Nigel Garston Crawford, who had died in the Boer War before succeeding to the title. Jonty, their son, had been born posthumously.

The 'schoolboy shape', as decreed by Paris, and enthusiastically taken up as a sign of feminine emancipation even in Glasgow, demanded a slender figure. She had looked at herself earlier in a mirror in her comfortable quarters upstairs, and thought that her legs 'teetered' in the right way into the gleaming patent leather shoes with their pointed toes, that her Milanese silk stockings shone discreetly, that their seams were straight, and that fortunately her knees didn't look bony in spite of their slenderness.

She had used, very discreetly, Icilma face powder faintly tinted, and a matching lipstick which had a tiny pencil attached by a chain for outlining the curve of her mouth. Lizzie had agreed that make-up gave the necessary look of sophistication for receiving the public, without looking 'common'. 'Common' was a word which made Lizzie shudder, and she avoided like the plague what she thought was the least manifestation of it.

But she had drawn the line at Ginny cropping her hair. 'You and I, Ginny,' she had said, 'are blessed with the McGrath hair. Yours is more the colour of Grandma's than mine, but Ernest likes what he calls my "copper nob".' Ernest was her mentor and her dear love although they had been married for more than fourteen years.

So Ginny had compromised French fashion, by copying Giselle, her niece in Paris ('niece' being a joke since Giselle was her senior by thirteen years), and sweeping her red hair to the top of her head while allowing little ringlets to curl on the nape of her neck and round her ears. Dressed thus it didn't spoil the schoolboy contour, and if she were feeling romantic on her evening off, she well knew the devastating effect it had on males if she let it fall to her shoulders in a rich, tumbling mass.

Annabel, Lizzie's and Ernest's daughter, deplored the fact that her own hair was scanty and of a dun brown colour—hence her pet family name of 'Mouse', no doubt—but she had persuaded her mother to let her have it cropped, so that she looked, as Ginny told her, like Little Orphan Annie.

Hutcheson Girls' Grammar School in Glasgow had taken badly to this departure, but when Lizzie had explained to the headmistress that Annabel's hair wouldn't grow long enough to be plaited in the regulation style, she had given in. Everybody ended in giving in to Lizzie, Ginny thought, even me.

When she had returned home to Wanapeake on the Hudson River in August 1918, her job as a Red Cross Auxiliary nurse had finished. Plans were afoot, Lizzie's plans, for a further conversion, an hotel. The days of the Hall as a family home were also over. Lizzie hadn't demurred at her departure. She knew that Ginny worried about her parents, and that Sarah, her sister, had written to say their mother was getting frail.

She had even advised her not to be too independent, at least not to show it. 'So you want me to twist my wrists, put on a soulful air and find a suitor in America?' Ginny had joked. She knew that was one of her faults, appearing to treat everything as a joke. Lizzie had been cagey, and wise.

Ginny had returned six months ago, ostensibly on a visit with other members of the family, in time for the Great Unveiling of the Sholton Hydropathic Hotel, still unmarried (although she had enjoyed the attentions of several American males), still unsure, but drawn by some force, some hint of destiny to be found in this cold northern country . . .

Once she had satisfied herself about her mother's health she'd had the old feeling that she intruded on her parents' settled life. Sarah was better at it. Besides, she was suffering, although she hardly realised it, from a malaise, a questioning, now that the War was over, whether all that suffering and bereavement, although it hadn't personally affected her, had been worth it. In fact, at twenty-two she had grown up, but was not ready to settle down.

Then Lizzie had dropped her second bombshell. She was clever, Lizzie, and intuitive. 'What I'd like you to do,' she had said, 'is to stay on and manage this place for me. I'll be away from home with Ernest quite a lot now that he's finished with the War. (Not that the War had finished with Ernest!) 'And now that my mind is at ease about Jonty.' Ginny could appreciate that. She and Jonty, Lizzie's son by her first marriage, had always got on like a house on fire.

'You would be,' she had continued, 'what they call in France a *Directrice*.' Lizzie's spell when she was seventeen at a finishing school in Versailles had given her speech a Gallic flavour.

Ginny had played Lizzie's game, being cool about it, but had been lost in admiration. What a planner she was! Not a word said until she had arranged everything, stables converted into two houses, one for her and Ernest and the children, one for the aunts. 'Just like my mother,' Aunt Maevy had said. Who could resist Lizzie when she had the bit between her teeth?

'How much?' she had asked, coolly, then had nearly fallen off her chair at the magnificence of the sum. Who, indeed, could refuse an offer of £500 a year, trips abroad, free accommodation? So here she was . . .

'Annabel!' she said, looking up as the swing doors swung and the slight figure in 'Hutchy' uniform pushed through with a huge school-bag on her shoulders. The felt hat perched on top of the thin, pointed face looked like an outsize pudding bowl.

'You look like a fashion model sitting there.' The girl staggered towards the counter, shook and wiggled the bag off her shoulders and plumped it down.

'Not on the counter, please. At your feet.'

'You're as bad as Mother.' She did as she was told. 'How are you getting on, with her in Paris?'

'Fine. It's quiet just now. Everybody's holding back for a blow-out at the Christmas week. There are just a few regulars staying, and we had the Crannoch Ladies' Society here for lunch.'

'Had they someone speaking? They usually do.'

'Yes. A man.' Ginny rolled her eyes. 'A real live man in captivity.' She didn't say that the sight of him, shabbily dressed but clean, had made her heart wince. He looked hungry. And he had a tick which twisted the left side of his face. Shell-shock, she had registered. She had seen them like that in the hospital, comforted them at nights when they cried out in terror. His shirt was frayed. 'He came home from the War and found his wife had gone off with another man . . .' Her fertile imagination had filled in a possible background. 'I think he had agreed to talk for the sake of the lunch. "War Poets" was his subject. We had quite a chat. I told him about Jonty.' She didn't say that she had given him a good glass of sherry beforehand. Nor that she couldn't forget his eyes.

'Oh, well, it's better than a talk on how to make rag rugs. They persuaded Mother to go once and she said never again.'

'I can't see your mother making rag rugs.'

'I can't see her wearing a dress like yours. She'd like to, but Father always wants her to look glamorous rather than up to date.'

'Well, so she is. How are you and your brother getting on staying with the three aunts at the Stables?'

'Oh, it's great! Kit loves it too. And I can run into our own house for anything I want. They're funny-peculiar, the great-aunts. That's the latest Hutchy word. Maevy's the boss, of course, Kate keeps the peace, and Isobel—well, honestly, Ginny, she's *really* funny-peculiar. She tells me stories about the family, about the McGraths when they were all young ages ago and lived in a miner's cottage in Colliers Row with Great-Grandma and Great-Grandpa. Can you believe it? When you think that Great-Grandma was actually Lady Crawford when she died!'

'That was after her first husband died. She was simple Maeve McGrath, wife of Kieran McGrath, for most of her life. A real love-match. The two of them eloped from Ireland to come here when she was seventeen. He worked as a miner first and then they founded the McGrath Carting Company.'

'I know. So romantic.' She sighed. 'Still, I wish I could have gone with Mother and Father to Paris to see Jonty.' Her little face looked sad. She and her half-brother, despite his being six years older, were close friends, even more so than her true brother, Kit. At eleven everyone said Kit was a real throwback to the early McGraths in his love of country life. He showed none of Ernest's sophistication. Rabbiting with the village lads was more in his line.

'You miss Jonty?' Ginny asked her.

'Yes.' Her brown eyes were moist. 'I still think of him as the big brother who came home from Eton and played with me, instead of someone who ran away to become a soldier in the War. And now he's an art student at the Beaux-Arts in Paris. Oh, I do admire him!'

'Yes, he's a grand lad.' She saw Annabel's dejected look. She's missing her parents, she thought, despite the aunts. 'Have you got a lot of homework to do?'

'Not much.'

'Well, what about us having a swim next door—it's empty just now—and then afternoon tea in the Palm Court—' she smiled—'with lots of tea-time fancies? Aunt Kate will stand in for me. She's in the linen room. She always checks it on Friday. Your mother calls her the *châtelaine*.' She laughed.

'Mother would. But, I haven't a costume with me.' She didn't relinquish the dejected look too easily.

'There are bound to be spare ones there. You go and get ready. I'll find Aunt Kate.'

'All right.' Her eyes brightened. 'It'll be a bit of a *tare*. Is Erik there?'

'I expect so. There are one or two old codgers staying who like their daily massage. Why, have you fallen for him?'

'Mr Atlas! Not a chance. I don't like muscly men. I prefer Daddy's type, thin, and wiry, and with a brain-box.'

'That's what *you* say!'

'And he's fair-haired. I don't like fair-haired men. It's cissy!' She's getting on for fourteen now, Ginny thought, seeing the pink face. She's vulnerable. I bet they talk at school . . . but she'd forgotten the Mouse's darting mind. 'And what about you and Mr Pearson? I saw you looking at him like a sick calf the last time he was here.'

'Iain Pearson! That . . . mole!'

'That's no way to speak of the General Manager of McGraths.' Annabel's brown eyes were mischievous now.

'He's still a mole. Obsessed with drains. That's why he was here. And I *have* to look at him when he's talking to me, even about drains . . . go away and get ready. For a wee lassie you get awfy queer notions.' She liked to use the Scottish vernacular. She thought, for an American, she had picked it up quite well . . . but Iain Pearson, of all people!

The thought of him niggled as she went in search of Aunt Kate, the Hostess as she was generally called. She it was who went with the guests to their rooms when they arrived and saw that their material comforts were satisfied. And he was still in her mind when she walked through the Palm Court, formerly the Hall conservatory, and beyond that to the swimming bath. It and the Turkish Bath were Lizzie's and Jonty's creation. They both had flair, Jonty more than a flair since he was now studying Art so that he could join the McGrath firm in their Auctioneering and Valuating Department. Lizzie, she knew, had grandiose ideas about setting him up later as a Fine Art Dealer in Sauchiehall Street.

It had been Aunt Maevy's idea originally to give Jonty a place in McGraths when she saw how he had been ousted from his grandfather's firm, Crawford Iron and Steel Works. And who, she had said, wouldn't have made plans for the lad and him losing his father in the Boer War? Nigel had died fighting in South Africa, and so had been unable to fight against that usurper, Sir Edward Hamilton, who had got the ear of his dying father, Alastair, Lord Crawford . . . but the McGrath way was not to have regrets but to look ahead.

The idea for Jonty's career had come to Aunt Maevy when she had seen the accumulation of fine furniture in the McGrath depositories, which had been abandoned during or after the War, or which they had been asked to sell. Sadly it was often because the husband had been killed.

'I feel like a vulture,' she had said, but then business was business, and it hadn't prevented Lizzie from buying some of the choicer pieces which she had segregated against the day when Jonty might have that shop in Sauchiehall Street. Nor had it prevented her from furnishing the Hydro from the same source, paying the market value, of course.

Business was business, Ginny thought, and McGraths wouldn't be the place it was today if the McGrath family hadn't had a keen sense of 'how many beans made five'. Her father in America, Patrick, the second son, was concerned principally with transport and shipping, and he in turn was ably helped by Robert, the elder son of his brother, Terence, now living in Ireland and breeding horses.

He was the only one who didn't seem to have that keenness for business. But then, the love of horses was in the blood too. Their father, Kieran, had been a groom before he eloped from Ireland.

Annabel, in a bathing costume drooping round her budding breasts, was sitting at the edge of the tiled swimming bath. She beckoned Ginny urgently. 'Hurry up! That Erik is skulking about! This . . .' she looked down, pulling a face, 'is far too big for me. I've got no . . .'

Ginny laughed. 'Two ticks,' she said, and went into one of the mahogany-doored cubicles. 'Everything of the very best', as Lizzie would say.

Later, as they swam together in the limpid water, aquamarine because of the tiles, she thought how happy she was. Water always induced that feeling of well-being in her. The caress of it on her limbs and the weightlessness of her body . . . she somersaulted to demonstrate it and Annabel spluttered and said, 'Don't do that!' The sheer smooth pleasure of it all, like soft fingers stroking away all the petty irritations . . . like Iain Pearson, for instance.

Mouse was quite right. She *had* been looking at him, admiring his strong profile, the straight, haughty almost bridgeless nose, the high cheekbones, the well-shaped mouth—she hardly knew if his teeth were good or not because he had a way of smiling with clenched molars. But his eyes were bright and his hair grew thick and dark from his brow. And yet all he talked about was drains . . . and Lizzie.

She it was who had wheedled him into being an unpaid adviser for the plumbing system at the Hydro which, because of the numerous demands made upon it, needed a great deal of water—baths for the guests, the Turkish Bath, swimming bath, showers, laundry . . . The only water not under his control was the supply from the old well beside the ruined monastery on the hill, which at tremendous cost Lizzie had had led to a fountain in the entrance hall, or, as she preferred it to be called, the Pump Room.

It was the *pièce de résistance* of the Hydro, she liked to say. It had special properties, beneficial to the health. (If you said it often enough you believed it yourself.) Anyhow, the guests believed it, and followed slavishly the programme set out for them by Lizzie—a morning drink at the fountain, one before lunch, one before dinner (more people got to know each other at the fountain than anywhere else and not a few romances were started), followed by swimming, riding, golfing, massage if desired—a healthy mind in a healthy body and a bit of fun and games and dancing thrown in.

Hadn't she booked a real-life jazz band from London, no less, for the Christmas festivities? Although that was Ginny's idea. 'Modern dances like the Black Bottom are all the rage, Lizzie, and you couldn't expect the Crannoch Silver Band to play for that! They're all right for Military Twosteps. Whole families come at Christmas, and some of the young ones are home from Oxford and London where they're into the very latest . . .' And all Iain Pearson could talk about was drains! It was a blow to her pride, she who generally found that every man succumbed to her at sight.

'I have to tell you that you have a very nice movement, Miss Ginny.' Erik, the Swedish masseur, was standing at the side of the baths, a short towelling robe over his impressive collection of muscles. The shoulders of the dressing-gown stuck out as if he had a coat hanger in them, his chin was square, his teeth were white, his hair was like lint.

'Do you think so?' she said, swimming even more smoothly beside Annabel.

'Keep your head down, if you please. It is necessary to have the straight line from the head to the foot so that the fine body glides . . .'

'See,' Mouse said, 'everybody's mad about you, even Erik!'

Ginny swivelled her face towards her, keeping the head down since it was necessary to have the straight line. '*You* can have Mr Atlas,' she said softly, 'all muscle and no brain.'

They both burst into laughter, and Erik, pleased, flexed his pectoral muscles so that the towelling robe had a life of its own. 'You make the little joke, *hein*? I like the little joke . . .'

2

Jonty had looked forward all day to going to visit Giselle and Terence. His class had been taken to the Louvre for life drawing, and as he sat on a camp stool looking at the opulent curves of some Greek goddess, he had been conscious of that little *frisson* of excitement which had nothing to do with the antique figure. How satisfactory some French words were—*frisson*, a tiny shiver, a trembling. He saw it in his pencil from time to time as he drew.

Of course he was very fond of Terence and Giselle. Terence, who had been badly wounded and gassed at Verdun, was always interesting to talk to because he was a painter—so different from his brother Robert McGrath, a businessman *par excellence*—but then again their father wasn't at all conventional, and he didn't mean his horses. That was trivial in comparison with the bombshell his mother had dropped when he came home from France at the end of the War.

'Terence's and Robert's father is mine too. I know it's a shock. I was going to tell you when you came home from Eton, and then you joined up and ran off, without telling us. Oh, it was silly of me to wait so long!' He had never seen her so upset, his happy, beautiful mother, and yet he admired her courage. She could have given the job to Ernest, but no, she had told him herself, sitting across from him in the Hall drawing-room upstairs, he still with the sling on because of that damaged shoulder.

Incredible as it seemed to him even now, it appeared that Uncle Terence in Ireland, when he was married to Robert's and Terence's mother, had had an affair with a girl called Bessie Haddow, and Mother was the result! And even more incredible, Uncle Patrick, his brother, had married Bessie Haddow to give Lizzie a name. The poor soul had died shortly after the baby's birth.

'It's all in the past now, Jonty,' she had said, 'but you ought to know.'

'What a business!' he had said, inadequately, and then, 'Was that why Uncle Terence came out of McGraths and went to live in Ireland?'

'Yes, in Grandmother's old house, Woodlea. And married Aunt Honor who was living there, as Irish as they come. And now they're all as happy as Larry with his horses and her three daughters. His first marriage ended in tragedy. He found his wife dead in her bath with her wrists slashed.' She had been rueful. 'Presumably because of his carrying-on with my mother.'

'My God!' he had said, the first time he had ever sworn in her company. 'I always knew the McGraths were a rum lot!' And, the way you do when you're shaken, he had laughed and she had too. She had got up and knelt beside him, and put her arms round him.

'You're not far wrong, Jonty,' she had said, 'but you have to hand it to them, they live dangerously. And don't forget, you're not all Crawford blood, in spite of being lord of the manor!'

'So I should be proud to have a bit of the McGraths through you?' he had teased her.

'Of course you should. It's better than being as dull as ditch-water.' And as she patted his sling tenderly, 'You can put it in your poems.' They had all been about the War so far, but there was no harm in trying something new.

He came back to his visit tonight. Now that he thought about it, Terence could be moody. Could this temperament be like his mother's who had committed suicide? No, that was too far-fetched. He'd had a bad time at Verdun and he wasn't able to shake himself free of the memories.

He could sympathise. For ages he himself had had those terrible nightmares of Jimmy McAlpine rising from the mud of the Marne and waving his bloody stump at him, but Ellie, that clever cousin in America who had been a surgeon in a War hospital near Paris, had shown him how to get rid of them.

'Think of him alive, Jonty, not dead. I had to do it.' He knew that her lover had been killed, bombed to pieces in a hospital tent. 'And go and visit his parents in Luss. It will give them comfort to be able to say that their dead son's friend, Lord Crawford, came to see them.'

She had been right, but unfortunately Terence still seemed to have the Spectre looking over his shoulder although he had the best of wives in Giselle, and two lovely children, Clovis and Jaime. Some day *he* hoped he might have children . . .

And then, Mother and Ernest being in Paris and having been invited to the apartment at Passy also was grand. He was lucky in having parents who never gave him any worry, although they could drop bombshells, at least Mother! But, strangely enough, he had felt quite tender towards her after she had told him about being Uncle Terence's child, protective, adult. And there was no doubt she was beautiful and clever, running that Hydro helped by Ginny—good old Ginny—and Ernest was tip-top, never rattled, always cool, with that wry smile of his. He remembered an expression for categorising people he had used at Eton: 'variable' or 'non-variable'. The parents were non-variable.

And Madeleine, Giselle's friend, would be there . . . once again the *frisson*. He had met her several times when he was visiting the apartment at Passy. He had called one Sunday and found them out. Madeleine was taking care of the children.

'I like doing it,' she had told him, 'I looked after Clovis when Jaime was born, and then the two of them when Giselle was visiting Terence in that Army hospital at Condé.' She wasn't like anyone he had ever met, especially someone who looked after children. 'You see, I haven't any of my own.' Her husband had been killed at Mons.

Giselle told him that she and Madeleine had been at school together. 'I think she's the most attractive woman I've met so far,' he had said, and regretted it when he saw how she looked at him. Perhaps there had been something in his eyes.

'What age are you, Jontee?' she had asked, smiling at him in that French way. By Jove, she was seductive too. 'Nineteen,' he had said, thinking that since he had fought with the Cameronians in that last final assault—his mind skipped over the terrible parts to that triumphant entry into Clary with the bagpipes playing and the flowers—it was a ridiculously young age to be.

'Madeleine is the same age as me, thirty-five.' Those great dark kohled eyes of hers had looked at him. Had they been saying, 'Be careful'?

* * *

She was there, with that animal quietness about her, a secret quietness, and so were Mother and Ernest. He went to greet them, enjoying like a child his mother's warm embrace, the perfumed beauty of her. 'Jonty, son! You look quite French, doesn't he, Ernest? I do like your cravat. Very Bohemian! Oh, you look wonderful!'

He laughed, pleased, as she released him. 'Ernest! Great to see you!' They clasped hands. Ernest whacked him on the shoulder.

'Good to see *you*. How are your studies going?'

'Fine. Florence next, I hope. I was in the Louvre all day drawing naked women.' He wasn't usually so *risqué* in his talk before ladies. He knew he was showing off.

Giselle had come from the kitchen to greet him, kissing him on both cheeks. 'Isn't it wonderful, Jontee? Your parents here in Paris especially to see you.'

'Not if I know Ernest. He'll have someone else to see, maybe Clemenceau himself!'

'Who knows?' Ernest was urbane. It was perfectly conceivable to think of Ernest having a civilised talk with the old *Tigre*.

'Hello, Madeleine.' He made himself walk casually as he went to greet her. Her hand was cool in his.

'Don't I get a kiss too?' Her voice was slow, and soft.

'Why not?' He bent and kissed each cheek in turn. They were like warm velvet and her perfume was different from Mother's, heavier. It seemed to settle inside his head.

'Madeleine has offered to sit with the children,' Giselle said, 'because Ernest insists on taking us to Maxim's. Isn't he kind?'

Ernest smiled. 'It's Madeleine who's kind. Especially as it's only to let Lizzie show off her new Patou gown.'

'Is it that one, Mother?' You could admire women's gowns in France. It was of grey chiffon on a copper satin base and it dipped on either side so that it showed her shapely legs. The copper colour matched her hair and she wore yellow opals.

'Ginny thinks I'd never dare to wear the short skirts. I'm getting the best of both worlds.' Lizzie made the side draperies lift and flutter, smiling. Trust Mother . . . He said to Madeleine:

'Poor you, missing all the fun.'

'No, no, *pas du tout*. The children are no trouble, and I will get some reading done. I work now, you know.'

'Oh, do you?' He was intrigued by the sheenless, honey-coloured hair, its thickness and heaviness, like a lion's mane, and the contrast of the dark eyes. Her nose was thin and straight, peculiarly French.

'Yes, in an office. I like it. I'm a modern woman, you know.' The heavy, dull hair swung as she moved her head. 'We have the vote now.' For women over thirty, he remembered.

'You should meet our Aunt Maevy,' Lizzie said. 'She was a Suffragette and still takes an active part in the Movement, besides running our firm when Ernest is away.'

'*Admirable*, but that is not my way.' Her smile was deliciously slow. He stood looking at her for a fraction too long before he remembered himself. Giselle was at his elbow with a glass of wine. 'To fortify you after a hard day's work, Jontee.'

'Painting naked women?' Madeleine said. Her eyes ran along her lids and she smiled again. That damned *frisson*.

'Where's Terence, Giselle?' he said, to hide his embarrassment.

'In his studio. Would you go and tell him we'll have to leave soon? We're meeting my mother and father there, so we shouldn't be too late.'

'It will be lovely to see Emily again,' Lizzie said. 'I've very happy memories of my visits to Monceau Park—when I was at school at Versailles. Your father was most hospitable, too.'

'When he was there.' Giselle laughed. This was a family joke, Jonty knew. Charles Barthe was supposed to have a love-nest somewhere—to escape from Emily.

Lizzie was laughing too. 'Remember he loaned you his Delaunay-Belville for our honeymoon, Ernest? We picked it up at your parents' country house at Château-sur-Epte. And how are your twin brothers? Is Olivier married?'

'No, not yet, but Marc's little Fabrice is a year and a half now. Yes, those were happy days, weren't they?' Jonty saw her face sadden momentarily.

'Is your mother still holding her salons?' Ernest asked.

'Oh, yes!' Giselle laughed. 'She regrets the end of the War in some ways. You know *Maman* . . .'

Jonty found Terence in his studio staring at a painting on an easel. He glanced quickly over his shoulder when he heard him come in. 'Hello. Have you been sent in to hurry me up?'

'Yes. How is it going?'

'Hopeless.' He looked down. 'It's this hand.' Jonty saw its deformity, the crooked fingers as if the tendons had contracted. It didn't seem to be improving in spite of several operations. 'Some days it seems to have a will of its own. Nothing goes right. I try and try . . . but I can't seem to get the likeness.' There was a half-finished portrait of a man on the easel. 'Then I spoil the whole thing by tinkering, the colour gets muddy, it's over-worked . . .' His thin face was drawn.

'They tell me it's best to take yourself away from it for a bit, then you can see it with a fresh eye. I . . . I find that with my poems.' He was hesitant, wanting to cheer him.

'I know. This is a bad day. But if I don't paint, and sell, we don't eat.' He began to clean his brushes, swilling them about in a turpentine jar. Drying them with a rag, he turned to Jonty as if making an effort to be sociable. 'So Paris is conducive to your writing?'

'Oh, it's only scribbling. But sometimes when I'm tired they seem to come more easily, maybe before I go to sleep.' He didn't say they were all love poems.

'Good, good!' His cheerfulness was forced. 'So now we're all going out for a jolly party? Ernest is always generous.'

'Yes, he was the same when I was at school, he spoiled me.

Maybe that's why I ran away to the War.' He laughed. 'But I'm glad I did.' He shouldn't have said that.

'Glad? Well, yes, I suppose we ought to be glad to be alive . . .' The cheerfulness had left him again. He said abruptly, 'I'd better go and get changed.'

When he went back to the sitting-room Madeleine was there alone. Her brown eyes seemed black in the shadow, and he thought how warmly pale her skin was, as if it reflected the tarnished gold from her hair.

'They've gone to see the children. They won't be long.'

'Terence is changing.'

'How did you find him?'

'*Distrait*.'

'Yes, that's a good word. Sometimes it's as if people don't exist for him. Even Giselle.'

'You're good friends. What does she think about it?'

'She's worried, of course, but nobody could be more practical. She thinks it may be because he loses a lot of sleep with coughing. That gas at Verdun ruined his chest.' She shook her head. 'Some times I think I was lucky that Paul died.'

'Your husband?'

'Yes. At least I didn't have to look at him day after day, still suffering . . .' That damned War, he thought. Everybody was still paying. The futility of it, the futility even of his 'noble' gesture . . . He sat down beside her.

'I have an American cousin, Ellie. She's very clever, a surgeon. She helped me . . . bury the dead.'

'That's what Terence needs.' She paused. There was a look of almost smiling disbelief on her face. 'You . . . you must have been incredibly young when you joined up!'

'Seventeen.' He laughed. 'I lied about my age. Now I . . . wonder why.'

'Lied?'

'No, went at all.'

'Oh, don't be too defeatist. Otherwise it makes Paul's death . . . unnecessary.' Her dark eyes were on him, considering, 'It probably made you grow up more quickly.'

'Do you think so?' He felt sure of himself, masterful. What luck to be sitting so close to her. He could see the velvet quality of her brown eyes now, and the fine texture of that colourless skin which wasn't really *pâle*.

'I think so.' She nodded, still looking at him. 'There are young boys in our office, but you do not look like them. You look . . . *mûr*.' It made him feel like a ripe pear.

'Mature,' he said, savouring the word nevertheless, smiling at her. He remembered saying to Ellie in response to some comment she had made, 'You cheeky thing. I'm a veteran!' 'Where is your office, Madeleine?' he asked her.

'Near the Beaux-Arts.' Her eyes met his.

'Near the Beaux-Arts . . .' He heard voices in the hall, said quickly, 'I could meet you after work tomorrow. We could have a coffee, talk some more about . . . things, Terence . . .'

'That would be nice.' She didn't jump at the invitation as a young girl might. 'The address is 33, rue Bonaparte.' She spoke in French, very quickly.

'Five o'clock?'

'D'accord.' Close to like this she didn't look like thirty-five. She looked no age, any age, the best of ages, a mature woman for a mature man. *Mûr.* He got up as Lizzie came into the room, smiling, her beautiful face lit up with pleasure. Would she see anything in *his*? Mothers were the limit.

* * *

He was trembling, and at the same time, very mature, *mûr*, nineteen and going to meet a wordly Frenchwoman of thirty-five . . . yes, you could call her *mondaine*. And she looked it as she came towards him in a narrow black hat slanting across her forehead with the thick honey roll of her hair showing smoothly underneath. Her coat was short, and narrow like her hat, her heels high.

'Quelle surprise!' she said, smiling, teasing him as they shook hands. He didn't dare kiss her in the street.

'Didn't you expect me to come?' he said. He was wearing a flowing black tie and a broad-brimmed black hat. It occurred to him they might look as if they were going to a funeral.

'I never expect, so I am never disappointed, yes?'

'I suppose that's wise, but I am very reliable. Non-variable.' He grinned.

'Qu'est-ce que c'est?' They were blocking the pavement, the *trottoir*—she even made him think in French.

'Shall we walk towards St-Germain?'

'Oui, certainement. Excuse me. I speak French all day long, but I love to practise the English.'

'It's good. Very good.' He wondered if he should offer her his arm but decided against it. It might look all right in some parts of France but here the students were much more informal. An arm round the shoulder, perhaps . . . '"Non-variable"? Sorry. It means I don't change. I'm faithful.'

'All men say that. I have not much time, Jontee. Is that right?' She pronounced it like Giselle.

'Yes. I'm really Nigel Jonathan, but that's too much of a mouthful.'

'Nigel Jonathan Garston, Lord Crawford. Giselle teaches me. A *bonne mouche*.' She smiled up at him, that slow, promising smile. Even in her high black heels she still only came up to his shoulder. Frenchwomen were *petite*, of course. Ginny, on the other hand, was only a few inches smaller than he was.

'I thought we might have a drink at the *Deux Magots*?'

'I thought you would say that.' Her smile was teasing again. 'Yes, of course, we go there.'

He couldn't have offered her his arm in any case. They were constantly separated. The streets were busy with students, *midinettes*, office workers, *tout le monde* hurrying home.

'You like the Left Bank?' she said.

'Oh, yes, it's the only place to be. Don't you live here?'

'No, I live in a little village.'

'Do you?' He turned to her in surprise. 'I thought you lived in Paris?'

'Of course, but it is a city of little villages. Mine is the Palais Royal, a courtyard off the rue des Petits-Champs. We were lucky to find an apartment in that *quartier*. Paul's parents bought it for us. They said I must continue to live there when he . . . died.'

'Isn't it a rich district?'

'Perhaps, but not in the usual sense. Its associations are rich. Paul was a writer. It suited him. Cocteau lives near us, although I don't know him. It's full of quaint little shops and streets. It has an *originalité*.'

'It sounds delightful, but I like it round here. Have you seen the Unicorn Tapestries in there?' They were passing the Cluny Museum. He was casual, as befitted an art student.

'Parisians don't go to museums,' she said, limpid, 'we leave that for the visitors.'

'Touché!' What a cliché, he thought. 'I like it here because it's young.' A young couple had passed them, arms round each other. He wished he hadn't said that. Did it sound as if he thought the Palais Royal was old, or that *she* was?

'Ah, yes,' she said, 'this is the place for students to dream dreams, and why not? How long are you here for, Jontee?'

'Only a year. Florence is really where I'll study. This is a general course to get me used to the French language.'

'You speak it very well.'

'*Pas du tout*. My mother is much better, but then she's good at everything.'

'You admire your mother. I can see it in your eyes.'

'Yes, I suppose I always have.'

'She's very beautiful, *lumineuse*, loved. One senses it. And Monsieur Murray-Hyslop is her second husband?'

'Yes, my father was killed in the last War. I have a younger half-brother and sister, a good deal younger than me.'

'Is that possible?'

'You're teasing me.' He put his arm through hers involuntarily and squeezed it. He would have done the same with Ginny.

'Yes, I mustn't. It's naughty. And stupid.' She seemed to lean slightly towards him. 'Giselle told me about you fighting in the War. That was brave when you didn't have to go. Perhaps because of your father? You were lucky to come home.'

'Yes, I know I'm lucky.' What had her husband, Paul, been like, he wondered. Had she been grief-stricken? Was that why she teased, to hide her constant grief? But it must have been four years ago, if he were killed at Mons . . .

When they were sitting in a tiny corner table at the *Deux Magots* —he had thankfully taken off the broad-brimmed hat—he said to her, 'Perhaps I have been a little tactless even mentioning your husband. Mother has told me of how she felt when my father died—he caught typhoid at Ladysmith . . .'

'No, no, Jontee.' She put her hand on his across the table, a white hand with long narrow fingers, a cabochon on one of them. 'I don't mind. People tend to keep quiet to spare one, they think. That is not the way. One wishes to talk and talk. There I was lucky. Giselle listened to me endlessly, wiped my tears often. Oh, she's a good friend! That is why I am pleased to do anything to help her now.' Did she mean accept an invitation from him? 'With her problem.'

'Oh, you mean Terence?' He tried not to look relieved.

'Yes. It is sad. He was beginning to be recognised as one of the best of the young painters before he enlisted. And having Charles Barthe as a father-in-law was a great asset. He is influential. He got him commissions. You know his forte is portraiture. But, *hélas*, he starts with enthusiasm, and then it goes. People don't ask him again . . .'

'He's ill.' He remembered the unease he had felt when he'd gone into Terence's studio.

'Yes, it is a malaise. You saw him in one of his bad spells, perhaps. When he feels well he is the most charming of men. You see the quandary it is for Giselle . . . Perhaps I shouldn't be talking like this.'

'He is a relative of mine. Family.'

'*C'est vrai*. Well, the commissions have grown less. If you don't work, you don't earn. And Giselle is very independent. She won't accept help from her parents.'

'It's early days yet. When he's really well things will improve.'

'Yes, that is so. At least he is alive. He is here.' She sighed. 'All I have left is a half-finished book, and memories. Paul liked to enjoy himself instead of . . .'

'Getting down to it?'

'What does that mean?'

'Getting on with the work. I know how difficult it is.' He said shyly, 'I'm by way of being a writer too. I've had a book of poems published.' *Sprowsing*, he thought, a family word. Mother kept them alive.

She nodded, appraising him. 'I am not surprised. You have the artistic temperament. It is a gift, but sometimes a worry for the wife. She sometimes wonders where the money is to come from. But you are different, of course. You are an English lord.'

He laughed. 'No, no, a Scottish one, if it counts for anything. To tell you the truth, Madeleine—' he liked the sound of her name—'I never honestly think of myself as one, but yes, you're right. I have the family backing and support. There's a place waiting for me in McGraths, that's the family firm, but if I choose to write or paint, that's all right. Yes, I'm very lucky, at the beginning of my career . . .' He felt ingenuous, nineteen, and yet he had fought in the War, seen and done terrible things. They had sloughed off, like a bad dream, as if they had never happened. It was strange. He would have to write a poem about 'Reality'. What was it, after all? *This* was real enough, sitting opposite this woman of thirty-five in the *Deux Magots* café in Paris. This was *living*. The War had been a grim day-to-day existence with occasional flashes of excitement or fear, and constantly being hungry . . .

'That's what I like about you, Jontee.' That seductive quality of her voice, its huskiness, as if it came from the back of her throat. 'You recognise your good fortune. Perhaps it is that you are more able to appreciate it having seen the back side, is that how you say it?'

'The other side of the coin perhaps,' he said, twisting his mouth in an effort not to laugh.

'Ah, yes, the other side . . . Were you an officer?'

'No, there wasn't time for that. I ran away from school, you see.' He remembered the decent letter he'd had from his master at Eton, not condoning, but understanding. 'I mucked in with the men. That's an appropriate expression. Muck. It's a Scottish word for "mud". I saw plenty of that.'

There was sadness in her eyes. He was always putting his big foot in it. How had her Paul died? In the mud at Mons? He thought of those terrible water-filled holes at Ravebeek, the bloated corpses floating in them, bits of everything, thought for the first time for many months of Jimmy McAlpine, that good friend. There were no more nightmares now, thanks to Ellie . . .

'Do you ever have *cauchemars*?' Madeleine said.

He shook his head, surprised that she was reading his mind. 'No, not now. I did when I first came home.'

'Giselle says Terence does. He shouts out in terror . . . oh, dear!' she had glanced at the clock on the wall, 'I must go now. Somehow we have become sad. That I don't like. I know you think of Paris as a city of gaiety. I must not destroy your illusions.' She was pulling on her black gloves with the white veining on their backs. 'Frenchwomen are very careful about the details,' Mother had said, as if *she* weren't.

'Shall I take you home?'

'No, thank you. I will take a cab. Someone . . . waits.'

'Yes, of course . . .' It *had* been a put-up job with Giselle. Or even if it hadn't, it would be foolish to imagine that there was anything more in it than a mature woman being kind to a young man, lord or no lord. He cursed his title, although ordinarily he never thought of it. And it had been a bloody nuisance to him in the War, like having a birthmark or a stain . . . funny, when he thought of the War he automatically swore.

'It was good of you to spare the time,' he said, rising to help her out of her corner seat.

'*Pour moi c'était un grand plaisir*. Next time perhaps we will talk about happy things.' Did she mean perhaps they would talk about happy things, or *perhaps* there might not be a next time?

He saw her into the cab. Her ankles were slim above the high heels, and her seams were as straight as a die. Mother would have liked that.

3

Aunt Kate came rushing into Ginny's office on the morning after Christmas . . . that is, if Aunt Kate's dignified but hurried gait could be called 'rushing'.

'Calamity,' she said. 'One of the gardeners has just come in to say that the girls' bus has gone into a tree on the drive!'

'My goodness!' She got up from her seat. 'Is anyone hurt?'

'No, he said definitely not. I should have said "slid". Walter was going slowly because of the ice. He skidded, went off the drive and came up against a tree.'

'I'll get the Morris out and go down.'

'Get one of the electricians.'

'No, they're all fixing up the lights. I'll go. Some of the old ones may have got a bit of a shock. Maggie and Bunty are over fifty.'

'"Older"' Aunt Kate said, 'not "old". They're younger than me.' Since she had taken on the job of hostess in the Hydro she had lost some of her sweetness. Or maybe it was living with Aunt Maevy that had done it.

'Would you keep an eye on the office while I'm gone, Aunt? I'm bringing the guests' bills up to date. Don't bother with that. When Aunt Isobel comes she'll relieve you.'

Before opening the Hydro Lizzie had put the three aunts on the board, more as a gesture than anything else, but they had proved their weight in gold. Aunt Kate welcomed guests, Aunt Maevy was available at weekends for anything to do with health or hygiene—although she was a partner in McGraths she hadn't forgotten her early nursing experience and liked to exercise it—and Aunt Isobel with her talent for figures was a valuable standby in the office if Nan Porter or her assistant didn't turn up.

She left Aunt Kate at the reception desk—her tranquillity had soothed many an irate guest—and hurried off to the garage to get out the Morris.

It *would* happen on the day of the big Ball. Most of the guests had arrived, fortunately, but the bus might be blocking the drive. There would be a constant to-ing and fro-ing of caterers' vans and so on, and in any case, the waitresses were needed for taking tea to the bedrooms and for waiting at breakfast.

The dining-room would have to be cleared up quickly so that they could have an early lunch. And the bus was needed again to ferry the girls who came specially to the Hydro to serve afternoon tea. Today's tea was going to be a party occasion in the ballroom for the children, with balloons and games, so that they would be tired enough to be safely in bed before the grown-ups began their festivities.

And there was that jazz band coming from London. Lizzie had over-stretched herself there, surely. They were costing an awful lot of money, but on the other hand, the Silver Tongues, she and Lizzie had agreed, were enough to draw the guests from as far as the Borders. There was actually a family coming from Newcastle-upon-Tyne! And there were plenty of smart young men and women amongst the regular families who had been attracted by the reputation of the Silver Tongues. Oh, it was going to be a wonderful night if everything went well.

She saw as she drove slowly down the drive that the concrete tennis court which they had flooded—Iain Pearson had been the guiding factor there—was satisfactorily frozen over. That had been a good idea. There were Jimmy and his cohorts fixing up the lights for the skating party which was to take place between tea and dinner. Then it would be hot baths for everyone, if the boilers didn't play up, and into their finery for the Ball . . . Oh, dear, she hoped the bus wasn't damaged. It was going to be needed all day.

Ginny, she told herself, you're unfeeling. What about the girls? How her mind skated about from boilers to buses and even Iain Pearson!

Ahead of her there were two stout figures walking briskly, and as she drew nearer she saw that it was Bunty and Maggie, arm-in-arm. And they were laughing! The nerve of it, and she worried out of her mind! She slowed down and drew up carefully, calling to them, 'Are you all right, girls?' The waitresses were 'girls' whatever their age.

'Och aye,' Bunty said, waving. 'It was a great tare. Walter couldny help it. Maybe it was the weans yesterday, sliding. "Here we go, lassies," he said. He couldn't dae a thing! The rough grass roon the trees stoaped him, luckily.'

'There's no one hurt?'

'No, they're all as right as rain. That wee Jenny is having a bit of a greet but she's only fifteen.'

'Hop in and we'll see how they're getting on.'

'No, no,' Maggie said. 'We'll keep walking. Your Aunt Kate will want us to get on with the bedroom teas.'

'All right. Thanks.' She waved and drove away.

She found a disconsolate Walter standing by the bus, surrounded by a chattering crowd of waitresses. By their flushed faces it seemed they had been trying to push it on to the road. She stopped the motor and got out.

'It wisny ma fawt, Miss Ginny,' Walter said. 'A just slid, nice and slow, aff the road, didn't I, lassies?'

'Aye, aye,' they chorused, 'it wisny his fawt.'

'No one's hurt?'

'No . . .' They looked at one another.

'Where's Jenny?' A thin little girl with her hair drawn back from a pale face came from the back. Her face was tear-stained.

'Suppose you come back with me in the motor, Jenny,' Ginny said, 'and any of the others who want a lift.' They all shook their heads. And to Walter, 'I'll tell the electricians who're working at the tennis court to come and help you get the bus back on the drive. I hope it's all right. We need it in good working order to meet the train today. And you girls, get back to the Hydro and see that you get a good cup of hot tea and a sit-down before you start.' They were all right, the Sholton woman, they had plenty of spunk.

The day sped on. The Silver Tongues were collected at the station by the bus, put on the road by the combined efforts of the electricians, the plumbers, and of course, Walter; the afternoon tea-party was going smoothly, helped along by the three aunts who dearly loved the children.

Aunt Kate had left her grandchildren in America to come to live here; Aunt Maevy wasn't likely to see hers for some time as Ellie's second child, Betsy Ann, was too young to travel; but Aunt Isobel, who had neither children nor grandchildren, was perhaps the best of the lot when it came to dealing with them.

Since her husband had died she had become a person in her own right—slightly eccentric, almost childlike at times, but a marvel when it came to figures. Nobody could add up a guest's account more quickly than Aunt Isobel. It was perhaps her very quaintness which made her a success with the little ones. Kate and Maevy, while the essence of motherly kindness, would never get down on the floor beside them as their sister did, the 'fragile wee thing'. Somehow, when you were thinking of her, you always added that.

Lizzie had invited Ginny for a pre-dinner drink at the Stables where she now lived next door to the aunts. Jonty was home and it would give her a chance to have a chat with him before she got swallowed up in the running of the Hydro from dinner onwards. There were endless things to be seen to, not least of all the ballroom. She must see that the floor was polished again after the children's party tea.

And the Silver Tongues must be made to feel it was worth their while to travel all the way from London. A brief glimpse of them when they had arrived had made her wonder about the name they had chosen for themselves. Four of them were insignificant-looking men speaking with a Cockney accent, and the fifth was black, a shiny black with an open white smile and broad shoulders, who at least looked the part.

She had a quick bath along the corridor (she had vacated her comfortable first-floor quarters for an attic bedroom because of the pressure on accommodation), and got into her dress (pale oyster satin, knee length), silver stockings, a white camellia in her hair. The silver theme which Lizzie had planned had to be carried out to the last detail. Silver, high-heeled sandals. Yes, not bad, she thought, taking a quick look in the mirror, a quick *skoosh* of that expensive perfume which Lizzie had brought her from Paris, her silver bag and fringed shawl, and off to the Stables.

What a good thing she had learned to drive, she thought, as she followed the road which ran behind the Hydro through the extensive grounds, then over the pack bridge where it became little more than a bridle path before it reached the cottages. Lizzie had said she would have the road broadened as Ernest drove over it every day *en route* for McGraths' Glasgow office. Aunt Maevy travelled with him. She had declared she would never learn to drive, but that was understandable, since Uncle Charlie had been killed in a motor car.

Belle Geddes, his assistant doctor in the practice, had been driving. Some said that was what had made her a spinster. I wonder what *she*'ll wear tonight, Ginny thought. Even now, at forty-two, Belle could still surprise with those strange eyes—no colour, really, except that in certain lights they gleamed silver. A strange woman, attractive in an unexplainable way. She had seen Iain Pearson looking at her speculatively. But, then, he was just as secretive. No one knew anything of his private life. Oh, to the devil with him, she thought, echoing her grandmother Maeve unknowingly, as she drew up at Lizzie and Ernest's front door.

Jonty opened it to her, smiling. 'Come in, come in. You aren't the last, although Mother says you run the Hydro single-handed!'

'Rubbish!' She put her arms round him. 'Oh, you're so smart! I expect you *slay* all those smart Parisian girls!'

'Naturally.' He hugged her in return. 'They're lying in rows in the rue St-Honoré.' When he released her she thought his cheeks were flushed. Was he involved with someone already? His good looks and charm were bound to cause a furore, not to mention his title. She believed the French were very susceptible to titles. She threw her shawl on a chair and went into the sitting-room, Jonty's arm round her shoulders.

What a satisfactory room Lizzie had made of it, she thought, by taking advantage of the height of the stables and having a gallery running round for the bedrooms which were approached by a winding staircase from the sitting-room—the McGrath flair.

'Here's Miss Hydropathic!' Ernest came towards her, always urbane, she thought, his sandy hair smooth to his head, more dapper than his son in his immaculate tails, his white buttonhole. 'Are you exhausted, Ginny?'

'No, not a bit of it. We had a *contretemps* with the bus this morning. It ran into a tree.' She glanced at Aunt Maevy, thinking, I shouldn't have said that, but her face was calm. She was the most 'complete' woman Ginny had ever known, always in command of herself, and of others if it were necessary.

'Kate told us,' she said, 'and if she hadn't, we got the whole story again from Isobel.'

The three sisters were seated on one of the huge sofas to one side of a cheerful log fire. Lizzie had said mischievously that she had got the sofas big enough to let the aunts sit together. 'They're entirely different but they have grown so close.' It was lovely to see, Ginny thought, bending to kiss them in turn.

'Hello, everybody!' It was Belle Geddes at the door and behind her the tall figure of Iain Pearson. 'Iain and I let ourselves in.'

'Quite right.' Lizzie went forward to greet them, in black this evening, severe, but backless, swinging diamond earrings, her copper hair dressed high. The whole effect spelled Paris. 'You've let yourself go tonight, Belle. Your dress is absolutely beautiful.'

'It cost me my entire month's salary, but I know what the competition is like around here.' She smiled at the aunts, taking in Ginny. 'I had to do something about it.' Ginny came forward to kiss her.

'It's a lovely dress, Belle. All that bead work. And the drapery! They'll be fighting to dance with you at the Ball.'

'That will be the day. Thanks, Ernest.' She took a glass of sherry from him. 'Just what the doctor ordered, for herself.' She laughed round at Iain. 'Nobody's complimenting the general manager of McGraths on *his* outfit!'

'Oh, I'm used to being eclipsed at the Hydro with all those

beautiful ladies floating around.' He was quite composed. I've never seen him flustered, Ginny thought. That's what's so irritating . . .

'Have you come to see about the drains, Iain?' she laughed, turning to Lizzie. 'Do you remember, Lizzie, when you and I were sitting in the Palm Court having tea—it was when you were offering me the job—and Iain came in . . .'

'That was over six months ago,' Iain said, straight-faced. 'I must have made a great impression.'

'It wasn't that.' She hid her discomfiture. 'It was just that the first thing you said was, "I've been looking at the drains."' She was losing out.

'Did I? Word for word, eh?' Everyone laughed.

'Oh, you!' she said, defeated. 'Anyhow, I'm not going to talk about the Hydro here. It's been quite a day, but it's always right on the night.'

'I'm sure it will be. You manage things so beautifully.' He was having difficulty in controlling a smile.

'Now you're trying to sugar me up.'

'I'm not, I assure you. I thought that Christmas Eve Carol Service you organised was really good. I'm glad you sent me an invitation.' There was a chorus of agreement from the others.

'That was all Ginny's idea.' Lizzie took over. 'The older guests tend to get left out with the younger ones dashing about skating and dancing and having parties in their rooms . . .' She laughed. 'Well, the less said about that the better. Jonty's great-grandfather would rise up in his grave.'

'Mother used to tell us about him presenting prizes at the Sunday School picnic,' Maevy said.

'And how she met his son, Alastair, at one of them.' Aunt Isobel looked too innocent.

'And the less said about *that* the better.' This was Ernest.

'Well, she *did* marry him when Grandfather McGrath died,' Ginny said.

'Let's not open family cupboards when we have company,' Ernest smiled wryly.

'All right.' She laughed. 'What surprised me about the Carol Service was the number of young ones who came as well. They helped me to light the candles. We had over a hundred. The lights were off, the room was shadowy, and when you looked out of the big windows and saw the snow on the park, it was beautiful.' She was still standing beside Iain Pearson.

'What did it remind you of?' he said. There was no teasing in his voice.

'Home, I suppose. Far across the sea.' She laughed but she knew her eyes were moist. 'Christmas always makes you think of home. They can't put up with me there,' she shrugged, 'but home's home.'

'Everybody wants to be at home at Christmas.' Jonty had joined them. 'Though leaving Paris was quite a wrench.'

'I know why,' Ginny said, 'you've left someone languishng there, a beautiful Parisian lady . . .' She thought she saw a tinge of colour again.

'I can go back to her again, can't I?' They had always teased each other. There might be nothing in it. And yet, looking at him talking to Iain, she thought, my boy is growing up (that had always been her secret name for him), he's becoming like other men, even to shutting her out of the manly conversation he was having with Iain about motors.

They would probably be staggered to know that she had changed a wheel on the Morris, and that under the bonnet was no mystery to her. She took her mechanical turn of mind from her father. Ah, but my boy's special . . . She realised that Iain Pearson was looking at her, contemplatively, as he listened. It disturbed her. 'I must have a word with Belle,' she said, moving towards her where she stood at the fire talking to Ernest.

'You look like a Greek goddess, Belle,' she said, 'in that beaded gown. A shimmering green column!' They both laughed and Belle's eyes gleamed in silver pinpoints through her half-closed lids. What a secret woman she was, so truly sophisticated. How did one acquire that poise? Through experience?

4

The Ball had just started when they arrived at the Hydro. The music of the Silver Tongues had drawn the guests like the Pied Piper from the Palm Court, the lounge, and even their bedrooms. The band, resplendent in silver tailed suits, were playing the appropriate 'Jingle Bells' with a great deal of panache and a waving of silver saxophones. The black man looked magnificent as he stepped forward and sang, full-throated, '"Jingle bells, Jingle bells, jingle all the way . . ."' giving an exotic sound to the words.

Lizzie turned, laughing, to Ginny who was standing beside her. 'You're smiling like a Cheshire Cat.'

'So are you. I must admit I had my doubts, but they're terrific!'

'Where are the men? We ought to start the ball rolling.'

'Maybe I should go and encourage the guests?'

'No, look, the Silver Tongues have done that already. There are some on the floor. And they're coming *pouring* in!'

And so they were: elderly ladies in long satin gowns with elderly escorts, young blades in white tie and tails and their girls in bright short dresses like tubes of colour, bobbed hair and scarlet-mouthed, swinging ropes of beads and bandeaux low on their foreheads. There was excited chatter all around them.

'We could have filled it three times over,' Lizzie said. 'We're complete, even in the extension. How many guests altogether, Ginny?'

'One hundred and twenty, not counting the children. That includes the twenty in Braidholme. Do the aunts miss not living there?'

'No, I don't think so. Susan's death was the end of an era. A valued servant is more than a friend. I remember her when I was a little girl living there with Grandmother Maeve after my mother died. That was before Aunt Maevy married Uncle Charlie and took it over. Oh, those were happy times!'

'And then you went to live with Aunt Isobel and Uncle John?'

'Yes, she had lost a baby and couldn't have any more. What a change! Grandma was full of fun, and Isobel in those days was always tired. She's a different person since he died.'

What a mix-up of a childhood she had had, Ginny thought. No wonder she had jumped at the chance to marry Jonty's father.

'I remember once long ago being taken to the Colosseum—that's a big store in Glasgow—to see the Christmas decorations. I thought it was Fairyland. Just like this. There were Chinese lanterns by the hundreds (Mr Walter Wilson, the owner, was the first to install electricity), and a miniature French Circus with a clockwork pony and a ballet dancer on its back, who pirouetted and dipped. I practised for hours in front of the mirror after that. Now we've got another fairyland here, thanks to you.'

'Nan Porter helped me to put up the decorations. Do you see that little lady coming in, Lizzie, the neat one with the *décolleté* red dress and the very black hair?'

'She must be sixty if she's a day.'

'Do you think her hair's dyed? But look at the daintiness of her. She's a Miss Letitia Wilcox from the West End of Glasgow. She told me she once knew Aunt Maevy. I forgot to tell her.'

'Maybe it's as well. Oh, that elderly gentleman has asked her to dance! Quick work.'

'Mr Cooper. He's a widower, a bank manager from Edinburgh.'

'She's balanced on his stomach. Oh, she dances just like my clockwork ballet dancer! Look at her ankles! You could snap them with a finger . . . here are our escorts, if you please. I bet they've been having a dram on the quiet.' Ernest and Jonty had joined them.

'We've been with Annabel and Kit,' Ernest said. 'She was dying to come, Lizzie.'

'Trying to get round you? Next year, I told her. I think fourteen's early enough.'

'You're probably right.' He had a 'soft side' for Annabel, Ginny thought, poor Mouse! But not for nothing was Ernest director of Globe Express Deliveries, the conglomerate which had embraced the McGrath Carting Company. Behind his urbanity he was as strong as steel. 'So, since I can't get to dance with my beautiful daughter—' he still retained some American modes of speech—'I'll have to ask my wife.' The look he gave Lizzie was not that of a disappointed man.

The tempo of the band had changed now. The black crooner was on his feet. '"I'm forever blowing . . . bubbles . . ."' Jonty sang along with him as he bowed to Ginny. 'Come on, we'll show them.'

She laughed, loving him unreservedly, 'I don't know if I should.

I ought to be behind the scenes, organising like mad. The buffet's at ten-thirty, and I'll have to arrange with the Silver Tongues . . . when they want to have an interval.'

'Just one dance,' he said, hand on heart.

'All right,' and as they danced off, 'did anyone ever tell you that you're irresistible?'

'Everybody. I say, do you know what I saw two of the guests doing?'

'Tell-tale tit . . .'

'Two of the young men. You know those rings which are hung from the swimming bath with ropes?'

'Yes . . . ? "Pretty bubbles . . . in the air . . ."' Everyone was singing.

'They were swinging from one side of the bath to the other . . .'

'In their clothes?'

'Full evening dress. I expect it was some kind of dare. For two pins I would have liked to join them, and then I remembered I was part of the management.' He laughed. When he had come back from fighting in France Lizzie had made him a director on the Hydropathic board.

'Gosh, I wish I'd seen them, the devils! I'll put up a notice tomorrow. Lizzie wouldn't like any accidents.'

The band stopped to vociferous clapping, and she found they were beside Miss Wilcox and her partner. 'Good evening,' Ginny said, 'are you enjoying the band, Miss Wilcox?'

'Very much indeed.' She smiled and the smile made creases in her face which was coated thickly with powder. It was even on the tips of her eyelashes. 'Dipped her face in the flourbag.' Grandma was always there. 'Mr Cooper and I were just saying it's quite an adventure for us.' Her look was arch, her neck scrawny, but her bright, deep-set eyes were intelligent.

'Allow me to introduce you to my second cousin, Nigel Jonathan, Lord Crawford.' Jonty was charm itself as he bowed. Miss Wilcox's chin raised, she was impressed, but not overwhelmed. Her partner, Mr Cooper, seemed more effusive as he shook hands, but bank managers had to be nice to everyone. The band struck up again.

'You're a devil, Ginny,' Jonty said when they were out of earshot. 'You know I hate that rigmarole.'

'That's why I do it, didn't you know, little boy? That Miss Wilcox, by the way, she told me she used to know Aunt Maevy . . . and Uncle Charlie.'

'Bit of a *femme fatale* in her day, I should think.'

'A bit skinny for that. Unless you like older women?'

'Experience is always . . . appealing.' He turned his head away.

'Come on, Jonty Crawford, I know you through and through. I don't expect you'd be in Paris and not meet loads of girls.'

'You're right.' He grinned at her. 'I *have* met loads of girls.' And he'll make them swoon with delight, she thought, that narrow artistic face—'a Crawford through and through,' Aunt Maevy had said, 'except for his eyes'. She decided on wile.

'As a matter of fact, I like older men too. Those of my age are just too silly for words. That caper with the rings above the swimming bath, for instance . . .' She wouldn't mind having a go herself. 'I prefer a more mature man, like . . .'

'Iain Pearson?'

'Iain Pearson? That stuffed shirt!'

'I don't think he thinks much of you either, at least not so as you'd notice. Maybe he prefers Dr Belle.' They had danced past, both dark-haired, tall . . . perhaps he preferred older women, too.

'Thanks very much. Of course I haven't the famous Crawford charm, like your grandfather, for instance, who charmed Grandmother into becoming Lady Crawford at the advanced age of sixty something . . .' Like your father, no doubt, who charmed Lizzie . . . no, she mustn't say anything flippant about him. Jonty idealised him.

'Well, if I have it I hope it works.' He was suddenly the old boyish Jonty, confiding in her. 'I met this marvellous woman in Paris—a woman, not a girl. She makes them all seem so . . . raw and giggly. She has real mystery and charm . . .'

'How old is she?'

'Thirty-five.' He mumbled it. Iain Pearson, she believed, was thirty-two.

'Well, of course you're right, in a way. They have a maturity . . . maybe it's what we admire. But they can make you feel awkward . . .'

'No, Madeleine isn't like that. She's quiet, and secret, but never rude. She . . . understands me, the way younger girls never do . . . except you, Ginny, otherwise I wouldn't be telling you. You've been a tower of strength, often.'

'Well, as a tower of strength, take my advice. I'm sure she's all you say, but . . . what about her husband?' Long ago there had been a duel between Giselle's father and his wife's lover, or it had been arranged, and at the last moment Grandmother Maeve had stepped in . . . you could never be sure with the French.

'He was killed at Mons.'

'Oh, that's sad. I'm sorry. Perhaps she's looking for another husband?'

'Oh, no!' He shook his head, and then a moment later, his tone changing, 'I never thought of that.'

'Most women want to get married, in spite of all Aunt Maevy's theorising. Maybe now they don't rush into it, and half the men were killed in the War anyhow so there aren't enough to go round, but that's their ultimate aim . . .' The band stopped. She put a hand on his arm. 'I'm glad you told me. I'm sure she must be very nice since you admire her.'

'I wish you could see her. You'd understand.'

'I'll come to Paris on my next holiday. Meantime, I'd better go and earn my keep. Could you bear to dance with one of those raw, giggly girls, as you call them, in that huddle down there? They do grow up, you know. Look at me.' She laughed at him.

'You're . . . Ginny. Yes, I'll do that. But purely in the line of duty.' He laughed and squeezed her waist.

* * *

In the kitchen it was organised chaos. Ginny had grown to understand and accept that the chef, Mr Armstrong (you could call him 'Dougie' if he was in a good mood), would always have everything ready on time. He had three sous-chefs, and some extra women from the village had been engaged to make the salads and trifles, trifle being considered a 'must' for a Christmas buffet.

He had a flock, it seemed, of roast turkeys which he was busily carving, and rows and rows of roast hams, and game pies, and mountains of potato salads and great tureens of various vegetables. Since working at the Hydro in such a land of plenty, Ginny had found that the sight of so much food being prepared each day had decreased her appetite, and even on this Boxing Day extravaganza, the chocolate profiteroles and the ice puddings had a limited appeal. It was remarkable how the guests, ostensibly here on a health cure, could forget all about their original intention.

She had put softly shaded lamps in the Palm Court, the lounge and the Pump Room where the guests were to eat informally. She had laid on extra Sholton women as waitresses. First as a private home, then a War hospital and now a Hydropathic, the Hall had always employed staff locally, although some of the older inhabitants were said not to be too happy with the latest transition. There was a grudging feeling that Lizzie was 'on the make', but her numerous charity commitments helped to dispel that.

In the Palm Court, when she was arranging tables, she met Erik Skolad as he came through the door which led to the swimming baths. He was wearing a white dinner jacket and black bow tie.

His fairness was striking. 'Will I do, Ginny?' he said. He radiated pleasure in his own appearance.

'Very nice, Erik.' She was noncommittal.

'I was just taking the temperature. There is talk amongst the young people about a midnight swim.'

'No,' she said firmly. 'Put up a notice and lock the door. I don't want any accidents. Did you know they were swinging from those rings which hang from the rafters?'

He expressed surprise. Too much? 'No, I wasn't there. I had an appointment . . .' Who would that be with, she wondered?

'Why don't you go to the ballroom now? You know Mrs Murray-Hyslop likes to have the staff there.'

'I was just going.' He pouted like a small boy. 'Why do not you come also? We could dance to the Silver Tongues together which would kill the two birds with one stone, eh?'

'Sorry, I'm too busy. I'm organising the band's meal here. Some of the guests are going to take their place at the interval. They've got together a substitute foursome of sorts. But there are plenty of spare ladies, Erik . . . old as well as young,' she added wickedly.

He shrugged. 'The old do not interest me. Remember, I see them when I give the massage. Not pretty, but they are rich . . .' Is he a gigolo, she wondered. She must speak to Jonty. He would know. 'Since you are not interested, I go and do my duty.' His white smile flashed, not even dimmed by his white jacket.

'Me too,' she said, and went dashing off to get the keys of the cellar from the office. The Silver Tongues deserved a good wine.

* * *

It was eleven-thirty, and the family and a few close friends were sitting down to a late supper in the Palm Court. Earlier they had waited on the guests along with the waitresses as a gesture in keeping with Christmas, and they felt they had earned this pause in the proceedings. The Silver Tongues, enlivened by some Château Yquem, were attempting to raise the roof of the ballroom. The steady rhythmic beat was heard even here.

'We deserve this,' said Nan Porter, the head typist, sandy-haired, freckled-faced, forty, unmarried and devoted to Lizzie. 'Especially when you remember we waited on all the staff at their Christmas party as well.'

'They appreciated it, Nan,' Lizzie said. 'I'm going to make the Staff Party an annual event.'

'And the Boxing Day Ball as well?' Ernest asked.

'If tonight's anything to go by, yes,' she said, smiling at him.

'But next time you must ask one or two of your directors from Globe Express in London. We'll make it free to them. It's good advertising.'

'And I thought you were being purely altruistic. What do you think, Dan?' Dan Johnson, whose father had been McGraths' accountant before him, nodded sagely. Ernest had told Ginny that Dan had changed greatly after he had married Ruby Carter, daughter of Bob Carter, another old stalwart of the firm, now dead. Ruby, at thirty-five, had produced a little girl called Davina, and Dan's eyes grew moist with love when he spoke of her. Ruby, she thought, glancing at her, having performed her marital duty, had lapsed into middle-age. And why was it that dark-haired, sallow-skinned women invariably chose beige?

'Lizzie's right,' Dan said. 'It's not a philanthropic institution she's running.'

'There speaks the true accountant.' Ernest smiled.

'And it's a modern business,' Lizzie went on. 'We have to move with the times. How do you imagine those young things would come here if it were like the old places I've heard about?'

Kate nodded. 'They meet and marry and have children and then their children come too. It becomes a tradition.' Aunt Kate's mind was never far away from children. Her sister, Maevy, not quite so starry-eyed, breathed down her nose.

'So long as it's not too lax.' Strangely enough, it was she who often displayed a high moral tone and not her sister, Isobel who, after all, had been a minister's wife.

'We certainly don't want to resemble a theological training house,' she said tartly, as she pecked at her food. Everyone laughed.

'We're going into the new world of the Twenties.' Lizzie, still seductive at forty-one, could be hard-headed without looking it. 'The worst is behind us. I'm quite content to let the guests look after their own spiritual necessities, and moral ones, come to that, so long as they appear to conform to what is accepted behaviour.'

'And drink the water from the fountain.' Ernest, with his dry smile, raised another laugh.

'They do, it's a ritual. And a meeting place. But can you imagine? In some hydros long ago the guests used to be fined a penny a day for coming in late to meals! And only square dances were allowed, no waltzes, because it was regarded as far too intimate . . .'

'I'm all for being intimate,' Jonty said.

'Oh, I expect waltzing would be *dull* in Paris!' Lizzie smiled lovingly at him. 'And no whist in case they got too excited, no fun and games like parties for the children, or if they did, all they could think of was tea and buns and Spin the Plate.'

'I love Spin the Plate.' Jonty looked wistful.

'Do you, little boy?' Ginny smiled at him. She remembered how at Claremont, her home in Wanapeake, she, Gaylord and Sarah used to play it with a wooden bread-board from the kitchen. Her heart was painful for a second as she thought of Gaylord's death. So unnecessary.

'All the same,' Belle Geddes said, 'hydros were established originally for health reasons. They followed a health regime, plain food, high thinking and washed it all down with water, not this,' she raised her glass. 'In one place I read about, there was a great tub of *boiling* water placed in the hall each night and each person had to take a cup of it to purify the system. But it didn't say what the ladies and gentlemen added to their cups in the privacy of their own bedrooms!'

'Oh, Aunt Maevy,' Ginny said amid the laughter, 'I meant to tell you, there's a lady here from the West End, Miss Wilcox. She says she knew you, and Uncle Charlie . . .' she saw her face change, the colour drain out of it.

'Is it Miss *Letitia* Wilcox?'

'Yes, that's right. The name suits her. A dainty little thing, beautiful eyes . . .'

'Charlie courted her for a while. Her father was his chief in the Royal. It would have made a fine match, but I scotched it.' She looked round the table, still white, but with a small smile.

'Good for you, Aunt Maevy,' Jonty said.

'I'll have a word with her sometime, Ginny. I'm not one to bear grudges, although she did try hard to nab him.'

'And aren't we all glad she didn't.' Ernest raised his glass, 'Let's have a toast to all those across the sea, to Patrick and Maria and Ginny's sister, Sarah, to Edie and Robert McGrath—both men stalwarts of McGraths in America—and to George and Victoria, my brother and sister, and all their children.'

'And don't forget Paris,' Jonty said. 'Aunt Emily and Uncle Charles, and Giselle and Terence "Magratt", as they're called there.'

'My, it's quite a collection,' said Maevy, sipping her wine. The three sisters nodded together, Maevy's still fair head, Kate's dark one, Isobel's spun silver, all without a hint of grey. The McGrath women kept their hair colour, even into old age.

'And since I'm only an outsider,' Iain Pearson said, smiling, 'what about a toast to the firm, eh, Dan?'

'Aye, you're right there.' Dan Johnson raised his glass. 'To

McGraths, who have kept us all out of the poorhouse.' He had gained a sense of humour since his marriage to Ruby. 'And while we're on that subject more or less, we want you all back in the ballroom at twelve midnight, on the dot.'

'For the quadrilles?' Ginny asked.

'No, after that.'

'Mysterious . . .' Lizzie didn't look at all perturbed. 'Maybe the spring's run dry, Iain?'

'Or the drains are blocked?' Ginny said. She saw the flicker of amusement in his eyes.

'Well, we'll do as we're told.' Ernest's expression was smoother than ever. He's in the secret, Ginny thought. There's nothing Ernest doesn't know. Lizzie had all the luck in the world being married to a man like that.

She danced the quadrilles with Jonty, although some of the 'young blades' had been besieging her earlier. Iain was in the same set partnering a dark, pretty girl called McCreadie, she remembered, who was there with her parents. Perhaps Lizzie had introduced them.

Jonty danced well, having no doubt been coached by Lizzie—she didn't think the quadrilles had been on the curriculum at Eton—but his English public school education had laid a veneer of restraint on him. It was the usually self-possessed Iain who let out the loudest 'hoochs', bloodcurdling yells which made everybody laugh. And when he whirled her in the sets his grasp was strong and powerful and he seemed to be a different person. There was plenty of fire under that smooth dark exterior, although he didn't often display it.

They were all exhausted and ready to sit down, ready to look with interest towards the platform where Ernest was standing, suave, slim, his hair gleaming against his skull. He held up his hand to stop the deafening roll of drums which the silver-coated drummer was producing with great panache.

'I feel like Mr Lloyd George himself with that introduction. What a disappointment for you!' His hand was in one pocket, he was completely at ease. 'But I'm merely deputising for my wife who was a Crawford before she became a Murray-Hyslop, but don't forget she was a McGrath before that, a true Sholton village lass.

'Anyhow, we thought you would like to share a happy little ceremony with us, which is the result of many heads getting together in the time-honoured fashion. As you may know, my wife's son, Jonty, Lord Crawford, has come back from Paris where he is studying art, to be with us—' he waved his hand towards

Jonty where he was sitting with Ginny and she felt his shoulder move against hers. 'What's Ernest up to?' she heard him mutter.

'Yes,' Ernest went on, 'today he's a student in Paris, but not everyone knows that he was a soldier in the last War—he couldn't wait to be called up—and he acquitted himself well on the Marne, being invalided home on the day the War stopped. He's not yet twenty.' The applause was immediate. Ginny heard someone say beside her, 'A soldier! My, he looks awfy young!'

'But I see I'm embarrassing him. Like most brave people he hates to have attention drawn to him, but nevertheless the Sholton people, backed by the McGrath Carting Company Limited, thought that his contribution to victory should not go unrecognised . . .' Why not Crawford's Iron and Steel Works as well? Ginny thought. She remembered Lizzie saying to her that they showed singularly little interest in the great-grandson of its founder.

Sir Edward Hamilton, whom she knew to be managing director, there, had applied for a suite before Christmas at the Hydro, but Lizzie had instructed her to say they were *complet*. 'And if he doesn't know what that means, tell him we're full up!' She knew there was no love lost between them.

'. . . and so I am going to ask the accountant of McGraths, Mr Daniel Johnson, to present a small token of the appreciation of Sholton Village to their young laird's courage and bravery. Come along, Dan.'

Dan Johnson stood up and walked to the platform carrying what looked like a silver casket. He faced towards Jonty, speaking firmly and precisely—he must have done it at board meetings hundreds of times. 'I know this is a great surprise to you, sir, but you fought like a man although just a boy, so come up and take this casket made of silver and chosen by the good folk of this village because they love you.'

'My God!' Ginny heard Jonty mutter, but he stood up and walked towards Dan with his back up. Discipline's been drilled in to him, she thought, watching proudly.

And the Crawford grace was evident as he accepted the gift from Dan, shaking hands with him, then Ernest. 'This,' he said, turning towards the rapt audience, handsome, boyish, 'has been as great a surprise to me as no doubt it is to you. I hope it hasn't spoiled your evening . . .' 'No, no,' someone called, carried away by it all. 'I'm not worthy, but I'm honoured and grateful. Thank you to everyone in the village and to McGraths who were involved. I shall always treasure this beautiful casket.' He bowed and walked, poker-backed, to his seat beside Ginny amidst a storm of clapping. That was the great thing about the Hydro, she could imagine the guests thinking, the personal touch (carefully fostered by Lizzie), and here they were actually sharing in a private family ceremony!

She read the inscription on the lid with him. 'To our young laird who fought gloriously in the Great War on the Marne from 1917 to 1918.' On the front there was an engraving of Sholton Hall with its towers and its sweeping drive.

Lizzie was beside them, putting her arms round Jonty, kissing his cheek.

'You're naughty, Mother,' he said. 'I bet you were behind this.'

'Me?' she said, wide-eyed, then in a whisper, 'Look inside later.' Well, Ginny thought, if he'd been cut out of Crawfords, his welfare was being guarded by McGraths.

'Oh, Mother, really . . .' He was Jonty, lovable, boyish. I hope that woman in Paris doesn't hurt him. She was surprised at her own fierceness.

5

After the presentation, and perhaps because of the excellent supper provided for them, the Silver Tongues seemed to be instilled with a new vigour. Ginny, relieved now of most of her duties, was besieged by Ernest's 'young blades'. They were charming, worthy scions for the most part of Glasgow trading houses, secure in their rich background of well-appointed homes in Pollokshields or Dowanhill, if not so secure in their lineage.

She remembered Magnus Muir whom she had turned down in spite of his title and Taquhair Castle. He had been more appealing as a convalescent in the Hydro when it was a War Hospital than in his own background with that formidable mother and lascivious father. 'Take a cat of your own kind,' they said. Maybe there was something in it.

'There's something wrong with the electric switch in my bedroom, Miss McGrath.' She saw the laughing face of Mr Hill of Hill Hardwares and General Goods bending towards her as they whirled on the dance floor. 'Do you think you could come up and see to it?' She pretended not to hear.

'Let's shimmy. Do you know it?' Mr Hill obligingly shimmied.

'The switch . . .'

'Oh, the Black Bottom now! Come on!' Mr Hill sighed, released her, and they went into a series of mad contortions facing each other. She felt her satin skirt whirl and slap softly round her thighs. Were her suspenders showing? Never mind, they were white satin too.

It was fun. She was only twenty-two, but already she had lived a fuller life than someone like David Hill with his conventional background of Glasgow High School and his father's string of shops. She was up to date, a post-war model like Ernest's Packard Twin-Six.

'It's the switch near the bed,' he said, putting his cheek against hers and pulling her against him. The black musician had decided he was Nick La Rocca and was leading the others in 'Tiger Rag', his silver trumpet swaying as he stood up, his body writhing.

'It's a marvellous tune, this,' she said, 'did you ever hear the Dixieland Jazz Band playing it?'

'Yes, when I was in London for Dad's firm. You didn't answer my question.' His cheek pressed closer. 'I expect instant service when I'm staying at the Sholton Hydro.'

'My turn, I think.' Someone very like David Hill but called Graham Liddell had tapped his friend on the shoulder. Mr Hill relinquished her reluctantly. 'Don't forget my switch,' he said, as she was whirled away in Mr Liddell's arms.

The music changed to a slower tempo, and she had time to notice the other dancers—Ernest and Lizzie looking like lovers as they always did, Jonty with a pretty young girl in a pink net dress like spun sugar, Belle, still enigmatic, now with Mr Cooper. They seemed to be using the dance for conversational purposes. Mr Cooper was animated, Belle was listening with that smooth, calm face which hid so much.

Had she long ago stopped crying in her pillow for Aunt Maevy's husband who had died beside her? Was it too late for her to marry now? Mr Cooper looked eminently suitable in age and appearance. Did career women hate to give up their independence, and did men regard it as a threat?

Mr Liddell only wanted to talk about Rugby. That must explain his close Rugby tackle which was crushing her dress, not to mention certain parts of her anatomy. 'Murrayfield . . .' he was breathing in her ear, '. . . last Saturday's match. Robson's tackling was a thing to see! You should have been there.' Why was it, she wondered, that young men who were interested in Rugby were invariably called Graham, in Scotland?

'You haven't ever seen the Fighting Irish?' she said. He stopped in the middle of some fancy footwork which would have graced any field. 'Who the hell . . . pardon me, Miss McGrath, but, I mean to say, where do they play?'

'America. Where else? Do you mean to say you haven't ever heard of George Gipp? The greatest player Notre Dame have ever produced? Do you ever go abroad, Mr Liddell?'

'Frequently, but mostly Holland, for the firm, cheese . . .'

'Try New York sometime. You might catch a game at the Yankee Stadium. You even might give up Rugby for baseball . . .'

'Excuse me, Graham, old son.' Another young man tapped him on the shoulder. Mr Liddell didn't seem to relinquish her quite as reluctantly as Mr Hill. The McGrath women could be nebby. She had better watch out.

It was the last dance but one before Iain Pearson claimed her.

'I couldn't get a look in,' he said, 'all those young men clamouring round you.'

'Fine excuse.' She got up and went into his arms. There she was, being nebby again. 'They're only trying to get their rates reduced,' she said, smiling up at him. He must be over six feet.

'Fine excuse!' He echoed her. 'I shouldn't think any of them needed to do that. Lizzie chooses her guests by the size of their bank balance.'

'Well, it's a business as she's fond of saying, and she's a McGrath.'

'How do you like working for her?' He was looking quizzically down at her.

'Lizzie . . . well, she's different from everyone else. I'm a great admirer of her, and as you know, she could charm the birds off a tree. She charmed me off my American branch anyhow.'

'What do you miss most?' The music was slow, lingering, sad. The lights were lowered. He was a good dancer. Of course, the waltz didn't demand such skilful execution as a quickstep, but he moved easily and smoothly, his feet were in the right place at the right time, his equilibrium was sure. But then, he was an engineer, precise.

'The weather. The hot summers, and the forest trees—you haven't trees like them in Scotland, it's too windswept. The Hudson River. Our Old Man River . . .' She remembered its noble breast, the view of it from Aunt Kate's house where Ellie and her husband, Kieran, now lived, seemingly happy with their two children—Betsy Ann, their own, and her elder half-brother, James, the son of Ellie and her dead lover. Perhaps since that terrible illness of Kieran's they had become close.

And there was her own home hidden by those tall forest trees, sturdily stone-built because it had reminded Father of grey Sholton, unlike Springhill across the river, now Edie and Robert McGrath's home and previously her mother's when she was a girl: a smiling house with its green skirts in the water and that river light indoors . . . 'I feel old,' she said.

'Old?' His voice was smiling, mocking. 'You're a young thing! And yet so confident, so good at your job, frightening, almost.'

'No, old.' She shook her head, trying to dispel the sadness. 'I think it's the War that's done it. Leaving home to come to nurse in Lizzie's hospital, and my life in America with so many memories, my brother Gaylord . . . who killed himself . . .' They had reached the doorway and he guided her through it, releasing her.

'Let's go and have a seat. Last waltzes are bad for you.' She felt a warmth, a kindness, coming from him. They walked through the lounge and into the softly lit Palm Court. They could hear the music coming faintly from the ballroom, 'Just a song at twilight . . .' 'Touching,' he said, cocking his head, '"And the flickering . . . shadows . . ." here's a comfortable seat.' He indicated a cane sofa, plump with bright cushions. 'You're tired.' He sat down beside her.

'It's been quite a night.' She didn't generally like to be cosseted —'cootered', they called it here. 'But everything went well, I think. We're establishing traditions, our first Christmas Ball. Did you see the photographers? They came from Glasgow.'

'Yes, you're efficient. Lean back. You were telling me about your brother Gaylord who killed himself.' He said it casually.

'Yes, shot himself. I think that's what took the life out of our house as well as out of him. Certainly out of my mother and father. Sarah, my sister, found her solace in religion. I ran away.'

'Everybody runs away from home sooner or later. Or leaves. Was he unhappy for a long time?'

'Yes. He was . . . different from other men. He hid it . . . because he was ashamed. Kieran understood, that's my cousin, and Ellie's husband. *He* got shot too for his pains, trying to wrestle the gun away from him . . . oh, it's a long story.'

'The sad thing is that if your brother had just gone on living the tragedy might not have happened. Manners and morals are changing fast, ideas, there's more tolerance. The War stripped us of our hypocrisy. And yet there's a sense of . . . loss, of . . . innocence. Young Jonty knows. He's sensitive, he knows that things will never be the same again. Ah, well, he'll be making up for lost time in Paris. And you,' his arm was along the back of the sofa in a friendly fashion, 'who would have thought of a young girl from a sheltered home running a hotel? In your mother's day they would have sat at home waiting for a husband.'

'*My* mother perhaps. Not the McGrath women. And I think I'm more like them, like Ellie, for instance. Oh, how I used to admire her!'

'Your Aunt Maevy's daughter?'

'Yes. She was a surgeon in the War at my age, now she's trying to be a wife and mother. It won't be good enough. I can tell that.'

'Would it be good enough for you?' he said.

'I don't know.' She met his eyes on her. She thought of the hot eyes of Magnus Muir, the innuendos of the gay young blades. Iain Pearson's look had curiosity in it, as if he had come across something which required close study, like . . . drains. She heard faintly a roll of drums from the ballroom. 'Goodness, that's the end! I ought to be there. The gathering of the McGraths.' She got up. 'They'll be starting to sing "Auld Lang Syne" now. Are you coming?' Maybe she was being bossy again. 'Unless you want to be beside Miss McCreadie?'

'No,' he said decidedly, smiling, 'I'm part of the firm, aren't I?'

The band had been applauded so vigorously that they had been persuaded to play once again. 'Shall we?' Iain said. They hardly spoke this time. In any case she had to smile socially to the guests, picking them out as they danced past, make conventional little remarks: 'Did you enjoy yourself?' 'Yes, it was good, wasn't it? 'The band? From London . . .'

She noticed Belle was still with Mr Cooper, Jonty with his spun-sugar fairy, Ernest and Lizzie lovingly entwined, secure. There was no sign of Erik. He should have danced with Nan Porter for the sake of appearances. Nor, she noticed, was there any sign of Miss Letitia Wilcox. But the aunts were there, not dancing but sitting on their gilt chairs, straight-backed, smiling, true McGraths, presenting a corporate front, giving that personal touch that Lizzie so desired.

They all linked hands, sang 'Auld Lang Syne', and then the gentlemen stood straight, if they could, while the National Anthem was played. 'God Save Our Gracious King . . .' Iain Pearson, she noticed, was straight-backed, but so was Jonty, both soldiers of the King.

Half-an-hour later, having received congratulations on all sides, praised the Silver Tongues with Lizzie, showed them their sleeping quarters, locked up the office and turned out the lights, she made her way upstairs. All the guests had gone to bed. The corridor on the first floor was silent, dimly lit and softly carpeted.

She passed her usual room with a pang of regret for its adjoining bathroom . . . how she would have liked to strip off her clothes and luxuriate in warm water to take away the strain of the evening. She was left with an unhappy feeling that she had talked too much about her own background to Iain Pearson while she had learned nothing of his.

She remembered it was Miss Wilcox who had her room. 'Pernickety', Nan Porter had said of her. 'Nothing but the best will do.' As she passed the door she thought she heard voices. Did she talk in her sleep, and was she dreaming of Erik? Or . . . oh, goodness, no, she thought, and then, being honest, why is your mind so full of thoughts like that? Of two people, close, in the final intimacy? Of Iain Pearson?

She had paused for a second but now walked on. Yes, there was no doubt, there *were* two people in that room, Erik and that elderly woman with the bright eyes, hungry eyes. Face facts. You wish it were you and Iain Pearson. 'Manners and morals are changing fast, ideas, there's more tolerance,' he had said. 'The War stripped us of our hypocrisy.' He had known what she meant. It was people like her, using the word 'different' about Gaylord instead of 'homosexual', who held back progress and understanding.

Everybody had to become honest with themselves sooner or later. Aunt Maevy had become a Suffragette, Belle Geddes had been locked up in Holloway for smashing a window, Lizzie had had to face the fact that she was Uncle Terence's daughter outside marriage.

She didn't like herself as she undressed in the chilly attic. She hadn't been a support to her parents, like Sarah, she had chosen to be a career woman. She had been so self-absorbed always that she had been unaware of Gaylord's agony. She had wanted only her own freedom and independence.

She wasn't thinking straight, she told herself. She was too tired, too hard on herself. It was men who had to come to terms with women's disparate goals . . . and yet when she went to sleep she dreamed of Iain Pearson. She saw him coming towards her, arms outstretched, saying he was now *free*. She couldn't understand. The dream was so real that it woke her up at six o'clock. Was it a fact of the human condition, she thought, that everyone had chains of some sort, but some talked of them more than others?

Lying there puzzling would solve nothing. She got up and went down to the kitchen where Mr Armstrong was sitting at the table making out lists. 'A cup of tea, Miss McGrath?' he said.

'Yes, please. Your buffet was a triumph, Dougie.' She hadn't used his first name before. 'I'll have to see Mrs Murray-Hyslop about a rise for you.' She sat with her hands round the hot cup, planning the day's activities.

6

Jonty knew he should visit Emily and Charles Barthe more often at Monceau Park, but he disliked the inevitable 'salons' she held, filling their lovely home with smart, bright people whose rapid Parisian French was too much for him to cope with. Ellie had told him how Emily had kept her salons going throughout the War. 'Sometimes I wonder if it would have been better had I never gone,' she had said to him. 'But, no,' her fine, beautiful face had softened, 'I don't regret it . . .' He knew from his mother that it was at one of them she had met Joe Gould, the father of her son.

He was happier with Giselle and Terence, or had been, but lately he was beginning to wonder if he was welcome. Sometimes Giselle told him Terence was too busy working. She seemed evasive, worried, her face drawn, but he had a feeling it was her loyalty which made her unwilling to discuss Terence's state of health.

He called one evening when she was getting Clovis and Jaime ready for bed. They were delightful children, and although only a year and three months separated them, they were quite different in temperament, Clovis at four-and-a-half a miniature Charles Barthe, white-skinned, dark-haired; Jaime with the sturdy good looks of his grandfather, Terence. He reminded Jonty of Kit.

He played with them while she was preparing their supper, noticing that she was unduly silent. He decided to be frank. 'You're worried, Giselle. Is Terence not well again?'

She turned to him, smart in her short skirt, her smooth black hair, her high-heeled shoes, 'Yes, I'm worried. I try so hard, Jontee, but he does not respond. Today he lies on his bed staring into space. *J'ai peur . . .*'

'Hasn't he any commissions?' Jaime was tugging at him to look at his train, 'In a minute, old chap.' He was used to children. Kit and Mouse had looked up to him, an older brother, had greeted his return from school with cries of delight.

'Less and less. You see, he never finishes them, or rarely. He starts off with great enthusiasm and then he loses interest. He stares . . . once I came in and he was sitting with his head in his hands in front of his easel. Oh, it was so piteous, my poor Terence . . .' she dashed a handkerchief across her eyes, 'I mustn't weep. One is enough. Yes, he weeps . . .'

'Try not to worry, Giselle.' He went over to her and put his arm round her shoulders. 'It's the damage to his hand. He thinks he hasn't the same skill, but that's because of the shell-shock. There were men in the hospital with me who were just the same. It takes ages for the effect to wear off. Has he seen the doctor recently?'

'No, he won't go, and when I made an appointment he flew into a rage . . .'

'It's hard for you. Sit down and have a drink. Let me get you something.'

'Perhaps that's wise. A small cognac. And you too, Jontee. I forget my duties as a hostess.' He poured the drinks at a side table remembering the word, 'neurasthenia', and those lettered cards he'd sometimes seen pinned on poor shivering souls in the Cameronians, 'NYD', 'Not Yet Diagnosed'. Why hadn't he had proper treatment? 'You can lead a horse to the water . . .' The McGraths were charming. They could also be damned stubborn.

He brought her a glass of cognac. 'Drink that. You'll feel better. You see,' he said, in an effort to cheer her, 'there's the effect of the gas on his chest as well. He's had a basinful, old Terence. I was lucky in comparison, didn't know how lucky I was with only a dislocated shoulder.'

'You deserved to be lucky,' she looked up at him, smiling, 'a schoolboy fighting for us . . .'

'*Maman, Maman*,' Clovis was at her side, '*Jaime est polisson*!' Jaime was hiding behind the sofa clutching his brother's clockwork train.

'Tell-tale tit!' She laughed and kissed him, got up and took the train from Jaime who howled with rage. '*Tais-toi*! You will both sit at the table and have a little drink of milk and a *petit gâteau*. See the instant smiles,' she laughed round at Jonty, 'a lovely *petit* gâteau, but you must keep quiet while I talk to Jontee.'

'*D'accord, Maman*,' they chorused, scrambling up on to their chairs. How polite French children were, he thought, or was it that the French language sounded polite to foreign ears? 'All right' sounded mundane in comparison.

'Did you know that Terence's mother was a *suicidée*?' She spoke in a calm voice as she sat down again.

'Yes.' He copied her calmness. 'Ginny, or perhaps Mother, told me. Luckily Uncle Terence has Aunt Honor now.' He saw what she was thinking. 'But Terence had a happy boyhood in Ireland with his brother Robert and Aunt Honor's girls. Mother always said you couldn't be unhappy at Woodlea. It was Great-Grandmother's old home.'

'Yes, but blood tells, does it not? That's what I say to myself.'

'You mustn't think like that. Look, you go and put the children to bed and I'll go in and see Terence. Is he in his room?'

'Yes. Don't be surprised if he doesn't wish to see you. At times he is in a world of his own. He shuts the door on me . . . that is what I find hardest to bear.' Her voice changed and she got up. 'Come, little ones, time for bed. Say goodnight to Jontee.' The two little boys advanced and held out their hands. Little French manikins, he thought, shaking each hand in turn. He would have liked to give them a good hug the way he did with Kit. Mouse was too grown-up for that now.

Terence was lying on his divan, his arms behind his head. Jonty sat down beside him. 'Thinking great thoughts, Terence?' he said.

He turned and looked at him, eyes half-closed, as if he was trying to focus. He didn't smile. 'Ah, it's you? No, wasting my time.'

'Work going well?' His assumed cheerfulness must surely sound false.

'Has Giselle been saying anything to you?' His look was suspicious.

'Giselle?' He tried to register surprise, blew out his breath, got up and walked towards the easel in the middle of the room. 'Is this the latest?' There was a half-finished portrait on it of a bearded man. The strong lines of the true draughtsman were there, but the paint was put on crudely like someone who hadn't paused to think.

'Yes, a friend of my father-in-law's. Much maligned man, Charles. Now he wants to lend us money. Did Giselle not tell you?'

'No, why should she?' He affected nonchalance. 'It's your affair. But I imagine he's rich enough . . .' He looked critically at the portrait. 'You draw like an angel, Terence.' There was a silence behind him, too long a silence. 'The effect of building up with blocks of colour, I see what you're trying to do.'

'Do you?' The voice was infinitely weary. 'Do you? Well, it's more than *I* can. God, I'm sick of painting! It holds nothing for me.'

Jonty went back and sat at the foot of the divan again. Terence had turned his face away from him. He could see how difficult it must be for Giselle, this withdrawal. Let him speak first, he thought. He waited. The silence lengthened, his discomfort increased.

He saw, probably for the first time, how art was an expression of one's personality and temperament. Perhaps his training was already helping. Of course, in his case, he hadn't any executive ability apart from his poems. What they're trying to train, he thought, is one's discrimination, one's selective capacity, and that's what I'll need when I go into auctioneering for McGraths, not to mention the antique shop which is Mother's dream. They were a stalwart bunch with their plans for him . . . He decided to be direct. 'Why don't you give it up for a time, Terence? Take your father-in-law's help. You're probably jaded, run down.'

'Become a beggar?' His voice was bitter. 'No, thanks. My estimation of myself is low enough without that. I *have* to paint to support my wife and family. I'm not like you, a young lord being fêted in Paris . . . how they love a title here!'

'I see your self-respect is important to you, but just for a while?' He had said the wrong thing.

'Self-respect? The terrible thing is . . .' he repeated the words slowly, 'the terrible thing is that it doesn't matter, nothing matters . . .' Silence. I won't speak this time, Jonty thought, it only makes it worse. 'Do you know that French word, *néant*?' Terence's voice was lifeless.

'Yes, I think so.'

'That's what life is like . . . for me,' he turned his head to the wall, 'nothingness . . .'

He sat, miserable, his heart aching for this unhappy man who had everything and yet seemed to have nothing. That damned War, he thought, nothing good came out of it . . . 'Is there anything I can do for you, Terence?' he said at last. And when there was no answer, 'Would you like me to go?'

'No, wait a minute.' His voice was muffled, 'Giselle would think . . . if I could *convey* to you,' Jonty heard the roughness of unshed tears, 'to *anyone*, this misery inside me, misery without real cause . . . I know other men who were at Verdun who have no sight, no arms or legs. They think I'm lucky! They don't realise *they're* lucky, that it's a question of genes, who you spring from . . .'

Should he come out with it, pretend, or be frank? He said, 'If you're thinking of your mother, forget it. It's in the past.'

'How did you know about her?' The voice was sharp now.

'It's family knowledge. Every family has secrets. The Crawfords are no better than the rest. My great-grandfather was a petty tyrant, soaked the workers to build the background that you reproach me with. Your grandfather, Kieran McGrath, could have told you all about that. He fought for the workers' rights in his own quiet way. But you're lucky. Try and believe that. You have Giselle, a winner, and those two lovely boys . . .' It was no good. He said after a time to the still figure, 'I'll go now . . .' Terence's voice cut across his.

'Did you read about Modi!'

'Modi?' He was at a loss.

'Modigliani . . . Amedeo. I met him sometimes in the cafés in Montmartre. "Hello, Modi!" "Hello, Terence!" Everybody was his friend. He drank himself stupid most nights, then it was drugs.'

'Yes, I know now who you mean. A tragedy. His work was very fine.'

'He died last Saturday, and the following day, Jeanne, his model, threw herself from a fifth-floor window.'

'Dreadful.' He knew nothing of that.

'She was nine months pregnant.'

'Oh . . .' He drew in his breath. 'Well, for every one like that there are ten successful ones.'

'But he was successful . . . he went . . . when it came to the end.'

'Perhaps, but think of all the good work he could have gone *on* doing. I think the end is never the end. You only think it is. There were many moments like that when I was with Cameronians. "This is it," I would say and then discover it wasn't. Little deaths. You must have felt the same. Terence,' he said, feeling he was on the right track, 'Why don't you get up and come for a walk with me? We'll go to a café for a beer. It will do you good.' It was a waste of time. He was out of his depth. 'What about it? Terence?'

He turned. His face was very white, his eyes wet. 'Thanks, Jonty. You're a good sort, ye know.' He heard the faint Irish intonation. 'I can't. It's the energy needed, you see. I'll get out of this myself, sometime. In my sane moments,' he smiled, and the smile was sadder than the white face, the wet eyes, 'I know it's the aftermath of the War. But in my not so sane moments,' he shook his head, 'that pit of nothingness, *néant*.'

Jonty stood up. 'I'll go, but maybe you could summon up enough energy to spend a little time with Giselle. It would make her happy.'

'How right you are.' The eyes were half-closed.

'I'll be back soon.' He put his hand on Terence's shoulder. 'I know I'm of no bloody help; all I know is you're ill and you need some help, for your sake and Giselle's, the medical kind. You're too good a painter to let your talent go to pot. Remember I'm an art student.' He saw the ghost of a smile on his cousin's face, saw it vanish and the eyes become unfocused again.

7

He took a cab to Madeleine's apartment in the little *place* off the rue des Petits-Champs. The district around the Palais Royal was unknown to him, as was most of the Right Bank. It was useful to have plenty of money to hire cabs whenever he wished. Ernest and Mother had never stinted him, he thought, as he bowled along by the Seine from Passy. Giselle had said that her mother, Emily, had chosen her apartment for her because it was also on the Right Bank.

The Eiffel Tower was the only landmark he knew. One of the family tales was of Great-Grandmother going to its inauguration during the *Exposition* of 1889. It was Giselle who had told him. 'Although I was just a little girl I remember her, that flame-red hair of hers, that proud carriage, like a queen. *Très belle.*'

He had told her how he had found Terence, and said that he felt he ought to see a doctor. 'Is there anyone whom he can really trust?' he asked.

'Not his local doctor.' She thought for a second or two. 'Yes, of course! Why didn't I think of it before? Dr Reynaud of the Condé Hospital. He was under his care there for a long time after he was wounded at Verdun. Terence thought the world of him. In fact, Dr Reynaud told me that if I ever needed his help to get in touch with him.'

'Well, there you are,' he said, relieved. 'That's the answer. Couldn't you telephone him, ask if you could bring Terence to see him?'

'He might not go.'

'Make the appointment and then tell him that he will disappoint Dr Reynaud if he doesn't keep it. If he cares for his good opinion, he'll go.' He thought of Terence's remark. 'In my sane moments I know it's the aftermath of the War . . .' Yes, Dr Reynaud was the man.

Giselle got up from her chair. 'I'll do it now. If he's still at Condé I shall regard it as a lucky sign. I believe in luck, don't you, Jontee?' He contrasted in his mind her silky black hair with the dull honey-gold of Madeleine's. One expected Frenchwomen to be dark-haired, and yet if one saw Madeleine in Scotland there could be no doubt that she was French even before she spoke. What was their charm? he wondered. Was it their very difference, their essential foreignness?

Giselle had asked him to wait while she telephoned, and he had listened to her rapid French, getting the gist of it. '*Je m'excuse profondement* . . .' '*Ici Madame Terence McGratt* . . .' '*Oui, le même* . . .' And then the launching into her request, seeing her face clear: '*Oui, d'accord. Vous êtes très aimable. Merci, merci, d'accord . . . demain à trois heures de l'après-midi . . . oui, oui, je vous remercie infiniment* . . .'

Her eyes had been shining when she hung up the receiver. 'He remembers Terence very well, he says. Is not that good? And he likes to follow up his cases. Did you hear the rest?'

'Yes, he's seeing you tomorrow. What about the boys? Would you like me to amuse them while you're gone?'

She shook her head, smiling. 'No, Jontee. I appreciate your offer, but they would . . .' she laughed and made a circle with her index finger, 'How do you say it?'

'Run rings round me?'

'*C'est ça*. I'll ask Madeleine. Oh, but . . .' she had put her hand to her head in dismay. 'She has no telephone.'

'You could write her a note and I could be postman. I can get a cab. It wouldn't take me too much out of my way . . .'

He saw what Madeleine meant when the cab drove through the gates. It was like a village with its narrow streets, the overhead lamps which gave the courtyards off them a mysterious air. Most of the little shops were still lit; he saw a man walking along with a long loaf under each arm, a middle-aged woman in black with a poodle on a lead, not a miniature poodle but a great, lusty frolicking animal which pranced along at total variance with its mistress's dignified gait. He saw a man in a broad-brimmed hat and cloak hurrying along. Cocteau, perhaps. He must make time to read some of his work.

The driver set him down with a terse '*Le voici, numero neuf,*' at a solid black door with brass fittings. To its left the window of a small shop was filled with a faded display of stamps. 'Laroche, Philatéliste', it said above. He lifted the knocker on the black door and let it drop, feeling suddenly shy, but at least, he told himself, he had a good excuse for being there.

He heard someone coming down the steps, and then Madeleine opened the door, her mane of hair tied back under a silk scarf.

She was wearing an apron and black slippers, not her usual high-heeled shoes. 'Jontee!' She was shy too, fingering the scarf, pulling off her apron and throwing it behind her. 'I was just washing up after my meal. Is there anything wrong?'

'I'm sorry to disturb you. I have a letter from Giselle. It was urgent and I offered to deliver it.'

'How you are kind! But what do I think of? Enter, if you please.' She held open the door and he went in, seeing a steep flight of stairs immediately ahead.

'Follow me. And please shut the door. It is a crush, *n'est-ce pas*?' She laughed, turning and going up in front of him. He saw the slippers flapping off her narrow heels. Her stockings were sheer black with seams running up a long way. He lowered his gaze.

He followed her into a large room at the top with a low ceiling and small window-panes which were curtained in velour. The room looked like a warm nest. There was a glowing fire in a small hearth and a cat sat swaying in the heat in front of it. It paid no attention to Jonty.

'Manon is an iconoclast.' She smiled at him. 'Please sit down. Is it bad news?'

'No, but Giselle wanted to get in touch with you quickly. Terence . . . well you know he is far from well.'

'That goes on for a long time, up and down.' She sat opposite him.

'I didn't notice it so much before.'

'You saw him in an "up" time perhaps. His mood swings. She has persuaded him to see a doctor at last?'

'I think so. I'm sure she will. She telephoned the one at the Condé Hospital who looked after him and he's agreed to see Terence tomorrow.'

'So she wants me to take care of Clovis and Jaime?'

'That's it. Could you? He was very sad and miserable when I saw him tonight. I'm sure he needs help.'

'Of course I will. What time does she wants me?'

'I'm stupid.' He smiled at her. 'I'm forgetting to give you the letter.' He handed it to her and watched her bent head as she read it. Her hand went up and pulled off the silk scarf. Her hair seemed to slide round her face and neck as if molten in its heaviness. He had never seen hair like that which had so much life on its own.

'Three o'clock, the appointment. I will be there at one. I can take the afternoon off. I may telephone in the shop of Monsieur Laroche but he is closed until tomorrow . . .' Her finger went to her mouth, considering. Her dark eyes were on him. The upper part of her face had a Slavonic breadth, but her chin was delicately rounded. He liked her mouth . . . very much. He had strange sensations in his body as he looked at her.

'My concierge has a telephone. I'll ring her when I get back.'

'Here I have not those advantages, but it is . . . private?' She smiled at him. 'You are kind. May I give you something to eat? There is some soup . . . ?'

'No, thanks. Dinner is laid on for me.' This was a lie, unless you counted the café along the street from his flat where he generally ate.

'A cup of coffee? It is still hot.'

'If you insist,' he said, laughing, he didn't know why. 'Although it's warm enough in here.'

'I like it so. I like the bare feet sometimes when I get home from the office. Take off your coat. I shall not be a minute.'

He sat down beside the cat and stroked it, feeling utterly relaxed, stretching his legs. When Kit and Mouse were small he used to go up to the nursery and play with them when he came home from Eton. The fire had danced like this. The cat turned and gazed at him with half-shut eyes as if it was aware of his thoughts, then turned away again, dismissing him.

Madeleine came in with a tray on which were two cups of coffee and a dish of bon-bons. She laughed when she saw him sitting on the floor. 'That is my favourite place. I am not a chair person either. I shall put the coffee on this little stool and join you.' She threw a cushion on the rug beside him and sat down. The cat slowly stalked away, its tail in the air. 'Manon is upset,' she said, 'she doesn't like to share me with anyone else. Here is your coffee, milord.' She laughed at him, and he saw that her eyes were dark brown, not black. They had golden specks.

'Thank you. You shouldn't have bothered.'

'Bothered?' She was puzzled.

'That's what they say in my village at home. They say that about everything, presents . . .'

'You shouldn't have both . . . bothered to come, but it is lovely to see you. I so rarely get visitors here, only the neighbours sometimes, friends of Paul's. I do not go out much. I am tired after working all day, and there is the . . . *aménagement*.' Frenchwomen laid great store on their household duties, he had noticed, particularly their shopping. Mother never spoke of hers, and yet she ran a beautiful house and a generous table.

They sipped their coffee in companionable silence. She said, 'The War has a lot to answer for, spoiling lives. In many countries.

The only one who truly realised that was President Wilson of America.'

'Didn't your Clemenceau?'

'He may have, but he wasn't called *Le Tigre* for nothing. And now since January he is out of the running. President Wilson knows War can never be good, that the price is too high. Did you read about the Peace Conference?'

'Not really.' He was ashamed. 'But I saw the placards.'

'Twenty-seven nations in an agreement that a League of Nations should be formed to prevent War. But many people will be against it.'

'Why?' I should keep in touch more, he thought.

'France wants to see Germany pay for what they did to us, and that only means more bloodshed in the end.'

'Perhaps Wilson is an idealist.'

'Be honest, Jontee, did *you* get anything out of the War?'

He shrugged, feeling immediately grown-up. He was a veteran . . . 'Experience, perhaps.' He laughed. 'I was so desperate to be in it that I ran away from school, and spent the rest of the time wondering why I had done it!' He smiled at her. It was beautiful, this intimacy.

'You're just a boy,' she said. 'So boyish, and charming. My heart', she put her hand over it, laughing, 'goes pit-a-pat.' She was like her cat when she put her head to one side. 'I can't believe you were in the midst of it, saw dreadful things. But perhaps it will help you in your life now.'

'I think most people grudged the lost time, don't you? In my case I should only have been at school.'

She bent her head and the heavy hair parted on her neck and swung over her face. 'It wasn't only lost time in my case. I lost my husband.' She hooked a heavy loop of the hair over one ear and he saw that tears were running down her cheeks.

'Here, here,' he said, totally at ease and putting his arm round her shoulders, 'please don't, Madeleine.' And thinking of Giselle earlier, 'I seem to make people cry wherever I go.'

'That is because you are *sympathique*.' She wiped her eyes with her handkerchief and smiled up at him the way Mouse had often done—a female look, ashamed and yet proud of the capacity to weep. She sniffed. 'There's only one tonic when one is feeling sad.' She got up and went to a nearby table where she poured two glasses of wine and brought them back. 'Let us drink to the League of Nations,' she said, giving him one.

'And to Terence's recovery.' He took a bigger gulp than he had intended, and another one to mask it. He was in fact very hungry.

Mother called it a healthy boy's appetite, and he remembered also the alacrity with which he had gone on begging errands for eggs during the War because of the meagre Army rations. 'This is the life,' he wanted to say, 'sitting drinking wine with a wonderful woman in her apartment in the Palais Royal. Better than the trenches.' He laughed, surprised that he felt slightly tipsy with those first two gulps. He took another one to test himself.

'What amuses you, Jontee?' Madeleine said. 'You are a funny boy.' The face which she turned to him glowed pearl-like from the reflection of the fire. Her teeth gleamed.

'Nothing. I get funny thoughts, that's all. Always when I think I'm grown-up, terribly *mûr*, in fact. It cuts me down to size.'

'You must explain that.' She put down her glass. '"Cuts me down to size," you say. What size?'

'My real size. A young student in a strange country.' He grinned at her, enjoying himself immensely.

'You never think of yourself as a lord?'

'No, not really. I'm very wary of people who are impressed by a title. But I used to be more aware of it in Sholton because the village people treated me differently—and so did the children.' He laughed. 'They wouldn't let me join in their games, for one thing. I thought all that difference had gone . . . until last Christmas.'

'Why?'

'The day after Christmas, at a Ball we were holding, I was presented with a silver casket from them. On it was inscribed "To our young laird". Ridiculous, really.'

'Laird? What is that?'

He thought. '*Châtelain*, perhaps? *Seigneur*?'

'Ah, yes. *Seigneur*.'

'It's only the old people who feel that now. With the growth of Glasgow our estate is too near the city to be really private, and Mother has turned our house into a Hydro.' He saw her look of puzzlement, 'a hotel, a *hydropathique*. My mother is always up to something. It was a hospital during the War.'

'Are you sorry?'

'No, I think it really came to an end when my father died in the Boer War.' He looked into the fire. 'His grandfather started the Crawford Iron and Steel Works. It's become a giant now, despoiling the countryside. I've been brushed aside. Not that I mind, nor would my father. I feel I know him, how he would have thought . . .'

'I expect your mother has been a great influence on you.'

'Yes, but a good one. And then there's Ernest, her second husband. You met him at Giselle's apartment. He's a fine chap. We get on like a house on fire.'

'Like a house on fire?' She knitted her brows. *'C'est bizarre.'*

'Not if you think of it. Nothing gets on more quickly than a house on fire, once it is set alight.

'Except love,' she said. The sight of her face, half-hidden by the fall of hair, made the feeling come back, stronger than ever.

'Look, Madeleine,' he said, 'I must go. It's far too comfortable here. And I've done Manon out of her favourite place.' He looked around. 'Where is she?'

'Probably sulking on my bed. She doesn't like men. She's a lesbian.' Her face didn't change. After all, it was Paris, liberated Paris. Why did his head suddenly swim?

'Be that as it may,' he had a ridiculous wish to giggle, 'I must get on.' He lifted his glass and drained it, and immediately a warm glow pervaded him. He didn't want to go. This was perfection, something he had been missing—home, the fireside, the *foyer*—since he was in France. Her voice broke the silence.

'Have you a girl friend, Jontee?'

'No.' He smiled round at her, he hoped, lazily. He was reclining now on one elbow, although hadn't he said he must go? 'Plenty of girl friends but not one particular one. Ginny, my cousin, an American, is my best friend, and a girl, but that's quite different.'

'So you have never . . . ?' Her dark eyes held his. There was no mistaking what she meant. For some reason he remembered the French farm girl who had sold eggs to him, and her firm breasts straining against the cotton stuff of her dress. The soldiers had joked when he went back, saying he could have had the eggs for nothing if he'd played his cards right. Her eyes had been the same. His head pounded between his ears as if it was going to burst. He felt blood rushing to his face.

'Plenty of time . . .' The words sounded strangled. He cleared his throat.

'Anyone would love you.' She put a hand on his arm. He looked down at it. He had noticed her hands before, narrow-fingered but not bony, loaded with rings. He had the absurd desire to lift it to his lips as they did in France, found to his surprise he was doing just that, what was more, that he was kissing each finger. They smelled of orange flower water.

She was so close to him that her breasts brushed his chest. He saw the fire through the shimmer of her hair. Still in some kind of dream he sat up and put his arms round her. 'This is terrible,' he said into her hair, 'I'm sorry.'

'What is terrible!' He knew she was laughing. 'You deserve a reward for being such a good messenger.'

'I'll go,' he said, not releasing her, 'before . . .'

'Before it is too late?' There was still laughter in her voice. 'Don't you think, since you're an old soldier . . .'

'A veteran, we call it . . .'

'A veteran, you ought to . . . become a man?' The words were whispered.

He was rigid with shock, and then the damned pounding started again, not between his ears this time. It changed to an ache, more than an ache, a pressing need, the greatest desire he had ever known. There was nothing in life he could compare it with, a total desire which had to be assuaged somehow. He knew she moaned, and that she gently pushed him back on to the rug, that she was lying beside him, leaning over him. Her hair was glowing red now, but that was the fire.

The rug wasn't particularly soft. He could feel the floorboards through it, pressing on his spine. 'You've an insatiable appetite, Jonty, but you never put on a pound . . .' Mother. She should see him now. She would know all about appetite. Madeleine was laughing above him. Her teeth gleamed. 'It is not as bad as facing the Germans, Jontee. Let me show you.'

That made him laugh too. He was laughing as he tore off his clothes, watched her taking off hers, saw her breasts revealed, then the smooth mound of her belly. Maybe it was just like bathing in the Sholtie Burn, the dread of the cold water, then the delicious sensation of being engulfed in it and swimming strongly away to the opposite bank.

The touch of her naked flesh on his made him cry out. The Cameronians had shouted like that when they were going over the firestep. Where were the pipes! But this wasn't going into battle, this was . . . there were no words for what this was, except that Madeleine was the captain. She knew all the routes towards their goal . . . and some delicious byways.

Why had he waited so long? Now he knew why Mother's eyes met Ernest's sometimes at breakfast, making him feel excluded, why Ellie had taken so long to come to terms with her marriage to Kieran. You had to experience it to understand, and yet it was so personal that you could never compare notes. (The soldiers had sometimes, but that was when they had been with prostitutes.)

When he looked at Madeleine at last her cat was sitting beside her with a female look on its broad, smug face, as if to say, 'How was it?'

'That cat,' he said weakly, 'it's staring at us.' He buried his head in Madeleine's breast. Tiny hard balls rolled against his cheek. He thought it might be damp talcum powder.

She stroked his hair. 'You,' she said, 'are going to make the ladies of Paris swoon.'

'Hey!' he said, pleased, if muffled, 'I'm not Don Juan, or Casanova.' Those were the only two he could think of offhand.

'Perhaps not,' she was still stroking his hair, 'but you have all the attributes.'

He was in too much of a daze for the next ten minutes to feel any awkwardness as he hurriedly dressed. Should he say 'Thank you', or 'I love you, Madeleine'? But he didn't. He didn't even have for her the tenderness he felt for Ginny sometimes, the feeling that they understood each other thoroughly, that they could talk about absolutely anything.

Madeleine was a womanly woman. He knew that by the way she disappeared and came back, brisk and fully dressed even to her high heels and her freshly powdered face, her lips reddened. 'You'll get a cab quite easily, Jontee. I know you have to be back for dinner. Don't forget to telephone to Giselle.' She smiled at him. 'It was a success?'

'Oh, Madeleine . . .' Did you talk of 'it' being 'a success'?

'No regrets?'

'No.' He felt like an empty sack and he was ravenously hungry, this time for food.

She opened the door for him and, putting her arms round him, kissed him on the cheeks. 'We will make good lovers, you and I.' Her eyes were deep and dark again. Perhaps he did love her.

He smiled at her, at a loss for words, feeling he had reverted to his boyishness despite everything.

In the cab he pondered. Did it mean he now had a mistress? But then you *paid* mistresses, didn't you? The desire had been mutual. She had sighed and groaned too, and once she had said in his ear, '*J'ai faim* . . .' He had been a little disturbed because he thought she said '. . . Paul', but it couldn't have been. He found as he thought of her that his desire returned. It had been like an *apéritif* only. That must be why lovers stayed all night. Had she hurried him away because she knew he would have to come back?

In the café, after telephoning Giselle, he laughed and sang with the other students and felt fine.

8

There were two Madeleines, the quiet, secret one he met at Giselle's, and the lover whom he went to frequently in her apartment above Monsieur Laroche's shop.

She was there the first evening he called at Passy to find out about Terence. Giselle greeted him with pleasure, Madeleine with discretion. There was no message in her eyes. Apparently the secret was to be kept from Giselle for the time being.

'Is Terence resting?' he asked.

'No.' Giselle shook her head. 'He's not here. He's at a small sanatorium in Condé, near Dr Reynaud. He is keeping him in for possibly a month to give him rest and treatment.'

'That's wise, don't you think, Jontee? Better for Giselle, and the children too.' How calm and composed Madeleine's face was, his mistress, if you could call her that on the strength of one night. It was strange to look at her and to know what she was like under that black dress, the full breasts, dark-nippled, the thin waist. Her legs were shorter than Ginny's, not that he had seen *her* naked, but you knew by how she walked, that free, easy stride. They had often taken long rambles before he went to Paris, and he had told her all his hopes and worries. 'Mind those Parisian women!' she had said.

'Yes, I do. What did Dr Reynaud say, Giselle?'

'It's a form of neurasthenia. His equilibrium has been severely disturbed by what he went through, and he has a delicate constitution. "Some pay all their lives," he said, "but we'll hope that won't be the case with him." He's to give up taking commissions, but paint for pleasure if he likes, and get plenty of fresh air and exercise. When he comes home Dr Reynaud thinks we might plan to go to Ireland for a little time to give him a fresh start. He's . . . hopeful.'

'That's a good idea. Uncle Terence and Aunt Honor will get him all right.'

'Perhaps he'll pass the time by painting his father's latest hope in training.' She laughed. '"This is the one, sure enough," he says.' It was a passable imitation of Terence's cheerful Irish brogue. '"Guaranteed to make all our fortunes," he says. Do you know what he calls it?'

'No.' He was pleased to see her gaiety returning.

'The Sholtie Flyer. What is "Sholtie", Jontee?'

'It's the local name for the Sholton river, the Sholtie Burn. It's bound to win with a name like that.'

'You haven't told him your other news,' Madeleine said.

'Ah, yes, my wonderful career! Can you believe it, Jontee, I'm going to become a working girl!'

'No!' He was surprised. 'What about the children?'

'*Maman* has arranged everything. They are to go to a kindergarten each day—she insists on paying for it—and I'll pick them up on my return.'

'Return from where?'

'Pierre's, Maman's couturier. He used to be mine too until I married.' She laughed. 'I start as an *assistante*, but who knows, perhaps I will become the *Directrice* in time.'

'Like Ginny. A career woman. She practically runs the Hydro for Mother. She's very competent. That's wonderful, Giselle.'

'At least I will earn some money. Dr Reynaud is very firm about Terence not saddling himself with commissioned work meantime, but he forgets we have to live.'

'You won't feel so lonely if you're working. Are visitors allowed where Terence is?'

'I should think so. I'll give you the address if you like. You have been so good to us, hasn't he, Madeleine?'

'*Très sympathique*,' she said. She lowered her head as if to hide a smile.

* * *

Of course, he was unable to keep away. It was as if he had been introduced to a wonderful new dish which titillated his palate, and he couldn't get enough of it. The irony of it was that he was now becoming acquainted with some of the girl students and being invited to parties in various *ateliers* where everyone seemed to be very friendly. He knew, of course, that it was partly because of his foreignness and his title, but even so, there were one or two who were appealing and who made it quite clear they were interested.

But he was drawn like a magnet to the other Madeleine—not Giselle's old school friend, but the one of the warm little apartment, the welcoming arms. No longer did they stretch out on the rug in front of the fire. They went to bed in her little bedroom which reminded him of a chocolate box with its rich, dark colours, its frills and bows, and he learned many things about women, and more about himself.

He began to think he must be in love with her. He longed for her body, to see her heavy hair turn inward on her bare shoulders, the French smell of her, the sheer physical satisfaction. The longing would come over him in the middle of a lecture, and he would press his elbows into his sides to control it. He could never have been so uninhibited with anyone else, he felt, even his own wife, whoever that might be. He thought of that unknown person as some shy virgin to be wooed.

Madeleine was delectable, and she also knew when to stop loving and listen. He would tell her all about his latest passion, 'apart from you,' he would say, kissing her neck (he was amused at how easily he had fallen into the role of lover), 'Piero della Francesca. You have the look of his women, so . . . complete in themselves, so calm, so monumental.'

'I am *grosse*?' She pouted.

'No, no, it is a very special quality. Like sculpture. Compact. I long to go to Florence. That's where my real studies begin.'

'And what shall I do then without you?'

He hadn't thought of her in Florence. That was another new adventure. There might be another girl. He might meet his shy virgin there, although when you thought of it men were the limit (he called himself a man now). They thought they could behave exactly as they wished but that women ought to remain pure. Ginny got hot round the collar about that—not that she was like Madeleine, but she hated to be patronised by men, talked about 'the double standard'.

But sometimes he felt very tender towards Madeleine, thought of her as typical of many women after the War. He saw life through her eyes, a young woman who had lost her husband, who had very little to look forward to except work since she was hardly likely to get married again at her age, even if there were enough men to go round.

Secretly he thought of thirty-five as being too old for marriage. He would feel sorry for her, and the sorrow would change to tenderness, the tenderness to passion, and he would make love to her until it was he who was exhausted.

Sometimes when he woke in her bed after one of those sessions, he would find Manon, the cat, lying between them. It had a habit of putting its head on the pillow, like a human being. There would be two pinpricks of light between its half-closed eyes.

9

Iain Pearson was a man of lists. He found it was the only way to get through the day methodically. There was a multiplicity of business and personal interests to be attended to, and this week was particularly crowded.

First of all there were the many details of McGrath's board meeting, the prospectuses to be prepared and printed. Then, Ernest had been in London at Globe Express Deliveries, their parent company, and he would have to be reminded to tabulate the matters arising there, hardly necessary as it happened, in Ernest's case. If there was anyone more logical than himself it was Ernest, coping as easily with his frequent trips to London as he had done with his duties in the Intelligence Service during the War.

They were a grand family, the Murray-Hyslops—the lovely Lizzie, the name he teased her with, sturdy young Kit, and that young girl Annabel, on the brink of womanhood with her touching awkwardness and Ernest's intelligent eyes. She was the kind who would develop into a beauty, and even more important, someone to be reckoned with.

And there was Lizzie's own son, that fine young man, Jonty, now training in Paris and no doubt sowing his wild oats.

It was a good thing that the trade depression in Glasgow which was slowly gaining momentum (he could date it from the Riot Act at the end of January, last year), hadn't touched McGraths as yet. Many firms had been affected. Crawford Iron and Steel Works had been clever enough to amalgamate into a group and save their bacon—probably that man, Sir Edward Hamilton, at the back of it, he who had managed to cut Lizzie's son out of the firm.

He had noticed before how terse-lipped Lizzie became if the subject was mentioned. He wouldn't be surprised if it weren't an act of vengeance on Hamilton's part for once having been spurned by her. He was known as a ruthless man. But it didn't matter. Jonty's future was assured in McGraths. He would lend lustre to it, and his title would look well on the notepaper.

The Lanarkshire coal fields were exhausted, the only reminder of them being the huge bings which reared over the landscape, and between them and the desecration of the countryside by Crawford's spreading steel works, Sholton was not the place it used to be. But the McGrath family—and Lizzie was a McGrath—had a flair. They were always in the right place at the right time, and Sholton Hall had moved with the times.

The Hydro was a success. There was still enough money and snobbery in Glasgow, despite changes, to make it a going concern. And as for McGraths itself, although many large industries had gone to the wall, in spite of the depression, or perhaps because of it, household removals had accelerated, the parcel business was flourishing, and their fleet of motor vehicles had increased steadily. Petrol had won over steam . . . he checked himself. All that would be gone over at the board meeting. Meantime, back to his list.

He would have to remind Miss Struthers, his secretary, to send out notices today to all the members of the board, and write a personal letter to the three aunts since they regarded it as an occasion. Tea and sandwiches. Maevy, still in command in the office, liked to show her two sisters how it was done in York Street. What a marvellous woman she was, fifty-eight and still going strong. She was going to be like that mother of hers—he often looked at her portrait in the board room, painted by young Terence McGrath. Character and beauty. He wished he had known her. Beth . . .

His face changed as his mind left McGraths to what was not on his list but always at the back of his mind. He hadn't been for a week. He would go tonight. He nodded, grim-faced.

Now, the plans for the dinner at the Hydro. That would be a pleasant surprise for everyone, his own idea to celebrate the satisfactory dividend paid on the ordinary shares. Members of the board, family . . . Jonty wouldn't be coming home, but all the same it would be a special celebration of the visit of Patrick McGrath, Ginny's father, and his nephew, Robert, all the way from America. Would Patrick throw in the sponge? He was sixty-seven. He didn't think so. He was the type of man who used his work as an anodyne for his own worries. 'Mother used to say,' Maevy had said to him once, 'that if Patrick hadn't any worries he would invent them.'

Ginny would arrange it all beautifully. He would go to Sholton and see her tonight, after he had been at Beth's. He sat staring at his hands, surprised at the gust of unaccustomed self-pity which swept over him. 'If onlys' were worse than useless. He shook his head impatiently at himself and lifted his pen again. Lists . . . In his neat hand he wrote busily for ten minutes, then locked up his desk and walked through the darkened office.

The covers were on the rows of typewriters, desks were tidy and cleared of papers, doors closed. Often he did his best work between five and seven o'clock when the place was quiet. The days were too busy. When Ernest was in London he took over his outside duties, calling on customers, having discussions with the Railway Company. 'Keep them sweet,' Ernest always said. They had been McGrath's bulwark before the War, but his own heart was in motor haulage.

He saw now that his apprenticeship in steam and petrol had been only a forerunner. 'Technical mastery and business acumen', Ernest had said of him in his speech at last year's board meeting, and he had cherished the phrase, tried to live up to it. 'I think I'll change my name by deed poll to McGrath,' he had said in reply, trying to conceal his pleasure.

York Street was in shadow, but the late evening sunlight was shining on the river and picking out the red of a steamer funnel as he walked to where his car was parked behind the solid sandstone of McGrath House. The name had been Lizzie's idea. A bit fancy, he had thought but, then, Lizzie had a flair. He drove steadily along the grid-iron streets, cobbled round the tramlines, his face grim again, in the direction of Pollokshields where Beth lived.

* * *

She hadn't had a good night, Mrs McDonald said, but she would be pleased to see him. He nodded, smiling, and gave her the flowers he had bought on the way, stopping at St Enoch's Station where the flower-women sat, surrounded by their baskets. Mimosa, there was always mimosa, dusty yellow, reminding him of some arid foreign place where it never rained, and ox-eyed daisies, all different colours—he didn't know their names—and gypsophila, baby's breath. Mrs McDonald was pleased. She would put them in a vase for Beth's room.

She was in bed, looking drawn and peevish. It must be because he hadn't been for a week. He hated the false cheerfulness he assumed as he went towards her, smiling. He didn't go in for effusiveness as a rule.

'Well, Beth,' bending over her, kissing her cheek, 'I didn't expect to see you in bed at this time of day.'

'My legs are worse. I tried to get up but it was no use. They were like jelly.' Her mouth had a downward turn.

'I'm sorry.' He sat down on a chair at her bed. 'Has the doctor been?'

'Yes, he can't explain it, the fluctuation. He says I've just to go with how I feel, not to force myself.'

He knew that the wasting disease she suffered from was probably progressive. Mrs McDonald, who was a sensible woman, had told him. 'I can't bring myself to tell her, Iain. She thinks it's only temporary . . .' She came in at that moment with a crystal vase of flowers. 'Here you are, Beth. Iain brought them. That'll cheer you up.'

'Thanks, Mother. It'll take more than that.' She looked down at her hands. Mrs McDonald took the hint and went away, glancing at Iain, her lips clamped. 'I think they're all keeping something from me . . .' Her daughter raised her head as the door closed. 'Mother and the doctor, the office people who come to see me. Has she said anything to you? Oh, don't sit there with that calm face of yours! You . . . hide behind it.'

He was at a loss. He leaned over and touched her shoulder gently, feeling pity which was even worse. 'I'm sorry, so sorry. I wish . . .' She didn't move. He straightened again, defeated. Two years ago he had loved her, or thought he did, a bright, healthy girl whom he had met at his golf club. They had planned to be married. What perturbed him was that his love had gone and he could not come to terms with it. He told himself that it was because of the change in her, but he knew in his heart it wouldn't have made any difference if his love had been strong. 'I can't help my face,' he smiled, but she was staring straight ahead. 'God knows I realise how dull it must be for you to be incarcerated here . . .'

'You say that, but you haven't any real idea.' She didn't look at him. 'Men haven't. That doctor rushes in and out, talks about his new baby half the time, how tired his wife gets looking after it, even brings me photographs of it . . .'

'He's trying to cheer you up.'

'Funny sort of cheering up when you think I'm not likely to have one . . .' Her voice quickened. 'When I think of what I was like at Campbells, joking with all the men, turning down invitations from half of them . . . I don't think you realise how popular I was.'

'Oh, I do, it was a real feather in my cap when you agreed to go out with me with all that competition.'

'It was between you and Robbie Spencer. He's not in Campbells now. He hasn't got on the way *you* have—Managing Director of McGraths Carting Company! *Robbie* would have had more time to come and see me . . .'

'Probably.' He didn't tell her that Robbie Spencer was married and had a child.

'Mother's getting fed up with me too. I can see it. She has friends in, and sometimes she goes out with them for tea and whist.'

'Well, you don't want her to stop playing whist, Beth.' He smiled.

'No, but it's the selfishness of everyone going on with their own lives and me lying here . . .' He heard the trembling in her voice and took her hands.

'I have a suggestion to make. Let me book you into a nice nursing home in the country for a few weeks. It would be a change for you and your mother.'

'Amongst a lot of old, ailing women!' She was suddenly outraged. 'Not likely! If you had said Sholton Hydro it would have been more like it! I was reading about it in the paper the other day—all the conferences and dances that are held there, and they've opened a nine-hole golf course now. That's what I'd call a *real* holiday.' She calmed, her mouth twisted in a smile. 'Remember, you and I playing golf out at Cow Glen?'

'Yes, you were good.' He had a sudden picture of her in his mind: the short tweed skirt, the yellow jumper, her sturdy legs in woollen ankle socks, always an outdoor girl, Beth, her brown hair blown back by the wind. She had never had it bobbed, was proud of its curliness. 'But you'll play again. Just you wait and see when summer comes . . .' His voice slowed. Silence.

She wasn't weeping. She often wept when he was with her, and he would kiss her and fondle her and think that perhaps he really did love her. 'Iain . . . ?'

'Yes.'

'I know you're tired coming here. I can see it. You get very . . . acute, lying in bed. Plenty of time to think. Too much time. Would you like to . . . stop . . . for *good*?'

He didn't believe she meant what she was saying. She had done this before, to test him. How could he say anything else but 'No' to a girl of twenty-six whom he had once loved and whose body had been taken over by an insidious disease which the doctors didn't seem able to cure?

He had made an appointment last year with an eminent neurologist. Maevy had given him his name, had looked at him curiously when he had asked her if she knew anyone. But she was as close as he was. She would never ask questions.

The man had explained the situation to him as far as he could without seeing the patient. 'It sounds like some kind of wasting disease as you say, Mr Pearson, motor neurone in character. We're not far enough advanced in that field yet.'

'Is it a matter of time . . . for her?'

'Isn't living a matter of time?' he had replied. 'She could go on for a long time or her kidneys could pack up and she could die tomorrow. But then, you might be run over by a bus tomorrow . . .'

He said it clearly and calmly. 'We've been over all this before, Beth. You know I would never walk out on you.'

'From a sense of duty?'

'I couldn't live with myself.'

'But could you live with me?' She sat up, her nightdress slipping and showing her thin shoulder and the deep hollows at her collar bone. Her beauty, which had been a combination of a fresh complexion and vitality, had gone. Her skin was mud-coloured. 'That's what I decided to ask you when I saw you.' Her dull eyes with their reddened lids brightened. 'What are we waiting for? My death? You have enough money to employ a housekeeper and even a nurse. I know that flat you have is sumptuous enough, but you could buy a house and staff it. I could at least be your wife in name.'

He smiled, shaking his head to hide his alarm. 'You'd be like Elizabeth Barrett Browning!'

'She had a new lease of life when she married. Half of her illness, whatever it was, was imaginary. Maybe I'd be the same. Oh, I know I shouldn't be saying this, Iain, but it occurred to me yesterday when I was lying here. The house was quiet, that afternoon quiet that all invalids know. Men are funny. They don't think of practical things. I could look after the house from my couch, or bed, give instructions to the housekeeper about meals, make out lists for shopping, and see you every morning and night. And maybe I'd become cured, mind over matter!' She was triumphant, and he was ashamed of the despair in his heart at her words. It would be hypocritical to marry someone he didn't love and it would be worse than hypocrisy to spurn her. He tried to think of something to say.

'It wouldn't be a real marriage, Beth. Would it satisfy . . . ?' She interrupted him.

'How do you know? You haven't been in bed with me. On my good days . . .' She went on, telling him of her fantasies. He could hardly bear his utter desolation as he listened. 'Of course, if you just want to sit there week after week and watch me die . . .' He made up his mind.

'We won't make any decisions until you see your doctor and ask him if it would be advisable . . .'

'I have,' she said calmly.

'What did he say?'

'That it was worth a try. I think he's hoping that if I move away he'll be rid of me. He likes patients a bottle of medicine will cure.'

'I still think you should see someone who would give you his expert opinion. I wouldn't feel happy otherwise. I know a man, a neurologist . . .' He knew he was beaten, that it wasn't a medical decision, but a moral one.

10

Erik Skolad was in his going-away suit, grey-striped, expensive-looking, his raincoat over his arm. He took off the soft hat which was set at a jaunty angle. 'Sit down, Erik,' Ginny said, and when he did she smiled at him, thinking how she had never liked him and it was a good thing he had decided to clear out. 'Well,' she said, 'all good things come to an end. I've put your cheque and your references in that envelope.' She gave it to him. 'You have a job in Switzerland?'

'Klosters,' he said, 'very exclusive.'

'Won't the snow be nearly over?'

'Not quite. But it is a health establishment also, much bigger than here,' he looked around disdainfully. 'People come to rest and recuperate. Some stay on who have broken the bones and need massage. The man which engages me says there are the wonderful opportunities for me.'

'I'm sure there are. I'm sorry you haven't been happy here.'

'Oh, I liked *you*, Miss McGrath. You run a good ship.' He preened himself. 'Very good, is it not, a good ship? But it is the old women. They bother me. "Erik, I need some treatment." Between you and me, they are past having treatment.'

She took the plunge. 'Miss Wilcox will be particularly sorry you're going.' She thought she saw his face redden, but it was so ruddily fair that it was difficult to tell. She had told Lizzie that she thought she had heard voices in Miss Wilcox's bedroom on the night of the Ball, that she had made enquiries and was pretty sure Erik had been there.

Lizzie had advised caution. 'We don't want a scandal. Tell him although we've been satisfied with him that we feel he should look around for something better. Say you can't give him an increase in wages, that you've consulted me. That should do the trick.' It had.

'Ah, yes, Miss Wilcox.' He nodded in an offhand way. 'Letitia. But demanding, oh, my God. And if you notice, it is the people with most money who hold on to it the tightest.'

'Perhaps.' Better to be diplomatic now that he was going of his own accord. And if Miss Wilcox was upset, then she ought to know better. Mouse was a different matter. She was at an impressionable age. Ginny doubted very much her sudden passion for swimming. Her excuse that she wanted extra practice in order to be chosen for her school team could scarcely account for her shining eyes and her guilty air after her daily lesson.

Ginny had been terrified that she would do something silly or, even worse, that Erik would. Lizzie was away a lot with Ernest when he had to go to London or abroad. They had a *pied-à-terre* near Regent's Park. On those occasions Annabel stayed with her aunts next door, but they were too trusting, with the exception of Aunt Maevy, and she was at McGraths all day.

The last time Annabel had called at the Hydro Ginny had taken her aside. 'Did Erik tell you he was leaving, Mouse?' She'd been casual.

'Yes, he did.' The girl had shrugged, had looked away. 'Why should I care? He wasn't much of a swimmer anyhow.' She was like Ernest in her urbanity, even if assumed. If there had been tears, they had been shed in the privacy of her own room. Ginny had hugged her. 'I was afraid to tell you. I thought . . .'

'Don't do that, Ginny.' She had released herself, her thin face haughty. 'I have to grow up sometime.' Yes, she had thought, remembering one of her father's Scottish sayings, Annabel would never sell her hen on a rainy day.

But Miss Wilcox was a different matter. She suddenly disliked this young man sitting facing her, talking about the beauties of Klosters. He looked cheap and flashy in the striped suit which was too tightly buttoned. He was at his best in his white flannels and white ribbed sweaters. She would engage some middle-aged Scotsman next time, perhaps a retired football coach . . .

She interrupted him. 'I'll say good-bye, then.' She got up. 'I have a million things to do.' She held out her hand to him and he took it, grinning at her. 'So you aren't sorry that I go?'

'Sorry? Why should I be sorry?'

'Those old women, and those untried girls . . . now *you* are different . . .' His grin was fading under her cold stare.

'Shut the door behind you, Erik.' She sat down and took up her pen, bending over her papers. She was aware he stood for a moment, undecided. It was a battle of wills. She wrote on industriously. The door banging behind him made her pen almost jump out of her hand. She said one of her private swear words and went on writing. She had a couple of hours before Aunt

Maevy arrived from McGraths for afternoon tea. She hoped Miss Wilcox wouldn't forget to come.

Later, dispensing tea to the two women in the Palm Court, she thought of the difference there was in their appearance although they must be about the same age, Miss Wilcox possibly a year older. But where she was wizened and rouged, Aunt Maevy had the fresh, fair complexion of the McGraths, and her hair was still like a new penny.

'I've been meaning to get you two ladies together for a long time,' she said, smiling at them. 'Lemon, you said, Miss Wilcox? I've learned Miss Wilcox's tastes, Aunt Maevy. She comes often to stay with us.'

'Milk for me, Ginny, not cream. It makes the tea such a sickly white. That's lovely. Well, I'm sure you couldn't find a nicer place to stay, Miss Wilcox. Just right in April, not too busy.' She looked around at the other occupied tables, the well-coiffured heads of the Glasgow matrons, the occasional elderly gentleman's bald pate. The younger element would arrive when schools and universities broke up. 'And we've still fresh air here, although I don't know for how much longer with all those Iron and Steel Works creeping nearer every day.'

'But the grounds are so lovely,' Miss Wilcox said, 'and the amenities, the swimming bath . . .' Aunt Maevy wasn't interested in swimming.

'Fortunately when you have such a large estate as this it protects you from everything . . . oh, dear, I do hope that didn't sound snobbish, but you know what I mean.'

'Oh, yes perfectly, Mrs McNab. I'm the same at the Botanic Gardens. That's why I never moved away, even when my parents died. They'll never build round the Kibble Palace—the Corporation wouldn't allow it—and we have a large area behind the house as well. With the Depression in Glasgow nowadays there are plenty of men dying to earn a few extra shillings. They walk out from Maryhill and places like that looking for a bit of gardening. My father would have shown them the door, but sometimes they have a child by the hand and they look famished, poor souls. I thought the War was going to make the world a better place to live in, but all it's done is take away the fine young men. There will be many women who'll never know marriage.'

'Aye, that's true. Maybe they'll be able to turn their minds to other things, fighting for women's rights . . .'

'Aunt Maevy's trying to recruit you,' Ginny said, smiling.

'Miss Wilcox knows her own mind. She's had to, left alone.'

Aunt Maevy accepted a buttered scone. 'And it's easy to see why she comes here for a bit of company from time to time. Yes, go on, try one. The chef here has a light hand with a scone. Yes, I well know what it's like. When my Ellie was in a flat in Hillhead —she's a surgeon, you know, but happily married now—I had many a lonely time even with Susan there, my housekeeper, who was a friend as well as a servant. But you wouldn't have got her to sit down in the drawing-room, oh, dear no. "I know my place, Mrs McNab," she would say. Aye, they don't come like her often.'

'They come and go in my case,' Miss Wilcox said. Her little face was humorous.

'You won't have had my luck, maybe. My sisters Isobel and Kate came to live with me when their husbands died and it's been one of the happiest times of my life.' Maevy paused to wipe her napkin daintily over her lips.

'Yes, you have the advantage over me,' Miss Wilcox said, 'Effie, my maid, who was a friend as well, left to be married, and we never got anyone like her again. Girls don't want to go into service now. It's lonely being an only child. Oh, when I think of how my father filled our house with dinner guests, often medical men from the Royal! But I'm forgetting, Mrs McNab, you worked there, didn't you? Miss McGrath told me.'

'Yes, indeed, and often acted as assistant in the theatre to your father when I became a Sister.'

'Well, I never!' Her eyes were her best feature, Ginny thought, watching her, especially when they lit up like that. 'So you knew him?'

'So I should. He was my surgeon when I had appendicitis. Oh, the state that my Charlie was in about that!' Ginny knew the story, how Aunt Maevy's husband hadn't approved of the surgeon's conservative treatment. 'But all's well that ends well,' she had said to her. 'When I saw how he was wearing himself to skin and bone worrying about me, I thought it was high time to give in and marry him and give up my wonderful career.' What had surprised Ginny was to know that even in those days there had still been that dichotomy in women's minds—at least, intelligent women.

'My father thought a great deal of Dr McNab,' Miss Wilcox said, nibbling delicately like a rabbit at her floury scone. 'Indeed he quite cultivated him.' Ginny smiled inwardly.

'Didn't I know it,' Aunt Maevy said serenely, secure in the knowledge that she had won in the end, 'always going to dinner at your house, and once—you may not remember this, Miss Wilcox,' her friendly smile showed there was no malice in her words, 'I saw him with you. It was at the Exhibition in Kelvingrove Park—1888, would it be? A lovely day. I was in charge of my niece and nephew, Robert and Sarah, and we were on our way to the new Lyon's restaurant where my brother had promised us a slap-up tea. Oh, that was Terence all right?'

'What a good memory you have, Mrs McNab.' Miss Wilcox put down her cup and clapped her hands. The gesture was too childish for her age. 'Yes, I remember that encounter! On one of the bridges over the Kelvin?' She said coquettishly, 'Can you remember what I was wearing?'

'Yes,' Maevy said, 'to the last detail. White ruched muslin with a narrow piping of black round the flounces. And a little white lace hat and a lovely parasol to match, black and white with white lace ruffles. I could have knocked you into the Kelvin!' Maevy laughed heartily. 'Fancy being able to discuss this with you after so many years! Well, if your father had designs on Charlie,' she was tactful enough not to say 'if you had designs', 'he wasn't to know how soon he was to lose his life in a stupid motor accident.' She lowered her head, to hide her emotion, Ginny thought. Everyone knew they had been the happiest of couples, deeply in love.

Miss Wilcox lifted her cup again. 'I saw it in the papers. So very sad. You were probably able to stand up to that better than I could ever have done. I'm not at all self-reliant now. I used to have a good brain—my parents never realised how much I enjoyed the *conversation* round the table—but the trouble was I was never trained in anything, and when marriage passed me by and my parents were gone, well, it's difficult to know what there is to look forward to.' She took a sip of tea, and Ginny noticed the cup shaking as she replaced it in the saucer. 'That's why I've found this place so pleasing. Restful, and yet plenty going on to watch.' She smiled tremulously at Maevy. 'Your niece takes very good care of me. She's into my little ways now.'

'You're not any trouble, Miss Wilcox,' Ginny said, smiling. 'A piece of Dundee cake?' Mr James, the elderly pianist who came in to play at afternoon tea, was giving a sentimental rendering of 'Love's Old Sweet Song'. She could have wished for the Silver Tongues at this moment.

'No, thank you, if you want me to do justice to your lovely dinner. Yes, plenty going on. Dinner dances. Everybody seems to have gone mad about dancing since the War, don't they? No programmes now, though, with tasselled pencils . . . I've kept all mine. And I hear the golf course is opening soon.'

'Yes, in a week's time. People will begin coming for their

summer holidays from May onwards. Mrs Murray-Hyslop likes to feel that all the amenities are within the Hydro grounds so that there's no need to go near Glasgow.'

'And that lovely swimming bath,' Aunt Maevy said. 'We had a little Miss Down-in-the-Mouth visiting us recently. Annabel,' she said to Miss Wilcox, 'Mrs Murray-Hyslop's daughter. You must have seen her about.'

'Oh, the thin child with the pointed chin and large eyes. She looks so endearing with that school hat nearly drowning her. I hope nothing has upset her.'

'Oh, you don't get Annabel going around crying like *some* young girls! She's like her father. Mr Calm-Cool-and-Collected, my sister Isobel calls him, but we could see she was upset. It was that swimming instructor . . .'

'Erik?' Miss Wilcox put down her cup. Some of the tea slopped over into the saucer. 'I'm sure . . . *he* wouldn't, and so . . . *genteel*. Those lovely manners . . .'

'Oh, I don't think he had tried anything *on*, Miss Wilcox,' Maevy seemed disturbed by the woman's reaction, 'but, looking at him I wouldn't have put it past him . . . No, it's with him leaving, and you know how vulnerable young girls are to men like that. We knew she was going to the swimming bath far too often, but we decided not to say anything . . . my mother used to say, "Don't precipitate . . ."'

'Leaving?' Miss Wilcox's voice rose in a little shriek. She put her hand to her mouth as if in apology. 'Did you say . . . *leaving*?'

'Didn't he tell you, Miss Wilcox?' Ginny said, thinking what a fool she had been not to warn her. 'He left at lunchtime. He's gone to work at Klosters.'

'Klosters?' The woman's eyes were staring out of her head. 'You mean, far away, in . . . Switzerland?'

'Yes. He didn't feel he had enough scope here . . .'

'It's temporary, of course?'

'No, I'm afraid not, I paid him off today. But don't worry, we'll get someone just as nice, perhaps a middle-aged man . . .' Had Miss Wilcox been giving him money in return for favours? She threw caution to the winds, 'He was a fly-by-night anyhow, we're better off without him, believe me. He was only out for what he could get.'

Miss Wilcox got to her feet. Her skin was grey, except for the two spots of colour high on her cheekbones, 'A fly-by-night! How can you say such a thing! He was considerate. And kind. I understood him. You young girls have not the experience. We were such . . . friends. He . . . promised . . . oh, oh!' Her hand went to her mouth again, 'It isn't true! It's a joke, isn't it? He'll be back soon, won't he? He . . . said . . .'

Maevy got up and went to the woman. She put her arm round her shoulders. 'I'm to blame, Miss Wilcox. I have a habit, my sisters tell me, of being too blunt. I should have known better. I'm . . .'

'Don't! Don't keep on *talking*!' Miss Wilcox looked round wildly. 'I've got to go. Where's my handbag?'

'It's beside your chair,' Ginny said. She was so ashamed of her own clumsiness that she could hardly speak. And Aunt Maevy taking the blame in her large-hearted fashion . . . 'Sit down again, please, I'm so sorry I've upset you. Let me give you a fresh cup of tea . . .' She heard herself being more stupid than ever in her distress, 'There will be someone else tomorrow, or the next day. The Agency are sending . . .'

'Agency!' Miss Wilcox was almost hysterical now, she screamed the word at Ginny. 'Agency! But don't you see, it won't be *Erik*!' She turned to Maevy, the tears streaming down her cheeks. '*You* tell her. She's too young to understand. *You* know. Tell her how I feel . . .' One or two of the elderly ladies at nearby tables were beginning to take an interest in theirs. Ginny fervently hoped they were deaf.

'I will,' Aunt Maevy said, 'don't you worry. Ginny's the last one to cause you any distress. Now, let me take you to your room. You've had a shock—a good friend, a very special friend, going without letting you know. There could well be some quite innocent explanation. Maybe there'll be a letter tomorrow.' She was leading Miss Wilcox towards the glass doors, Ginny at their heels feeling like a whipped dog. 'You'll have a wee lie down and things won't look so bad as you think. I'll stay with you, if you like, we're of an age . . .' She turned round. 'Hot water bottles, Ginny, and some hot, sweet tea.'

'Yes, of course.' She opened the door and they passed through, her aunt's arm round Miss Wilcox's waist. She was leaning against her like a child. Thank God for Aunt Maevy—once a nurse, always a nurse. Ginny left them.

She went quickly to the kitchen and took two rubber bottles from the shelf, wishing they were stone pigs but the Hydro was too up to date for that. She filled them from the steaming kettle, and as she infused fresh tea, thought how strange it was that the two women who had been involved with Uncle Charlie so long ago should be again united. And that the situation was typical of Aunt Maevy. She had always plenty of love and pity to share. I've a long way to go, she thought, chastened.

11

'It was good of you to let me come so late.' Iain and Ginny were in her flat on the first floor of the Hydro, a pleasant sitting-room with a bedroom and bathroom adjoining. Lizzie didn't believe in crowding her employees into inferior accommodation, and besides, Ginny was 'family'. When the chalets were built in the grounds, she was to have first choice if she wished. He said, looking around at the high walls, the corniced ceiling, 'This is nice. When the proportions are right, everything's right.'

'Yes, I wonder sometimes if Lizzie and Ernest don't regret turning the Hall into a Hydro, but neither of them is sentimental by nature, except with each other.' She laughed. 'I call them the lovebirds.'

'It's the only time I see Ernest with a soft look in his eye. Usually he's as hard as steel.'

'He says *you* are.'

'I wish I were.' He looked away.

'Coffee?' she said. 'Are you sure you won't have anything stronger?'

'No, I have to keep my head clear when I'm dealing with a McGrath.' He laughed.

'Cheeky thing!'

'Maybe I am, disturbing you at nine o'clock.'

'I don't go to bed until late. I was glad you phoned.' She wouldn't tell him, of course she wouldn't, that when she had heard his voice she had been excited, her heart had raced.

'It's this board meeting next week. I thought I ought to discuss it with you. I want to combine it with a dinner, and I wondered if you had a suitable room, or suite?' Foiled again, she thought. Well, she might have known.

'We have two on this floor, a Conference Room and a Wedding Suite. That has one room leading off the other. I could let you see them, and then we could decide on the menus. The suite would be more expensive, of course.

'Nothing but the best is good enough for the McGraths.' He

smiled at her, making his face light up. She wished he wouldn't do that. It was upsetting.

'Well, there's no problem. We'll make it the Wedding Suite, which will give us a separate room for dining in. How long would you want it for?'

'Let's see. A couple of hours for the meeting, drinks six to seven, dinner finishing nine or thereabouts. Six hours?'

'Fine.' She said jokingly, 'They wouldn't want a swim in between?'

'Not a chance. I've a feeling some of our members might lose their dignity with their clothes.'

'It would do them good. Don't you find some people put up fronts all the time? I do in this job. I've had to learn. At home in America I used to say the first thing that came into my head. My parent's favourite remark was "Trust Ginny". I suppose I've learned discretion—' not always, she thought of Miss Wilcox—'and maybe how to see behind other people's fronts.'

'That's just you growing up.' He smiled at her again over his coffee cup. 'I suppose there's nothing better than a hotel or a hydro for that, a microcosm of life.'

'Maybe. You should have seen my front when I had to sack our swimming instructor, or rather, cause him to give in his notice. Lizzie gives me all the dirty work to do.'

'She trusts you. But she didn't trust Erik, evidently. Was he a bit of a lady-killer?'

'Yes, especially with ladies of a certain age, lonely ones.'

'Either end of the scale is very vulnerable. You fall nicely in between.'

'Is that a compliment? Yes, you're right. It was bad enough when it was a certain guest past her first youth, but I was principally worried about Annabel.'

'Yes, she'd be vulnerable. You're very fond of the Murray-Hyslop children, aren't you? I've seen you with them. For such a pretty girl you have quite motherly instincts.'

'Me?' Was that supposed to be a compliment. 'I'm a career woman!'

'Don't protest too much or you may have to eat your words. But Jonty won't give you any worries. He should be able to look after himself.'

'I hope so. He's learning all about life just now in Paris. He's found a teacher, and I don't mean Art. Let's hope he can get out of the situation as easily as he got into it.'

'See, I said you had motherly instincts.' His eyes laughed at her, and then he was speaking soberly. 'That's the difficult part.

Whether it is cruel to be kind, or kind to be cruel.' He looked away, his face grim. Unassailable. You could point the way with Jonty. Not this one.

'My goodness,' she said, brash, the old Ginny, 'you look as if you had all the worries of the world on your shoulders!' And another Scottish saying coming into her mind, she said, 'Who stole your scone?' He turned towards her, his face opening, his smile broad. She felt the warmth again, the racing of her heart. She would do anything for him if he smiled at her like that.

'You'd be good for me.' He shook his head delightedly, 'if you could have heard yourself, saying that, in your American accent . . . oh, yes, you'd be good for me! Here, what did you put in this coffee!' He set down his cup, 'Come on. Let's have a look at that Suite. We've wasted enough time.' Thank you very much, she thought. She got up.

She admired his thoroughness and capacity for instant decision. 'Fine, fine,' he said, looking at the two rooms, commenting favourably on the décor, the space for tables. 'It'll take around thirty people very comfortably. Six or seven tables should be ample. Shall we discuss the menu now or will you send one or two on to me?'

'I'll make out a special business one. Much cheaper than our wedding banquet.'

'What an advantage being in with the management!' He was at ease with her, she felt, it was a good feeling. *She* knew they fitted. How long would it take him to discover it? It wasn't as if she was unattractive. She knew that from the number of men who made what Nan Porter called 'Suggestions, dirty pigs'. And there had been Magnus and Hamish Muir, and young men at home—Craig Trumbull who took her sailing . . . she couldn't remember the rest.

But her heart hadn't been engaged. Why was that? Was it because she hadn't wanted commitment? Now she had changed. She would like to be the object of this man's attentions, she would like it very much.

They went downstairs and he said good-night to her at the door. The night air was soft, and if it hadn't seemed familiar, she would have walked to his motor car with him. 'I'll send off that stuff to you tomorrow,' she said.

'Thanks.' He hesitated, looking at her. 'You iron out my problems, Ginny McGrath.'

'All part of the service.' She tried to keep her voice steady.

'Some day,' his eyes seemed sad, 'I'm going to come to the

Hydro and say, "I would like an injection of Ginny to make me feel well again."'

'I didn't know you were ill.' It was difficult to sound light-hearted.

'I'm not. Not in my body. That would be easy to cure.' He hesitated again, looked at her, then said quickly, 'Good-night, and thanks.' She stood and watched him go swiftly to his car and get in before she shut the door.

She checked that her office was locked up, that John, the night porter, was in his usual place. She had installed a comfortable chair for him behind the counter. He wasn't a young man.

She went up the stairs slowly, feeling unsettled. Perhaps it was because it had been a busy day—the influx of golfers eager to try the new course, a new laundry maid to engage, Erik's replacement to be shown the ropes—not with his exotic appearance but seemingly steady enough. Almost too ready to please, too voluble. 'Aye, aye, Miss McGrath,' this Angus Galbraith had assured her, 'I'm an old hand at the game.' Was Iain Pearson an old hand at the game, unsettling her?

On the first floor, as she went towards her flat, a door opened and Miss Wilcox came walking towards her, wearing a lace boudoir cap and a flowing Japanese kimono on top of a pink satin nightdress. She looked flurried and odd, Ginny thought, and she was muttering to herself.

'Good evening, Miss Wilcox,' she said, 'can I get anything for you?' The woman stopped, stared at Ginny as if she hardly knew her, then gave a little start. 'Why, it's that nice Miss McGrath, of course! I thought it was . . . Effie.'

'Effie?' she said, racking her brains. There was no one of that name here, either among guests or maids, as far as she knew.

'Yes, *you* know. She was to be my companion . . . but she left. A man wanted her. I warned her . . .'

'I'm afraid you're making a mistake, Miss Wilcox. Let me take you back to your room. Perhaps you've just wakened out of your sleep?'

'Out of my sleep? Oh, do you mean, I was dreaming? I've such terrible dreams these days. Frightening . . .' Her lips trembled.

'Come, Miss Wilcox.' She put an arm round the woman and led her back to her bedroom, helped her off with the silk kimono and tucked the covers round her when she got into bed. She had bony ankles, Ginny noticed, like her wrists. She looked badly nourished, the poor soul. Maybe she could get Dougie to tempt her with some of his specialities, keep her in bed for a day or two.

She might ask her if she would like to see a doctor. Belle Geddes would come.

'I miss Effie.' The small raddled face on the pillow was pathetic. 'I miss her more than my mother. She didn't understand. She was a big woman, heavy. She frightened me, but of course she didn't know that. My father wasn't much better. So pompous. And desperate to get me married . . .'

'Try and get some sleep, Miss Wilcox. You'll feel better in the morning. You've had a bad dream.'

'I'll have a massage . . . from . . . Erik.' The woman's eyes closed. Her heavy lids were wrinkled like a bird's.

12

On her first afternoon off, Ginny got out her clubs and went to have a round on the new golf course. She couldn't extol its virtues if she hadn't tried it out.

It was a relief to be out of the Hydro even for an hour or so. Quite a number of guests had already arrived for the Easter week, and she and Lizzie had been busy making out a full programme of activities—*divertissements,* Lizzie liked to call them, always mindful of her French education.

For the children there was daily pony riding, treasure hunts and a wagonette picnic to the Crannoch 'Tumshie', the local name for a well-known hill, on Easter Sunday, so that they could roll their eggs. And swimming competitions and tuition, of course. Angus Galbraith was proving popular. He was a wiry, slightly bow-legged Glaswegian with a cheerful manner.

To Ginny's mind the swimming bath didn't have quite the pristine air which it had enjoyed when Erik was there, but then he had been a perfectionist when it came to personal cleanliness and his surroundings. Angus was careless. Twice he had left the bath unlocked at night. But he had accepted her rebuke with good grace.

She had asked Peter Kennedy, the minister at Sholton Church, if he would officiate at a small service on Easter Sunday for the older people. The others could take the hotel bus, if they wished, and sit 'under the minister'. She was rapidly beginning to understand the idiosyncracies of the Scottish dialect. Peter would give them a warm welcome since their contributions filled the collection box as much as their bodies filled the pews.

After she had tried out the course she would work on the details of the golf competition which would suit those who didn't wish to take part in the tennis tournament. And for the older members there was the putting green. In the afternoon she would have to drive to Crannoch and buy the prizes for all the events, including the *pièce de résistance,* the Easter Fancy Dress Dance. 'Give them a busy programme,' Lizzie had said, 'to convince them that everybody who is anybody is at the Sholton Hydro for Easter.' 'Such snobbery!' Ginny had said, laughing.

Meantime it was enough to be out in the fresh morning air. The grass was a vivid green, the flowering almond trees pink against the blue sky, looking exotic and strangely un-Scottish; there were drifts of daffodils under the oaks. Tall as they were, they couldn't compare with the forest trees back home.

What would it be like there just now? Hot instead of merely warm, Father complaining about the city heat when he arrived home from the New York office of McGraths, Mother still busy about her domestic duties, although they kept plenty of servants. And Sarah would be out and about on her good works.

'I'm interested in a Club for Fallen Women,' she had written in her last letter. It would do her good to fall herself, just once, Ginny had thought. No one should reach the age of thirty-seven without knowing those hidden joys which Jonty, for one, was experiencing at this moment, according to his last letter. Oh, take care, Jonty! Still, everyone did sooner or later. She hoped she herself wouldn't die without having known them.

The contractors had made a good job of the laying out of the golf course. The club-house was pretty, a copy of the chalets which were to be grouped round it, although larger, and the greens looked fresh and inviting. They had taken advantage of the natural inclines and valleys of the ground, they had spared the best of the trees, and although it would never be another Royal St Andrews, the guests would be able to pass a pleasant hour or so in healthy exercise. If they topped it up with a glass of spring water from the fountain in the hall, they would surely feel they were getting their money's worth—six pounds per week full board now because of the golf course. It had to be paid for, Lizzie had pointed out.

She took up her position on the first tee and drove off, not badly pleased with her swing. She remembered it was Iain Pearson who had helped to plan the course. Lizzie said he was one of the best players at Cow Glen, although he was the last person to boast. 'He's very reticent,' Ginny had commented, 'as if there was something he had to hide . . .'

It would have been nice to have a partner. Ahead of her she could see two people, a man and a woman. She walked briskly, filling her lungs, looking around her at the smooth swelling curves and dips of green, the golden shadows of the bunkers, lifting her eyes to the old monastery set up on its wooded hill. Yes, she was lucky: a good job, independence—Belle Geddes had once said it was enough for her.

She realised that the woman ahead of her *was* Belle Geddes, and in another second that the man with her was Mr Cooper who had been staying at the Hydro for Christmas and was now back again. She remembered booking him in herself a day or two ago.

'Hello!' she called as she drew near. 'What a surprise to see *you* here, Belle! I thought you were much too busy.'

'My day off.' Belle, in a grey knitted suit, a brilliant scarf round her dark hair, looked relaxed, cool, her odd silver-grey eyes amused. The exercise had brought a faint wash of colour to her usually pale cheeks. She's beautiful, Ginny thought, maturely beautiful.

'Hello, Mr Cooper,' she said. 'You haven't wasted much time in sampling our course. Is that what brought you back to the Hydro?'

'I wouldn't say that,' he said, looking at Belle as if they shared a secret. He seemed much younger in his sweater and plus-fours, a different person from the suave dinner-jacketed man of the Boxing Day Ball.

'I thought doctors could never take time off,' Ginny teased. Belle's eyes were characteristically half-closed. The sun caught the silver glint in them.

'Norman can be very persuasive.' She spoke slowly, a seductive, husky voice.

'Join us, won't you, Miss McGrath?' Mr Cooper said, smiling with great good humour.

'Thanks, no. I'm only playing a few holes to get the feel of it for the competitions.'

'Norman was looking for his ball,' Belle said. 'Why don't you try over there?' She pointed in the direction of a shrubby hollow.

'Right,' he replied cheerfully, 'whatever you say.' Ginny smiled at Belle as he turned away, *her* smile was coolly amused. She was like Iain Pearson, she thought. You could never get anything out of her about herself, only other people. That reminded her.

'I was going to come and see you,' she said as they walked on together, slowly, so that Mr Cooper could catch up. 'There's a guest at the Hydro, Miss Wilcox, who's acting rather strangely. I met her wandering about the corridor last night, in a dressing-gown.'

'Was that so strange?'

'She was muttering to herself.'

'Ah! What age will she be?'

'About the same as Aunt Maevy. As a matter of fact they knew each other long ago. I gathered her father was Uncle Charlie's chief at the Royal when he was a surgeon there.'

'Ghosts from the past.' Belle was no longer amused, but still cool. 'Everyone fell in love with Charlie McNab. It's hard to find anyone to measure up to him.' Her glance fell reflectively on Mr Cooper who was beating a patch of shrub with his club.

'Do you think you could just sort of turn up and see her? I'm a bit worried about her. She doesn't take part in anything, stays in her room all day.'

'No, Ginny, that wouldn't do. Everyone is captain of their fate. Suggest it if you can, but keep a canny eye on her. Perhaps your problem will be solved and she'll decide to go home. She may simply be here for the Hydro's recuperative properties.' The cool amusement was back again.

'Yes, perhaps. Now that Erik's away . . .'

'Oh, him!' She was derisive. 'That peacock! You're well rid of him.' She wondered if she should tell her more . . .

'Belle! I've found it!' Mr Cooper was beside them, holding up his golf ball triumphantly. He was like a small boy waiting for a pat on the back, or a kiss.

'Good for you. Let's have another go, then, shall we?'

'I'll walk on,' Ginny said. 'I'm giving up after the next hole. Have a good game.' Belle smiled. How did one achieve that state of amused nonchalance, Ginny wondered, as she took a swipe at her ball and lifted a divot from the new turf.

13

'Who's that talking to Ginny in the far corner?' Lizzie said to Ernest. Iain Pearson had asked them to welcome the board members as they arrived, 'not forgetting Lord Duntocher,' he had said with a grin. Ah, well, his lordship's nose would be put out of joint when Jonty officially joined the firm.

Ernest looked at his love lovingly. Only the other day Mouse had said to him, 'Have you noticed, Daddy? Mother's getting as blind as a bat.' 'Do you mean to say you've forgotten the man who was once your father?' Her blue eyes darkened, making them more beautiful than ever, her mouth trembled, she put up a hand to cover it, 'Uncle Patrick! Yes, he was my father at the beginning . . . well, of course, I recognised him, almost at once, but it's such a long time since I saw him. He's gone quite white.'

'He's sixty-four now, love. What a pity Maria and Sarah couldn't come with him.'

'It's more of a business trip. And where's Robert?' She peered. 'They came together.'

'He's standing beside him.' He laughed at her. 'My dearest dear, you must promise to ask Lamond to drive you in future or you'll be killing all the hens at the farm if you're at the wheel. And perhaps it would be a good idea if he drove you to the opticians while he's at it.'

She smacked him indignantly on the wrist. 'What nonsense! Grandma didn't wear glasses until she was well over sixty, and Aunt Maevy doesn't have them yet. The McGraths are famous for their eyesight!'

'Ah, but you're half Bessie Haddow, don't forget. Maybe all her ancestors had steel spectacles from the age of nine!'

'You're teasing me.' She was flustered and beautiful and he loved her more than ever.

'No, I'm serious. We'll get a pair with gold rims and a handle of mother of pearl on a gold chain, and you'll wear it round your neck like a duchess.'

'Well, I might have a lorgnette, but never spectacles.' She was partly mollified. 'Just think what they would look like under a hat like this.' She touched the tulle confection, a froth-trimmed helmet on her copper hair. Ernest had advised her against a brim at a board meeting.

'Ah, Lord Duntocher!' Ernest extended his hand to the man who had joined them. 'I'm glad you're here. Now we can go in.'

'Not before I shake hands with this beautiful wife of yours.'

'It's Lord Duntocher, dear,' Ernest said, controlling a smile. Lizzie froze him with a look.

'As if we weren't old friends, Murdoch,' she said, giving Lord Duntocher her hand. 'And here's Dan Johnson to show you to your chair. But I don't have to introduce you two, do I?'

She and Ernest fell in behind his lordship and the firm's accountant. 'Just look how skilfully Ginny is rounding everyone up,' he said to her. 'Such a capable girl, the way she keeps an eye on the clock, yet manages to be pleasant to everyone.'

'Well, didn't I train her?' She smiled sweetly at him, then opened her eyes wide in pleasure. Robert McGrath had come to speak to them. 'Robert, I saw you talking to Uncle Patrick!' She kissed his cheek. 'How lovely to see you. When we've more time you must tell me all about Edie, and that lovely little girl of yours, Sophie, and how Springhill is looking. Such a happy home on the banks of that grand river.'

'We're all well, including Springhill.' Robert's serious face broke into a smile. No one can resist my Lizzie, Ernest thought. 'Edie's just sorry she couldn't come too but Sophie's too young to leave. Although Ellie said they would welcome her at the nursery at Wolf House. But you know mothers, how devoted they can be.'

'She'll just have to have some more. Anyhow, we'll have a lovely talk later about all our American cousins once this boring board meeting is over.' Ernest smiled to himself as they moved forward, the smile serving for any members of the board who were also making their way in. Boring business indeed! She was a true McGrath with a mind as shrewd as anyone here. Look at the success she had made of this place. She was Grandmother McGrath all over again, talented, beautiful, and she knew how to delegate.

'I knew you'd get them shepherded in before long,' he whispered to Ginny who was beside him at the moment.

'You make me sound like a wardress at that prison in Glasgow.' She laughed at him. 'What's it called?'

'Barlinnie.'

'What a funny name!' No, he thought, smiling with her, it was Ginny who was the living embodiment of Maeve McGrath—the same red-gold hair, the brilliant complexion, that never-dowsed air of vitality, an inherent thing, unique.

Who was going to measure up to her requirements? Where she differed from her grandmother was in the time of her birth. She was a modern woman, a flapper as they called them, who had sought her own independence by leaving home and crossing the sea. Maeve McGrath had had to elope at seventeen to gain hers.

'Excuse me, Ernest.' She was away. Iain Pearson was there, serious, businesslike. He should carry his duties more lightly.

'Did you get all the figures from Jack, Ernest?'

'Yes, and your analyses. You've made a good job of them. Why don't you take my place? You could explain them much better.'

'Don't be modest.' The swift smile lightened his face. 'Besides, there's a copy for everyone. And no one but you can report on the goings-on at Globe Express.' The man looked drawn, Ernest thought, despite the smile. Of course he worked all the days God sent him, especially when he himself had to be in London so much. They were lucky to have him as manager, although it was a pity he couldn't look happier. Perhaps he had some personal worries, but he wasn't the type of man to confide in you. Ah, well . . . Ernest made life easy for himself by minding his own business.

'Right, Iain.' He had no worries about speaking . . . in fact he rather liked it. Lizzie said he was a performer, and he had said, laughingly, that it took one to know one. She was inundated with requests to speak at charity functions in Glasgow. It was said she could bring in more money than anyone else.

Iain had said a few words of welcome. He also showed no nervousness. He had the assurance of a man who knows his job thoroughly. 'And now I'll ask Mr Ernest Murray-Hyslop to speak, our chairman and emissary who will bring us news from the capital.'

Ernest bowed to the applause. 'I feel like the man who brought the good news from Aix to Ghent,' he smiled round at them, 'and it *is* good news. But first of all I would like to welcome the two members of our family from America who are here today, Mr Patrick and Mr Robert McGrath from New York State.' Patrick bowed briefly into his beard, Robert smiled with his eyes, probably doubtful about being too effusive beside his dour uncle. The applause, however, was genuine.

'I said it was good news. The parent company, Globe Express Deliveries, are more than pleased with our progress for this year —indeed, I got the distinct impression that we were propping them up.' Everyone laughed.

'Since the War, our parcel business has improved. There have been several innovations, refrigerated lorries for one, which we now have running from Aberdeen to Liverpool and London, the two main ports of entry for imported meat.

'We have also acquired tankers for the transport of liquids in bulk, the most important being petrol. I see nothing but improvement here as more and more people begin to own motor cars. Who knows? In times to come the average family might even own two!'

'That'll be the day!' someone said.

'Naturally, with this increase in bulk motor traffic, suitable premises for garaging and maintenance are required, and fortunately, due to the foresight of Mrs McNab, we have plenty of room at Parkhead. We have installed there an up-to-date plant which cleans by the injection of steam, and which is going to more than pay its way . . .' he stopped to look round. Yes, they were impressed.

'The figures for all those items are on your balance sheet, but, as a small indication of our progress we have at the moment one dozen 1,000 gallon petrol tankers in use, which is far removed from that humble old Dobbin, God rest his soul, with which this firm began. Wherever he is, may his feed bag be always full!' He enjoyed watching the laughter. Even Patrick grinned and nodded appreciatively. He, like his brother, Terence, now breeding a different type of horse in Ireland, had known the time when the only employees were carters, and when their father, Kieran, had fought for their rights.

'Of course, our chief earner is and always has been removals, and there again we score by having the necessary storage space in the East End. We have a reputation for safe deliveries, and I'm eagerly awaiting the day when we will have pneumatic-tyred vehicles for even greater safety. Mr Pearson tells me that this time isn't far off.' He looked at him. 'What's your estimate, Iain?'

'Nineteen-twenty-four.' He nodded decisively.

'There you are, gentlemen. You can trust your Crown Derby and Spode soon to McGraths. And, of course, in the wake of removals we have the auctioneering and valuating business which is growing at a steady pace. You will see that we have acquired premises in Sauchiehall Street. The offices will be on the first floor, with a showroom at ground level. As you know, my stepson, Lord Crawford, is at present undergoing a training in Fine Art on the Continent, and hopes when this is completed to join the firm. We couldn't make an engineer out of him like Iain Pearson, but I have a feeling he'll hold his own in Sauchiehall Street.' Ernest glanced at his notes to let this sink in. There were some who didn't approve of his latest move, but the answer lay in one word, 'diversification'. He wouldn't hesitate to tell them that.

'By the way, there is one point which I should have mentioned in connection with heavy haulage . . . We have now instituted a back-loads system which we hope will cut out fly-by-night operators who use ex-Army lorries. I assure you that outward journeys are carefully monitored from Head Office, and we make sure that no lorry makes the return journey empty.' There were nods of approval. That had a canny Scots ring which pleased them.

'Railways.' He paused. 'That is a saga in itself, and you will see that the present state of affairs has been fully explained in the prospectus. Your company will keep a watchful eye on developments, and fluctuations will be noted. We always try to keep on good terms with the railways, but', he glanced round, smiling, 'one step ahead . . .' He raised his head confidently.

'This is exemplified by our latest development, a Travel Service. We have already set it in motion by taking over a private firm which makes coach tours to the Swiss Lakes, but this is just a beginning. There will be substantial reductions to any member of the board who would like to book a holiday.' Everyone laughed. 'Do I see surprise on your faces? Ah, well, you have only to talk to Mr Patrick and Mr Robert McGrath who will tell you that the Travel Section is a going concern in our American branch. Isn't that so, Patrick?'

Patrick rose to his feet, portly, white-haired, severe. His Scottish accent had almost gone. 'It sure is. In a country the size of America, people take to coach trips like a duck to water. They want to see their own country. They are curious about its many marvels, Niagara Falls, Arizona—well, gentlemen, and lady,' he bowed to Maevy, 'why don't you come and see for yourselves? We have two of the younger generation already working in that department, Benjamin Vogel and Sam Murray-Hyslop. One or the other is ready to come to Scotland any time and give you a few tips.' He sat down, inclining his head to the applause.

'There, gentlemen,' Ernest said, 'that's how it's done in the New World, push ahead, go with the times; but if we have anything to do with it in Glasgow, the Old World won't be far behind! We have come through a dreadful War triumphantly, but at a terrible cost to our young men. Unemployment is now the spectre as one by one heavy industries go to the wall, but I can confidently claim that McGraths is doing its bit to provide jobs, and what's more, a link with the country which came to our aid, the United States of America.'

He sat down, well pleased with the look of satisfaction on the faces round the table as they applauded him. The dividend paid was the chief reason for that, but there was no doubt about it, McGraths was a thriving concern. He looked across at young Terence McGrath's portrait of Grandmother Maeve in her gold gown. She seemed to be smiling too.

Ginny moved swiftly about the room where they were to have dinner. At the moment the guests were drinking cocktails, and Dougie Armstrong, who had worked in a Glasgow bar at one time and knew something about them, had concocted a special one for the occasion and called it the Sholtie Flyer.

It was a good talking point. As she helped the waitresses to dispense the glasses, she explained to anyone who was disposed to listen that it was the name Uncle Terence in Ireland had given to the racehorse he was training. 'Keep it in mind for the Grand National,' she said, laughing. 'Get your bets in early!'

Jonty had written to say that Giselle and Terence were in Ireland at the moment. Dr Reynaud, who was looking after Terence, had thought he was well enough to travel. 'I miss going to their little *appartement* in Passy, but, of course, there is Madeleine's place . . .' 'Madeleine's place,' she had thought, but remembered that he had then gone on to extol the beauty of Claudine, a student at the Beaux-Arts.

'I'm having a wonderful time, Ginny,' he had written. 'Perhaps I've let Paris go to my head, although the main thing still in my mind is Florence, and my career. But it's the atmosphere here, the gaiety after the War, the change in manners . . . and morals. I was terribly naïve when I first came. I'm afraid you wouldn't recognise your boy Jonty now . . .'

She stopped beside her father with a tray of drinks. She had welcomed him earlier when he had arrived with Robert. He was talking to Iain Pearson, and she stood beside them, waiting for a chance to interrupt.

'Yes, last month,' her father was saying, 'President Wilson refused to give his vote. Of course, he's an ill man.' They were talking about the League of Nations, she realised. Aunt Maevy was a great one for politics and had fired her to take an interest. 'You should have a broader view than most, Ginny,' she had said, 'an American living in Scotland. Take advantage of it.'

'He always had his principles,' Iain said. 'Where would we have been without the United States in the War? I always remember his words: "The world must be made safe for democracy." It was a hard struggle for him, a man of peace.'

'Aunt Maevy was the same,' she said. 'She laid aside her interest in the Suffragettes until the War was over. ''First things first,'' she said.'

'Trust Ginny to get her oar in.' Her father could still put a damper on her. She wouldn't get annoyed.

'We're being too serious,' she said airily. 'What about a Sholtie Flyer to cheer you up?' She saw the slight look of disapproval on his face. Sarah would never be found passing round a tray of alcoholic refreshment, oh dear, no!

'What's that?' Iain said, smiling at her. He was losing weight, surely, and he had hardly any colour at all. 'You need a good holiday,' she thought of saying, 'you work too hard.'

'My father could tell you.'

'Could I? This lass credits me with more knowledge than I have. There's the Sholtie Burn . . .'

'Maybe Uncle Terence hasn't told you. It's the name he's chosen for his favourite racehorse.'

'Well, well!' He shook his head, smiling. 'Trust Terence! He's remembered where he comes from at least.'

'Try one, Father,' she said. It mattered to her at that moment that he should take the drink. It would signify approval of her as a daughter, as an independent woman who nevertheless loved her family although she had to live her own life. She saw the frown, the pursed lips above the beard. Go on, she said silently, everything's going all right for you now, maybe not the way you wanted it, but Gaylord's at peace, Sarah is happy with her Fallen Women, I'm standing on my own feet, you have a loving wife . . .

'Ah well, maybe I will,' he said, 'though I'd rather have a dram.'

'I'm all for an experiment,' Iain said, following suit. 'You won't find it wanting in a touch of the hard stuff, Mr McGrath, if I know Dougie.' And to Ginny, 'You've done things well for us.'

'Wait till you see the menu Dougie and I have thought up. And we've lobsters for you and Robert, Father, so that you'll feel at home. I remember the ones we got at Wanapeake.'

'We still do. They're brought from Maine, packed in ice. By McGraths,' he added. They laughed. The Sholtie Flyer was helping already, Ginny thought.

'I'm looking forward to meeting the two younger members of your family who run the Travel Service,' Iain said.

'Sam and Benjamin? Ben, they call him. Yes, they're bright lads. You ask my sister Kate about them and she'll heap them with praises. That's the only thing she misses living with Maevy, her grandchildren. But it was a wise move. Sometimes I wish I'd made it. Too late now . . .' He looked around. 'I haven't had a word yet with the sisters. Where are they?'

'They're missing out on the drinks. Aunt Isobel can't stand for a long time. They've gone back to the Stables to see Kit and Annabel to bed since Lizzie and Ernest had to be here to officiate. But I've placed them next to you at dinner. You can have a good chin-wag then.'

'Aye, a real old crack.' He shook his head. 'It's not so much places you miss when you come down to it, but people, your ain folk.'

'Yes, I understand that,' Iain said. Ginny saw the genuine look of kindness on his face, of appreciation of her father and his longings, even of his nature which would never be completely happy with the *status quo*, and fell in love with him. It was instant, and certain. There was that in the look which exemplified the man, a largeness of spirit. No one else will do for me, she thought, and there was a feeling of rightness which stayed with her as she left them and went round the room, greeting, smiling. She overflowed with the feeling of certitude.

Here was Dan Johnson with his Ruby, now a stout matron, and Jack Richardson, the firm's secretary, with his smart thin wife with the new shingle which didn't suit her thin neck. And here was their banker, Alex Crichton, with that lovely Highland wife, Catriona. Scotsmen stuck to their wives at parties, unlike America. Were they afraid they might lose them, or had the wives said they mustn't be left? Now Mr Gregg, Sandy, an old member of the board and at his last meeting before retiral. Wife gone, his old friend, John Drummond, gone. She stopped to chat to him before she brought over some of McGrath's office staff to join him, dressed in their best and all aglow with imbibing one or possibly two of the Sholtie Flyers. And she waited long enough to see Sandy Gregg brighten considerably with the attentions of that pretty typist called Muriel from Accounts.

The guests who sat down to dinner were a very merry party indeed. Iain Pearson was beside her, and she thought how strange it was that when she had arranged the places she hadn't been in love with him and now she was. Or had she always been and hadn't known it? He said in her ear as he pushed in her chair when she sat down, 'I'll see you in the office afterwards to square up.'

'There's no need for that. You won't run away.'

'I'll want to congratulate you.' He raised his voice and said to Robert McGrath who was sitting opposite them, 'Have you any more in America like Ginny?' The swift smile which she loved.

'No. I'm afraid not.' Robert shook his head. 'Ginny's always been adventuresome, to the despair of Uncle Patrick and Aunt Maria at times. Just like our little Sophie.'

'Ah, away with you. Sophie's ten times nicer.' And as Robert turned to speak to Lord Duntocher who was beside him, she said to Iain softly, 'You should wait till you sample the food before you talk of congratulating me.'

'That was just an excuse. I have something to tell you.' She was happy, indescribably happy. She felt she was exuding happiness, and kindness. She loved Robert, burly Lord Duntocher with the hair growing out of his nostrils, Mr Gregg with his widower look partly banished by the good wine and food and perhaps the attentions of Muriel from Accounts, Jack Richardson and his thin wife—she even loved her shingle—she loved the whole world. She loved Iain Pearson. And he had something to tell her.

14

She was sitting in her office making up accounts, or trying to, when Iain came in.

'Sorry if I kept you waiting. Your father wanted me to have a nightcap with him. I could hardly refuse.'

'You should consider yourself highly honoured.' Maybe, she thought, he's thinking of him as a son-in-law, seeing if he would do. 'He doesn't take to everyone. That's why I thought he would be happier in the Hydro where he can be alone occasionally. But he'll be off to the Stables tomorrow morning to spend the day with his sisters. They're putting up Robert.'

'You're a close family.' He was walking up and down, looking at her pictures. He seemed restless.

'Yes, it's always been like that. The McGraths and the Murray-Hyslops are hopelessly intermingled. And yet we've spread far afield, France, Ireland, America. I think it was my grandmother, Maeve, who made us close. Her influence is still there.'

He stopped in front of her. 'People say you're like her. I see it in her portrait.'

'Oh, I'll never look like her! She was a beauty! Lizzie favours her, and she favoured Lizzie. But I *feel* like her in temperament.'

'Robert said you were adventurous.' He lifted a paperweight on her desk, examined it.

'Yes, I always want to see round the next corner. That's why I left home. But it's all right now . . . Could you sit down or something? You're making me feel . . . oh, never mind! I felt for the first time tonight that my father accepted me as I am, didn't understand me but accepted me. That's all children want.'

'He speaks highly of you. And admires you. I could hardly get away.' He didn't sit down.

'Isn't that typical? *Sprouses* to other people!'

He smiled at her. She could hardly bear to look at him because of her love. 'Where did you get the word?'

'It's a family one. Probably my grandmother's.'

'I told you you were like her.'

'Well, she was a businesswoman. Which reminds me,' she lifted an envelope, 'There's your bill since you asked for it. Ernest wanted to pay it for you, but Lizzie and I said no, it was a business proposition. We have to make the Hydro pay.'

He laughed and took it. 'That's the way I want it . . .' He hesitated, looking at her. She looked down at her blotter. 'My head's full of cigar smoke and whisky fumes. Would you like to go out for a walk?'

'A walk!' She forgot her shyness. 'It's nearly eleven!'

'It's the Roaring Twenties. The night's a pup. That's another Glasgow expression.'

'I'll add it to my vocabulary. I don't mind. I could do with some fresh air.' She got up, putting her cardigan round her shoulders. 'I don't feel like sleeping in any case.'

'Nor do I. And I've something to tell . . .' Now that he had at last come to the point, she wanted to prolong this interval between knowing but not saying.

'And I want to check that the garden door to the swimming bath is locked. This new man we have is careless.' She took a bunch of keys from a hook beside her desk and he opened the door for her. Their glances met. His eyes seemed to be full of sadness. Why should he be sad when she felt so happy? Did he think she didn't love him, or could it be—her heart suddenly hurt—that what he had to tell her was something entirely different? But at eleven o'clock! He was so complex. So withdrawn. With Jonty she could have put her arm through his and said, 'Come on, spill the beans . . .' This one was . . . austere.

The grounds were different at night, strange. The smooth lawns and the beds of flowers looked like a painting, not real, the edges razor sharp because of the contrast between dark and light. There was a painter, Chirico, she thought his name was, who painted like that. Like a dream. The red blaes paths glistened here and there with mica, the pink cherry blossom was no colour, and she could smell the heavy scent of the wallflowers.

'Night's the nicest time of the day,' he said, she knew he smiled, 'you know what I mean.'

'Yes. Restful. Much better than taking a pill.'

'You've no need of that, a young girl like you.'

'My brother often did. Gaylord.' She didn't know why she wanted to harp back. 'Laudanum. Father would like to keep it all a secret, but it's better to be frank.'

'Yes. But some find it easier than others. And you have to think how it's going to affect other people.'

'No, you have to come out with it and damn the consequences, or it festers inside you. Kieran understood him as well as loved him. That's the important part, the understanding. I was too young to understand. He shot himself because he couldn't come to terms with his homosexuality. There, it's said, the dread word. There are so many skeletons in family cupboards which need a good airing. Have you any in yours?'

He smiled at her. 'How direct you are! Not as far as I know—a happily-married sister, parents dead, unfortunately, but they were happily married too. No, there are no skeletons there.' He stopped and put his hand on her arm. 'I'm the one . . . oh, it isn't a skeleton unless I make it so. I have no doubts about what I'm going to do, no doubts at all, but the thing is, Ginny,' he spoke quickly, 'it's got so complicated because I've fallen in love with you.'

The swift piercing sensation which went through her heart was new. Exultation. There had never been for her a feeling which deserved that word. All doubts gone, no longer any need to hold back. 'But that's fine! I love you! I knew it tonight, quite suddenly!' She raised her face to him, and a spatter of huge raindrops splashed on it. The wind blew round them, she heard the trees rustle, and then the heavens opened. She laughed, standing beside him, her thin dress already soaked. She put her cardigan over her head. 'The great moment of my life and we're going to get drowned! Doesn't He like me up there? Have we offended Him?' She was laughing, delirious with happiness. She spat out a strand of wet hair which had blown into her mouth.

He paid no attention. 'You're saying you love me?'

'Yes.' She put her arms round his neck. It was the natural thing to do. 'Just kiss me once and then I'll know I haven't been brash and forward and all the things I'm trying to grow out of.'

His arms drew her towards him, he bent his head and they kissed. Their mouths were wet, their faces, their hair. There was no tenderness, but she didn't want that. There was strength, and tears, or the rain, or both, and a terrible wish for him to take her completely there and then, which was ridiculous for her to think of even if it *was* the Roaring Twenties. There had to be a courtship, and words of endearment, and visits to relatives and this is my intended . . . how did people wait? She was shivering with delight and excitement and he took it for cold.

'You're soaked. We'd better get back in.'

'There's a fire in my sitting-room. I'll make some coffee.'

'There's something I have to tell you, Ginny. Oh, my God, I've been a fool.'

'For standing in the rain?' Why was he so solicitous? It was better to think like that, disregard the warning bells. It had been too good. 'Look, I've just noticed it. We're at the door of the swimming bath.' She tried it. 'And it's open. That man . . . well, it suits us as it happens.' She went in and he followed her. 'There, it's locked now.' She turned the key. 'I won't tell him off this time.'

They stood for a moment, not seeing. 'Do you know where the switches are?' he asked.

'No, but my eyes are getting adjusted now. There's a sort of reflected light from the water. And it's all glass. Take my hand, Iain.' There was something he had to tell her. It couldn't be all bad. He was only thirty-two, he hadn't shot his cousin, like Gaylord. And in his dealings in the firm he was above reproach, Ernest had once said, a man of integrity. Too much at times. Of course he would have had girls. She didn't mind that as long as it was behind him now. But supposing, allowing that he loved her but that he had an . . . understanding with someone else? 'Iain,' she said, plunge in, damn the consequences, 'you aren't by any chance . . .' she stopped beside him, her hand tightening on his, her heart pounding, the other hand to her mouth.

'What?'

'In the water.' She pointed. As if in a dream, her voice wouldn't come. She tried again. 'In the wa . . . ter. Has Angus left some things . . . floating about . . . ? I told you he was careless. Things . . . to teach with . . . like water wings?'

'It isn't anything like that.' His voice was brusque, no intimacy in it now. He went to the edge of the bath and knelt down, peered. He said without turning, 'Is this the deep end or the shallow end?'

'Shallow.'

'I'm going in. It's a body.'

'A body.' This was the second time this evening she had experienced a new feeling. But this was not at all like exultation. It was a mixture of shock, disbelief, a slow conviction, a sick pain in her heart, then her head cleared. 'I'll help.'

'No. Stay where you are. I'll bring . . . it to the edge. Perhaps it's all right.' Not a chance, she thought. No one would choose to float on the water like that as a joke, especially at midnight.

In his shirt sleeves, the water up to the knees of his trousers, he was wading heavily towards it, his arms outstretched. Once he stumbled. When he reached the body he stood for a second, turned, then began to push it towards the side like a boy pushing a sailing boat. He was panting when he got to her. 'Grab hold of the clothes!' He scrambled out as he spoke. She knelt down, grasped, not looking.

He stood for a second beside her to get his breath back, his clothes dripping wet, not rain wet, his hair plastered on his brow, his ribs showing through the soaking shirt. 'Now!' he said, kneeling down. Together they heaved, both panting with the exertion until whoever it was, was lying on the tiled walk.

'See if you know . . .'

'Yes.' She was calm now, quite calm, but breathless. A woman. Nightdress, a sodden Japanese kimono, bare, bony feet, thin, large-knuckled hands. Look at the face . . . plastered black hair, black streaks on the brow. Dyed. Not young. It was Miss Wilcox. The bright intelligent eyes were dull in death.

15

Belle Geddes folded her silk nightdress, then the matching negligée, and put them in her case along with the mules of the same soft turquoise colour. Silk underwear, a dress, not as short as Ginny wore but short for her. The underwear should be black, and the dress scarlet, she told herself as she put cosmetics in the toe of one pair of shoes, rolled-up stockings in another pair—those at least were black since she was going for a sinful weekend.

When Norman Cooper had proposed to her she had said truthfully that she didn't love him. 'There's only been one love in my life and it couldn't be repeated. And that's that.'

'I'm not asking for a mad passion,' he had smiled at her. He was a humorous man, which had been the first thing which had appealed to her, 'but something more than companionship. I can get that from my dog.'

'I can get that from mine,' she agreed. 'Jock keeps a better eye on me than any husband.'

'And Shoonagh's the same with me.'

'West Highland?'

'Yes, they're the best.' It had been another point of agreement.

He drove her up through Stirling and Callander with all the lovely mountains, lochs and glens to nod to—Ben Ledi, Loch Earn, Glen Ogle and Glen Dochart, and on the way they stopped to have a look at Rob Roy's grave and the ruined church with the odd cupola on top of it. And also to have a drink in the nearby inn. She thought that if she ever stopped working at Sholton she might come up here to die since one seemed to be much more in touch with fundamentals than when surrounded by Crawford's Iron and Steel Works. The shepherd who sat dreaming over a dram with his two collies gave her the same feeling.

They stopped at the best hotel in Killin and she deliberately didn't listen when Norman registered them as Mr and Mrs Cooper. There was no point in being squeamish now, and, remembering the shepherd, one might as well be hung for a sheep as a lamb.

When she was seated at the dressing-table putting in her earrings—she had always favoured earrings with her black hair and white skin—he came up behind her and kissed her neck. She saw his face in the mirror, middle-aged, a little anxious, but essentially kind, and she thought, could I stand him doing that to me every night if I were married to him, and then even *more* in bed? It was in for a penny, in for a pound when it came to marriage, and she had become used to her own company. But she would be old some day, and lonely . . .

She smiled at him, and saw them in the mirror, objectively, as a couple, quite a handsome couple. They could have quite a good time together—jaunts like this, concerts, theatres . . . but no work? Her heart sank. Could she live without her doctoring? He wanted her to have 'an easy time', as he put it.

The dining-room was cosy, with a log fire in its stone fireplace, and the other diners looked like them, well-heeled Glasgow or Stirling couples who had decided to spend a weekend in the Highlands for a change. That was a favourite word in Glasgow. 'I could do with a change, doctor.' Well, this was a change for her, letting her see how the other Belle Geddes might live if she became Mrs Cooper—an attentive man at her side, plenty of money to spend, golf twice a week, bridge, which he said he would teach her . . . but what about her doctoring? Look at that poor woman, Letitia Wilcox, who had led a perfectly useless life because she had never been trained to do anything else.

'I heard there was a tragic accident at the Hydro,' Norman said as if he were reading her thoughts. 'In the swimming bath.'

'Lizzie tried to keep it out of the papers.'

'It was someone in the Athenaeum Club who lived near the lady, I think. No, the Press didn't get hold of it.' They were having Trout Rob Roy, which meant that it had been rolled in oatmeal before it was fried, and then flamed in whisky. His lips were glistening with the fat, and there was a grain of oatmeal in the corner of his mouth. He was enjoying his Trout Rob Roy.

'Oh, well, I can safely tell you. I was called out last Saturday night to see this woman. Ginny and Iain Pearson, you'll know him, the general manager of McGraths, found her floating in the swimming bath, drowned.' He's not medical, she thought, and I shouldn't be telling him this. That's what would happen if she were married to him . . . careless talk. And then if you lived alone you didn't talk at all as a rule, so that in a situation like this you talked too much. But the wine, mixed with the fumes from the Trout Rob Roy, was loosening her tongue.

'What do you think it was?' he asked. 'Suicide or an accident?'

'The Procurator Fiscal will treat it as an accident, I think.' She knew him well. She had had a talk with him. 'There's no proof otherwise, and Ginny found both doors to the swimming bath unlocked. Carelessness of one of the staff.'

'Did you know the woman?'

'Yes, vaguely. As a matter of fact she had known Mrs McNab's husband when he was a surgeon in the Royal. This woman's father was his chief. Isn't life strange?'

'Mrs McNab?'

'The famous Aunt Maevy.' She smiled. 'You know the three sisters.'

'Yes, of course, they're becoming an institution in the Hydro. There's the fragile one who's in the office sometimes, and the other one who shows you to your room, Mr Murray-Hyslop's mother, I think . . .'

'Step-mother.'

'And the stately one who's in McGraths. That's Mrs McNab?'

'That's right. It's a sad story about the drowned woman.' She put her knife and fork together on her plate. She found the trout rather heavy, used as she was to the light meals Mrs Lawson prepared for her. 'She had never married. Perhaps at one time she hoped Charlie McNab would marry her, and because she had plenty of money she kept on going to places where she would meet people.'

'Like the instructor in the swimming bath? Swede, wasn't he, Erik something or other? I heard some women talking about how she hung round him.'

'Poor soul. I've no doubt tongues clacked. Ginny got rid of him.'

'Ginny is Miss McGrath who runs the Hydro? Any place would succeed with someone like that at the helm.'

'Yes, she's a chip off the old block, Ginny. Her paternal grandmother, Maeve, was beautiful. Not many people to whom you can apply that adjective. Pretty, yes, but beauty is . . . extra.'

'So Ginny saw there were goings-on between Erik Skolad and Miss Wilcox?'

'You *knew* who I was referring to?' She couldn't remember ever having been so unethical.

'Oh, yes,' he smiled at her, 'she had a go at me. I got the impression, though, that behind it all she had quite a good brain.'

'Which was in process of atrophying through disuse. That was condescending of me. Sorry. But there must be thousands of women like her, unmarried with money, trying . . . to fill in their time.'

'Precious few these days. You should know that. And there are worse days to come. Depression is on its way. It'll be a long time before we climb back to our former pre-war glory, if ever. I can see the signs. Anyone in business can see them. Glasgow will go down the nick.'

'Is that the general opinion?' She reflected that medical people were poor at politics, especially country doctors. They hardly saw beyond the next surgery. But she was lucky. If she hadn't had a career and had been forced to live like Miss Wilcox, would she have been any different?

Her mind stayed on the dead woman as she listened with one ear to Norman's reminiscences of happy holidays spent climbing here when he was a boy. He was genuine, and good, she decided. Would he have been shocked if she had told him of Ginny's belief that Miss Wilcox was paying Erik for his favours?

And would he have had a fit, after the shock, if she had pointed out to him that he was paying her for *hers*, in advance, by taking her to the best hotel in Killin, dining and wining her *à la carte*, for the sake of getting her into bed?

Men had queer little blank spaces in their brains, dead ends, she thought. Charlie wouldn't have been like that. How do you know? she asked herself. He didn't marry you. He chose Maevy. She would never tell if there were any flaws in him, but you may be sure there were. No one was perfect . . .

Norman looked better with his clothes on, which were expensive and well cut. She was now reflecting in the bedroom upstairs in the best hotel in Killin. As he came towards her in striped pyjamas. The Paisley-patterned dressing-gown on top made him look like a bag of potatoes tied round the middle.

She, fortunately, had grown thinner as she grew older—maybe not so alluring as before, but she could wear fashionable clothes, and she spent money on them. And why criticise Norman when she had no idea how Charlie might have looked if he were here? It was fourteen years ago, a lifetime. But, ah, Charlie, you were different, you were my dearest love. Did you ever guess?

And now he was in the four-poster bed beside her. (Extra for the four-poster, she had read in the prospectus.) And it took the poor soul ages! He was aiming, of course, to emulate the Royal Scot, but with his puffing and blowing and backing to get a better run at it, and stoking up again and then full speed ahead—except that *his* full speed was more like the Cathcart Circle on a foggy night than an express train, it wasn't exactly overwhelming as far as she was concerned.

The truth of the matter was that he was past it. She had to restrain herself from putting a finger on his pulse. And to be even more truthful, she was too. At least Hamish Black from Crannoch, with whom she had had a long-standing affair after Charlie died, had been virile, but there had never been much love between them, simply a common need, or rather that she had a ghost to exorcise. It was he who had supplied the motor car in which Charlie had met his death.

On the second night she was thinking longingly of Jock and her own fireside, and Mrs Lawson bringing in her Sunday supper on a tray, instead of the rich Highland fare here which was overloading her stomach. She was thinking of a good book to read, peace and contentment. She had had it all now—a real love which had never been consummated; a make-do-and-mend love for the sake of her sanity; and now this nice man who thought it would stave off death if he took her into his bed, a poor variation on the theme.

'I enjoyed it, Norman,' she said when they were driving past Rob Roy's grave, 'you gave me a fine time.'

'What about it, then, Belle? If you really want to keep on your practice, I could buy a piece of land at Sholton and you could have the house of your dreams.'

She wanted to say there was no house in her dreams, that it had gone long ago with Charlie, that and all thought of children. Now it was only work that counted and a simple place where she could be comfortable for the evenings.

And a good bed for Jock. He wouldn't like to be uprooted either. He had that lovely padded one she had bought him, with sides to keep out the draughts (although sometimes he came into hers), and a rubber bone and his own dish with 'DOG' on it, and the old shoe he preferred to worry rather than the rubber bone. And his walks by the Sholtie Burn.

'Jock and I have no territorial ambitions,' she said. He looked discomfited. He didn't like that sort of talk. It was ambiguous. He was a man who liked to know where he stood with a woman. He himself thought they would get on very well together, and he had stretched over backwards (that was apt) to please her and give her a good time.

'It couldn't have been nicer,' she said meekly, 'but I'm afraid I'm too set in my ways.' She broke the hurt silence which lasted until they were through Stirling, by suggesting that he might try Crieff Hydro for his next break instead of Sholton. That it might be more in his line.

16

Jonty read the letter for the second time. '*Cheri, pourquoi . . .*'

> . . . have you not visited me last Tuesday? I think that now the little *appartement* in Passy is closed, you would make this one your refuge. I keep it nice for you, I buy the food you like, the *saucisson* from the little butcher near the Gates, and for a special celebration, the *pâtisserie* which you adore, *les religieuses. Mais, pas de Jontee!*
>
> Are you tired of your Madeleine? She longs to see you, to stroke the hair back from the noble brow, to listen to your so strange voice, and much, much more which you know I cannot put in this letter. It is lonely here without you when I have only Manon . . .

For some reason, as he read through the letter for the second time, Jonty had a clear picture of the cat sitting primly with its paws together and its mouth pursed. 'I'll be glad if you don't come back,' it seemed to be saying, 'she was mine first.' What on earth was wrong with him? He ruffled his hair. It was a perfectly ordinary cat.

The truth of it was that his ardour had cooled along with the improvement in the weather. Or was he satiated? A disturbing thought. Paris in the late spring was enchanting. The chestnut trees were freshly green in the boulevards. In the clear, thin sunlight the pale grey stone of the buildings became pearl-like, the Seine glittered silver, and there was a vitality in the air which seemed to seep through the grimy stones of the Beaux-Arts, making the students restless.

The pavement cafés were crowded with people who talked, gesticulated and laughed as if they had been released from prison, and now that it was warm, there were the *flâneurs*, mostly young people, who filled the streets as they strolled, no longer wrapped in their cloaks and long scarves. The girls were bare-headed, short-skirted, they walked often four abreast so that he had to move aside to pass them. Their laughing repartee often escaped him. Perhaps it was as well he didn't understand their street argot.

Then there was Claudine. The relationship he had with her was like that with Ginny, a meeting of interests, a comradely affection. There was nothing flirtatious in her manner. It was that of a girl who had brothers, and she mothered Jonty in a non-compromising fashion which was a pleasant relief after Madeleine who was becoming . . . well, cloying. It was the only word.

They had struck up a friendship in February in the annual Vin Rouge parade, marching along behind the costumed band through the Latin Quarter, shouting, dancing, brandishing bottles, and when the gendarmerie had charged in, she had led him through the narrow streets away from the crowd. He was grateful to her that he wasn't forced to spend a night in jail, because there was no doubt, the wine had gone to his head.

She went round the galleries and markets with him—their favourite was in the rue Mouffetard, or sometimes the one at Clignancourt on Sunday. He fell in love with la Sainte-Chapelle along the Seine from the Beaux-Arts, and when he told Claudine she suggested an outing to see the Écouen stained glass. He developed a good eye. He knew his executive ability was less than mediocre, but that didn't matter, he told himself. His job would be to sell, not produce.

Because of his interest in the history of art they spent one Sunday at Fontainebleau. Claudine had no time for the grandeur, her favourites being the small apartments which Napoleon and Josephine had occupied. 'Small is relative,' she told him, 'wait till you see my home. I've to take you there for supper tonight.'

It was a little terrace house near Saint-Lazare, where Madame Sechel and Claudine seemed to rule the roost over Monsieur and four brothers. One had been killed at Verdun. Monsieur was lost in admiration at the clever daughter he had produced. 'Think of it, monsieur, a working-class girl who studies art! *Mervielleux, n'est-ce pas*? From her earliest days she draws like an angel!'

Madame Sechel deferred to Jonty. She dusted his chair before he sat down and presented him with great pomp and ceremony with a bowl of weak-looking tea. Her husband, not to be outdone, offered him some of his pipe tobacco in a tin. Jonty politely declined. Monsieur's black moustache was stained ginger at the edges, and he soon filled the little room with a thick pall of acrid tobacco smoke.

But the brothers soon rescued him, taking him into the small plot of ground behind the house while Madame and Claudine were preparing supper. While he admired the ornamental hens they kept at the end in a small pen, they plied him with questions about 'Aston Villa' and 'Huddersfield'. Their pronunciation was so bizarre that until they said, '*Les équipes*!', he was at a loss to understand them.

They were all for taking him to the *gymnase* there and then, but Claudine came out and stopped them in their tracks. 'No, no,' she said severely to Jonty, 'they will have you wearing a striped jersey soon.' And to her brothers, 'This is an English milord, understand?' Jonty regretted he wasn't wearing the Cameronian kilt. He was tired of insisting that he was Scottish. But he enjoyed his visit. The cramped little house was far removed from Madeleine's velvet-lined *appartement*, but it seemed more wholesome.

'Have you a girl in Paris?' Claudine asked him one night when they were walking by the river. The lights were reflected in the dark water, le Pont des Arts was like a lit pathway to the Louvre. The couples who passed them had their arms round each other.

'Not exactly.' He put his arm round her shoulders and drew her close to his side. He would have made the same gesture with Ginny, or Mouse.

'That is the first time you put your arm like so.' She laughed. 'I do not ask, but *c'est la coutume*.'

'When in Paris do as the Parisians do.' He bent and kissed her cheek as they walked. Perhaps it was his upbringing which told him he had to be off with the old before he began with the new.

'You don't have to do that,' she said. 'It is a relief that you don't grab and squeeze and *feed* on me the way some of the boys do. We girls laugh at it together. We are free, independent, we do not want to be a man's plaything.'

'I have an aunt like you,' he said, 'I don't mean she was ever a man's *joujou*,' he laughed at the thought of Aunt Maevy being anyone's *joujou*, 'but she has always fought for women's rights. Before the War she was a Suffragette.'

'Yes, we have them here too, but not so militant. Mostly it is the women writers who carry the flag, many of them American, like, let me see, what was her name . . . ah, yes, Natalie Barney. My professor said he had been at one of her salons in the rue Jacob. Then there is the rich one, Edith Wharton, but they are *all* rich, and the strange one, Gertrude Stein. They come here for freedom, to express their views. America is, how do you say it, puritan?'

'Puritanical.'

'They form a coterie here of their own with their poets and writers—Ezra Pound, you know of him?'

'I know of Hemingway.'

'*C'est ça*. There are our own poets as well, like Claudel and Valéry. They all live around here, in the sixth or seventh *arrondissements*.'

'Is Proust one of them?'

'Yes, when he gets out of bed, I suppose. At least, that is what my professor says. He chatters while we paint. But I think we grow tired of the Americans. We are so poor and they are so rich, and they keep asking for the War debt to be paid. Imagine! This country is bled dry, my brother killed, and they ask for more!'

He changed the subject. 'Do you read poetry, Claudine?' He had had a pang of guilt when she spoke of Claudel and Valéry. He remembered writing poems in the dirt and noise of battle, and here in a beautiful city surrounded by works of art he had had no desire to put pen to paper.

'No, it is too *exaltée* for me.' But that was what *he* had been. 'I am a working-class girl with working-class hands which like to paint. That is where I find my *métier*. My hero is Matisse. Such radiance, and then, when he discovered the structure of Cézanne, he was . . .'

'Home and dry?'

She turned to him, laughing, 'Home and dry. I like that. You are a charmer, Jonty, with your English politeness.'

'Scottish. Remember?'

'I tease you. You are a gentleman in any case. It is in you, and how you look. Don't throw yourself away. And don't be afraid that I might seduce you. You are too young for that kind of thing.'

'What a nerve!' He swung her round to him and attempted to kiss her the way he would kiss Madeleine, but it didn't come off. Her body didn't naturally fall to his, and she was impatient.

'Let us walk on,' she said, and when they were strolling again she said, 'Don't tell me you have a lover already. You English!' He was annoyed. She was too small for him anyhow, but then all French girls were small. She had wonderful eyes, certainly, but a sallow skin. They should see Mother's, or Ginny's, the fineness, the tea-rose beauty of it. And all the McGrath women were tall.

'Scottish,' he said dourly.

'Is it different?' She was still laughing at him. 'Anyhow, you are the fast workers.'

'I may look young,' he said, 'but I fought in the War. Right to the end. Came home wounded in November 1918.' It was the first time in his life he had boasted about it. He hoped it would be the last.

'But that would make you a man! My brother, Alphonse, was twenty-five!'

'I was a schoolboy. I can't understand it now. But there was a fever . . . the young men probably had it here as well. I used to sit at my desk and think what nonsense it was learning Latin when all that was going on. Lots of us enlisted. My cousin here, for instance, Terence McGrath. He was born in Scotland, lived in Ireland but married a Parisian girl. He would never have been called up but he volunteered.'

'He is dead?'

'No, but he suffers from neurasthenia. He's convalescing in Ireland at present. He is a painter.'

'Ah, it is difficult to paint if one is not well. I have the right constitution, sturdy, like an oak tree. That is good. The aristocrats die young because they don't know how to take care of themselves. One day I shall be famous.' She didn't sound boastful, only factual.

Claudine will never dog my footsteps, he thought, as he listened to her explaining Cézanne's painting methods. She is her own woman. She accepts the temporary nature of our friendship because she has her own plans for the future. It was just as well. She wasn't the kind of girl he was looking for. She was too . . . masculine. He would know the right one when he met her, but there was no hurry. Meantime, there was the problem of Madeleine . . .

He called one day at the Passy flat when he was nearby and to his surprise and delight found it occupied, but only by Giselle.

'Yes, I am alone,' she said when she had greeted him. 'Have you forgotten that I am a working girl? Pierre gave me leave to go with Terence to Ireland, but they won't keep my job open indefinitely.'

'I can see that. It must have been a wrench leaving him and the children.'

'That is true.' He saw there was a new line on her face running from her nose to the side of her mouth. It wasn't easy to have an ailing husband who couldn't work. 'But he seemed more relaxed at Woodlea, and Honor urged me to leave him with the boys for a few more weeks. They're young enough to absent themselves from school. It was a hard decision but . . . we have to live.' Terence was lucky with a wife like Giselle, he thought.

'You'll miss the children especially.'

'Yes, but they adore being there. The house is always full of grandchildren and dogs, and outside there is all the freedom in the world, not like Paris. Terence's father is the best grandfather you could imagine. He takes them with him when he goes to the Irish fairs in the . . . jaunting car? And they play about the stables and the lads there spoil them. They were looking so fat and rosy that I steeled my heart.'

'And Terence?'

'Well, he has his bad moments, but somehow they're not so bad in the Irish countryside as they are in a frenetic city like Paris. There isn't the same pressure. He paints the horses, and he's done a wonderful portrait of the stable-hand, Liam, and some watercolours, which is a new departure for him. He says he just takes some of the moist Irish air and colours it.'

'That's really good. Is he doing the wonder horse, the Sholtie Flyer?'

She laughed. 'No, it's too young and skittish yet. It wouldn't stand still for long enough. Uncle Terence thinks it will be a few years before it's ready for the big races. He says it is a flyer all right, but it hasn't any road sense yet.'

'Well, you look better for your holiday too. How do you like working in a *couturier*?'

'I like it. It is in the doldrums just now because of the *garçonne* look, you know. Coco is to blame for that. All those little *passementières* are out of work because of the plain silhouette. I see your look of bewilderment, Jontee, but your mother would understand. It will come back. But, yes, I like my work. I have discovered I have a flair, I have even been asked to put on a little show by the great Pierre. I suspect my mother is behind that, but *que voulez-vous*?'

'So you may be a *Directrice* any day now?'

'No, no, I think that may take as long as the Sholtie Flyer . . . I talk about myself too much.' Her face sobered. 'Jontee, I had a visit from Madeleine yesterday. I didn't realise things . . . had gone so far. She wonders why you don't visit her.'

He coloured, embarrassed, 'I've been . . . rather busy.'

'She's unhappy. She weeps. You see, she lost her husband, and she had hopes . . . oh, I know I shouldn't interfere, but I feel I'm to blame in a way for introducing you. It is not unusual in Paris for a young man to have an older lady friend, but Madeleine was perhaps a wrong choice. Once she has an *idée fixe* . . . you understand?'

He was miserable. How much did she know? 'We've been good friends, of course, well . . . more than that.'

'I have to say this. She surprised me beyond words. She has formed the idea that . . . you are going to marry her.'

'Good God!' He was horrified. 'There was never anything like that. She was lonely, I liked her . . . ' *you lusted after her*, 'one thing led to another . . .' She put up her hand.

'I don't want to hear. She is my friend, my friend for a long time. I know her nature. She is . . . determined. She has surprised me sometimes at what goes on in here,' she pointed to her forehead, 'and yet, we are tied by the years we have known each other. That is friendship . . .'

'I never led her to believe that there was any question of marriage!' The words burst from him.

'Then you must make it clear to her. Staying away won't help. I stand in the middle, I see both sides. Your mistake was in choosing someone like Madeleine.' 'But she chose me!' he wanted to say as an excuse, a poor excuse. 'But I can't interfere.'

'I wouldn't ask you to, Giselle.' And yet it had been at the back of his mind, or even more ridiculous, that he might write to Ernest, man to man, and say to him, 'Look, Ernest, I've got myself into a bit of a fix . . .' Wasn't that what men said when they had got a woman pregnant? He blanched. Maybe that's what she wanted! A child! Her husband had been killed. She loved looking after Clovis and Jaime . . . Oh, God, what a fool he'd been! Ernest could have advised him, *should* have, that urbane step-father of his who hadn't married Mother until he was in his late thirties, and he certainly wouldn't have been celibate. But all along they had left him to make his own mistakes. They had never even tried to get him out of the Army . . .

'This has been a shock for you, Jontee?' Giselle was saying. He pulled himself together.

'I've been . . . stupid. I'll go and see her.'

'That's best, but be gentle with her. Poor Madeleine.'

Women stick together, he thought, but, then, why shouldn't they? There was nothing praiseworthy in *his* behaviour.

He nerved himself for three days before he went to the Palais Royal. It was worse than climbing over the firestep and throwing himself into battle. He castigated himself, saying to himself that he was less of a man now than he'd been as a soldier. But life had been simple then because he had gone by the rules, and now it was complex because he was making rules for himself.

He had got himself into this situation. He would have to get himself out of it. Florence was like a star ahead. He had only until mid-July to spend in Paris and then he would be at home before setting off for Italy. Perhaps he would visit Craven in Bucks before that, and, of course, he would join the family in Arran in August.

* * *

She welcomed him with her quiet smile, her secret eyes, but there was no resentment in them. 'I am so glad to see you, Jontee. I begin to wonder if you were ill. You did not mind my writing to you?'

'No, but I've been busy, very busy. You see, I'll soon be going to Florence and there are examinations, things to clear up.'

'Oh, that is not for a long time yet.' She was a trifle impatient. 'Sit down, my darling, in your favourite chair.' Manon, the cat, was in her usual place in front of the fire, swaying in her usual dream. At the sound of her mistress's voice she turned and gave Jonty a supercilious stare before she turned back again.

'Madeleine, I have to tell you . . .' All the tactics that he had worked out went by the board, the gradual introduction of the idea that it was purely a temporary affair, with no substance, seemed impossible, useless. 'I don't think I'll be able to come any more. As I said, there's a lot of work to be done and I have to let my flat, be in it to see people.' He took a deep breath, 'I'm afraid I've been coming here under false pretences.'

'How you chatter on, *chéri*!' Had he spoken at all, or had his embarrassment made him unintelligible? '*Par des moyens frauduleux*? What do you mean? You came because you wanted to. Isn't that the truth? Now, see, I have this lovely Muscadet for you. You will sip it with a Boudoir biscuit or two and then we make love.'

'I don't think that would be wise.'

'Why?' Her eyes were veiled.

'It is . . . unfair.' He felt like an awkward nine-year-old, instead of going on for twenty. 'I am . . . too young to settle down.' Ridiculously he remembered a Scottish song, a jaunty kind of song that had been a favourite with those ladies who visited Mother and liked a sing-song round the piano, 'I'm owre young tae marry yet . . .'

'You don't love me?' Her heavy hair had gained a flickering reddish-gold hue from the fire. She looked desirable. Claudine had talked about the boys 'feeding' on her. That's what he had been doing, coming to Madeleine as if to the fountain in the Pump Room at the Hydro to give him pleasure and release.

'Of course, but . . .' He touched the swag of hair which hung over her left eye, 'you see,' he sounded infantile to himself, 'I don't want to get married . . . not for a long time.' Could he say, 'Unless I have to?' But *she* would have said, thank God. And she was as slim as a reed.

'But that's all right!' The hair swung back from her face as she raised it. 'We are still getting to know each other. I want you to feel that you cannot live without me, that I am part of your life. It takes time. You have to grow up and then we will be the same age, no?' She laughed. Her laughter had always intrigued him, a chuckling kind of laugh in the back of her throat. 'You enjoy me, don't you?' She turned round, still on her knees, came in between his and put her arms round his neck. The heavy muskiness of her perfume filled his nostrils. The heat from the fire was making one side of his face burn. He was burning in other places too.

'Madeleine, I should go . . .'

'Bring your wine with you, *chéri*. We will be more comfortable in the bedroom.' He lifted his glass meekly and followed her. He was aware that the cat stalked behind them, tail in the air.

* * *

He was disgusted with himself. He walked by the Seine for a long time, and since it was Paris he behaved histrionically, banging one fist into the other hand, sometimes grabbing his hair, swearing, 'Oh, foolish, foolish, spineless *séducteur*!' He hissed it at the river. But who had been seducing whom?

When he got back to his flat he couldn't sleep. What had happened to him? Someone who had fought in the War and then had crumbled at his first encounter with a determined woman? Was it better to have something to fight for? But you *have*, he told himself. You have your future and you know it's not going to be with Madeleine. If you haven't the guts to tell her, write to her, but keep away. He got up and sat shivering at his desk in his nightshirt.

> Dear Madeleine, I am ashamed of myself. I came to tell you that our affair was over and then went to bed with you. If we both felt the same that would be all right, but I know you would like a permanent situation. I understand this. You are lonely and want someone in Paul's place. I know I wouldn't suit, *believe me*.
>
> There is no point in coming to your apartment any more. It is dishonest, and it only makes it more difficult when I have to leave Paris. Believe me [no, he wouldn't underline it this time, for why *should* she], there is no one else. But I have a million things to do with my life, which precludes any permanency. If you can forgive me, would you meet me for dinner in the Trocadéro and we can talk together? I shall always be grateful to you, *chère* Madeleine, for giving me such pleasure and companionship, and I feel very badly about writing this letter at all. Your friend, Jonty.

She didn't reply. He met her by chance at Giselle's and she was the quiet and discreet Madeleine whom he had been originally introduced to. He excused himself as soon as he reasonably could. Giselle didn't speak as she showed him out. She shook her head sadly, making him feel guilty and miserable.

* * *

The remaining weeks before he left Paris were purgatory to him because of the letters which came on an average of twice per week. They were neither quiet nor discreet. He thought of showing them to Claudine, but feared her frank tongue. She would have a few choice words to describe what a fool he had been.

Help came, strangely enough, from Terence, who had returned from Ireland looking much better. 'I'm not cured,' he told Jonty, 'I never will be completely, but Dr Reynaud says he will see me through the bad times. My salvation will be in getting older. Age blunts feelings and memory, he tells me. I have to believe that.'

And when Jonty said how pleased he was he gave him a whack on the shoulder. '*Your* feelings are far from blunted, eh? Giselle tells me the fix you're in with Madeleine. Of course, women stick together. You were a damn fool to take up with a withdrawn type like that. They're always trouble. What's wrong with all the young girls you meet at the Beaux-Arts?'

'You're right,' he said, 'I thought the difference in ages . . .'

'It doesn't mean a thing with Frenchwomen. I'm younger than Giselle, come to that. Don't forget you're quite a catch!'

'I'm worried sick that she might be having a baby.'

Terence laughed. 'Baby! She would have told you if she were, believe me. I'll have a word with Giselle. She has more influence on Madeleine than anyone I know.'

'The damned awful thing about it is that I feel so *sorry* for her.'

'That, my lad, you have to live with.' Terence's thin face looked bitter. Was that all life offered, having to live with one's mistakes or misfortunes?

A few days before he was due to leave Paris he had a letter from Madeleine. He winced as he read it.

> I think you are despicable, but perhaps that is how the English aristocracy behaves. [Scottish, he muttered . . .]
>
> Believe me, if Giselle had not persuaded me, I should not have written this letter, but she is a good friend and has her

own worries with Terence. That is her cross. I have to bear mine.

In the end I have to accept that I never mattered to you except as a dalliance. At first your letter made me feel that you had killed any capacity for happiness in me, but I have begun to think more kindly of you. You were too young. Maybe it was misplaced maternal love on my part. Giselle says so, and she is very wise.

I am going to take her advice and join a few societies and begin to meet people who are more in tune with me. Perhaps in time I will meet someone who will give me what I long for, the married life which was denied me.

C'est la guerre, and it has much to answer for. I will try to think of you kindly. You have a lovable nature, and perhaps in years to come you will write and tell me what has happened to you. Or Giselle will tell me. I can't as yet wish you happiness, but the bitterness will pass . . .

He felt years older as he went out for a walk, but young enough to trot along by the Seine when he thought no one was looking. The relief was great.

17

One thing, Ginny told herself, sitting in her room behind the reception desk, my boy, Jonty, will be home soon, and the other good thing is work. In front of her was a pile of mail. They were turning away bookings now that they were in the high month of holidaying for the monied Glasgow folk, August. July and the Fair fortnight were for the ordinary lot, although there would not be much holidaying for them with the unemployment figures growing all the time. Many were beginning to ask what they had been fighting for.

She had asked Lizzie if she didn't feel guilty about catering only for the comparatively well off, and she had said, not at all. 'The McGraths grew from nothing by hard work. And we never did it on the backs of the poor like the Crawfords. We've paid good wages, looked after our employees, and here in the Hydro we give good value for money. What's wrong with that?' It was a good argument, and she hadn't mentioned the amount of charity work she did in Glasgow. She was organising soup kitchens now.

There were the menus to be changed and then duplicated. Dougie was rightly proud of his soups, but she had decided on a larger choice of alternatives than melon and grapefruit. Glasgow had a fine reputation for seafood, and what the guests could get in Rogano's, they would expect to find in the Sholton Hydro.

What else? That list of new arrivals for Aunt Kate so that she could swan up to their rooms and give them her special welcome which everyone valued so much. 'Swan up' was perhaps rather unkind, but Aunt Kate had never forgotten that someone had written in the visitors' book, 'and special thanks to Mrs Murray-Hyslop Senior, who has already become an institution.' At times the McGrath sisters seemed almost too capable, especially Aunt Kate and Aunt Maevy.

What was next? She looked through her notes. 'See to the fire precautions being completely overhauled.' Iain would have done that for her . . . she put down her pen and stared at the opposite wall which had a fine picture of the Falls of Docharty by a local artist. The turbulence of the water echoed the turbulence of the heart. When would she be able to accept that he was not for her?

He had been a tower of strength that night after the terrible discovery of Miss Wilcox's body floating in the swimming bath. Together they had carried her to a small changing-room and laid her on the bench, and then he had stayed there while she telephoned Belle and the police. There had been no chance to talk, to touch each other.

He had come the next day and helped her with the necessary interviews and questioning, been discretion itself in keeping the news from the guests and the staff. Of course, the family had been there, and Aunt Maevy had been especially helpful with her calm practicality. And then, when they were alone, he had come up to her and taken her hands. She thought at first it was to draw her to him, but, her face uplifted, she saw his, and the expression on it.

'What is it, Iain?' she had said. 'It's over now. Don't take it so badly.' She couldn't understand. He had been businesslike and competent all day . . .

'Miss Wilcox? God, it isn't that. The poor woman's at peace now. No, it was before . . . when I told you I loved you . . .' She still didn't understand.

'And I said I loved *you*.' She smiled to hide her fear.

'The joy when I heard you say that!' His face lit up for an instant. 'I've known how I felt about you for a long time, but . . . it was too late to tell you, much too late.' He said roughly, 'Sit down. If you look at me like that I'll never have the courage to . . . do what I have to do. Here, sit there.' He pointed to the sofa and sat on a chair opposite her. 'I daren't touch you . . .'

'Go on.' Now the fear was real.

'Ginny,' he leaned forward, 'I love you, always will. I've never been more sincere in my whole life. Last night, I was going to go on and tell you the . . . circumstances, and then, Miss Wilcox . . . happened.' His grimness terrified her. 'There's a sick girl, Beth McDonald. We formed an attachment once, pleasant, golf, companionship, I made certain promises . . .'

'Go on!' She was hoarse, trembling.

'She has an incurable disease. The one thing she wants in life is to be married to me . . .'

'But you love me!' She couldn't listen to this any longer.

'I'm committed. I shouldn't have said I loved you. I blame myself totally.'

'You're telling me . . . that this girl . . . you can't back out?'

'Yes, that's what I'm telling you!' He shouted, and yet his face was a white mask, registering nothing. She could see he wasn't going to plead for understanding. It was, she realised, a moral dilemma, and he had decided on his course. Nothing would change him. He was that kind of man.

She sat straight-backed and suffering in the silence in a way she had never suffered before. The one man she had ever wanted was telling her that he had a commitment to someone else, someone who had a greater need than hers. She sat waiting till some of the bitterness went, till her sore heart eased a little and she could speak. She felt she too had been through a serious illness. She got up. 'Well, that's that,' she said. 'It's the bitterness, *here*!' She was aware that she struck her heart dramatically, she who hated dramatic gestures. 'Why did you *say* . . . ? If you hadn't *said* . . . !'

'I know. It burst out. It's strong, permanent. But I couldn't live with myself if I chose happiness with you and . . . walked out on Beth.'

It was her turn to burst out. It was like an abscess. 'How noble! How satisfactory for you! Your conscience at rest, your halo firmly in its place . . . !' It was then she really ranted and raved . . .

Belle Geddes had come up to see her in her sitting-room a few days later after her evening surgery. 'You can forget about it now, Ginny, it's all over. Death by drowning. The Procurator Fiscal will treat it as an accident since there's no letter.'

'It was because of Erik,' she had said.

'Do you think so?'

'I'm sure.'

'Well, that's one thing I'd never do, kill myself because of a man, would you?'

'Not likely,' she said, then burst into noisy tears, made a fool of herself, threw herself into a corner of the couch, did everything but drum her heels on the carpet.

Belle didn't cuddle or comfort. She wasn't that type. She let her go on until she herself felt she was making a fool of herself, and stopped. She said, drying her eyes, 'I'm ashamed of myself.'

'It's more than Miss Wilcox, isn't it?'

'Yes. I'm sorry, of course, really sorry for her, I only wish I had tried to talk to her, befriend her, let her see what kind of man Erik was . . .' she drew in her breath, 'It's Iain.'

'Iain Pearson?' Belle would never have dissimulated by saying, 'Iain who?'

'The night it happened we walked in the garden and the rain came on. We took a short cut into the house by the swimming bath . . .'

'I know all that.'

'We had discovered we loved each other. At least I had.'

'So?' She looked impatient.

'When all the noise and shouting had died down he called—the day before yesterday—and told me he was sorry about misleading me, that it was incredibly stupid of him,' her smile had no mirth in it, 'but that there was someone else.'

'Who is someone else?'

'Someone called Beth McDonald whom he's had an understanding with for years. She's ill, she has a disease called, myasthenia, I think, yes, that was it . . .'

'Myasthenia Gravis! Good God! That's not a picnic.'

'Is it fatal?'

'Sometimes, not always. It may be long-drawn-out, or quick. There are all kinds of unpleasant symptoms, diplopia—that's the eyes—difficulty in swallowing, indistinct speech, the worst thing about it is the overpowering fatigue which gets worse in the evenings.'

'Not bad enough evidently to stop her wanting to get married.'

'She wants to get married!'

'Yes, he was committed, he said. He apologised for the night before, putting his arms round me, saying he loved me, that kind of thing, that I was to forget it. Just like that.' She shrugged.

'He's either a saint or a fool.' Belle looked at her. 'Well, that was a slap in the face all right. What did you say?'

'Oh, you know me.' Her throat was dry and burning now. 'I ranted and raved and wept for five minutes, then calmed down and said I was sorry and that, of course, he must do whatever he felt was right. I wish I could learn to be as calm as you, Belle. I'm ashamed.'

'Better out than in.'

'In a way Miss Wilcox's death helped me to regain my sanity. I thought, that poor woman killed herself because of a man. I'm damned if *I* will. They aren't worth it.' She wished she sounded more convincing.

'Some of them are. It remains to be seen whether Iain Pearson is. You look terrible.' Her voice was gentle. 'Now I'm going to give you some bad advice. Practical. I wouldn't dream of telling you how to think. That's your affair.' She had opened her handbag and taken out a small phial. 'There are two pills in there, a sedative. But if you wash them down with a tot of whisky you'll sleep like a log. You look starved of sleep.'

'Only two?'

'I told you I was practical. Not that I think there's a chance in hell . . . now for the homily. Fifty years ago or less women didn't work outside the home, except the poor. When they were under emotional stress there was no real way to work it off. If they were rich they had to sit and twiddle their thumbs, and if they were poor their stress was exacerbated by toil and moil and kids. You're lucky. You know perfectly well the Hydro would fall to the ground if you were to take to your bed with the vapours.'

'Rubbish!' She was faintly pleased. 'There are the aunts.'

'Their usefulness is limited by their age.'

'And Lizzie.'

'Lizzie has learned to delegate. And at the moment she's sunning herself in Arran with Ernest and the children, as you well know. Jonty might have joined them, if he can tear himself away from Paris. He's a handsome lad. Women will always throw themselves at him, but once he meets the right girl he'll be faithful. He's like Ernest there, not by blood, but by example.'

'Yes, he and Lizzie are a good advertisement for marriage.' Despair swept over her and she began to weep again, softly, the tears spilling out. This time Belle put her arms round her.

'Yes,' she said, 'a happy marriage is one of the blessings of men, they say. I turned down what might have been one a month ago.'

'Did you?' She was interested enough to stop weeping.

'You know him. Norman Cooper.'

'That nice man who used to come here quite often? I wondered what we had done to upset him.'

'It wasn't you. I suggested he should change his venue and he might meet someone more suitable. That I preferred the quieter joys.'

'You're a one-man woman.' She wiped her eyes.

'If you mean Charlie McNab, yes. And I was never his, as they say. He could never see past your Aunt Maevy. Now, you get into bed because I don't want you falling all over the place when I give you your tot and the pills. There's one thing that doctoring has taught me. There isn't much that doesn't look better when you've had a good night's sleep.'

* * *

Towards the end of August she felt sane again, except that there seemed to be a hole where her heart had been. She seemed to swim through the days, her own efficiency surprising her since she didn't feel *real*. She looked up one morning from her desk and saw Aunt Isobel at the glass door of her office, her thin shape in the grey dress and white lace collar which she wore for 'business' as she called it. She came in quietly, as she always did.

'Good morning, Ginny. I've brought in the accounts for you to look over. We'll have to watch that plumber. He's getting above himself.'

'I'll tell him I'll stop recommending him to other people. That should fix him.' And then, 'You look well, Aunt Isobel.' She didn't think so. She was interested that she could even *think* about her aunt. She knew the china-doll fragility had proved to be misleading. It was the spirit behind the delicate façade that mattered. Aunt Maevy said that she would outlive them all, but Ginny had noticed how attentive she was to her elder sister's health: 'I've got a fine recipe for beetroot wine that'll put some colour into your cheeks . . .' She smiled at her aunt, with love.

'I can't say the same thing about you. But the family will be home today from Arran and Lizzie should be in fine fettle to take up the reins again. You've had a bad time recently.' How much did she know? 'And you're working too hard. You're shilpit-looking.'

'I don't get out much.'

'It's those late nights. I'm told you're up till all hours.'

'We always have dinner dances every night in August, Aunt, and the guests like to see one of the family there.' She didn't say that she danced the night away in the hope of making herself sleepy. Belle's pills and tot hadn't been repeated.

Each night, sleepless, she lived through her despair, her rage against fate and her resentment against Iain, until she reached through weariness a plateau of pity and understanding. Each night was a repetition of the one before. She asked herself endlessly when she was going to learn that it was useless when the circumstances could not be altered. And then she would conjure up his face when he had said he loved her, and she would writhe and turn and know there was only one answer . . . when she gave up loving him.

'Maybe Kate, Maevy and I could take turns?' Isobel was saying.

She had to smile. 'No, thanks, Aunt. You all like an early bed. It's only for the month, and then, don't forget, my boy—' she smiled again—'God's gift to womankind, will be here soon. He can take my place on the dance-floor.'

'My, you dote on that lad, don't you? He'll have some fine tales to tell you, no doubt, about his high jinks in Paris. You always were as thick as thieves.' Her face sobered. 'I . . . I brought in the papers.'

'Oh, thanks.' She glanced at the pile. 'Have you given special orders to Sam about them?'

'Yes, and I told him to look slippy. People don't want their morning paper at eleven o'clock, especially our business gentlemen who have to see to their stocks and shares. Though they'd have to be gilt-edged these days. He's a chatterbox, that lad. He goes into the office and keeps the girls off their work.'

'They should know better. I'll speak to them. He's collecting the shoes for cleaning early enough?'

'Yes, Kate keeps an eye on him there. Ginny,' she paused, 'I don't like to say this, but I think I should warn you. There's an announcement in the *Herald* about Iain Pearson's wedding.'

'Is there?' She knew she was brusque. 'Let me see.'

She took the paper her aunt held out to her, flicked through it. The two or three lines of print seemed to find *her*, jumping out of the page, saying, 'See, it's over! I told you it's all over . . .'

> 'Iain Robert Pearson, son of Mr and Mrs Robert Pearson, both deceased, of Muirend, Glasgow, to Miss Elizabeth Mary McDonald, only daughter of Mrs Rachel McDonald . . . and afterwards at the Windsor Hotel, Glasgow, on the . . .'

Had it said 'married quietly'? Or had she imagined it?

Aunt Isobel came to her and put her arm round her shoulders. It was feather-light. 'We know how you must feel, Ginny. It was in the evening paper as well. We talked about it last night and Kate said . . .'

'There's no reason for you three to sit gossiping about my affairs,' she said, shaking herself free. 'I knew he was getting married. He told me. It's no concern of mine.' She looked up and saw the hurt on the thin face, the soft, ash-blonde hair, the blue McGrath eyes, not so brilliant as Grandmother's had been, but still that indescribable blue blue, like a river seen through the trees, all the bluer for being half-hidden. My eyes, she thought. 'There was never anything between us, Aunt Isobel.' She spoke politely, apologising for her rudeness. 'Now, we must get on. I've got the tennis competitions to do!'

She was quick. 'Yes, of course, Ginny.' She went back to the other side of the desk. 'I had an idea about the first prize. Why don't we call it the Suzanne Lenglen Trophy since everybody's talking about her. There's a picture in the paper of her curtseying to the Queen.'

'All right. That's a good idea.'

Her aunt was looking at her. In her eyes was understanding and love, and the quirkiness that was the essential Aunt Isobel. 'She has an awfy big nose, all the same, that Frenchwoman.'

'Yes,' she mimicked, 'she has, but it disnae stop her playin' tennis.' She smiled, comforted.

18

Jonty came with all the family to see the presentation of the Suzanne Lenglen Trophy a few evenings later. It was held between tea and dinner as the audience was made up chiefly of the young. Annabel had competed during July, but had missed out on August, and although a good player, nimble and quick-witted, she wasn't eligible for a prize.

Ernest, Kit and Annabel looked bronzed and fit, Lizzie glowing, but her skin had obviously been protected from the sun. Grandmother, she had told Ginny, had been a great believer in gloves, parasol and hat, and that must have influenced her. Ginny herself was not a great sun worshipper. She, too, had the delicate McGrath complexion, but she had thought this morning that her reflection in the mirror was wan. She still wasn't sleeping. Iain still took charge of mind and heart when she got into bed.

Jonty was pale, a city paleness, but he was full of vitality and pleasure at being home. She thought he was more handsome than ever, and with a greater assurance. Even as a child he had never been awkward. He had his father's elegance. 'Wait till I tell you all about Gay Paree,' he said.

'And your love life?' She smiled, happy to be with him again.

'After you've told me about yours.'

'I don't want to shock you, little boy.' Ernest was with them. His eyes were knowledgeable. Of course he would know about Iain's marriage. Why didn't he warn me, she thought, or had Iain kept his own counsel? He should have kept it with me too. The bitterness was like bile.

Rows of chairs had been laid out in the Palm Court, and Ginny had had programmes printed commemorating the inauguration of the Suzanne Lenglen Trophy. The three aunts were there, beaming, as if they themselves had invented the French tennis player. Aunt Maevy must have come home early from McGraths. It had to be something important which would make her do that.

There was to be a tennis hop afterwards in the ballroom at the special request of the players. It seemed sometimes that however bad the state of the country, the more people wanted to dance. Dancing on the graves of the men who died for us, she thought. Often she felt that there was another catastrophe ahead in spite of that War to end all Wars. She told herself she must stop thinking depressively. It would show on her face.

She saw Lizzie who was beside her, peering at her programme. 'Is it all right, Lizzie?' she asked. 'I've changed our printers.'

'It's small.' She peered again, 'You have to take account of the older people.'

'Not many of them play tennis. Just look at the audience.' They were surrounded by young people, the boys in white flannels, the girls in white dresses with the Suzanne Lenglen headband low down on their foreheads, which was *de rigueur* this summer. 'Don't you have your lorgnette?'

'Oh, I don't like it! It makes me look so ancient, like an old duchess. The thing is it doesn't go with modern clothes, somehow.'

'Never mind, I'll tell you who the prizewinners are. It could have been Mouse if she hadn't been in Arran.'

'Oh, but we had a grand time, fishing and sailing and golf, although it might as well be Great Western Road nowadays. You meet all your friends there, except that the men are in khaki shorts!' She laughed. '*You* could do with a holiday, Ginny.' She was peering at the programme again. 'I know what you've been through.' That was Lizzie. 'No post-mortems. When we get quieter I'm going to pack you off to America for a good rest. Oh, who's that?' She had looked up at the platform.

'It's Mr Bird from Crannoch, the Mayor. You couldn't miss him with that gold chain hanging round his neck.'

Mr Bird, round like a robin, gave a neat little speech about the advantage to the county in having a place like Sholton Hydro. 'A worthwhile contribution to the unemployment which seems to be endemic now. Endemic,' he repeated, liking the word.

'Some of you older people,' he looked round hopefully at the young, fresh faces, 'may remember when the pits were working full blast and it was not unusual to meet groups of men in the village here, black-faced, their cans slung from their belts, walking home from their day's toil. But that's only a memory now. Certainly Crawfords have absorbed some of them, but they're concentrating on their steel works now, and Sholton isn't what it was.

'Times are changing. We must look forward to the future, to plenty of jobs for everybody in new industries since the old ones are dying. But we must keep our spirits high while our dear country tries to gain its feet after the most terrible War in history.

Let's hope there will never be another one.' The young, well-heeled audience looked blank.

'Not much to do with tennis,' Ernest whispered, who was on Ginny's other side.

'He thinks he's at a Trades Council meeting.' But the Mayor's words had given her a sense of foreboding. I'm run-down, she told herself, Lizzie's right. I'll go off for a holiday soon.

'However, we're only young once,' Mr Bird was chirpier now, having delivered himself of his peroration, 'and it's a case of "Gather ye rosebuds while you may," or in this case, prizes, and without more ado I'll read out the winners.' There was a rustle of excitement. 'The Suzanne Lenglen Trophy will be the last. We'll start with . . .' He had no difficulty in reading his list so the printing was all right. 'Ages fifteen to eighteen, tennis singles, Arthur Campbell and Craig Rintoul . . .'

Everything moved with a swing now. The prizes were awarded, the Mayor thanked graciously and with aplomb by Ernest, then they trooped into the ballroom where the orchestra had already struck up with 'Me and Jane on a Plane . . .' The floor was soon a mass of couples shimmying and shaking in the approved manner.

This was the post-war generation, Ginny thought, plenty of youths under eighteen, not so many above it. At the dinner dances in the evening it wasn't unusual to see two douce ladies dancing together. You couldn't decimate the young men of a nation and expect there would be a partner for everybody. Craig Rintoul, a strapping seventeen-year-old from Trinity College, Glenalmond, was bowing in front of her. His eyes were sparkling with excitement. Was it a 'dare' by his friends? 'May I have the honour, Miss McGrath?' he said in best McEwan Dancing School manner.

Her usual high spirits had deserted her. Normally she would have responded willingly to an overture like this. Miss McGrath wa a good sport. He was so young, and the only arms she wanted round her were Iain's . . . desolation swept over her and she smiled too brightly to cover it. 'I'd love to, Craig, but I've just remembered, there's a crowd going to the Ritz in Crannoch tonight to see Rudolph Valentino. I have to telephone to book the seats. But I'll be back!' Her face would crack if she smiled any more.

'I'll be waiting.' He was unsure now, wondering if it was an excuse. She could see it all in his uncertain smile. His friends would tease him unmercifully when he rejoined them.

She cast a quick look round the ballroom. Mouse was with a nice little boy—she knew his parents—Ernest and Lizzie had vanished, Jonty was whirling the same dark-haired girl so that her short skirt spun. He looked across and saw her, and she thought, well, there's always my boy. He'll come over tonight after supper and we'll have one of those long talks which we used to have. It will be balm to my soul . . .

* * *

He sat on the rug at the empty fireplace which she had filled with flowers—it was too warm for a fire—and she was curled up on the couch, her feet tucked in. She had put out the sherry bottle and a plentiful supply of canapés which Dougie had made at her request, filled with creamed mushrooms, smoked salmon and anchovies. He would still have his healthy appetite. 'Tell all,' she said. 'Did you manage to get rid of Madeleine?' His dark eyes met hers.

'It sounds awful, put like that, but, yes, I did. Terence helped in the end. I'm not proud of my behaviour.'

'He who fights and runs away, lives to fight another day. As long as you didn't make her pregnant.' She saw him flush.

'Trust you, Ginny, to come right out with it. How do you know it was . . . like that?'

'Oh, come on! I know young men. The only thing that keeps them back is when a girl says there's nothing doing, and apparently Madeleine didn't.'

'You're crude.'

'But truthful. Madeleine had been married, hadn't she? She needed a lover. You came along.' She wouldn't say that he was too handsome and lovable to resist, even if he hadn't been the leader in the affair. 'As a matter of fact, I wouldn't be surprised if Ernest didn't let you have a year in Paris in order to sow your wild oats as well as study the history of Art. He's pretty suave, Ernest. I think he was born that way.'

'Still, I behaved like a cad.' His long eyelashes fell on his thin cheeks. Anyone who looked like that would melt any girl's heart.

'What an old-fashioned word to use! You want to stop thinking like that. It takes two to tango.' She laughed at him. 'Was she very sad when it was all over?'

'I expect so, but I think she accepted that I was too young for her.'

'What was the difference in ages?'

He looked away. 'About . . . eighteen.'

'Good God!' She shook her head. 'Well, I must say you got in at the deep end. Was there nobody else you were interested in, nearer your own age?'

'Yes, there was Claudine, a student at the Beaux-Arts. But there was nothing like that between us. I think she was a lesbian.'

She opened her mouth in astonishment. 'Well, you *have* been learning in Paris!'

'Oh, there's any amount of *that* there! I expect it's the same in all big cities, but Europe's more advanced in its thinking. Can you see there being that sort of thing in dreich old Glasgow?'

'I don't know dreich old Glasgow as well as you, but Lizzie once told me there used to be a lady who wore a collar and tie who haunted the Central Station, called Jenny Willocks.'

'Mother told you that!'

'You really must stop thinking your parents aren't worldly wise. They've been through a lot. Life teaches you, and experience, as you found out in Paris, and don't forget they've travelled about. They're sophisticated . . .'

'I know, but Mother . . . !'

'Oh, have an anchovy canapé for goodness sake! Dougie made them specially for you. I think he's got a yen for you.'

'Ginny!' He spluttered with laughter. 'I don't think you're a proper person to run the Sholton Hydro. You'll give it a bad reputation.'

'Oh, we see life here too! We had a woman who drowned herself in the swimming bath.' She told him of Miss Wilcox.

'Who's discovered her?'

'I did. Not on my own. I'd been walking in the grounds . . .' she hesitated . . . 'with Iain Pearson, and we came into the Hydro that way.'

'I'm glad he was with you.'

'Yes. We got the body out and carried it to the women's changing-room.' She looked away. 'I remember thinking, isn't it absolutely stupid, the men's is nearer, and then, no, that won't do, she's a woman . . .' She felt the weight of the body as she spoke, saw the bare feet, the night-clothes plastered against the limbs, remembered how she had kept her head up in case she looked at Miss Wilcox's face, in case she was sick . . .

'Yes, strange how one's mind works . . . why did she do it?'

'She had been having an affair with Erik, and I got rid of him. I knew, you see.'

'You knew!' He blew out his breath. 'Well, I take it back. You *do* see life.'

'Even if you stand still it passes in front of you. But me,' she shrugged, 'I'm crazy! I always want to put my oar in, direct things, organise. I thought . . . I thought . . . go on, eat up those canapés. They're for you.'

'Thank you.' The formal Crawford politeness. 'May I pour you another sherry?'

'Why not?' She held out her glass, saw that her hand trembled. If Jonty noticed, he made no comment. 'So you're looking forward to Florence, are you, now that you've shaken the dust of Paris from your feet?' He ignored this. His voice was gentle.

'Ernest was telling me about Iain Pearson . . . and you.'

'He had no right to!'

'Keep your hair on. You know there are no secrets in our house.'

'Except about lesbians?' She mocked him.

'Don't be stupid. He was saying it's a bitter blow for you, his getting married.'

'Was he? Well, of course, your precious Ernest knows everything. He was born knowing everything. Kieran, his own half-brother, used to say that about him.'

'He says it's even worse for Pearson, that he's a man of integrity.'

'Is that so?' The bitterness was there again. She gulped the sherry, banging the glass down.

'Look at it like this, old thing. He meets this girl, long before he meets you, and they drift into some sort of relationship, perhaps he even committed himself. Then she becomes ill and he's stuck with her . . .'

'Stuck with her? How nicely you put it.'

'Well, that's what it is: he's stuck with her, chicken comes home to roost and that sort of thing. She gets the idea that she would like to be married, maybe because she's ill and knows she may die at any time. Moral blackmail in a way. What could he do?' She was silent. 'Have you seen this girl, Ginny?' His voice was still gentle.

'No, how could I? I only heard of her when I'd been stupid enough to say . . . to say . . .' she dashed her hand across her eyes, 'I've done with weeping . . . to say that I loved him!' She shouted the words. 'I knew, you see, because there had been others, and the feeling for Iain was so different, so sure. I don't know if you remember Magnus Muir? The Honourable, no less. Funny, the titles you have here. I can tell you, his brother wasn't at all honourable. Magnus was here when it was a hospital during the War . . .'

'Vaguely. I was at school most of the time.'

'Or fighting in France.' She looked at the elegant young man sprawled at her feet. 'That's difficult to believe now. Didn't it teach you *anything*?'

'Yes, about death,' he said shortly. 'You're fed up with yourself. That's why you're being so rude.'

'Yes, you're right. I'm fed up with myself because I knew this was at last the right thing. I thought for a little—I was only your age—that Magnus Muir was the man. Think of it, I should have been a countess one day if I had married him, once that old targe of a mother of his had come to a sticky end, thrown by her horse, no doubt. But I knew it was no good. Neither Magnus nor his brother were right for me, nor I for them. I was waiting for something, someone . . .'

'And it was Iain?'

'Yes. You'll know too, Jonty, when it comes. Oh, I'm not railing against him, I'm railing against fate because I can't alter it. Ernest was right. It's a bitter blow.'

'He's in a hell of a fix too, Pearson. You have to see that. He must know that it's wrong ethically to marry this girl when he loves you. It's a dilemma. He has to put her wishes first.'

'There are mine also.'

'He must think you're strong enough to bear it. And so you are, Ginny. You've always liked a challenge.'

'"A Daniel come to judgement!" I never liked Shakespeare at school but there's always one that fits.' If she hadn't liked a challenge she wouldn't have left home in the first place and come to nurse here. But that hadn't been enough for her, oh, dear no. When the War was over she had accepted this new challenge, to run the Hydro. Was Iain at the back of that, although she hadn't realised it at the time? 'Maybe you're right, Jonty.' She wouldn't drink any more sherry.

'I told you I was the one to buck you up. Tell you what, let's go and have a swim. There's nothing that makes you feel better.'

She shook her head. 'I haven't been in since Miss Wilcox. I can't. It would bring the whole thing back.'

'Rubbish! You've got to get rid of those ideas. You were just waiting for me to come home, that's all. Are there any swimming trunks in the men's changing-room?'

'Plenty. Agnus is always complaining about people leaving them.'

'Well, I'll borrow a pair. They'll never know.'

* * *

He was in the water when she went in and she stood, hesitantly. He hadn't put on the lights except in the changing-rooms, but there was enough of the blue summer dusk coming through the glass roof to let her see where she was going.

She dived in, which was the only way to tackle it. Miss Wilcox, here I come. The silky coolness of the water was immediately therapeutic. She joined Jonty and he said to her, 'Four lengths first. It's ages since I had a proper swim.'

'It's that indoor life you were leading.'

There was something essentially satisfying in swimming easily beside him, her boy, sometimes turning to laugh at each other in the sheer joy of the sensation.

'The water cure!' he shouted. 'Is it working?'

She nodded at him, forging ahead. She was the better swimmer. There was something in what he said, something in getting on with things, not letting the thought of Iain fester inside her and spoil her life. If she did she would end up here like poor Miss Wilcox. The tears running ceaselessly out of her eyes became part of the blue water.

She remembered Aunt Maevy telling her of the spineless creature Aunt Isobel had been when her husband the minister was alive, and how when he died she had been born again. 'Resurrected, Ginny, a terrible thing for me to say when I think that I fell in love with him as a girl and was broken-hearted when he chose Isobel!' And Jonty thought things only happened in Paris! 'But I didn't know he was going to turn out to be such a bully! Nor that Charlie would come along and make me the happiest woman alive . . .'

It's the surprise element in life, she thought, that keeps you going, bad or good, but if you give up expecting to be surprised you might as well die . . .

'You're better than me,' Jonty was saying, puffing comically, 'let's see who can swim along the bottom the longest.'

'Right,' she said, 'but I'm coming up again, don't forget.'

'You can do that whenever you want,' he laughed at her, 'just slant your arms.' It was he who had taught her.

That night she slept for the first time without dreaming.

19

They had worked all morning at the mail which had accumulated while Lizzie had been in Arran.

'That'll do for the time being,' she said at last. 'I've to meet Mouse in Glasgow at one o'clock. She's going to the Mitchell Library in the morning and we thought we'd make a day of it and get her fixed up with what she needs for going back to school. Thank goodness she's beginning to grow at last.' She smiled across at Ginny. 'How would you like to join us for lunch?'

'I'd like to, but . . .'

'Oh, come on!'

'I'm not in the mood, Lizzie.'

'Is it because of Iain? I'm truly sorry how it has turned out. We knew there had been someone, but I thought it was all off . . .'

'I'm putting it behind me. No, it's not that. I promised Nan Porter I would relieve her at the desk at three.'

'Aunt Kate would take her place.'

'I happen to know she wouldn't. She and Aunt Isobel have gone off to Crannoch to see about some new curtains we ordered there. I knew it was a mistake. Far better to have gone to Wylie and Lochheads in the first place.'

'Maybe, but it's in our own interest to give the local firms our custom. Well, never mind, you take it easy, sit in the garden for an hour or so and we'll start working on the holiday rota tomorrow.'

'Right. Enjoy yourself on your . . . trail.'

'A trail round Glasgow. You're learning. How I used to enjoy a trail with Grandmother when I was living with her! She swanned about those shops as if she owned them, and they nearly went down on their knees to her. Of course, she had a way with her.'

'I doubt if they would do it for anyone now. Things have changed, and not for the better.'

'You talk like an auld wife. What age are you, for goodness sake?'

'Twenty-three.'

'A mere babe-in-arms with your life before you.' She stood up. 'Take my advice, Ginny, you may feel Iain Pearson has robbed you of your happiness, but don't let him rob you of your youth. There's as good fish in the sea as ever came out of it.'

'I've no intention of being robbed of my youth,' she said loftily.

'You don't know what it's like after forty. The best time's past. In a bright light you can see the wrinkles, frailties appear . . .'

'Oh, Lizzie!' She laughed. 'I know you. You're fishing for compliments.' She looked at the picture she made in her white linen suit with the black blouse. There was a white-brimmed hat to match with a black crown, hanging up on the hook behind the door to complete the costume. 'Besides, you get plenty from Ernest!'

'Oh, I know I do, but they're much better coming from a woman!' She took the hat down from its peg and went to the mirror to adjust it on her copper hair. She would make Mouse look like a . . . mouse.

* * *

There was nothing she liked more than a jaunt to town, she thought, sitting in her first-class compartment. Of course, Paris and Amsterdam and Vienna and all those wonderful cities she had been to with Ernest—even New York—had their own beauty, but was there anything nicer than knowing your way about, going straight to the shops you knew and where they knew you, and getting the attention which was your proper due considering how much you spent in them?

It was such a pity that Mr Walter Wilson of Trérons had passed on two years ago. She remembered the funeral to which she and Ernest had been invited, and seldom had there been a more impressive cortège. Ernest had said it was a bit of Grandmother's world dying, and that was true enough. There was not the same leisurely pace in the big shops now; the special attention, the deference of the shopwalkers, was largely missing except perhaps in Tréron et Cie, nor did the customers have the same leisured air. Their faces were often strained-looking because it was not only the workers who were facing unemployment, but the owners of factories and shipbuilding yards who were seeing their order books dwindle. Some of them, no doubt, would be wondering how to keep up their big houses in Park Drive and the like.

McGraths was fortunate. Transport was the lifeblood of a country, prosperous or not, and if ever she felt smug about that, and the fact that her new venture, the Hydro, was making a handsome profit, she had only to call in at that soup kitchen she had organised with a few other ladies on her charity committee to see what straits some people were brought to.

She enjoyed talking to them, mostly men, and helping to fill plates from the great steaming pots of broth. One of them had told her he went round the middens in Hillhead at night with a candle or a torch to scavenge for bits of discarded food or any object he might sell or use. Another that he sung in the back courts with his wife, in the hope that one of the tenants would push up her window and throw them a few pennies or even a jammy piece in a poke to take 'hame to the weans'.

She took care to pass on those anecdotes to Annabel and Kit so that they would know how the other half lived. It was better than preaching.

But she wasn't here to feel gloomy. Here they were, crossing the Bridge, and everyone was getting up and lifting down their cases and putting on their coats. A very nice gentleman opened the door for her, lifting his hat. Really, there wasn't much wrong with things when there were people about like him. She gave him a ravishing smile as a reward.

She looked at the clock as she walked blithely through the Central Station. She had more than half-an-hour before she was due to meet Annabel. They must give up the habit of calling her that ridiculous pet name of Mouse. She was becoming too grown-up for that.

Ernest had talked about a book he would like to buy, on Covenanting times. He took a great interest in Scottish history in spite of, or because of, the fact that he had been brought up in America. She would give him a surprise and buy it for him. She remembered the author's name, and there was always a nice assistant in Smith's in St Vincent Place who would help her out. Sometimes you got the impression that the world was *full* of nice men eager to help, but it wouldn't last. She had warned Ginny . . .

She went out of the Gordon Street entrance, taking care as she crossed the street because of the taxis which were rushing in and out of the Station all the time. On the other side she dawdled past the shop windows of Forsyth's. Yes, it was as she thought. The windows were full of the winter outfits for all the best schools. There was no doubt about it, this was where she and Annabel would go after lunch. You could always rely on Forsyth's.

Her eye fell on the shoe shop directly opposite. She must have a look at that. It wasn't as good as Rayne's in Sauchiehall Street where she generally went, but it might be more *avant-garde*. It would have done Ginny good to come with her and buy something new to cheer herself up. It always worked.

She stood at the kerb with a group of people waiting for a gap in the traffic to appear. Sometimes she had the impression that Ginny thought she was—how to describe it—rather shallow in her liking for clothes. She would have liked to explain to her that it was part of one's armour against life's vicissitudes. Grandma had taught her that: 'Rise to the occasion,' 'Put a brave face on it.'

It went deeper, in fact. The psychological effect of being admired restored your morale. After her last baby died she had come to terms with the loss by taking pains with her appearance. What good would a drooping, badly dressed, unwashed woman have been to Ernest? Or Kit and Annabel, for that matter . . .

'Come on, missus!' A woman nudged her in the ribs, and she crossed with about a dozen other people, safely in the middle of them. She didn't even have to look.

But what a difference in Glasgow streets since the War, she thought, as she stood in front of her goal, the *avant-garde* shoe shop. No, quality always paid. Her eye rapidly ranged over the display and rejected it. There was something in cut and style which you would never get in those flashy shoes. Not for her. They were for the young.

But, so many cars rushing about! It made you quite dizzy! Ernest said the Baxters at Drymen had two now, one chauffeur-driven and the other a runabout for Mrs Baxter! She herself wouldn't feel at all sure driving amongst all that confusion and tooting of horns. It was all right in the quiet roads around Sholton. But Ernest had been a bit high-handed saying that she should ask Lamond to drive her anywhere she wanted to go. She was a businesswoman, wasn't she? She had organised and run a successful hospital for the Red Cross during the War, and now she was doing the same again with the Hydro.

She regretted, of course, that the Hall was no longer a private house, with Grandmother there and her second husband, that dear man, Alastair, Nigel's father. Sometimes she longed to be back again in that wonderful, tremulous time when she and Nigel had been married, both so young, but she was sensible enough. It was her youth she was longing for. Ernest and she, however much they loved each other, had never known that special joy together, young, innocent love. Nothing lasts . . . don't think of it, she told herself. Live in the present.

St Vincent Place was solid and successful-looking with all those offices and banks, and here was Smith's. Yes, the book would be a nice surprise for Ernest. He was so appreciative. That was what some of the young-married of today hadn't learned, to appreciate each other, and to show it. She and Ernest had never taken each other for granted. Sometimes her heart failed her when she thought of life without him, as it did now, like a little cold wind, making her stop for a second and pretend to be looking in Smith's windows which she had just reached. Desolation, that was it, a cold finger on your heart. Maybe the apprehension was worse than the fact, if that were possible. Now, that book . . .

It was a pity they set some of them so far back. It was difficult to read their titles. And she could have made a much better display than that by arranging the books with the brighter covers in groups, half-opened, to attract the customer to go inside. Jonty took his good 'eye' and his discrimination from her. He would be a success. No doubt he had got to know some girls in Paris, suitable or otherwise, but after all, that was what education was all about in the broad sense. She had been a different person when she came home from her finishing school in Versailles, more assured, and with a *je ne sais quoi.*

He was going to McGraths this morning with Ernest. Maybe when they were seated behind Lamond being driven up to Glasgow he would tell him about Paris, and if he . . . a man-to-man talk. And then afterwards Ernest would tell her . . .

Ten minutes later she was out again with a neat parcel which had been personally wrapped by the manager himself. He had told one of the assistants to find the book for Mrs Murray-Hyslop —he knew it, of course—and he had said he would mention to his window-dresser the little matter of putting the books with the largest print on their dust-covers at the back. He had asked kindly after Ernest and the family, and their annual holiday—'All the best people go to Arran in August'—and said what a pleasure it was to serve her, any time.

There was no doubt about it, she always got on well with men. It was the old story. You just had to give them your whole attention, appreciate them. That was all there was to it.

When she reached Fuller's, Annabel wasn't there, but checking the clock above Simpson, Hunter and Young, she saw there were still ten minutes to go. Maybe she had had to wait for a tramcar to bring her from the Mitchell. Which way would she come, Argyle Street or Sauchiehall Street? Or, knowing her nimbleness of foot, would she race down St Vincent Street *without* waiting? She was like a young hare, Ernest said. She had the same build as himself.

She would walk on and see what MacDonald's had in for their autumn wardrobe. It would fill in the time. She had an account there, and if she saw anything enticing she and Annabel could always pop back after they had had lunch.

Buchanan Street was busy. She walked along, enjoying the warmth in the air, the crowds of women shoppers. Some of them came almost every afternoon, she had been told, and whiled away their time sitting chatting in the tearooms, but that wasn't for her. They didn't know the word 'involvement'. The McGrath women had too much intelligence for idling their time away in Glasgow shops, Grandmother had always said. The very rarity of the 'trail' was what made it so enjoyable.

She was glancing across the street when she saw Annabel, trim in her white skirt and blue blazer, her panama hat with the blue ribbon. Why was she on the other side for goodness sake? Girls of her age didn't listen, in one ear and out the other, dreaming of boys . . . what a good thing they had got rid of that Erik! They had nipped *that* in the bud in time.

'I said Fuller's, distinctly,' she said to herself as she stopped, watching the neat little figure dashing along. Yes, it was Annabel, always half-running. She won all the races at the school sports. But she was turning into the Argyle Arcade! What was she thinking of? It had always had a fascination for the children, that welter of little shops which sold everything and were permanently lit, making the Arcade like a jewelled cave. Kit liked the one where they sold model trains, and Annabel had twin boy dolls—trust her to be different—which she had bought there and called Marc and Olivier after her French cousins. The silly girl, she would be swallowed up in that maze of wee shops, dawdling, going in and out asking prices, and she would never be able to find her . . .

She launched herself into the stream of traffic without pausing, because she saw, or thought she saw, a lane through it. She'd catch up with Annabel before it was too late, and what a telling-off she would give her! Maybe she wasn't as quick as Mouse, but she'd been crossing Glasgow streets all her life.

She skipped between two taxis and saw one of the drivers, red-faced, waving a fist at her. Her smile didn't seem to have the usual effect, but she had no time to bother about that. You had to have eyes in the back of your head for this. But there was a rushing kind of wind coming towards her, making her hesitate. She would have looked that way but you couldn't do two things at once, and she had to keep her eye on the opposite side in case . . .

She swayed, frightened. The rushing wind was filling her ears, enveloping her like a cloak, there was a loud screeching of brakes and then a woman's high-pitched scream, 'Oh, ma Goad! She'll get killed!' It couldn't be her, could it? She was nearly across, she could see the entrance of the Arcade, black dark in the sunlight. The thought came at the same time as she felt a violent blow on her side and immediately she was in a dark cavern of her own, deep as death . . .

Outside Fuller's windows filled with cream cakes, Annabel stood, glad that she had been here first. Mother was a stickler for punctuality. She couldn't understand why a crowd had gathered farther down the street, why people were running . . .

Book Two

SEPTEMBER 1920–JUNE 1930

1

It was the summer of 1921 before Ginny was able to have a holiday and go home, and looking back on that terrible time after Lizzie's accident, she realised it was a mixed blessing. Iain was still there in her mind; her love for him, instead of dying now that he was married, seemed to grow stronger. Had it not been for the anxiety about Lizzie, and all the responsibility which had been suddenly thrust on her, she thought, in retrospect, that she might have given up the job and gone home long before that.

But the McGrath discipline stood her in good stead. It was true that Lizzie had been away as much as she had been present in the Hydro, but she had never left without discussing with Ginny what was likely to crop up during her absence. She had an incisive mind. When she left with Ernest on one of their trips, both Ginny's mind and her own were perfectly at ease as regards the day-to-day running of the Hydro. Like Maeve McGrath, she knew how to delegate, but she chose the right people to whom she gave responsibility.

But all that had changed after her accident. When Ginny visited her for the first time in the Royal, she was appalled at her appearance. Her beautiful copper hair had been shaved unbecomingly where there was a large gash running from her forehead, her arm was in a sling, and there was a cage over her leg.

'I thought the War was over . . . oh, Lizzie!' In spite of her resolve to keep a brave face she had to wipe away the tears after she had kissed her cousin's cheek.

'Here, what's all this?' Lizzie smiled wanly. 'I'm the one to cry if there's any crying to be done, not you.'

'Your beautiful hair . . .' She tried to smile, ashamed of herself.

'It will grow again. Ernest quite likes it. He says it gives me an intellectual look.'

'Ernest would.' Lizzie's accident had tried even Ernest's urbanity. When he had first called at the Hydro to tell Ginny, in the middle of his account he suddenly got up and stood looking out of the window, his back to her. She had slipped out and brought back two cups of strong coffee. It had also given her the chance to go into one of the cloakrooms and repair her own face. She cried far too easily these days. 'Has Mouse been to see you?' she asked Lizzie.

'Annabel?' She would use that name consistently until they all followed suit. 'Yes, poor wee soul. She hates the place. Every day when she gets out of Hutchy. Sister Thoms mothers her. Gives her a cup of tea and a piece of cake to keep her going.'

'Everybody's asking about you. I can't tell you the calls I get at the Hydro, and it must be the same at the Stables.'

'Yes, everybody's most kind.' Her eyes were black underneath, making them bluer than ever. Nothing could dowse their blueness.

'I could kill that van driver! I believe it was one of Fraser's. Careering along as if he owned Buchanan Street.'

Lizzie shook her head. 'It wasn't the man's fault. It was mine. I just didn't look, or I didn't see. When I'm up and about I'll go to the optician and get spectacles.'

'You hate them!'

'But I need them or I wouldn't be here.' She drew in her breath, looked away. Ginny put her hand on hers.

'We'll call you Mrs Mazawatee, then. You know the advert?'

'Thanks for the compliment. That old granny!'

'I'm only joking. Nothing will ever spoil your looks, Lizzie. You're the pick of the bunch.'

'That's what Ernest says, but I doubt it will be a pretty dilapidated bunch he's left with—a scarred face, a broken arm, a broken hip, maybe. It'll have put years on me. I haven't dared to ask nurse for a mirror.'

'You're fishing again. I know you. But since you're an invalid, I'll spoil you for once.' She said, seriously for her, 'Nothing will ever spoil your beauty . . . no, don't make a face . . . it's like Grandmother's. It'll last as long as you do. It's not only your face or hair or your figure or your colouring, it's something else, something that distinguishes you from other people, a vitality, an inner glow—I can't describe it. You should get Jonty to write a poem about you.'

'He has. He brought me one today. In fact, I think he's going to have another book ready soon. Wasn't it good of him to go to the new office, the Auctioneers and Valuators, instead of setting off for Florence?'

'Very, but it's only deferred. He's been a great comfort to Ernest, not to mention keeping an eye on Mouse—I mean Annabel. She's beginning to look more *like* Annabel these days. It must be because she has a young handsome brother to go about with. And he's been a great help to me as well. He comes often to the Hydro and lends a hand wherever it's needed.'

'It sounds as if the Hydro and everything else has closed over my head.' She looked pathetic.

'If you saw Ernest's woebegone face when he thinks you aren't looking, you wouldn't say that.'

'It's good of you to try and cheer me up, a stupid, short-sighted old woman . . .'

'Don't lay it on too thick!' Ginny laughed.

'I haven't let anyone read that poem Jonty wrote for me. It shames me.' Her eyes were moist.

'You have a devoted family, Lizzie. I know Ernest cancelled a lot of his London trips. And Jonty collects Kit and Annabel from their schools every day. Well, you know that.'

'Yes, every day. They weren't allowed in here at first, but Sister Thoms let them stand in the doorway and they waved, my tall, handsome Jonty, Kit beside him trying to be as tall, my little Annabel. She's got the make of Aunt Isobel. She'll never be buxom.'

* * *

Lizzie was in the Royal Infirmary for six weeks. As she grew stronger and the days grew shorter, she got Ginny to bring her pencil and paper, and together they planned the Christmas festivities. Nothing must be allowed to interfere with the smooth running of the Hydro. They must consolidate last year's success. People would expect more and better. If they didn't get it they would go elsewhere.

So together they drew out the winter programme and chose a fine winter scene of reindeers for the front of it. There were to be table tennis and badminton tournaments, and a children's Magic Show, held conveniently when the parents were having dinner so that they could dine in peace. There was to be a Candlelight Carol Service with mince pies and coffee to follow, a Gala in the swimming bath, a children's film show, and for the days when the weather was too inclement, colouring competitions, Hunt the Slipper, and a Grand Fancy Dress Parade which would keep all the mothers and many members of the staff busy with their needles.

'If you can keep the children amused, the grown-ups will enjoy themselves, and it's they who pay the bill,' Lizzie said.

And for the parents there were bridge and whist competitions, dancing every night, and finally a Farewell Dance, as well as golf matches and a regular morning exercise class run by Angus Galbraith, who declared he would make a football team out of the ladies before they went back home.

'And in between all that they can have regular health-giving drinks from the Fountain,' Ginny said. 'We have to remind them they're at a spa.'

'I never told you,' Lizzie said, lying back on her bed exhausted, 'the well at the monastery didn't supply enough spring water so we've had to augment it from the mains.'

Ginny stared at her, horrified, then broke into gales of laughter. 'Oh, Lizzie, you're the limit!'

'That'll do you good.' She smiled wryly. 'You've been looking far too solemn lately. Don't let anything, or anybody get you down.' She knew she was referring to Iain.

Lizzie was discharged from the Infirmary well before Christmas so that she could spend it at home. Aunt Kate, who had briefly seen her since the aunts lived next door, gave Ginny a report the following morning.

'She's changed, almost as if her youth had left her. Of course it's early days yet. She's distressed about the sensible shoes she has to wear. The injured leg, although it's mended now, is slightly shorter than the other one, and she has to wear a thicker sole. And the glasses!' She shook her head. 'Well, it gives our Lizzie a different look, earnest, somehow. It just isn't her. But she was bright enough, putting a brave face on it for them all. Jessie had a wee greet into her apron when she showed us in.'

She telephoned Ginny in a few days and asked her to bring the business letters which had to be attended to. 'I'm all right, Ginny. I'll get round to coming to the Hydro once I get my sea legs again. But my arm's fine.'

'How do you really feel, Lizzie?' Ginny asked her when she arrived. Ernest had taken Annabel to the Hydro for the jollifications and left Lizzie in charge of Jessie. He would far rather have stayed at home with his beloved, but she had been short with him and said she didn't want him hanging around her all the time.

She met Ginny's eyes, her chin up. 'Fine . . . in myself. I can throw away this stick when I get used to the new shoes. Talk about props!' She touched the glasses selfconsciously. 'That isn't the worry. I've had a good innings with Nigel and then Ernest praising me, telling me . . .' Her voice broke, 'It's my spirit, or lack of it. I'm disgusted with myself.' She laughed, her eyes sad. 'I've lost my *je ne sais quoi.*'

'You've still got plenty of something or other sitting there like a queen.' She said seriously, 'Your body's had a great shock. I've heard Aunt Maevy telling you that more than once in the Infirmary, and no one knows better than she. You need a tonic. Do you think you could travel?'

'No.' She shook her head. 'I couldn't face it.'

'You loved it with Ernest. Maybe not yet, but why not set a target for yourself? Say, in the spring. If you had to choose, where would you like to go?'

She looked thoughtful. The tilt of her head was beautiful, Ginny thought, in spite of the scarred forehead. 'A bit of my heart lies in France. I spent a year there, remember, for my education. Grandmother paid for it. To give me some *savoir faire*.' She laughed. 'Then when Ernest and I were married we toured Normandy. The Barthes have a house there, La Hirondelle. Madame Jacques was the caretaker. It all comes back to me. It's like a . . . like a golden dream.'

'Well, make it a reality. You know the Barthes would do anything for you. Emily's written several times, and Giselle . . .'

'La Hirondelle . . .' She wasn't listening. 'Isn't that a lovely name? That little village, golden in the evening light, Château-sur-Epte, and the house set back where the two roads crossed, the *carrefour*, and that little river, the Epte, at the foot of the garden. There was a ruined castle above it, on the top of the hill. Why are all memories golden, Ginny?'

'That kind are. Not all of them.' Hers were anguished, dark and bitter.

'Ellie, our clever cousin in America, spent a weekend with her lover there, you know, the American surgeon, before he was killed.'

'We're a passionate lot.'

'Anyone worth their salt should be passionate. Life's nothing without it. Grandmother could have told you that. But, France! Did I say "dream"? It's a day-dream. You have to go home in the spring. I don't want *you* breaking down,' and, scarcely pausing, 'have you got over Iain?'

'No,' she said.

'Best to be honest. Have you seen him?'

'Yes, he calls occasionally on business matters. I ask politely how his wife is. He says, "No better, no worse." That's how it is.'

'Are you going to be another Belle Geddes?'

'I could do worse.'

'Think hard about it. Belle isn't a McGrath. She thrives on

solitude. But the McGrath women are only fulfilled completely when they have a home of their own, a man, and children.'

'It takes two, and I could never take second best.'

'I'll remind you of that.' And then, just as directly, 'You aren't hoping his wife will die soon?'

She flushed. 'You're a devil. I try not to. I've asked Belle about his wife's disease—I can't say "Beth". She even showed me a picture in a medical book. She says it's sometimes recognised by a "snarling" smile. Isn't that pitiful, and terrible? As it progresses there's difficulty in swallowing, in speaking, weakness of the muscles. The head falls forward. It can . . . finish with paralysis.'

'Poor Beth. See, *I* can say it. I've told Iain to bring her to the Hydro when the weather gets better, free of charge, maybe at the spring holiday.'

'Well, since you're so good at arranging for other people, you get busy and make your own plans for spring as well. Go to France. I can quite well wait until summer for mine, and I'll only go then if you're fully recovered.'

'I'll make a point of being fully recovered as you put it. An objective is a great thing to make you stir yourself.' She looked suddenly tired, or she was in pain. She lay back on the pillows, her face drawn.

'Are you all right, Lizzie?'

'Of course I'm all right.'

'Then I'll get back. I like to keep an eye on the young ones when the parents are dancing. They try to slip down and have a swim. After Miss Wilcox I'm . . .'

'Aye, that was another one, poor soul. Don't get like Miss Wilcox, Ginny.' She held out her arms, a rare gesture, and Ginny bent down and kissed her. The rush of love was of a different kind than she felt for Iain, but as strong.

2

Lizzie was safely packed off on holiday with Ernest at Easter, an unusually tremulous Lizzie who had taken to wearing a small veil to hide the scar on her forehead, longer skirts in the hope of drawing attention away from her sensible shoes, and, reluctantly, rimless glasses.

Ernest looked bemused, amused, but still loving. 'If Mother looked like one of those old tramps you see coming stotting out of the pubs in Glagow, he would still think she was perfect,' Annabel said to Ginny when she called in on her way home from school. Ginny, in fact, had suggested she stay at the Hydro while her parents were away, but Lizzie had demurred on several accounts.

'She would take up a good room,' she had said, 'and you know we are in danger of being overbooked for Easter. She's perfectly all right at the Stables. There are the three aunts next door, and now that Aunt Kate and Aunt Isobel are getting on a bit they don't turn out every day at the Hydro. Have you got replacements for them, by the way?'

'Yes, Lizzie.' She had been patient, recognising the source of the anxiety, 'I've taken on two more staff in the office and I can fill in for Aunt Kate.'

'You're everybody's dogsbody. I shouldn't be going away.'

'You should. Besides, I like being the gracious dowager to the guests. Lady Muir taught me!'

Lizzie had laughed, reassured. 'That's fine, then. And Annabel has to learn to stand on her own feet. Not that there will be much chance of her doing that with Jessie waiting on her hand and foot and doting aunts next door . . .'

'Will you get away with that doting husband of yours and forget everything?' she had said. Lizzie had looked her straight in the eye.

'I intend to. By the way, Ginny, talking about welcoming people, don't forget that Iain Pearson and his wife will be coming . . .'

How could she when she lay awake at nights wondering what she would say to them, how his wife would look, how she would remain the cool, businesslike Miss McGrath . . .

Annabel was sitting in a comfortable chair in Ginny's office, very inelegantly, her legs draped over one of its arms. 'If your mother saw you like that you would get your head in your hands to play with.' Ginny glanced up and resumed her writing.

'I wish I had good legs. These are like *spurkles*. Do you know what *spurkles* are, Ginny?'

'How could *anyone* know what your heathenish language means? Go on, tell me.'

'Wooden stirring spoons, for porridge. Have you porridge on your menu for the guests?'

'Och aye, and a piper dancing round the table every morning. This is a civilised hydropathic, not a Highland gathering.'

'Pipers don't dance. You've no idea of things. It's very posh to have pipers *marching* round the table. All the dukes and duchesses have them. Did that boyfriend of yours, Magnus, not have any?'

'Oh, all the time, squealing in my ear.'

'*Skirling* is the word.'

'And dances where the men made terrible, ear-splitting sounds . . .'

'*Hooched*.'

'And leaped . . .'

'*Louped*.'

'Louped to the ceiling and whirled . . .'

'*Burled*.'

'Burled you round and round till your eyes fell out. No, when I marry I'll have someone like Jonty . . .'

'If I know him he'll be getting off with someone in Florence right at this minute. I wonder what it will be this time—a fat opera singer maybe?'

'The Italian girls are very seductive, I hear. Big,' she cupped her hands round the front of her white blouse and rolled her eyes, 'low-cut cotton dresses, black curly hair, even their lips curl . . . in fact, everything *you* aren't, skinny-ma-link.'

'Thanks a million. Just because I'm rather slender, there's no need to rub it in.' Her disdainful expression changed, 'Is there any chance of tea and cakes, Ginny?'

'You're like your brother. You must both have worms, otherwise you wouldn't stay so thin. I'll ring for some if you'll promise to keep quiet and stuff yourself. I've an awful lot to do.'

'Don't you wish you could chuck all this and get married? I thought at one time you and Mr Pearson . . .'

'Keep quiet and stop thinking.' She knew her face changed. 'Mr Pearson, if you want to know, is arriving today with his wife. Look, go to the kitchen and ask Dougie to make you up a tray of sandwiches and fancies while I finish this.' She saw the girl's hurt face, 'I'm sorry if I shouted, Mouse, I mean, Annabel, it's just, it's just . . .' she bent her head to her work, sick with herself.

'I'll go and get the tray,' Annabel said in a quiet, small voice.

* * *

She was at the counter relieving Nan Porter when Iain arrived with his wife. She greeted them with professional warmth. She had rehearsed it often enough. 'Good afternoon, Iain.' She had decided to use his first name. 'Did you have a good journey?' And smiling, still professionally, 'Welcome to Sholton Hydro.'

'Thank you. It's not so far.' He looked amused, 'This is my wife. Beth, I told you about Miss McGrath. Ginny's an old friend.'

'How do you do.' She took in the woman's appearance in one sweeping glance as she rang the bell for the porter. 'I hope you'll be comfortable. I've arranged a room for you on the first floor. Just leave the cases, Iain. The porter will follow with them.' She took a key from the rows of hooks, 'If you would follow me, please . . .'

Not as pale as she would have imagined, nor as thin. A bit of colour, but it might be rouge, and despite that the skin had an indoor look. Brown hair. She had evidently paid a visit to the hairdresser before she came. It was perfectly waved, with henna tints in the small troughs of the waves. There was a diamanté clasp holding it back. The lips were full; they pouted over two rather prominent front teeth. Her eyebrows were like a man's, dark and heavy.

'This is lovely,' the woman said when they were in the bedroom. 'Isn't it, Iain!'

'Yes, very nice.' Of the two he was more gaunt, his eyes shadowed. Oh, she loved him . . .

'I've been ill, you see, Miss McGrath. This is my first outing.'

'I hope you'll feel better for the change. Everybody who comes says they do. Be sure and drink plenty of our spring water from the fountain.' He must know too that half of it came from the mains supply.

'I'll make sure she does,' Iain said. His eyes were dark, either embarrassed or sad, she couldn't tell which.

'If you like I could arrange for you to have dinner in your room,

Mrs Pearson?' She stood, the fixed smile on her face, misery behind it.

'What do you think, Iain?'

'Perhaps for the first evening, Ginny, but after that,' he turned to his wife, 'our intention is to get out and about, remember?'

'Oh, I haven't forgotten!' She looked wholesome for a second, ordinary. 'Well, only for the first night, Miss McGrath, till we get settled in.'

'Certainly. Breakfast in bed?' She revived her smile.

'I'd like that.' She seemed apologetic. She was a woman who liked to please.

'Just for one.' His voice was curt. 'I always get up for mine.'

'Porridge and bagpipes?'

'What?' He looked astonished.

'Oh, I'm sorry.' His wife would think she was mad. 'It was just something Annabel was saying, Lizzie's girl . . . It slipped out. What time, Mrs Pearson?'

She looked doubtful. 'What do you think, Iain?'

'Eight o'clock, and just tea and toast.'

'And orange juice?'

'No, it doesn't suit me,' Beth said.

'Grapefruit?'

'Yes, please. You seem to think of everything.'

You couldn't dislike her: anxious to be on good terms, perhaps stubborn in private. But she didn't look ill. She searched her face while she reeled off the times of meals, the facilities available. She had colour, her eyes were clear. The only thing she noticed, and perhaps even that was her imagination, her mouth was a little slack. It trembled above the two white teeth at the front. She could see the tremor in the lips. And she had thin arms and legs—*spurkles;* that would be through lack of exercise.

'The *Glasgow Herald* will come with the breakfast tray, but if there are any magazines you want, Mrs Pearson, just tell the waitress. We have most of them. There's a programme of events on your blotter. Enjoy your stay.' She felt her cheeks pull in before she smiled to cover it. What claptrap it all was, role playing. But she had never felt that before. She noticed the tremulous smile in response to hers. You couldn't dislike her. Not under any circumstances.

She ran into Iain on the stairs later, when he was carrying a glass of water. 'Has the cure begun?' she said brightly.

'She has such a lot of pills to swallow. She might as well try it.'

Her resentment vanished. The love was there, as strong as ever.

In *his* eyes too? 'It must be wearisome for her. Will you be sure and let me know if there is anything you specially need?'

'You've done everything possible. She's an appreciative girl, Ginny.' He seemed to be pleading. 'I'd like you to get to know her better. She talked a lot about you, thought you were lovely . . .' She didn't want to hear.

'There's a cocktail party tonight before dinner. If you would like to bring her?'

'No, thanks, it would be too exhausting. I know now to a hair's breadth what she can take. Why not slip up for a drink with us while it's on?' It would have been ungracious to refuse.

'Thanks. Well, I will if I have a minute. Aunt Kate's off today. She's gone to Glasgow to meet Aunt Maevy at York Street, and Aunt Isobel goes home at four for Annabel. It makes me more busy than usual around dinner time . . .' She gave up. 'Well, just for a minute . . .'

The room was a large one and Ginny had given instructions to have the sofa shifted in front of the fire. The evening was chilly. Mrs Pearson—she must learn to call her that—was seated in a corner of the sofa wearing a brightly-patterned dress. She looked up, smiling. 'Iain has been singing your praises. Sit down beside me, Miss McGrath. That's better. Sometimes my eyes don't focus properly. I know you and Iain are old friends. He'll have told you what's wrong with me.'

'Yes,' she said. 'How is your health just now?' She saw the unsteady smile.

'There's been a steady improvement, hasn't there, Iain? Oh, good, gin and orange. I can take orange when it's mixed with gin.' She laughed, sipping. The glass shook a little in her hand. 'Yes, a steady improvement. Must be something to do with getting married.' She bit her lip, looking up at Ginny, as if to stop it trembling.

'I hope it goes on. Had you thought of swimming?' She remembered Lizzie in her direct way asking her if she wanted Iain's wife to die. How easy it seemed to be in water, how painless . . .

'Oh, dear no, I haven't the strength. But Iain's going to take me for nice runs in the country. *You* won't get much time for that sort of thing.'

'No, unfortunately. I scarcely know the countryside around here. Now, where I live in America . . .'

'You come from America? I thought there was something different in your voice.'

'Yes, we used to drive up by the Hudson River, cross the Tapanzee Bridge into Bear Mountain . . .'

'It's funny, an American girl coming to work here. Do you ever regret it?'

'Sometimes.' She didn't look at Iain who was sitting in a chair opposite them. She had the uncomfortable feeling that she was being questioned too closely. For what purpose? Did she suspect anything? Invalids had time to think . . . 'I'm going home in the summer and who knows what may happen? I may never come back.' She looked directly at him as she spoke and he turned his head away. His profile was austere. Well, at least he was faithful to the promise he'd made to his wife long ago.

Beth laid a shy hand on hers. 'I hope we're going to be friends, Miss McGrath. I don't have much energy to walk about, but I do like to have a chat occasionally, if you have time.'

Ginny put down her glass and got up. 'I'd like to but Easter's very busy,' and feeling she had been too abrupt, 'I'll do my best.'

'How is Lizzie?' Iain asked. He had risen too.

'Brave, as you would expect. She's gone to France with Ernest.'

'Iain told me about her,' Beth said. 'I'm not the only one with problems. And she used to be a beauty, didn't she?'

'Oh, she's still that! Nothing can spoil her beauty. But she'll sort herself out. You can depend on Lizzie. Now, be sure and ask for anything you want.'

'You've been very kind.'

Iain opened the door for her. Their eyes met. She took a deep breath but it didn't stop her eyes filling up. She turned away before he noticed. Once she conquered this tendency to weep, this weakness, she would be fine. 'Thanks again, Ginny.' His voice followed her as she ran downstairs.

There was a little queue of late arrivals at the desk, and the McGrath charm came to the rescue. 'Oh, I'm so sorry to have kept you waiting!' It was second nature now, and so useful when you wanted to dampen down that absurd desire she still had for a married man. Surely it would go away, the feeling of desolation, she told herself, as she entered names in the ledger, handed over keys, smiled. Look at Lizzie with her problems. Hers was nothing compared with those.

3

The drawing-room at Monceau Park was as Lizzie remembered it. She and Ernest were shown in by René, the footman, who ought to have been pensioned off by this time, she thought. But that you couldn't do with an old faithful servant if he wanted to stay on. She remembered Susan at Braidholme, dying in her chair at the kitchen fire.

Ernest's sister was coming forward to meet them from that elegant Louis Quatorze fireplace with the great mirror above it, and on the mantelpiece 'the monstrous ormolu clock with its cupids'—so she had described it to Aunt Maevy and Grandmother. Charles, her husband, was a step or two behind her on the Aubusson carpet, quiet, secretive, but fulfilling his duties to those strange relations from Scotland. 'Oh, la, la!' Emily was crying, kissing Lizzie's cheeks French fashion, 'What have they done to you, those doctors!'

'What a way to greet your dear brother's wife!' Ernest said, unruffled as always and embracing his sister, then shaking hands with her husband. 'How are you, Charles?'

'Well, I thank you. Our house welcomes you.' He kissed Lizzie's hand, his dark eyes meeting hers. Don't pay any attention to my wife, she's scatter-brained. That's why I have my little love-nest on the Left Bank . . .

'Am I so awful, Emily?' But Emily was only saying what everyone else was too polite to say.

'Of course not! My tongue runs away with me as usual. But sisters-in-law can be frank with each other, *n'est-ce pas*? Come and sit bedside me on this *canapé* and we'll be more comfortable. Not very, Lizzie thought, surveying the straight back and the elegant lines of the sofa. What a difference from the huge lounging ones she had in the Stables, had had in the Hall when they lived there.

'Thank you, Emily.' She sat down. You haven't changed anyhow, not even in the colours you choose. 'The little humming-bird', Grandmother used to call her, or was it parakeet? And, didn't she even begin to look like one with her sharp little beak? But she wouldn't be as rude as Emily.

'Tell Raoul to bring in the tea, please,' Emily said to René. He bowed and went out. 'We're surrounded by ancient minions here. Raoul was our coachman so I thought he would be happy pushing a trolley . . . Ah, I remember being driven through the Bois by him with your beautiful grandmother. Those lovely parasols! Happy days before the War . . . Charles won't hear of them going. I mean, the servants.'

'They are our friends as well as our servants. It is a Barthe tradition.' Charles turned away. Come, Ernest, tell me about Scotland. Has the Depression hit you as badly as here in France?'

'Probably worse. Miners' strikes, coal rationing, unemployment, murder in Ireland by the Sinn Feiners . . . that, of course, is a running sore.'

'Like the German reparation debt. There is talk of the Army advancing in the Ruhr if they default . . .'

'How utterly boring,' Emily said, waving her hands dismissively. They were beginning to resemble little glittering claws, Lizzie thought with some satisfaction. Her hands, at least, had escaped injury in that stupid accident—white, beautifully boneless with pearl-pink nails, Ernest's emerald emphasising their whiteness. 'Ah, here's Raoul with the tea. Just there, thank you.' 'Just there' was a Boule table with girandoles glittering at either end. 'That will do. Leave it to me.'

She certainly has drawing-room skills, Lizzie thought, watching the expert way she interrupted the men, found out their preferences, served them, then Lizzie and herself. Everything was beautiful. The Barthe Second Empire tea service, the miniature iced cakes—she ought not to indulge—the choice of Orange Pekoe or Darjeeling. Emily's hands flew like parakeets over the array of silver and delicate Limoges china.

'You don't take offence, Lizzie, at what I said?' She settled back comfortably, difficult on such a sofa, her cup poised exactly over her saucer.

'Goodness, no, I have a mirror, Emily. I know I'm a freak!'

'A freak!' A small screech. A ruffling of feathers. 'What is that? You are a beauty! Nothing will change that. It is God's gift to you. But that veil for a start . . . why do you wear it? It is quite *démodé*.'

'I have a scar on my forehead. The hair hasn't grown yet.'

'It will, it will, but meantime you'll go with me to my *coiffeuriste* tomorrow morning. He will cancel his appointments for us, and he will give you a little *pièce fausse*. I have one, see.' She touched her hair at the front and it wobbled slightly. 'My hair has always grown too far back for my liking. Had I lived in medieval times when they actually plucked out their hair to give them a noble brow . . . but we are in the twentieth century, praise be. Tomorrow, then, without fail, nine-thirty. You will stay here, I hope?'

'No, I regret, Emily. You may remember Grandmother and Aunt Maevy stayed at a hotel in the rue St-Hyacinthe near you, also Ernest and I when we were here on our honeymoon. It's a McGrath tradition.' She glanced at Charles. 'We love it here, of course, but we'll stay at the hotel for . . . sentimental reasons. You understand?'

Emily shrugged. 'Monceau Park is turned down. Ah, well, yes, I understand sentiment. I have to search for it elsewhere.' She gave the men who were talking together a sideways look and put her finger to her lips. 'But what's sauce for the goose is . . . shhh! Well, I give in about the hotel, but you must have some fresh air. I insist that you stay at La Hirondelle. The last time you turned it down because you were touring, but this time is different?'

'Excuse me, Ernest,' Lizzie raised her voice, 'Emily has just offered us La Hirondelle for a few days. Shall we accept?'

'If you hadn't, Emily dear, I was going to ask you.' He smiled at her, then turned to his host. 'With your permission, Charles, of course.'

He bowed his dark head. He could do with some fresh air himself, Lizzie thought, that dead white skin, contrasting so dramatically with the thin blackness of the moustache. 'It is more than a pleasure. I'm sorry the Delaunay-Belville is no longer there, but you may have my Mercedes.'

'No, no, I wouldn't dream of it. We just want to relax for a few days and have quiet little walks.'

'That's settled, then,' Emily said. 'You two go on with your talk about *les affaires*.' She turned back to Lizzie, 'Of course, you are going to see a couturier while you are in Paris?'

'I think Pierre. And now that Giselle is there . . .'

'Oh, didn't you know? She left Pierre to become *Directrice* to a smaller house, Capel et Cie. She will take care of you. There are shoes,' she frowned at Lizzie's sensible ones, 'hats also. She will help you. She's made for the job. Such flair! And such patience!'

'How is Terence?'

She sobered. 'He comes and goes. That is Giselle's cross. We all get them. But when he's well he produces good work, and when he's bad he goes to spend a week or so in Dr Reynaud's clinic at Condé. He believes that Terence is slowly getting better. And he has the right wife in my Giselle, so understanding, so uncomplaining. I'm ashamed when I see them together . . .' She shrugged. '*Que voulez-vous*? Would you like to see my doctor while you're here? We could have a little *tête-à-tête* dinner. Armand is so . . . *comme il faut*.'

'I don't need to see a doctor. We couldn't have a better one than we have in the Royal Infirmary at home. My leg doesn't give me any pain now.'

'But . . . excuse me, those glasses, Lizzie, are they strictly necessary?'

'Well, for distance . . .' she touched them selfconsciously.

'Can you see the door?'

'Perfectly. I'm not blind.' But you didn't see that van when you crossed the road . . .

'Paris is full of ladies sailing about far worse than you. They peer! People think it is a sign of aristocracy. Armand will test your eyes. One of his pet interests is ophthalmology. It's the coming thing. He will tell you exactly what you need. Is that agreed?'

'You are certainly taking me in hand.' Lizzie smiled ruefully at her over her cup.

'My dear,' Emily patted her hand, 'it's like this. You are the one whose beauty I have most admired. Even as a girl when you were at school at Versailles I was jealous of you. You never knew that, did you? Well, I want to preserve that beauty. It is there. It only needs a few aids because of that unfortunate accident and you'll be more beautiful than ever, and I'll have had a hand in restoring you to perfection. You wouldn't deny me that pleasure, would you?' Her little face was sincere enough. Underneath the glitter there was a good heart.

'How can I?' She leaned forward and kissed Emily's cheek. 'You've made me feel better already.'

The next few days were crammed with appointments, Ernest acting only as companion in the car and chauffeur he had hired. He had refused the loan of Charles Barthe's Mercedes, saying that he wouldn't have the courage to drive in Paris because of *la circulation*.

The *tête-à-tête* dinner with Dr Armand Duval did not materialise. Emily had had second thoughts and said it might be a little indelicate to invite Charles and Ernest—Lizzie didn't pursue this —but they had tea in his beautiful consulting room which felt like being in a dove-grey velvet envelope, safe from the harassment of the noisy boulevard outside.

He was professional enough in his approach to Lizzie, but the way he practically ignored Emily made her think there was more in their relationship than met the eye. She wasn't the originator of a war-time hospital and a flourishing Hydropathic for nothing.

'You are certainly myopic, my dear lady,' he said, 'but not to a great degree. I find that with certain ladies this varies a little from time to time—the constitution, the weather. Your eyes are perfectly healthy, and I am almost certain they won't grow worse. In fact, you can look forward to a possible improvement when you reach the stage of requiring glasses for reading . . . a long way off.' He flattered her with his glance.

'I shall prescribe spectacles for you which are non-reflective—this makes them less noticeable—and suggest that on certain occasions you may leave them off, provided they are to hand.'

'But my dear Armand,' Emily said, 'you don't want my sister-in-law fumbling in her handbag every time she wants to see something or someone in the distance?'

'Certainly not.' He didn't turn his head to look at her. 'In this life we must make advantages of our disadvantages. That is the secret of comfortable living. Now, I imagine that with a beautiful wife like you, your husband will wish to buy you some trifle in the jewellers, *n'est-ce pas*?'

'He had mentioned . . .'

'I know an optician who makes the most beautiful chains set with stones which a lady wears round her neck to anchor the spectacles. You will set a vogue in Scotland. They will talk of you as a setter of fashion. And this friend of mine will make the spectacles so fine that your eyes will look more beautiful than ever, if that is possible. I have noticed,' he said in aside to Emily, 'that myopic people have often the most beautiful eyes. The pupils are enlarged.'

'That doesn't sound like a compliment to me, Armand.' He smiled but didn't turn his head.

'And he will be careful of your long eyelashes also,' he said to Lizzie. This man is an artist. You will look divine, glasses or no glasses, and you will throw away those horrible *pince-nez* which do as they are named. Already there is a red mark.'

She left his rooms, after a delicious 'four o'clock' served by his footman, walking on air. 'I don't care if he charges the earth,' she said, 'I feel better already.'

'Oh, he won't charge!' Emily looked horrified. 'That would be infra dig. It is a favour because of me. Now, the *coiffeuriste*.'

This visit was more businesslike—no tea—but even more comforting. Madame had beautiful hair. It would grow again, without a doubt, it was strong and healthy. But meantime he would make a little 'piece' which could conceal it *comme ça*, and her beauty would be unsullied. 'It is not often we see hair of your colour in Paris, Madame,' Jean-Jacques said, 'here it is usually the black.' He gave a disparaging look at Emily as he spoke, but perhaps seeing her expression, changed it to one of admiration. 'Of course there is black and black. Madame Barthe's is of a richness you cannot imagine . . .'

The visit to Capel et Cie took the best part of a day as they had arranged to have lunch with Giselle as well. She was a different Giselle from the girl Lizzie remembered from her previous visit, slender to the point of thinness in her straight black dress, three rows of pearls at her neck, large pearl studs in her ears, shining straight black hair, rouged lips. But the way she embraced Lizzie was the old Giselle, whole-hearted, generous. 'Oh, how good to see you, Leezie. I call you that now, not *Aunt*? I was so sorry to hear of your accident.'

'You were kind to write.'

'Ginny kept me informed of your progress. She's a wonderful girl, so *vivante*. Terence and I love her very much.'

'How is Terence?'

'At the moment he is spending a week at Condé. Dr Reynaud calls it "taking the pressure off". It is the best solution. There is a rare rapport between them, and he can work at his own pace there. Each time he goes, he is less . . . *affligé*? And he comes out of the depression more quickly. "The War fades," Dr Reynaud says, and the scars with it. There are men like himself in the clinic, and they talk out their experiences. It is part of the treatment.'

'And his painting?'

'That is flourishing.' She smiled. 'He worked well in Ireland and came back with quite a few portraits of horses. Dr Reynaud calls him the French George Stubbs! He's sold them all except one, which he won't part with. It's of the Sholtie Flyer, the horse his father is training to be a winner, and it has a special significance for Terence.' She laughed. 'I tell my father-in-law, try out your horse at Longchamps or Chantilly first.'

'And then the Grand National?'

'That's a dream. Not many of us get our dreams.'

'Don't you think we should get started on Lizzie?' her mother said.

Lizzie laughed. 'Get started, indeed! I feel like a motor car, a badly broken-down one. But I haven't asked about Clovis and Jaime.'

'Ah, they're *mignon*,' Emily said, her face lighting up.

'You will come for dinner with Ernest and see them. We shall make an appointment, but now let us see this badly broken-down old car you speak of. If all my clients were like you I would not do any business at all.'

The dresses were cunning, with side draperies whose movement would conceal the damaged leg but show off her good points, her full bosom, her slim waist. Being Lizzie she looked closely at how the mannequin walked and decided to emulate her, just a trifle.

The shoes were a masterpiece—high fashion with long toes and centre bars to slim the bad foot and . . . *thin* soles.

'The extra thickness is inside,' explained the little man who knelt humbly at her feet. 'Quite invisible, style, elegance, concealment and comfort. With the beautiful gowns which Madame Magratt (McGrath, Lizzie realised) has arranged for you, you will be able to stroll down the rue St-Honoré and they will make a path for you.'

'I should come to Paris more often,' Lizzie told Ernest when they were driving back to the hotel. 'It is a city to restore a woman's morale.'

'Your eyes are shining,' he said, kissing her. 'Let's set off tomorrow to Château-sur-Epte for that second honeymoon, or is it the third?'

'The day after tomorrow. We have to visit Giselle at Passy and see the boys, and she is having her twin brothers, Marc and Olivier, because I knew them when I was at school here. They made me laugh so much with their quaint ways. Marc has one child, Fabrice, Olivier isn't married.'

'We never met them at Monceau Park. Why is that?'

'There are very few family parties there, haven't you noticed? Only salons.'

'Not like the McGraths,' he said.

'The Magratts,' she said, laughing, 'that's what the little shoeman called them.'

* * *

'I wonder if the second honeymoon is going to be better than the first,' Ernest said, watching Lizzie at the dressing-table. He was already in bed.

'Not after this performance, my darling,' she said. 'First I unpin this hairpiece and expose my noble but scarred brow, then I take off this beautifully-cut dress which does wonders for my stupid leg,' she put her foot up on a stool. 'Then I take off the shoes which level me off instead of making me walk like a drunken sailor . . .'

'Then the glasses,' he said.

'Ah, yes, I leave them on so that I can see what I'm doing.' She lifted the gold chain over her head and it made an expensive rattle as she laid it down. 'Then the rest of my clothes . . . the beauty of a dress like this is that it's like a sculpture, supported in just the right places, and so there's hardly need for corsets, or even lingerie . . .'

'You've forgotten to unscrew your wooden leg.' She was standing naked.

'Don't be cruel. Oh, dear, I shall have to put on my glasses. I can't find my nightdress.'

'Didn't you put it under your pillow?'

'Oh, yes, probably.' She came towards him, and when she bent to search for it he grasped her hand and pulled her in beside him. 'No, it isn't cold. I've forgotten what you're like under all those lovely clothes Giselle designed for you.'

'You've nothing on either! You're bare scuddy!'

'It's a French custom. See, let's lie like this together and we'll talk about the wonderful day we've had,' he had one arm round her and with his free hand he gently stroked the scar on her brow. 'The little village with the old main street. And the café where we had our glass of wine.'

'And the island where the river divides where we had our picnic.'

'Like the first time.'

'Yes, like the first time.'

'And you and I preparing the dinner in Emily's flagged kitchen with the copper pots.'

'Madame Jacques offered.'

'But we didn't want her, did we?'

'And the dinner with the candles glowing and the logs crackling.'

'And the wine.'

'And the wine. I don't know how we got upstairs.'

'Or you got your clothes off.'

'Or you. But you hadn't bits and pieces like me.'

He stopped stroking her forehead and took her tightly in his arms, 'Oh, my love, if I'd lost you that time.'

'Are you saying you couldn't have lived without me?'

'A kind of a life, for the sake of the children.'

'Annabel and Kit, growing up, and Jonty, my first-born, my handsome laddie.'

'And probably in bed with a woman at this very minute.'

'He won't be so silly this time.'

'As he was with Madame Delage? No, he's learning, I think, and we have to leave him be. He proved himself a man in France . . .'

He made love to her, caressing the broken places with mouth and murmured words. This was his dear love. He hoped Jonty wouldn't throw himself away on inferior love but wait until someone like Lizzie came along, who would satisfy his every need.

They let themselves go in the old French house—no servants, no children. They groaned together, they shouted, they ended up on the floor in a welter of sheets and blankets, and towards morning groped their way back again, slightly ashamed of themselves at forty-odd and fifty-odd, that they had made such an exhibition of themselves.

At least that's what Lizzie said, not too seriously. He had no regrets. Only she held his secret, that under his urbanity there was the devil of a man.

4

Before Ernest and Lizzie had gone to Paris they had talked about making it a really momentous trip and flying there, but in the end had decided that Lizzie had had enough trauma to last her for the rest of her life. It was a restful holiday they were going for this time, but it wouldn't be long before they would be flipping over there by air for a weekend.

Now that Ginny was at last going home, the thought crossed her mind that some day it would be possible to fly the Atlantic also. But for the time being she was well content with the luxurious sea trip. Aunt Kate was going with her on her annual visit to see her grandchildren. Aunt Maevy would go alone when they returned, Maevy being regarded as more stalwart, and, of course, under no circumstances could the two sisters leave Isobel on her own.

It was over two years since Ginny had been home, and often, on the trip, while Aunt Kate was chattering away about her grandchildren, she turned over in her mind all that had happened to her in that time. You could day-dream with Aunt Kate. She wasn't as forceful as her sister, Maevy, who commanded attention. Perhaps it was a good thing, because if she had been installed in her daughter, Ellie's house, as was natural, Ginny and Ellie would have found it difficult to have the intimate talks that Ginny was looking forward to.

Ellie would understand her, her ambivalence about her home, her deep love of it, and yet her inability to remain there for long, her decision to refuse Magnus Muir, her love of Iain. But she would be careful not to moan about that. Iain was alive whether married or not: the love of Ellie's life and the father of her first child had been blown to pieces in France. You couldn't complain in the face of that.

And also, during those few placid days on the high seas, she thought of Iain's wife and the bond which had grown up between them while she had stayed at the Hydro. She had developed the habit, at Beth's insistence, of slipping up to see her whenever she had a spare moment if she knew Iain wouldn't be there. Beth didn't seem to have the confidence to venture downstairs on her own.

There was something infinitely pathetic to Ginny in the girl's assumed cheerfulness. It was easy to see by the glancing eyes and the hands which shook occasionally that it was only skin deep. Once she had said to Ginny, 'I haven't talked about this to Iain because it would only distress him . . . Sometimes I lie awake at night dreading death. It clutches at my throat, squeezes my heart, I want to scream with terror. I sweat . . . sometimes I have to get up and change my nightdress and he thinks I have a temperature, but it isn't that.'

'You should tell him.' And although it twisted her heart to say it, 'He would comfort you, soothe you. That's what husbands are for.'

'Maybe.' The mouth had trembled above the front teeth. 'I know he would be sympathetic, but somehow he's grown . . . aloof. Oh, he's kindness itself, but the old Iain is gone. I torture myself with the thought that he's regretting marrying me . . .'

'That's nonsense. He's . . . serious. Was he ever fun to be with?'

'Oh, yes. We used to laugh together when we were golfing at Cow Glen. He has this dry way of saying things which made me double up . . . he has, or had, a great sense of humour. But he was always ambitious, and when he got the job of managing director at McGraths he became . . . different. He's over-anxious, he sets very high standards for himself, he would never allow himself to slip from those.'

'I wonder what made him like that?' Talking about Iain to his wife was the next best way of talking to him. There was a vicarious pleasure which she despised as she encouraged it.

'I don't know. Of course, he's always known responsibilities. His father was an invalid, and so Iain supported his mother and sister. I think he liked coming to our house because it was different, lighter. Mother's outgoing, and we've never known money worries. The world outside was always hard for Iain. All his achievements are his own. Not like that young heir of the McGrath fortune he's told me about, Mrs Murray-Hyslop's son. He's had everything handed to him on a golden plate, hasn't he?'

'It looks like that. Things are never what they seem, Beth. Ernest isn't his real father for a start. He was killed in the Boer War before he was born. Maybe because of that he ran away from school and joined up and went through one of the bloodiest battles of the War at seventeen—Passchendaele.'

'And here's me thinking he'd sat in the lap of luxury all the time! I think of you in the same way.' Her look was shy and glancing.

'Me! Oh, I had a hard life,' she joked. 'I ran away from home, almost. It was luxurious enough, I'll give you that, but I wanted to see the world. And I came here. It wasn't easy. I had terrible feelings of guilt, still have, especially as I have a sister, Sarah, who's so holy that she lives half in heaven already.'

'That would be enough to make anyone run away from home.' This Beth had a sense of humour. 'I'll tell you something. I never envied riches or high living. I didn't even want Iain to get on. It only took him away from me. All I wanted was a nice suburban house and a game of golf in the evenings, and maybe in time some children.'

And the resentment went finally one day when she ran up to see if Beth was all right and found her in bed, lifeless, her face drained of colour, her mouth slightly open. There was a dribble of saliva from her lips and Iain was wiping it.

'Is she . . . ?' she stopped herself in time from saying 'dying'. She had seen the slight tremor in the girl's hands, the quiver of her lids.

'It's one of her bad days.' He looked round at her, dark, anxious. 'She feels the most awful fatigue. I'm beginning to understand it.'

'Iain,' Beth's voice was faint, 'stay with me.' Her eyes rolled, took in Ginny standing at the bedside. 'Who's that?'

'It's Ginny, darling. Just come in to see how you are.'

'I don't want her . . . here. I want you.'

There was no place for her in this room. They were married, an inseparable bond, stronger than most, because of her condition. She went out of the room sick at heart and ran downstairs. She burst into the office, her face hard. 'Nan! Have you got those figures for the takings of last month?'

'I'm just on them, Ginny. You said there was no rush.'

'Well, there is now. I'm going to Glasgow to see the accountants.' She could almost hear her mortified tones behind the door as she shut it, not too gently, 'I wonder what's eating *her*?'

* * *

But, oh, the joy as she and Aunt Kate sped along in the train from Grand Central Station to Wanapeake, that sing-song call of the guard was so familiar in her ears that she could have joined in: 'Harlem, Yonkers, Ardsley, Dobb's Ferry, Ossining . . .' And the broad river outlining its route sometimes lapping almost at the station platform.

Then the reception at Wanapeake Station. Father, Mother and Sarah standing at their stately imported Daimler; Sam and Zach, two of Aunt Kate's grandsons, jumping out of their yellow sports car and racing forward to meet them: Sam freckle-faced and broadly built, betraying his Dutch ancestry on his mother's side, Zach, elegant as befitted a young man from Yale. Kate's eyes were shining with pride as she hugged them in turn. 'We're deputising for Father and Uncle Kieran! Hello, Ginny! They had a board meeting in the city.' The vitality of them. The exuberance. So definitely New World.

But, first, her mother and father. Sarah had come forward with her cousins, definitely dowdy in dress now but with a face which radiated goodness and serenity. 'How are the fallen women, Sarah?'

'Trying to get them up on their feet. Oh, it's good to see you, Ginny, my little sister!'

'I'm a few inches taller than you. Mother! Father!' The tears came as she went into their arms in turn. They had aged. She should have come more often.

'Welcome home, daughter,' Maria said. She was still fussily dressed, as if to make up for Sarah's disregard.

'Oh, it's good to see you both! How have you been keeping?'

'Fine! Fine!' Father's beard tickled.

'Sometimes,' his wife said. 'You know, Ginny, at sixty-eight your father still travels up to New York every day.'

'He probably thinks McGraths couldn't run without him. You should look for a deputy, Father, take it easy.' Immediately she realised her mistake. Gaylord might have taken that role. She saw his mouth tighten.

'So they keep on telling me. It's finding the right person.'

Sam interrupted. 'I have a mesage from Mother, Uncle. She would kill me if I forgot.' Ginny remembered Abigail and her formidable mother, Mrs Van Dam—the uncrowned queen of Wanapeake, Gaylord used to call her. 'We're having a family get-together tomorrow evening and everybody's coming, even the children, so that Grandma can see them. Uncle Kieran and Aunt Ellie are bringing their two. They'll have a party in the afternoon, then the nursemaids will take them away and the grown-ups will sit down to dinner when Father, Uncle Kieran and you, Uncle Patrick, get home. And me, of course, I'm the smaller fry, along with Ben Vogel. We'll beat the train from New York in our motor.'

'What kind is it?' Ginny asked, curious.

'A Yankee Hispano. It goes like a bird. There's room between

Zach and me if you'd like to ride along with us. We'll drop you off at Claremont.'

'Right!' She shouldn't have said that. 'What about Aunt Kate?'

'You'll drop her off at Wolf House, won't you, Uncle Patrick?'

'I'm only too pleased to fit in with your arrangements.' He hadn't changed. He didn't like to be ordered about.

Zach put the tin lid on it. 'It's much more your style, Ginny, than the Daimler,' he said in his lofty Yale way.

'See you at the house, then,' she said. Difficult love swept over her as she looked at her father. He had taken a day off to come and meet her.

She changed her mind. 'I'll have a ride in your yellow peril later.' She smiled brightly at the two boys. 'I'm anxious to get home. ' She got in beside her father. Sarah and her mother were already ensconced in the back. 'This is nice,' she said, turning to him.

5

George Murray-Hyslop, Aunt Kate's elder step-son, couldn't have been more different from his younger brother, Ernest. Where Ernest was suave, a man in his own right, George was serious and dignified, yet paradoxically happily hen-pecked—not surprising since Abigail, his wife, had a commanding presence rather like her mother, Mrs Van Dam.

Maria had said to Ginny when they were preparing to go to Albany House, the Murray-Hyslop residence, 'You'll find it as untidy as ever, all dogs and children. The Van Dams may be real old gentry, but Abigail's mother didn't teach her to be tidy. It's not at all like the Vogel place where Victoria keeps everything ship-shape. Victoria's sister in Paris, Emily, has a lovely house. You've been there, haven't you?'

'Yes, Mother. Lovely.'

They went in the afternoon to see the little ones, to please Aunt Kate. Ginny had hoped Ellie might be there with James and little Betsy Ann, but she found them in the charge of Rachel, the same competent nursemaid she had known before. 'Miss McNab' was operating this afternoon (Ellie used her maiden name professionally), but she would be at the evening party with Mr Kieran when he got back from the office.

Ginny remembered that Kieran and his half-brother, George, had inherited the family business from their father. In the early days, Ernest had told her, the family export firm hadn't been extensive enough to absorb the two brothers (himself and George), and his father had encouraged him to accept the offer from McGraths to join them. Much later, when Kieran, his half-brother, had been ready for a career, the Murray-Hyslop firm had by then expanded enough to welcome him. The thought of her true son following in his father's footsteps had pleased Kate.

Ginny romped with the children—James, quite unlike either Kieran or Ellie with his long eyes and golden skin, and Betsy Ann, pale, golden-curled like her mother and with the same thoughtful yet sweet expression, but she giggled when she was tickled, which was a good sign. Little Sophie McGrath from Springhill across the Hudson, daughter of Edie and Robert, had to be tickled too.

'Robert and Ernest did a swap in McGraths a long time ago,' said Sarah who was down on the floor with her. 'You were just a child. Robert came to be Father's assistant in New York, and Ernest went to the firm in Glasgow so that he could be near his love, Lizzie.' She did not say that Robert had been in love with her and her father had forbidden the match because they were full cousins. Her face was serene. Perhaps she had put away worldly things.

Then there were Victoria's five grandchildren. Ginny had a natural affinity with children, and she thought she probably enjoyed them better without the presence of their serious young mothers who, Ellie has told her, gave *her* such well-meaning advice when she was pregnant.

'How we've spread,' she said to Sarah, 'all starting from Maeve and Kieran McGrath who eloped from Ireland.'

'Yes, all over the world—Scotland, France, Ireland and here . . . I've got them all in my birthday book.'

'You don't mean you send cards to them all?'

'I do,' she said. 'I'll never have children of my own.'

'Who knows? Maybe neither shall I.'

'I thought you would have been married ages ago,' Sarah said without rancour, 'all the boys after you. It will be the same again while you're here.'

'No, I've changed. I'm nearly as serious as you now, Sarah. Hi!' Two of the children had launched themselves on her and began to climb over her.

'Watch your Aunt Ginny!' Sarah said severely. 'She's a lady.'

'I'm far from that. Leave them be, Sarah.' She took a little boy under each arm and squeezed them till they shouted. 'I'm not hurting you, am I? You're big strong boys. Oh, I *am* hurting? Dear me!' She rolled them on the floor, where she tickled them until they were giggling uncontrollably. She looked up and saw two nursemaids looking down severely.

'Its time for their tea now, Miss Ginny,' one of them said, 'we don't want them upset.'

'No, of course not, poor delicate little things.' She smiled up at them and their authority fell away from them and they broke into laughter themselves.

'They love a rough house,' one of them said, 'you're right up their street.'

When eventually Ginny drove her mother and Sarah home to get ready for the evening party, they felt, as any one of the Scottish aunts might have said, as if they had been dragged through a hedge backwards.

'But nothing that a good hot bath won't set to rights,' Maria said when they were in the hall. And then, 'You noticed you have a bathroom suite of your own now, Ginny?'

'Yes, I noticed, Mother.' She should have commented on it. It was an innovation at Claremont, but she had grown used to one in the Hydro. 'It's lovely. What a lot of work and upset it must have meant! It's a pity I couldn't use it oftener.'

'It's yours, kept for you whenever you can get home to visit. And who knows, you might come some day with a husband.' She wanted to say something outrageous like, 'Then we'll be able to bath together . . .'

'Would it be terrible if you had *two* unmarried daughters, Mother?' she asked.

'Well, every mother longs for grandchildren, it's natural, but your father and I, we've learned not to expect too much, and we haven't forgotten your little sister, Mary, who died when she was three, as sensible then as she was at birth, which isn't saying much. No, we have two dear girls and we count our blessings.'

She kissed her, difficult love moistening her eyes. 'I love you,' she wanted to say. 'Well, Sarah's not been a disappointment. Come and give your mother a cuddle as well, Sarah.' They stood entwined, the three of them.

'Neither of you are.' There were tears in Maria's voice. 'The only one who gave us real heartache, as you both well know, was Gaylord . . . doing that to himself. That's what made your father and me different, well, serious . . .'

'We like you that way, don't we, Sarah?' She spoke lightly to hide her emotion. 'Well, I'd better go up to my lovely bathroom suite now and wallow.'

'You'll find everything you need in the cabinet—bath salts, talcum powder, perfume, all the same make. Houbigant. Your father bought them for you in New York, in Madison Avenue.'

'Do you mean Father went into that shop for *me*?'

'Yes, he did,' Sarah said, smiling. 'We couldn't get the right things in Wanapeake.'

She wept in her bath, tears of guilt and happiness and resolve. She would forget the resolve, she knew, but not the happiness. And no doubt the guilt would stay.

* * *

Whatever the state of the house might be, Abigail Murray-Hyslop, *née* Van Dam, could set a fine table. She had been used to gracious living, and her dignified demeanour proclaimed it. The table was glittering with Van Dam silver and crystal, huge epergnes of fruit gleaming under massive candelabra. It had a Dutch plenitude. Unfortunately the great Mrs Van Dam was indisposed—a touch of gout, typically enough—and she had sent along as her ambassador her youngest son, Roland Van Dam, known as Rollo, apparently.

Ginny, watching him when they were all having a pre-dinner sherry in the drawing-room, saw how his charm seemingly fluttered the hearts of Victoria and Jason Vogel's married daughters, Deborah Sandburg and Judith King, both rather nondescript girls, she thought, probably because of their pompous father—no, she mustn't think like that, they were young mothers absorbed both in rearing children and their small-town activities.

The surprising thing was that even Victoria, their mother, seemed enchanted with Rollo Van Dam, although one couldn't have found a greater contrast between her and her sister Emily in Paris. Where one was a humming-bird (or a parakeet), the other most nearly resembled a small brown wren, almost a facsimile of 'our own dear late-lamented queen'. She whispered that to Ellie who was sitting beside her on one of the untidy leather sofas, a pale, finely featured Ellie with a new look of serenity. Kieran, at her side, had filled out, and she had noticed earlier that his limp was almost gone. He looked like a man who was happy in his marriage.

Well, she would hear all about it from Ellie. Tomorrow, being Sunday, she had been invited with Sarah and her parents for afternoon tea and a 'post-mortem', Ellie had said, mischief in her eyes. She wasn't all sweetness.

At the table she was placed between Sam Murray-Hyslop and Rollo Van Dam, probably an effort an Abigail's part to let her meet her brother again. On Sam's other side there was a delectable young girl called Lucy Springer whom he seemed more interested in. It was typical of Abigail, Ginny thought, that she should include her children's friends. The Vogels would have been much more conventional. Priscilla, the unmarried Vogel girl, had no companion, nor had her brother Ben, but then, they were invitees. Abigail could do whatever she liked in her own house. She had the total self-confidence of people who have always known their proper place in society.

Rollo Van Dam had the same self-confidence: tall, chestnut-coloured wavy hair well pomaded, as suave and insouciant as Ernest, but more talkative, not the occasional dry remark which was Ernest's forte. 'Where have you been all my life, Ginny McGrath?' he said, turning to her. He was finely tanned, he had fine brown eyes, a fine line of a moustache above a smiling mouth, nothing the least bit uncouth in his appearance. His bearing was handsome and assured.

'Mostly in Scotland,' she said smiling at him, 'but I haven't been purposely avoiding you.'

'Quite right to get away from Wanapeake. A one-horse town. I live in New York. Work in Wall Street, as a matter of fact.'

'Buying and selling millions?'

'Incidentally.' He smiled at her with his eyes. 'It isn't the only thing, the money, you know. It's the excitement. Like a drug. I like excitement. Do you?'

'I suppose so, otherwise I should have stayed at home like Sarah.'

'Shows your character. Tell me what you do in Scotland.'

'I run a hydropathic hotel for my cousin, Lizzie, Ernest's wife. She inherited the house from her first husband, but she thought it was too big for them eventually. It goes to her son, of course.' She couldn't resist this, 'Nigel Jonathan Garston, Lord Crawford.'

'Phew, what a mouthful! Puts the Van Dams in the shade, I'll tell you. But what a brilliant idea!' He looked impressed. 'Took a lot of money to get started, though? Where did that come from?'

'McGraths, I suppose.' He certainly asked questions.

'Now that they're doing so well, and I should know, your father, if you don't mind me saying this, is perhaps . . . over-cautious. So is Robert, for that matter. I've pointed out a few quick returns on the Stock Exchange to them.'

'It's Scottish canniness. But they're shrewd. I know Ernest worries about the increasing signs of unemployment in Scotland, the fall of the German mark, and so on. He's a citizen of the world, Ernest.'

'Yes, I've always admired old Ernest, but he should spare a little time to study the markets. There are fortunes being made . . . but what am I doing talking business to a glorious girl like you? Ma says I've to learn to leave it in the office . . .'

Sam said, overhearing and momentarily deflected from his Lucy, 'Don't listen to a word that fellow says, Ginny. He's got a reputation in Wanapeake.'

'Has he? What kind?' But before he could answer he had turned back again to his enchantress.

'Now, there's a bright lad,' Rollo Van Dam said. 'He and Ben have got in on the ground floor of this travel business. It's the latest thing. It used to be only for the privileged, but everyone's going to start moving around. Just wait until the first commercial aeroplane flies the Atlantic. There have been tries before.'

'Why don't *you* do it?'

'Haven't time. Too many irons in the fire. But this travel thing . . . there will be companies which take the bother out of it, hotels booked for you, guides and all the rest. All you'll have to do is sit back and enjoy yourself. Oh, yes, there's money to be made there.'

'I thought you weren't going to talk business,' she said, laughing at him .

'God, what a fool I am!' he said, striking his forehead. His smile was engaging, his eyes creased when he laughed. 'The returned beauty beside me, and I wasting my time! Has anyone ever told you how utterly fascinating you are?'

'You're laying it on too thick. They don't talk like that in dour Scotland.'

'Well, they should. What shall we talk about, then? Let's see. What's your favourite place for holidays?'

She thought for a second. 'Oh, I think France, without a doubt. You know Emily, Sam's aunt . . . she's lived in Paris since she was married, and I'm very fond of her daughter, Giselle. Her husband, Terence, and Robert McGrath are brothers. He was badly injured at Verdun and hasn't fully recovered.'

'Poor chap. I was in at the end. Had the luck of the devil. What's his trouble?'

'Neurasthenia. A complete breakdown. I think he's slowly mending. It's been hard for Giselle and the children.'

'Sure. Do you like Paris?'

'Love it. It has an effect on me, makes me feel gay and dying to throw my cap over the windmill.'

'You could do that here, too. New York's the same.'

'I don't believe it. To me it's only a shopping place.' She remembered her Houbigant perfume and looked over at her father who was sitting opposite her. Their eyes met and he smiled, even nodded appreciatively, as if for once she was doing the right thing. 'And I went to school there. Travelled with Father every morning.'

'Ah, but you don't know the fun New York. Have you ever been to the Waldorf Hotel?'

'No.'

'Corner of Fifth and Thirty-third? Where have you been? It's a great place to be with a girl. Like a palace, and *so* romantic. Do you believe in romance, Ginny?' Of course he knew how charming he was.

'Not any longer.' The old feeling of desolation swept through her. Iain . . . marrying Beth even although he loved *her*. Oh, those

Scotsmen with their high morality, and their stubbornness. No lightness . . . but would she have him any different? He was worth ten Rollo Van Dams.

'If you went to the Waldorf with me I bet it would make your pulse beat faster.' His smile was engaging. His voice had lowered.

'I don't believe it.'

'You'd turn everybody's head there. I'm surprised one of those hairy Scotsmen in a kilt hasn't made off with you to his cave long before this.'

'One tried. A very large cave, a castle to be exact.'

'Aristocracy?'

'You could say that. His mother was a battleaxe.'

'I hope you aren't casting aspersions at my own dear Mama?'

'Oh, gosh no!' She spluttered with laughter. 'I *would* put my foot in it. I didn't mean . . .'

Polly, the unmarried daughter of George and Abigail, looking pert, called to her. 'Watch out for that wicked uncle of mine, Ginny! Prissy and I call him the American robin!'

'Do you?' A large bold bird, bigger than the round-breasted British one . . . 'Don't worry, Polly. I'll put him in his place if it's necessary.' She met Rollo's twinkling brown eyes and suddenly liked him very much. You could forget with him . . .

'What about the Rainbow Room at the Waldorf, Ginny? An evening of unalloyed pleasure with the most eligible bachelor in Westchester?' He looked it when he smiled. Dashing. She smiled at him.

'What crass conceit!' And then, 'I'll think about it.'

'I'll pester you till you do.'

'Pester away, then . . .' Inconsequential banter was fun. She had been bashing her head against a brick wall for far too long.

The rest of the party went with a swing. Her father looked contented enough sitting with his wife. They were seldom apart.

It was a great joy to her to meet Edie again, whom she had known before she married Robert. Her liveliness as Edie Barnes hadn't changed, in spite of being a mother and being pregnant again. Her quick dark smile was still there as she questioned Ginny about the doings of 'the Scottish clan' as she called them, especially Jonty.

'What good fortune to be studying in Florence,' she said. 'Oh, how I wish I had done something like that before I settled down . . . but I've no regrets.' The cleft at the side of her mouth appeared and disappeared as she smiled. 'Robert and I are very happy, and I still get time to do some reading on art and slip up to the New

York galleries. I see the newest works—N. C. Wyeth, for instance. Have you heard of him?'

'No.' Ginny shook her head, seeing for a second unknown worlds, non-personal worlds which she would have to discover for herself.

'Will you tell Jonty that if he comes to visit here he must stay with us and I'll take him up to see my favourites?'

'He'd love that. He and Terence McGrath get on famously, although he doesn't paint himself.'

'Nor do I. But Terence is good. I've heard about his troubles. I took the liberty of writing to him as he's Robert's brother. He'll be all right in time, I'm sure. His painting must be a great solace to him.'

And there was Kieran and Ellie to talk to, he with a new assurance because of his fatherhood.

'Do you remember the poor soul Kieran was when he was in bed with that Spanish flu?' she asked Ellie.

'And you saved his life by nursing him till I got home?'

'Oh, rubbish! He was as good as gold. But you've still to take me on the trip we were going to make that Sunday, Kieran. To the Catskills. They'll still be there.'

He remembered. 'It's never too late. We'll have a family picnic. Grandmother Maeve loved family picnics. Mother still talks about them, especially one when she went on the *Mary Powell*, the old paddle steamer. It's one of the family Great Days, enshrined in the collective memory.'

'And the collective unconscious,' Ellie said.

'You clever people.' She looked around, smiling, happy. 'Aunt Kate?' she called. She was sitting with Victoria and her husband, Jason Vogel. 'Could you spare a moment? We want you to put on your thinking cap.'

She rose and came over to them, gracious, sweet-faced, happy to be surrounded by her step-children and their children's children and her own dear Kieran. Every detail would be retailed to the sisters when she got back to Scotland. 'What is it?'

'Have my seat, Mother.' Kieran got up. Maybe she was glad to get away from self-important Jason, Ginny thought as she leaned forward to her aunt.

'Kieran says you used to tell him of a lovely picnic you had with Grandmother, when you went on an old paddle steamer.'

'My goodness! That was a long time ago.' She paused, smiling, 'And yet I remember it as if it were yesterday. It was a lovely day, and we took the *Mary Powell* to Kingston. She was a sidewheeler, George and Ernest told us. You weren't even thought of, Kieran.'

'Hard luck! I should like to have been there.'

'Ah, my poor love!' Ellie smiled at him. Yes, they were happy now.

'There were Maria's parents, Uncle Terence and Aunt Caroline —Maria was my great friend. What a bright, lovely girl she was then, and my dear James and all the children—no, Emily and Victoria would be at their finishing school in Paris. We wore our summer muslins and our shady hats, and mother had on a new Indian shawl we had given her. She was *that* proud of it.'

'She always liked clothes,' Ellie said.

'Like Lizzie,' Ginny agreed. 'She had a field day in Paris recently, Ellie.'

'George and Ernest told Mother the whole story of General George Custer, if you please, because we were going to sail past the place where he'd been buried. I remember her lively, beautiful face quite clearly. She had always infinite patience with children because she was a child herself in some ways. That was her greatest charm, the interest, the curiosity, aye, right up to the last, like the clothes. She loved the boys, and I remember Isobel, who had come with her from Scotland, like a fragile fairy with that lint-white hair. The Hudson Highlands we sailed through. Well, you know all this, Ginny. You were born and bred here.'

'But I certainly wasn't on that trip, and I doubt if I know much about General George Custer. You'd pass West Point and the Military Academy?'

'Yes, we did. We were all so happy. James had his hand over mine as we sat on the slatted seats . . .' her face was soft. 'There was a gentle breeze, and the tulle veil which hung from Isobel's hat kept blowing over that delicate face of hers . . .' She shook her head, sighing. 'Then we got off at Poughkeepsie to see Maria's school, and when we'd been shown all her remembered haunts we spread out our rugs and set up our chairs by the riverside while Caroline and I laid out the food we'd brought in a wicker basket. I wish you had seen the size of the basket!'

'You're making us see the scene anyhow, Mother,' Kieran said, smiling at her. What a sweet mouth he had, Ginny thought.

'Anyhow, that's it, but years later Mother said it was one of those glowing days that stayed in her mind for ever . . . and that there was one thing she was glad of . . .'

'What was that!' Ginny said. She had never felt nearer her grandmother, nor more part of her family.

'She said she knew it at the time, that when she was sitting watching the boys playing in the water, she had said out loud,

"Today I'm happy."' She was silent for a second, her head bent. 'That was Mother's secret. Each day was a day in itself. She hardly ever looked back. She had few regrets.'

'I wish we could all say that.' Ellie's beauty was luminous, her eyes sad. When Aunt Maevy asks me how her daughter is looking, Ginny thought, I'll tell her I've never seen her look more beautiful. She jumped up and put her arms round Kate. 'It must be the Irish in you, Aunt! Sure and begorrah you're a wonderful teller of stories, isn't she, Kieran?'

'Yes, she's that. Do you remember Leerie, the lamplighter, Mother? You used to tell us about him in the nursery. I could see, and feel, the misty Glasgow darkness. That was *my* Scotland, the wee man going round with his long pole to light the street lamps . . .' His eyes were tender. 'And then, there was "Wee Willie Winkie runs through the toon . . ."'

'"Upstairs and downstairs, in his nicht goon,"' Ellie said, smiling.

His eyes were on her, full of love.

In the Daimler going home Ginny sat with her father in the front. The feather trimming of her evening cloak was soft and cool on her flushed cheeks, its satin slid against the satin of her dress and against her skin. She liked the feeling. She felt happy. Life was good.

'I saw you were sitting beside Rollo Van Dam at dinner,' he said. 'What do you think of him?'

'Rather nice. Entertaining.'

'He's certainly handsome,' Maria said from the back. 'The only unmarried Van Dam.'

'What did *you* think of him, Sarah?' Ginny asked. She didn't like this concentration on herself.

'I'm no judge of modern young men. You ought to know that.' There was no resentment in her voice.

'He's got his foot in with a good Wall Street firm.' Her father wasn't going to drop the subject, 'Mather and Robb. He's a live wire, but a bit too daring for me. Still, I suppose we have to move with the times.'

'We might ask him to dinner some evening while you're here,' her mother said, 'some young company around the house.'

'I've got Sarah, Mother. That's enough for me.'

'Oh, but I might drag you out with me to visit my fallen women,' Sarah said. 'You'd be better off with Mr Van Dam.'

'Maybe he's a fallen man! I shouldn't be surprised.'

'Ginny!' Her father's voice was reproving. 'You have to curb that brash way of talking about people. You're no longer a young girl.'

'Twenty-four, Father,' she said. 'Not so young.' Maybe it would be a good idea to have Rollo. She could call Craig Trumbull if he weren't married. And have Kieran and Ellie, and perhaps Edie and Robert. It would be a change for Sarah.

It wasn't Rollo Van Dam she thought of when she was in bed. It was Iain, who had few social graces. If they'd been able to marry she would have teased and loved him until his taciturnity went and he could have matched her high spirits. Regrets were useless. She should remember Grandmother who had believed in living a day at a time.

6

She set off on Sunday afternoon with her mother only. Sunday was Sarah's Big Day at her church, and she was fully occupied. Her father liked to rest in the afternoon.

'I know he feels the strain of travelling to New York every morning,' her mother said as they drove to Wolf House, 'but he's the last to admit it. I notice his breathlessness, and he has a tendency to drop off after Sunday lunch, when he's relaxed, or sometimes after dinner.'

'I haven't noticed.'

'That's because he's making a valiant effort while you're here. He was so looking forward to it.'

'I wish I could stay longer, Mother,' and then, making a decision, 'would you like me to give up the job at the Hydro and come back home? I would willingly do it.'

'Willingly?' Maria said.

'I would be glad to do it. I know I'll never be as good as Sarah, but I could help you in other ways, see more of you all.'

'No.' She stole a glance at her mother, and saw the square chin under the frivolous hat. 'A bright lively girl' Aunt Kate had said. Was it circumstances which had sobered her, or living with Father? 'One daughter at home is enough. I've accepted that Sarah will never marry, and the main thing is she's happy. I know your father never approved of Robert McGrath as a prospective son-in-law, but Sarah has enough of the McGrath character to have married him if she really wanted to. I can't fathom her . . . saintliness. Your father and I are just conventionally religious which isn't saying much, but she finds her real happiness in the Lord—it even embarrasses me to say it.'

Ginny smiled. 'It must be difficult for parents to accept the vagaries of children. I never thought of it till now.'

'We had to accept little Mary's death, and once we had accepted Gaylord's suicide, for that is what it was, nothing was really difficult.' Had they accepted his homosexuality? There were some things you couldn't ask parents.

'But I mean it, Mother. I'll come back to Wanapeake.'

'Only if you really want to. It's a small town. There aren't many openings here for a bright girl like yourself. Only if circumstances make it attractive . . . now we'll say no more about it.' Only if I marry and settle down here? Was that the unspoken thought?

Maria was welcomed warmly by Kate who bore her away to her own room to have a long 'chin-wag'. Kieran was working in the garden and would appear at tea-time with the children. James was 'helping' him and Rachel had taken Betsy Ann for a walk.

'It's Ladies' Day here,' Ellie said. 'Decks have been cleared for talking. Come along to my study, Ginny. I've two comfortable armchairs there and it's cooler out of the sun.'

Her study was meticulous, like herself: rows of books in glass cases, mostly medical tomes; pictures of the children, her mother and Kieran on the tidy desk, good prints on the walls. 'Edie influences me there,' she said. 'When I have a little more time I'm going to start buying originals. We can afford to with both of us working.'

'That works well?' Ginny asked, settling down on one of the leather armchairs.

'Yes, like clockwork. I guess because I'm methodical, my besetting sin.' Ginny looked at the immaculate pale gold hair, the finely featured face, the simple lines of her dress, the well-kept hands. 'Mrs Vanaressi, the back-bone of the house—I think Mother-in-law and Aunt Maria will be having a chat with her in the kitchen right now—has a blackboard where I write all our comings and goings, telephone numbers and the like.'

'I remember it when Kieran was ill. She knew exactly where to find you.'

'September 1918. That was a turning-point in more ways than one.'

'And since then Betsy Ann has arrived and everything in the garden is lovely?'

'Oh, it isn't paradise on earth—only Sarah has that—but we have a good life.' She looked at her hands, then up at Ginny. 'You learn to settle for less.'

'Joe Gould? Do you still think of him?'

'Not in a conscious way, but he's become part of me, and yet at the same time I can look at James who's the living image of him, and five times out of ten not even think of Joe. That began to happen once Kieran was able to accept him. And then Joe's sister, Holly, helped. I have a good friendship with her.'

'Do you still see her?'

'Occasionally, but it was the first time that mattered. From then on I accepted Joe's death as part of my life and let Kieran share it. Now that's enough about me. Why did all that come out? Still, you're family. Tell me all about everybody in Scotland. Tell me about Mother.'

'She's fine, a moral support to everyone and a power in McGraths. She stands in for Ernest when he's away in London and elsewhere, she's on tap for the Hydro if anything goes wrong there, she's everybody's mentor and there's no holding her back now since women got the vote.'

'Mother . . .' Ellie shook her head. 'If you could have seen her as a fully-fledged Suffragette before the War. The things she got up to! No wonder I wanted to have a career. Anyone would with a mother like that.'

'She will be over to see you when Aunt Kate and I go back. She's dying to have a look at James and Betsy Ann, although she isn't quite as matriarchal as Aunt Kate. Maybe she'll bring Aunt Isobel, though we all think she's too frail for long journeys.'

'We'll go on thinking that about Aunt Isobel when she's celebrating her one hundredth birthday.'

'Those three sisters, Ellie! Lizzie and I have many a laugh at them, but we couldn't do without them.'

'And has Lizzie recovered from her accident?'

'Yes, I think so. Nothing that a few dresses from Capel et Cie couldn't cure. Not to mention a second honeymoon at La Hirondelle, the Barthe house in Normandy.' The colour had drained out of her cousin's face. 'Oh, my God, I'm sorry,' she said. 'You and Joe . . .' Ellie shook her head, keeping it bent. 'Leave me a minute.' There was silence, and then she looked up, trying to smile. 'Ghosts walking over my grave.'

'Oh, Ellie, I wouldn't for the world . . .'

'Don't be sorry. I got James out of it. Go on talking. Tell me about Lizzie.'

She tried to find things to say about Lizzie and her Parisian trip, about Giselle and Terence. 'Lizzie's like Grandmother, I think, resilient. I'm beginning to think that's the only virtue worth having, resilience . . .'

'Yes, I think so. Life gets impossible without it. You're all right, Ginny. Mother and I have always said you're even more like Grandmother than Lizzie is, except,' she smiled, 'and these are Mother's words, not mine—she didn't "breenge" as much as you. Do you know that Scotticism?'

'Know it! I'm an authority on Scottish words! How else could I have survived there? "Breenge" . . . to rush in where angels fear to tread. Well, I can tell you, I've done with that.'

'You've something on your mind.' Ellie bent forward, put her hand on hers. 'Come on, out with it. You and I see each other so seldom that we can't waste time with the preliminaries. Go on, tell the doctor . . .' She smiled at her.

'You asked for it. I fell in love with a man who's now married. It's as simple as that.'

'It doesn't sound simple. Why on earth did he marry someone else?'

'Because she's ill with Myasthenia Gravis and she wanted to be married and he felt obliged to, or so he said. There are several possibilities there. Maybe one since I'm a *breenger*, two that he is the soul of moral rectitude, and three that he loves her. Or it's a combination of all three.'

'That doesn't sound like you, Ginny. You've never been bitter.'

'Everybody becomes bitter when they're coming to terms with the fact that they're not going to get what they want. You were bitter when Joe Gould was killed.'

'By God I was.' She looked away, 'I cursed fate, God, anybody. The bitterness went when his son was born. It flooded out of me when the waters broke.'

'Well I'm not having a baby to Iain nor is there any chance of that.'

'Did he ever tell you he loved you?'

'Yes, we had one night . . . no, it wasn't one night of love. Now I wish it had been. It was an evening stroll but bells rang in my ears because he said he had something to say to me. I walked on air and then we walked through the swimming bath and found the dead Miss Wilcox floating in the water. That was guaranteed to put an end to most things.'

'Mother wrote me about that. What is he like, this Iain?'

'He's dour and handsome and haunted. Underneath there's a lovely and humorous man but circumstances have been against it. And living with a very ill woman isn't likely to bring out your funny side!'

'You make him sound dull.'

'Oh, compared with Rollo Van Dam whom I met at Abigail's party, he's dull, but then he doesn't come from a feather bed and he doesn't work in glamorous Wall Street. Mostly he deals with drains.'

'Oh, Ginny! Drains?'

'No, that's a joke. He's managing director of McGraths, a competent engineer and a man of integrity. He does look after the plumbing and water supply and that sort of thing for the

Hydro in an advisory capacity. And,' she laughed, 'Lizzie's famous fountain. You've heard about that, haven't you?'
'Yes, and where it comes from. The cheek of her!'
'No, she's on the right side of the law. It's only augmented by main drainage.'
'I see you're a disciple.' And without a pause, 'Are you going to go out with Rollo? I saw him captivating you at the dinner party.'
'Did it look like that? Oh, he's very "taking", as they say in Scotland.'
'Priscilla Vogel would like to have been "taken".' Ellie laughed. 'I think they went around together for a little while.'
'Well, he is a charmer, isn't he? A bit of light relief. Yes, I might go out with him, if he asks me, just to see what he's really like. I never could resist a challenge. And talking about charmers, I've never seen *you* look better!'
'Kieran likes the new shorter dresses, but it isn't as short as yours.'
'This is my Sunday one. What should I do about Iain, Ellie?'
'Help him. He's got a lonely furrow to plough with a sick wife —mortally sick, maybe. You'll either meet someone else or you won't, or you'll find comfort in your work, as I did. Whatever happens, somehow I don't see you as another Sarah.'
'Ah, Sarah. There's the devil in me sometimes. I like to shock her.'
'You're probably afraid. She's away beyond being shocked. But she's a rare creature. You and I will never be like her. We have something she's devoid of.'
'What's that!'
'The McGrath passion. Speaking for myself, I wouldn't be without it. Now come away and we'll gather up the children and the aunts and Kieran and have a family tea. I love my Sunday family teas. I go back to work after Sundays refreshed, but glad to be back at work. What would Sarah think of me? But wait till you see Kieran with his little daughter. And her arms round his neck and the look on his face . . . well, there's nothing to beat that.'

7

Rollo Van Dam telephoned her at six o'clock that evening. His voice had a racy American twang after the flatter vowels of the Scots. 'Hello! Remember me? It's Van Dam. Have you recovered from meeting me?' There was laughter behind it.

'*Did* I meet you?' she said, playing his game.

'There! I knew you would have forgotten me. I must be losing my touch. Look, a crowd of us are driving up this evening to a friend's house in Kingston. There will be some fun and games when we arrive—midnight bathing, that sort of thing. Care to come?'

'I'm sorry. We've invited the Vogels for supper, and some of their family, I think.'

'Oh, skip out of that! You'd be much better off with me.'

She laughed at the sheer effrontery. 'I said I'd be in. I never break promises.'

'You're just the girl for me, then. Promise you'll come up to town and meet me next week. We'll go to the Waldorf and then on to a nightclub. I know one where you can get it under the table.'

'Get what?' she said, pretending ignorance.

'Hooch, what else? I know Scotland is swimming in whisky, but have you forgotten what it's like here?'

'I'm afraid that would make me far too late going home.'

'Oh, you wouldn't go home!' He sounded horrified. 'I could get you put up with the greatest of ease.'

'My father would have a fit. I'm only here for a short time. I must keep on his right side.'

'I see your point. Well, let's cut out the nightclub. Pity. You might have heard Louis. He's in town. Great chance for you to hear genuine New Orleans jazz.' She would have liked that. In Glasgow Lizzie wouldn't have turned a hair if she had stayed out all night. In fact, she needn't have known. No, she thought, living at home would be impossible unless it became a necessity. 'Half a loaf's better than no bread to a starving man,' she heard Rollo say, 'What about Monday?'

'Make it Tuesday.'

'Fine. Could you take a cab from the Station and meet me in the foyer of the Waldorf? That way I shan't keep you waiting, or at least you'll be waiting in comfort and seeing who's in town. Things might blow up on the Exchange at the last minute. Seven o'clock?'

'Right. I'll get a train to suit. 'Bye.' She hung up, pleased but apprehensive.

But she needn't have been. Her father greeted the news of her appointment with Rollo very equably. 'Well, you're young and you need a bit of excitement. We're dull for you here. Wanapeake must seem like a one-horse town after Glasgow.'

'At least they don't have Prohibition laws,' she said, smiling at him.

'I don't approve of them,' he said, surprising her. 'They've only led to a lot of undercover drinking. The McGraths have always felt that liquor used in moderation is all right. My brother, Terence, would endorse that.' He even smiled at her.

'Did you ever visit him in Ireland?'

'It's a long way but I'd like to go. As you grow older you long to see your ain folk. Many a good time Terence and I had when we were young. We once got roaring drunk together by accepting whisky from an old tramp. Mother nearly killed us.' He laughed at the recollection. 'I've invited him and Honor over here often enough, but these horses of his are his life. He can't bear to leave them.'

'He's training a winner, Father. Remember the Sholtie Flyer?'

'Aye, well! We'll all have to go to *that* race. What a turnout of the McGraths that would be!'

* * *

Rollo was waiting in the foyer for her when she arrived. Her drive through the thronged street had stimulated her: she had forgotten how vibrant and intoxicating New York was. He looked handsome and at home in his surroundings as he came forward to meet her. He led her to the lounge with an attentive waiter following. 'You quite melt my heart, Ginny,' he said when they sat down, 'That incredible freshness you have, a dewy rose freshness.' He laughed. 'Is your skin ever so slightly moist? Let me touch. ' He put a finger on her cheek.

'I don't know whether to take that as a compliment or not. Slightly moist?'

'It's an original one, you must admit.' His lively eyes were twinkling on her—like a robin's, she remembered. 'And truthful, too. A complexion like yours is a rarity in New York. It must be the Scottish water.'

'You haven't seen Lizzie's, Ernest's wife. Everybody would turn their heads here if she came in.'

'Trust old Ernest. He's like me. He likes to be surrounded by beautiful people. Thanks.' This to the waiter who had placed their drinks in front of them, tall, frosted glasses with a single flower floating on their surface, 'Yes, they're a pleasure to look at.'

'You mean the Waldorf Specials.'

'You're ribbing me. No, beautiful people, like the McGraths. *They're* quite special in Wanapeake, did you know that? They have a certain "something". Your Aunt Kate . . . she must have been a beauty in her time, and nothing to compare with the old lady, I understand. And Ellie, Miss McNab . . . now there's a cool one. They all have an air.'

'Grandmother certainly had.' She sipped her drink. Even if it was non-alcoholic its flavour was interesting. Better not to enquire too closely. 'Have you had a busy day?' she asked.

'A busy day, she asks? Let's say the market was buoyant. I made some interesting purchases.' He pulled in his cheeks. 'Some day I must take you to the Stock Exchange. I've just bought a second seat. You'd marvel at the noise and colour, the millions that change hands in a day. It makes you feel . . . terrific. That's the attraction. You were asking me about that at Abigail's, I think. It's the power to make or mar, skating on thin ice . . . yes,' he said, raising his glass, 'that's the life for me.'

They went in to dinner and the quiet opulence was reassuring. High Renaissance, she thought, seeing the gold and burgundy hangings. Almost *too* much, or was it? This was, after all, her proper setting. Her father was a rich man. There was nothing quite like it in Glasgow which, despite its size, somehow seemed parochial. Even in a first-class restaurant people met and greeted each other as if they were old cronies who lived in the same street. It had no style.

She asked him to choose from the menu for her and he showed a sure touch: smoked salmon, a delicate veal dish, strawberries in kirsch—a summer menu. And the names of some of the people Rollo pointed out to her were famous world-wide—the Vanderbilts, 'built the railway line you travelled in on tonight', well-known actresses, playwrights, and a sprinkling of foreign aristocracy.

'This is the place for you, Ginny,' he said. 'Do you see Sturteyvant at that table? At Yale with me. Can't take his eyes off you.

I wish we could have gone on to dance later. I could introduce you to some jolly people. You're sure you couldn't change your mind?'

She shook her head. 'Impossible. I've lost all touch with any friends who live in the city, and I'm sure they'd faint with horror at Claremont if I stayed in a hotel.'

'Would you, though? To please me?' He was beguiling.

'No,' she shook her head again, smiling. 'I see enough of hotels. Don't forget I work in one.'

'What a thought! You could stay in my apartment! That's it! There's plenty of room and a housekeeper for the proprieties if that would make you feel easier.'

'Perhaps another time.' There was no point in letting him see she thought it was a rather bold suggestion on their first meeting.

But there was no doubt they got on like a house on fire. They laughed a lot, and he told her of being at Groton, his first school. 'George and Ernest were in some sort of establishment in Albany, I believe—their father had some odd ideas but then he was a Scotsman too . . .' He was determined to tease her. 'But, of course, they're much older than me as they are the children he had by his first wife. Kieran is your Aunt Kate's son, isn't he, his second wife? But he's older than me as well.'

'Yes, I suppose so. Gosh, he'll be forty-three now.'

'I did know Thomas Vogel, Ben's elder brother, at Yale. Same age as me. Although he's never around at Abigail's parties. I think the War changed him. An oddball.'

'Yes, he's a dark horse. So you're about thirty, then, said she, making a rapid calculation?' She laughed at him.

'Thirty-one. Is it indelicate to ask *your* age?'

'No, I'm still young enough not to mind. Twenty-four.'

'Seven years' difference. We'd make a perfect couple.' His eyes were so bright and his smile so engaging and the way he gave his whole attention to her was disarming. Ellie had asked if Iain were dull. Well, of course, he would never be that, but he hadn't the lightness of Rollo Van Dam. On the other hand, it was easy to be carefree in his position. Or was it? She noticed the air of tension when he spoke about his work, how he followed with his glance someone leaving until they looked round and acknowledged him with a wave. Maybe he was right when he said his job at the Stock Exchange was like skating on thin ice.

He drove her home, saying that he couldn't bear to put her on the last train. He would stay at the Van Dam residence and go up to the city in the morning. The moon shone on the Hudson, the car was an open tourer, a Hispano-Suiza, and it was pleasant to race along the curving road, the wind cool on her face. Except that she wished it was Iain beside her, dark, difficult, complex, foreboding almost, in comparison with this light-hearted man singing as he drove, '"Three o'clock in the mo . . . rning",' or, rather, *bawling*, as she told him.

'You should take singing lessons.'

'Ah, but you should hear me tickling the ivories. My "Kitten on the Keys" would bowl you over.'

Ian was like a rock compared with him, a rock of integrity, damn him. What do you want him to do? Her inner voice was there again. Make love to you when he's married to Beth McDonald? You can't bear the thought of it, can you, he in bed with a sick woman, caressing her, pleasing her . . . a jealous love like this does you no good, warps your character, makes you an unpleasant person. Forget him, forget him, *forget* him . . .

He swerved off the road suddenly, ran on to a landing stage at Dobb's Ferry, and stopped. 'Just the place I've been looking for!' He leaped out of the car and, coming round to her side, lifted her out and set her on her feet on the wooden boards. 'Isn't it romantic here?' he said, smiling down at her, 'Come on, let's dance!'

'Hi! I can't dance . . .' She was laughing at his craziness, stirred a little.

'"Three o'clock in the morning . . ."' He sang as he whirled her round.

'We've no music. Rollo, would you stop that caterwauling? You'll be heard all over the place.'

'Are you pouring scorn on my singing? I'm known as the Yale Crooner, I'll have you know. Our sextet travelled all over the globe . . .'

'You're mad, absolutely mad,' she said, adoring his craziness as he whirled her until her head spun. They were both breathless when they staggered back to the car and threw themselves into it.

'What *you* need,' he said, panting, 'is a little sustenance.' He pulled down the locker lid which made a small table, and produced a bottle and two glasses. 'My own private bar. This was the only thing we needed to make it a perfect evening. Now, don't tell me you don't drink.'

'I couldn't,' she said, 'not truthfully, at least. Ernest chooses the wines for the Hydro, and after all, it was you who said Scotland was sailing in whisky.' She recognised the bravado. 'Just . . . that it seems funny to do it . . . like this. What if the Law appeared?'

'I'd offer him one too. Come on, down that stuff. It's real fire water. Jersey Lightning.'

It was. It made a fiery path down her throat, not at all like the occasional mellow sherry she had at the Hydro, generally to please the guests. She looked at her watch. 'It's after midnight, Rollo. After this we must get on. I hate to think of Mother or Father sitting up for me. That's their way. I'm really a guest now in the house.'

'Right!' he said, surprisingly. He had finished his glass, and he rapidly poured out another drink and downed it. 'Shop shut!' He took her empty glass, placed it inside his own, and put them and the bottle back in the locker, closing it with a decisive click. 'Right! See your point. Musn't offend Mr Patrick McGrath. Mr Patrick McGrath is a very important man in the city. Looked up to. Want to keep on the right side of him. I have designs on Mr Patrick McGrath, so shall we go?' He revved the engine far too loudly and swerved off the landing stage with a squeal of tyres and a crashing of gears.

He sang all the way home and she decided she didn't like him so much. Was it because he hadn't kissed her? She was used to men wanting to kiss her. No, of course, it wasn't that, she was past casual kissing nowadays; it was another thing, some element in his character which disturbed her, a kind of . . . excess. A sort of recklessness. Dangerous recklessness. And yet he had been perfectly behaved, dinner, taking her home, no attempted lovemaking. The drink? But she mustn't be prudish. Illicit drinking must be going on all over the place.

And yet when he deposited her quickly and safely at the door of Claremont, his smile was charming and disarming, and he seemed sober enough. He kissed her then, and she didn't mind. She would rather it had been Iain, but as Ellie had said, you couldn't get everything you wanted.

8

For the remainder of Ginny's stay the time flew, partly because Rollo was always in the background—on the telephone, suggesting meetings in town, calling in at the weekends, and so on. Her mother and father liked him. They beamed. In the city he seemed to be well known. He said jokingly, when they were at a party together, that of course, he was popular because he was the next 'President-elect'.

'Of the country?' she said round-eyed to make him laugh. She had told him he was 'too full of himself'.

'No, of the New York Stock Exchange, stupid girl.'

'You're joking, of course.'

'What do *you* think?' He was tantalising. She was intrigued, flattered at his attention, that was all.

Then there were visits to Springhill where, sitting on the lawn with Edie—her baby was due in November and she didn't feel like walking much in the heat—they watched the river traffic.

'We talked about a picnic on the *Mary Powell*,' Ginny said.

'Ah, that's gone, sadly.' She shook her head. 'They took her off last year. We regarded it as *our* boat at Vassar. Some of the girls came to school on it. Happy days!'

She went by Royal Command, as she told Ellie—they were soulmates—to Victoria and Jason Vogel's grand house. Priscilla, the unmarried daughter, seemed to enjoy making veiled comments about Rollo who, she said, took a fancy to every new face which appeared.

She decided she much preferred Giselle in France, and the jolly daughters of Aunt Honor in Ireland. As Aunt Maevy had once said, unlike Aunt Kate who was blinded to any faults in her step-children and *their* children, you could choose your friends but not your relations.

More to her liking were the picnics on the river with the younger element—Ben Vogel, and George and Abigail's children, Polly, Sam and Zach Murray-Hyslop, with any of their friends who came along, such as Lucy Springer. They were all round about her own age. She could be silly and frivolous with them and realise she was still American, that here were her roots. Her only regret was that Sarah didn't join them. Every morning, off she went in her dowdy clothes and with her serene smile.

Why did holy people make one feel so guilty? she would wonder. But it was no good. She was worldly—that is, she liked the world and all that went on in it, and she had no great desire for the heavenly mansions which Sarah seemed so intent on.

Then, towards the end of her holiday, there was Mother's Grand Effort as Ginny secretly called it. With her own knowledge of catering gained in the Hydro she could have taken all the arrangements in hand, but Maria became again the strong-willed woman she once had been and would brook no interference.

'Your father has said no expense has to be spared. We're having professional caterers, but of course there's all the business of invitations and seating arrangements, and I want to do some refurbishing of the house, drapes and carpets and so on. It's a good opportunity. We've been a little lax recently. And the family silver has to be taken out of the vault. It was given to me by my parents.'

She knew why there was all this fuss. The great Mrs Van Dam had accepted an invitation and would be coming, escorted by her son, Rollo. Everything must be perfect. Ginny was given the task of taking Sarah up to New York and choosing an evening dress for her.

This, strangely enough, was her father's idea. 'Your mother can't get her to take any interest in clothes. Not like you, Ginny. I know *you* won't let me down on the night.'

He was unlike himself, unsure; he gave her a resumé of the history of the Van Dams, how the old grandfather had been a power in New York, how they were descended from the noblest of Dutch families, how great things were expected of Rollo.

'Do you like him?' He fired the question at her, looking into his beard. She was puzzled. Was he matchmaking, or was he considering Rollo from a business point of view? He couldn't be going to offer him a place in McGraths, as financial consultant? She had heard him say that they needed someone with flair since the American side of the business was expanding so rapidly, that money had to be made to work . . . Maybe she would drop a hint to Ernest when she got back to Scotland.

The party was a great success. It was a calm September evening, and the caterers had put Chinese lanterns amongst the trees in the grounds. Two large buffet tables had been set out, one in the stone gazebo now heavy with a grape-bearing vine whose great purple bunches were cunningly illuminated, the other in the dining-room which could be easily reached through the french windows leading off the lawn.

People drifted from one place to the other, the older members to find a comfortable seat, the younger ones to climb the steps to the gazebo and view the Hudson with the moon glittering on it.

There was a small orchestra set in a niche amongst the huge rocks which led to the wood by a spiral iron stair. The bright colours of the women's dresses appeared and disappeared amongst the trees, the music was a background to the laughter and talk.

Ginny, going about efficiently to see that everyone was getting enough to eat, found Sarah lurking in the dining-room in her new short dress of green chartreuse, her silver slippers. 'Why aren't you out there with all the young ones?' she whispered.

'I'm . . . keeping an eye on things here. Honestly, I'm quite happy.' She looked anything but happy.

'Your ladies won't miss you for one night, darling.'

'I know, oh, I know. Ginny, there's far too much food. I thought if, when they've all gone home, I could pack the leavings up and take it to them tomorrow? They never see things like this.'

'What a good idea.' She was touched. 'I never serve left-overs at the Hydro. It's false economy.'

'Who does it go to, then?'

'The pigs on the farm.'

'Jellies, and roast ham, and . . . ?'

'Don't, Sarah.' Ginny hugged her. 'Don't make me feel more guilty than ever.' She would have liked to say, 'I love you, my dear sister,' but it was neither the time nor the place.

Despite the tug of guilt, she had a wonderful time. She, Ellie and Kieran gravitated together, and when Rollo arrived, late, of course, with his mother, a stout, dignified woman in old-fashioned evening dress, he deposited her with Patrick and Maria and made straight for Ginny.

'Hello! Ellie, you beautiful ice-maiden! Hello, lucky Kieran! You've no idea the trouble it was to get Mother here. I'm feeling quite faint. Could you feel my pulse, Miss McNab? Half-an-hour ago Mama was tramping over the estate with the dogs to see if she could catch those poachers and I had to lead her back to the house and get her into her bath!'

'Oh, Rollo!' He could always make her laugh.

She danced with Kieran because Rollo had said he ought to be in a doctor's care until he recovered, and had swept Ellie off.

'What do you think of Rollo Van Dam?' she asked him.

'Are you thinking of him as a possible suitor?' His mouth was quizzical.

'Not a chance. My heart is given to another.' She spoke lightly, then wondered if Ellie had told him about Iain. 'I've been away so long. Is he well liked generally?'

'Well, the Van Dams have always been regarded as uncrowned kings of Wanapeake, haven't they? Won the American Revolution single-handed. And one of them was First Lieutenant Governor here, if you remember.'

'Yes, I suppose you're right. They've just always been there, like God. You didn't answer my question. Is he well liked generally?'

'In Wanapeake, yes. In the city, no. Sorry to be blunt.'

'But he's the same there as here!'

'Oh, yes, he's the same. But charm isn't everything. Some people in the city are . . . wary.'

She was unaccountably annoyed. 'Some of those old city men resent any young man with confidence.'

'Not if it's backed up with knowledge. You're making me say too much. I'm speaking generally. But these are tricky times, especially on the Stock Exchange. The German mark's declining. Don't forget, there are more people ruined in Wall Street than make their fortunes, and everybody's feeling this is the time to be cautious.'

'Thanks for the lecture,' she said, hurt. Should she warn Father? But she knew so well what his attitude would be. His business and home life were kept strictly apart, and the last thing he would permit would be a discussion about his business affairs. He gave lip service to her independent way of life while expecting her to be simply a feminine member of the household when she was there.

Later she and Rollo strolled in the wood in the far reaches of the grounds, away from the Chinese lanterns. She felt the moisture from the grass soaking through her thin shoes, saw the moonlight falling on the statues which her father, or, rather, the landscape gardeners he had hired when they moved, had placed at strategic intervals. His arm was round her, her head was on his shoulder. So what? she said to herself. You're only young once.

'How are you getting on with Father?' she asked.

'I've made a conquest there. I'm quite proud of myself. I asked him to a business lunch in my club last week. He's quite human, and approachable. And I get the feeling that he wouldn't mind seeing you and me hitched. He talked about Gaylord . . . that surprised me. Said I reminded him of his son.'

Realisation dawned with his words. Her father had found his lost son in this man, the same lightness, the same charm. Why hadn't she seen it before? 'Wouldn't mind seeing us hitched!' She laughed and raised her head to look at him. 'This is the Twenties! I do my own hitching, thank you very much.'

'Quite right, sweetie. But, if I happened to come to Scotland to see how his firm works there, and renewed our friendship, you wouldn't mind, would you?'

Forces were moving. Had her father already arranged it? She said lightly, 'That would be fun. Let me know when you're coming.'

They were at the stone wall separating the grounds from the road running at the foot of a ravine. The tall trees made it so dark that she could hardly see him. He took her in his arms and she didn't resist. 'You're very aloof, Ginny,' he whispered in her ear. 'What would it take to . . . fire you?'

She shrugged. 'Am I?' Iain she loved, but this man attracted her. And yet she longed for love, to be loved, apart from Iain. It was the very devil.

'Is there someone else?' She felt the hopelessness of her situation creep over her.

'Not a soul. I'm footloose and fancy free. Let's go back and dance. We've been away long enough.'

'One kiss?' She hesitated, then turned to him. She couldn't wander in dark places and not expect him to ask.

It was a different kiss this time, long, hard and searching. It stirred her, which was again the very devil, but then she realised she was imagining she was in Iain's arms, not Rollo's. She shook herself free, trembling. 'I said, "Let's dance!"' She turned towards the lights and the music, half-running, so that he could scarcely keep up with her.

* * *

They had a smooth return crossing on the *Mauretania*, she and her Aunt Kate sitting, metaphorically, with their feet up.

'I'll need a rest cure after all that excitement,' Ginny said to her.

'Yes, you appeared to be having a grand time, dear.' One black wing of her abundant hair showed under the veiling round her head, her profile was sweet. 'Dashing about all over the place and Rollo Van Dam paying court to you all the time. That would give George and Abigail something to crow about, another Van Dam in the family.'

'Oh, I'm not thinking of him in that way, Aunt Kate,' she said. 'He's very . . . lightweight.'

She frowned at the word. 'Very taking, I would say. He's a model for young Zach, that I know. Apparently he made a name for himself at Yale. Rowing, I think . . .' She was vague.

'That wasn't very academic,' she said with some asperity.

'I shouldn't dismiss him so easily.' Aunt Kate looked into the distance. There was nothing to see. 'I can't tell you the joy there is in seeing all your children and step-children happily married, and their children. Maevy and Isobel and I were just saying that it doesn't do to long for the unobtainable . . .' quick glance, 'but I know you don't like your affairs discussed.'

'I wasn't aware it was *my* affairs you were referring to.'' What is it about you McGraths that you want everyone to *breed*? she thought. Father and now you. She had the sense not to say it.

Kate put an arm through hers. 'Forgive your old Aunt Kate. It's just that your welfare is very dear to my heart, my brother's girl . . .'

'I wonder,' she said, still haughty, 'that with all the pleasure you seem to get seeing your spreading family, you don't live in America amongst them.'

Kate took away her hand. 'I see I've offended you and you're quite right. Maevy tells me I'm becoming gossipy. I wasn't like that when my dear James was alive. And we weren't discussing you. She wouldn't allow it. But do you want to know something?'

'I want to know plenty,' she said, smiling now.

'I'd trade the whole lot of them for my two dear sisters. You'll understand that some day. For us to finish up together in a house, the way we started with our own father and mother, is all I ask for, and I thank God every day for Maevy's kindness in asking Isobel and me.'

Ginny put her hand through her aunt's arm. 'I'm glad to hear you say that because we couldn't do without the three Musketeers at the Hydro.' She laid her head on Kate's shoulder like a child. The sea glittered in her eyes making them run.

Yes, you had to be where your heart lay. Hers was with Lizzie and Ernest and Iain, whether or not he was married to another woman. In Scotland she was an adult, managing her own affairs, doing a worthwhile job. She was no longer Ginny, the baby of the family. She loved her parents, but you couldn't cleave to them, unless they needed you.

Sitting there, her head on her Aunt's shoulder, she felt a kind of contentment, of being part of a line whose destiny would work itself out with little or no help from her. She could alter the details from day to day, perhaps, but not the grand design. Aunt Kate said softly, as if she had been following her thoughts:

'Whit's fur ye, will no' go by ye.'

9

Jonty blamed his Scottish roots for the fact that he hadn't 'taken to' Florence for the first year or so. Eton ought to have rubbed smooth the harsher edges of his Calvinistic heritage, but its effect, in fact, was minimal. As he said to Ginny in a long letter in September 1923, 'the old devil won.'

'If I see another Child on the lap of another Madonna, I'll give up and come home. If they were all *nice* babies it wouldn't be so bad, but some of them have heads too small for their bodies, some heads like turnips, and most of them make me believe in the Immaculate Conception for purely anatomical reasons!' She laughed at that. Good for her boy.

'The exception is Lippi,' he went on, 'who draws really good *bambinos*. The Madonna in his famous picture with two angels has what the Sholton village women would call "a real steerin' wean", and the boy angel looking over his shoulder with a grin seems to be agreeing!

'I'm a romantic at heart, there's no doubt. I could stand all day in front of Uccello's "Rout of San Romano", and strangely enough, although it was far from romantic when I was fighting in the north of France, it reminds me of it. There was the same chaos, except that Uccello has turned the chaos into order by treating it as a perspective study, and the same slaughtered horses. Apart from Jimmy McAlpine, it's the horses I remember most, with their guts steaming on the ground . . .

'But a far cry from all those stylised Madonnas and angels are the sturdy portraits of Federigo da Montefeltro and his wife, by Piero della Francesca. Remember I was talking about him even before I went to Florence? I haven't been disappointed. That landscape, and those faces! A touch of the Dutch, but the completeness of it all, the abstraction, and yet the construction That's how I'd like to write poetry. QED. My puny early efforts ought to be burned. When I think of the temerity I had to have a book published! Maybe the excuse was that it was a celebration of life, that I had come home from the War alive.

'Yes, the fifteenth century for me. And Italy. Its lovely hill-top towns. Siena has a peculiar effect on me. I always seem to write a poem when I've been there. That Cathedral, crouched like a sleeping tiger on top of the hill. But what a right royal tiger in its magnificence! It's the most purely medieval of all the places I've seen since I came here.

'But my spiritual home is Arezzo, I think, because of the Piero della Francesca frescoes. There's another visit scheduled next week with the Accademia. I wish you could come too.

'I'm still at the Ponte Pensione in the narrow medieval street behind the Lungarno. The Signora tells me that if I had one of the expensive rooms up the beautiful spiral staircase, I could see the Arno from its window, but I'm so near it doesn't matter.

'Florentine buildings are flat-fronted but hide so many secrets—corridors, unexpected stairs, alcoves—and the rooms themselves have such lofty ceilings that you could put in another floor quite easily. Strangely enough, they aren't cold in winter because of the huge heating stoves, and fortunately my room has a parquet floor, not marble, as the grand ones have.

'Your eyesight has to be good to read the titles of the pictures on the walls. I imagine they've been left by grateful tenants because they're good but not good enough—"Piazza del Duomo", pencil sketch by one Francis Sacchetti, "Torino Piazza Castello" by Michael . . . Angelo? No, that took me aback at first, it was Angelus! Thought I'd stumbled on an undiscovered masterpiece.

'The Signora mothers me and gives me addresses of places to eat run by friends of hers, and tells me not to believe everything Luigi tells me, who relieves her in the evenings. He has curly hair and a curly mouth which he seems to have difficulty fitting into its place in his face, and he sleeps in a cubby-hole where all the suitcases are stored.

'He says I'm a "beautiful person", but I imagine he has enough trouble keeping his mouth in order without having any designs on me. Italian men seem softer than the women. When the Signora gets going you could hear her on the other side of the Ponte Vecchio, and that's when she's being friendly!

'But almost the best part is the little Borgo with its shops which look tiny until you go in and find they stretch back and back, full of hidden treasures. There is the leather-worker, and the *farmacia* with the fair lady—many of the Italians are fair—the *latteria* where I have my morning *cappuccino*. the *lavanderia* who launder my shirts, *il mercato*, which sells everything from newspapers to *grappa* . . . I know them all by sight and they greet me in the morning when I hurry to the Accademia, "*Bon giorno*!"'

10

She was a bit prim, and he called her Battista Sforza to tease her, because she had the habit of pressing her lips together while she was listening, which gave her a quaint schoolmarmish air. And her hair was done in plaits over her ears.

'Are you one of the Shaker sect, Delia?' he had said to her.

'How do you know of them?'

They often met in the Della Robbia loggia where the statues were mostly headless and their bases made convenient seats for the students. As space was limited the girls would sit on their boy friends' knees, but Jonty and Delia were more circumspect. Their relationship was platonic at this stage.

Sometimes, however, they would be swept along with their class into the Via Ricasoli and from there into the noisy San Marco for sandwiches and coffee. It was in his second year that he formed the habit of walking her home to her flat in the Street of the Twenty-seventh April (they never found out why it was so named), and they would drink a glass of wine in the Piazza della Independenza nearby. He began to think of it, with its dusty trees, as their private square.

'How do I know of the Shaker sect?' he had said to her. 'I've American relatives. One of them is married to my mother. Another runs the Hydropathic Hotel which Mother started in our house. It became too big for us. And you told me you came from Albany. I remembered about the Shaker Museum near there.' She disregarded this.

'It must have been quite big if it could be turned into a hotel.' He had kept his title dark. He doubted if any of the students knew about it.

'We still live on the estate. In the stables.'

'With the horses?'

'No, silly. Mother had them converted. I have a flat under the roof there. Marvellous views.'

She returned to the Shakers. 'My parents couldn't have been a member of the Shaker sect, could they, or I wouldn't be in existence, would I?' She was like a teacher reprimanding a recalcitrant pupil.

'It took you a long time to think that one up,' he had been amused at her. 'The Amish, then.' Perhaps it was then that he became intrigued.

The day they all went to Arezzo, in May 1924, was perfect, a high blue Italian sky, a soft wind. He and Delia sat together in the train and looked out at the soft contours of the Tuscan landscape with the Apennines beyond the serried rows of vines, spring green and young yet.

'That would make a painting,' he said.

'I should abstract it.' She considered. 'Otherwise it would be banal, like a greetings calendar. 'It's those straight rows.'

'Mondrian uses a ruler.'

'Ah, yes, Mondrian,' she said, as if that wouldn't do for her. She gave the impression that she only said part of what she was thinking.

When they left the station, they walked in a straggling group to the Piazza Risorgimento where the tutor said they could collect any leaflets they wanted from the Tourist Office, but after that they were on their own.

'When you walk up the Via Madonna del Prato, you will find the Chiesa di San Francesco closed for lunch. That means three hours, but be sure and see it on the way back. The Duomo will be the same, so eat if you wish at the Piazzale del Campanile beside it. If you look round the medieval part of the town after that, you'll manage to fill in the time. I have a kind friend who gives me lunch.' He raised an eyebrow at a comment from someone in the group. *'Mi scuso?'* The laughter rippled. He spoke with sternness.

'You heard much from me yesterday about the frescoes. Do not waste your time when you get inside.' He strode away from them with the look of all Italian males—as if they owned the world, or at least that part where they found themselves.

Carlo Martelli, a classmate, standing beside Jonty, made some remark in rapid Italian. He guessed at the drift. Carlo tended to shadow him on excursions like this as he was passionate about learning English. Luisa, his girl friend of the moment, was hanging on his arm. Delia made up their little group. She and Luisa, with two other girls, shared a flat. *She* tended to shadow Luisa because she was passionate about learning Italian.

They strayed rather than strolled up the Via Madonna del Prato towards the Basilica, and arrived in time to see the last visitor being ushered out and hear the false *'Un momento'* from the verger as he shut the door in their faces and shot the bolt. They groaned and laughed.

There was a somnolent air now in the streets as they began climbing, their laughter and talk echoing against the flat golden fronts of the ancient buildings. The Piazza del Duomo was empty except for a child running after a red ball. It was the hour, or rather the three hours, of the *pranzo*.

Jonty, walking with Delia, noticed that the sleepy quietness had the opposite effect on Carlo. His arm was round Luisa. From time to time he stopped to kiss her. Passionately. Her arms would wind round his neck; her hands stroked the back of his head. Jonty and Delia were forced to stop also, an audience of two.

'It's a good thing we have some time to spare,' Delia said primly, or at least it sounded prim in comparison with Luisa's abandon. He turned to look at her, and then looked again. Yes, there was something different about her. The strangeness had been there when they were sitting in the train.

'What have you done to your hair?' He realised also for the first time that she had a complexion like his mother's when he saw the faint pink dye its fineness, a flawless tea-rose complexion which somehow she had managed to protect from the sun in the last two years.

'Oh, is it terrible?' She put a hand up to it. 'It was Luisa and the other two. They said I was ruining it by screwing it into plaits and insisted on me letting it out for air. That's how they put it.' She laughed shamefacedly, 'Let it out for air . . .' She touched it again. 'I know it's *awful*.'

'It isn't,' he said, 'it's beautiful. It's corn-coloured, wheat-coloured, maize-coloured, I don't know which. And your plaits have given it little ripples.'

'I know. They won't come out.'

'But you don't *want* them out. They make a net for trapping the sun.' Poem . . .

'Of course, I shan't have it like this at the Accademia. It would trail into the paint.'

'You could tie it back loosely with a ribbon. My mother comes down for breakfast on Sunday like that. Hers is copper-coloured. Ernest won't let her cut it.'

'Who is Ernest?'

'My step-father. He's American. I told you.'

'That's interesting. Do you remember your own father?'

'No, he died in the Boer War before I was born.'

'Oh, that's *very* interesting. Don't you wish you'd been old enough to fight in the last one?'

'I did.'

'You did? Oh, that's *very* interesting.' She must have seen his mouth because she suddenly laughed at herself. The laughter was as much of a surprise as the hair. It couldn't have been more different from the pursed mouth, it was . . . hearty. She threw her head back, her hair slid with it, exposing her white throat. He saw her white teeth, her tongue. She couldn't be prim with a laugh like that. At Arezzo that day, 8th May, 1924, he had to change his whole conception of Delia Wallace of Albany, twenty-three minutes from Old Chatham, home of the Shakers.

They found the park beside the Duomo, and the kiosk where they bought lemonade and sandwiches. Some of them sat at the tables provided by the signora who ran the kiosk, others lay on the grass or sat on the benches placed round the park with the great monument in its centre. Jonty chose one of the wooden benches under the trees, where he laid out their picnic; Delia wandered over to the statue to find out who it was.

In the soft May sunlight he watched her coming towards him, her white dress, the Renaissance gold of her hair lifting from her brow, and knew that this Delia Wallace was no longer simply a fellow-student, she was his love, the girl he was going to marry.

'It's Petrarch,' she said, 'looking over his town. You know, Dante and Boccaccio.'

'He wrote love sonnets,' he said.

'Did he?' Her eyes, velvet-brown Renaissance eyes, met his, stayed with them. Then she seemed to give herself a small shake and said in a housewifely fashion, 'What did you get? Prosciutto and cheese? Oh, good!'

They studied their leaflets with an assumed air of earnestness during their lunch, and went like tourists to see what had once been the intellectual quarter of the city, Petrarch's house, the Palazzo Pretoria, the Santa Maria Della Paeve; they talked determinedly about those medieval marvels, but when they walked along Vasari's Portico, their fingers were entwined. In a Lippi dream, he thought . . .

'Don't you find that Lippi's people always seem to be looking out of a dream?' he said, having to voice the thought. She didn't answer, but her face between the twin falls of hair was also dream-like. 'There's still an hour before the Duomo opens its doors. Shall we go and have a look at the Medici Fortress?' She nodded gravely.

The town lay below, glimpsed at intervals through the trees, another world. This was theirs. He hoped Delia felt the same way.

She walked sedately beside him. He looked occasionally at her profile between the two waterfalls of corn-coloured hair.

'Do you like it here?' he said as they stopped again to look at a new angle of the buildings beneath them.

'It's not a question of *liking*,' she said, 'it's something more. I'm *tasting* it inside me. It's something . . . quite different from what I've ever felt before.'

'It's happiness.' He spoke quickly, excitedly. 'My mind is as clear as crystal. I understand myself, I understand Arezzo. It's the epitome of a Tuscany hill town for me. It's a working hill town. Not so elegant as Florence.'

'Florence is . . . Botticelli?'

He nodded. 'And Arezzo is Piero della Francesca, workmanlike and solid, like where I come from in Scotland.'

'Where is that?'

'Sholton.'

'Is it small?'

'It was, but like Arezzo again the industrialists moved in and the workers moved in and we had strikes, but not the killings and beatings they had here. Carlo told me.'

'Mussolini?'

'Yes. The Sholton villagers would have chased him for his life, but they wouldn't kill.'

'The Italians are hot-blooded.'

'It looked like that with Carlo and Luisa.' He wanted to talk about love, not killings.

They walked on and his rich feeling about Arezzo changed to a rich, tender feeling about Delia, tender but strong. It suddenly engulfed him, and he stopped, stood against the rampart and drew her towards him. 'Delia . . .'

'The grass is white with daisies . . .' She looked down. Was she shy?

'We're crushing hundreds of them, I know. Delia . . . this feeling inside me, it's strange, new . . .' But a part of it wasn't new . . . he thought of Madeleine, 'I never felt so *translated* before.' He laughed, his mouth trembling.

'Maybe you haven't a head for heights.'

'A rarefied atmosphere? Do you think I shall come down with a bump?'

'If you do, so shall I.' He saw her eyes, brimming, melting, moist, the lashes seemed touched with gold paint.

He drew her even nearer and kissed her, knew that her arms hung at her sides. When he felt her hands on the back of his neck, and then on his head, he had to restrain himself. He hadn't learned restraint with Madeleine. 'I love you,' he said. There was release in saying it.

'I love you.' Her lips were against his ear. Madeleine had used her tongue, but even so he shuddered and wanted her to know the effect it had on him. He slipped his hands to her waist, drew her very close, and her body seemed to mould itself round his. She wasn't prim, thank God. He released her quickly in case . . .

'We'd better get down to the Basilica.' He knew his voice was trembling. Her eyes avoided his.

The stunning beauty of the frescoes prevented it from being an anticlimax. They studied the cartoons first of all, becoming through habit Accademia students instead of lovers, then went to see the reality of them in the choir. There was the same feeling he had experienced on the ramparts, of revelation almost, as if he had been given the clarity of thought and vision of Piero della Francesca himself.

The detail of the Queen of Sheba's retinue seemed magical, the footmen were a solid displacement of colour and volume against their background, the battle scene made him shiver and remember the bloated corpses in the French swamps. When he half-closed his eyes he felt that the whole of the composition was revealed to him.

But, walking down the hill with Delia, once more with the other students, he saw that the background of the frescoes was the same as what was before them, or its essence. He had seen into the heart of Arezzo, as if love had given him a new perception.

'I'll never forget this place,' Delia said. 'It's been a perfect day.'

'Because of the frescoes?'

'And you.' Her gaze was clear-eyed. He put his arm round her shoulders, completely happy.

'We'll remember it together.' Never, even after he had been with Madeleine, especially after he had been with Madeleine, had he felt like this.

11

Dear Ginny,

I have always shared good and bad with you, and this is good. Suddenly my life makes sense, as if I had at last found myself.

In France I used to think I was no end of a man, fighting alongside men, watching them die often. No one could see the terrible things I saw and still remain a boy.

And then when I visited Terence and Giselle and saw what the War had done to him, I realised that physical injury was not the worst thing that could happen to you. My inability to help him made me realise that I had a great deal to learn.

Then came Paris when I went back to being a boy again amongst boys and girls, a student, until I met Madeleine and knew I had a man's feelings, and lusts. I feel I can say that to you because we've always been frank with each other.

I'm not proud of that episode, and yet, looking back, I'm grateful beyond words to Madeleine, and Delia would be too, if she knew. I didn't love Madeleine, but I was infatuated by her, and she taught me how to show my feelings.

It wasn't a thinking time but it was a necessary time because it let me see that I had a capacity for love. In Italy, Carlo tells me, mothers generally arrange for their young sons at puberty to meet a 'sympathetic' lady older than themselves who 'indoctrinates' them.

It sounds simple, but it isn't. Madeleine showed me that as well as poets not being lily-livered, sympathetic ladies can be hurt. She used me as a substitute for her dead husband, I used her as an object. All we got from it was release, and experience. I hope I didn't hurt her too much. Men are marauders, especially young men. Does all this sound like sententious nonsense to you? Probably it is.

But now my life's beginning to shape up. Florence has been very valuable to me, although she still seems to me like an old, rather faded courtesan with dirty petticoats, but the light, and the satisfaction to the eye of the buildings and the Tuscan countryside, have a permanent place in my heart,

A truly cultivated man, they say, needs two countries, one a reality, one in his mind. Italy is that. Yours, I think, is France. I know it's Mother's. Grandmother did a good thing for her by sending her to be 'finished' at Versailles. She and Ernest have done an even better thing for me, giving me two choices, France and Italy.

And if I were in any doubt which was my favourite, Delia has decided it for me. I always imagined that the girl I would marry would bowl me over when I met her, that I would be reduced to a gibbering wreck, but it isn't like that at all. I hardly noticed her for the first two years, and it was only when she unbraided her hair one day when we went to Arezzo that I even noticed her face!

She's a paradox. She has elderly parents, and so she looks prim, 'old-fashioned' they say in Scotland. But that's only the exterior. She's bubbly, with a rich sense of humour, and she has definite opinions on nearly everything whether she's right or not. And she has a rich sense of beauty. I've seen her in tears in front of a picture, and then the next minute clowning when she trips going up those spiral stone stairs which you meet everywhere in Tuscany. Maybe she's clumsy-footed, I don't know, but she laughs heartily at herself, and there she's like you. She's not worried about what people think.

She's many-layered, like an onion. I shan't make a poem out of that! I've a long way to go yet, and I don't want you to think I've discovered all there is to know in the first five minutes. But we like being together—no, it's more than that, we are complete when we are together, so complete that we aren't making any plans. The present is enough.

Sometimes in the evening we go up to Fiesole and look down on the huddle of buildings which is Florence, and pick out the landmarks. We wander other times in the Boboli Gardens, not like a pair of lovers because we talk too much, but sometimes she falls silent and won't be teased, and I know there's still another layer. Maybe one shouldn't probe and pry, especially men, in their desire to know everything, possess everything. 'What are you thinking about?' Once I said that to Delia and she looked at me coldly and said, 'That's my business.' After I got over the shock I liked her for that . . .

How terribly selfish this letter is, Ginny! Me, me, me! And

I wanted to cheer you because I thought in your last letter you were becoming like wine which should be *pétillant* and had gone flat. I know what's causing it: Iain Pearson and his sick wife. I know you're sad sometimes, but don't let it spoil your life. I don't think it will. You and Delia are like each other with your sense of the ridiculous. It's a good standby.

I've really let myself go this time. But we're friends, always will be, and I wanted you to share my joy. My three years are up here, and I'll soon be home, and in spite of my love of Italy, there's no place like home. See you then. My love, Jonty.

* * *

Lizzie had arrived at the Hydro that morning to 'put in a good day's work', as she said. The holiday crowds were thinning now that September had come, but it had been a successful year. She was her usual bright self, dressed soberly, but being Lizzie, with a diamond and sapphire brooch pinned in the lapel of her tailored suit, and her spectacles on their jewel-encrusted chain at the ready. She adjusted them firmly on her nose.

'A good year, Ginny.' They were in Ginny's room behind the reception desk. 'Numbers up in spite of the increase in charges, and the state of the country. There are always people with money to burn.'

'Even under the Labour Government. It's not fair shares for all yet.'

Nan Porter came in after a brief tap on the door. 'Some letters just arrived, Ginny. I thought Mrs Murray-Hyslop would like to see them.'

'Thanks, Nan.'

'Nan, your hair's different.' Lizzie peered through her glasses. 'It is a Marcel, isn't it?'

'No, it's a Eugene Permanent Wave!' She looked smug. 'I've always envied you McGraths your lovely hair, so I said to myself, here goes, it can't kill me.'

'I heard of someone who was electrocuted,' Ginny said.

'Pay no attention to her. She's a tease. It's lovely. Did you say it was permanent?'

'Well, permanent till it grows out. It was as bad as going into the Royal for an operation, all the same. They screw your hair into rollers and then attach you to the ceiling and turn on the current.'

'You were lucky to come out alive,' Ginny said, limpid.

'Yes, I was scared stiff. Halfway through, one place on my head began to burn, and I thought, here goes, I'm going to look like one of those wee boys you used to see in the back streets with a bare patch.'

'Ringworm,' Lizzie said. 'I've seen them coming with their mothers at my Gallowgate club.'

'Worse if when they unscrewed the rollers, your hair was left *in* them.' Ginny eyed Nan, laughing.

'Nothing venture, nothing gain.' The girl touched her crimped hair. 'It turned out fine and I'm very pleased with it.'

'You'll be bowling over all the men,' Lizzie said.

'That'll be the day. Ginny and I are on the shelf now.' She went out of the room with a swagger of her fat bottom.

'Touché!' Lizzie said, laughing.

'You Scots are famous for your tact, I must say.'

'And giving as good as we get.' She bent to her papers again, 'When we get this work done I want to discuss holidays with you. I know you generally take a week or so about this time, but I thought . . .'

'What did you think?'

'Well, with Rollo Van Dam arriving . . .'

'What difference does that make?'

'Don't be coy. You can't deny he's shown you a lot of attention on his visits here.'

'Oh, I'm not coy, whatever else. Yes, you're right. I like him. He's good company . . .' How could she even mention Iain? Everyone accepted his situation, that he was married to Beth, that they seemed happy enough—indeed, that her disease had got no worse, if anything, seemed to be in remission, or even cured . . . She searched around. 'No, it's Jonty's homecoming I don't want to miss. Will he bring Delia with him?'

'I don't think so. She has to go back to her parents first. He's being sensible this time. He wants to discuss things with Ernest. And he's going to start work for McGraths! Oh, I *am* excited about that. A dream come true. I've got the shop in Sauchiehall Street ready, and Aunt Maevy has all the pieces of furniture in apple-pie order at the repositories. He's to choose what he would like. He knows all about art now.'

'And about love.'

'Everything turns out all right if you wait.' Her look was shrewd. She'd never been a fool. 'How I worried about that Madeleine! I felt she wasn't right for him. He didn't need a mother. He has a perfectly good one.' She touched her diamond and sapphire brooch. 'But Delia sounds sensible and another link with America.

Ernest went to school at Albany before Yale. That's her home town. He feels he knows her already.'

'Everybody's happy, then. Lizzie, I think I'll go to Ireland for a week if you don't mind.'

'Has my father been writing to you?'

'No.' She had to jog her own memory. Lizzie's father . . . ? Of course. 'No, it's Aunt Honor. She says it's high time I paid a visit. Giselle and Terence would be there, but I'd really like to see them.'

'Well, you go off, then. You look jaded. Maybe you need a Permanent Wave!' She let out a peal of laughter. 'No, Ireland's better than that. I'll hold the fort. I'll have to be around to get Jonty established. Maevy and Ernest are looking into a place in Union Street for our Auctioneer and Valuators premises as well. Oh, can you imagine it? My Jonty going to be a working man!' And then, peering at her, 'You're sure you aren't escaping because of Rollo?'

'You're a clever thing. Well, in a way. He's been . . . bothering me.'

'Bothering you? You mean, asking you to marry him?'

'Yes.'

'"Bothering", she says. Well, he's a charmer. Everybody seems to like him.'

'Do you?'

'I hardly know him.'

'I know you, Lizzie. Ernest doesn't, and you take your colour from him.'

'No, you don't know me. No one ever knows anyone else thoroughly. But in any case, you're old enough to make up your own mind.'

'Yes, being on the shelf, as Nan reminded me. Well, I'll go to Ireland next week if that's all right with you. Now, what about this paper work? I want to get things sorted out before I go. There's a great list of repairs. You wouldn't believe the damage guests do. And the white rings on furniture because of your blessed water . . . !'

'It's a hydropathic establishment, don't forget.' She studied the lists. 'Wireless. I see you want three in the downstairs rooms . . .'

'Yes, and I think the suites ought to have a private one each. Everybody's dying to know when Ramsay MacDonald topples.'

'It was running his Daimler on biscuits that did it, Ernest says.'

'Ernest says . . .' Ginny looked fondly at her. 'I only hope whoever I marry, or if I marry, I'll think as highly of him as you do of Ernest.'

'Ah, but he's special . . .' Her beautiful eyes were moist behind her glasses.

12

It was an invidious situation, Ginny thought, to be a friend of the wife of the man you loved. She hardly knew how the friendship had developed to this stage, not at Iain's instigation certainly. He had never begged in his life, and he would have considered it a lack of taste to encourage her to see Beth. The first invitation had come from her in a letter which Ginny had read dubiously.

> Dear Ginny (if I may call you that), This is to thank you for the special attention you gave me when I stayed in the Hydro with Iain.
>
> As you know, I am confined to the house a great deal, and I wondered if you would care to drop in and see me any time you are shopping in town. As you can see, we're quite handy, and I would be glad to give you a cup of tea any time. It would be nice to have a chat. Yours very sincerely, Beth Pearson.'

Curiosity had taken her the first time, not concern. She despised herself for that. She wanted to see where Iain lived so that she could picture him in his own surroundings. (She wouldn't admit the baser thoughts which lay deep in her subconscious, the bedroom, where they . . . if they did . . .) What have I sunk to? she asked herself.

She had found the place easily, a flat with its own front door in a quiet street between Woodlands Road and West Princes Street. She thought they might have had a more impressive address, but realised that Beth would scarcely be able to run a large establishment.

Her first visit was pleasant, and any anxiety she had about 'dropping in' was quickly dispelled by Beth's welcome when she was shown into the drawing-room by a middle-aged housekeeper. Beth got up to greet her, smiling, holding out her hands.

'Ginny! How good of you to come! Iain gave me a good telling off when I told him I had written to you. Said you were far too busy.' She still had an indoor look, a muddiness of skin, but her hair was professionally done, and her dress fresh and up to date with its low waist and scooped neckline. She wore a swinging string of amber beads. She looked, Ginny thought, like someone who was sitting waiting for something to happen.

She had been almost vivacious, chatting brightly as she served the tea which Mrs Simpson, the housekeeper, had brought in. Her mouth seemed rouged against the whiteness of the prominent front teeth. She was eager to know what was in the shops—not only clothes but furniture and household equipment. 'Iain won't let me have a good trail round them. He says I'll get tired. He's very protective, too protective at times.'

Ginny had made no attempt to steer the conversation towards Iain, but while Beth was talking she had taken in the room, the comfortable sofa with a rug folded on its back, footstools at the easy chairs, fresh flowers everywhere, a preponderance of magazines of all types—women's, the *Spectator*, *Scottish Field*, *Punch*. There was an open roll-top desk with a well-worn leather top, and the pictures on the walls, although not known to Ginny, at least looked authentic.

It was a safe enough topic. 'I'm interested in your pictures,' she had said. 'We try to encourage artists to use our walls in the public rooms at the Hydro, and I keep a list in my office of their prices. It helps them and us.'

'You and Iain would have a lot in common. He collects painters whom he likes. That one above the desk is a Sam Bough. And that one,' she pointed to a picture hanging near the window, 'was done by a kind of hermit who lives up the Clyde Valley in a corrugated iron shack. Iain says he's Neo-Primitive, or something like that. I wouldn't know.' She suddenly looked excited. 'I bought two hats yesterday! I got them sent up from Daly's. I must let you see them!' She got up, staggered a little and then laughed, her mouth half-open, her lips moist. 'Silly me! I've been told not to jump up too quickly.'

She walked smartly enough to the door, went out, and in a few minutes was back with a striped cardboard hat-box. 'I put them together. Easier to carry. But at their prices they were in a box each.' She produced two cloche hats in brushed fur felt. 'Don't you like the way they've caught that one up with a sparkling ornament at the front? And this one? It has a bigger brim. And look at the fur pom-pom at the side. Smart, eh? Try them on, Ginny. They'd look lovely on you.'

'No, thanks.' She smiled. She had never been in the habit of trying on clothes with other women. She knew it was a favourite pastime with many of them. 'They'd look much nicer on you.

That one with the pom-pom looks as if it would really suit you.'

Beth lifted it, went to the mirror above the fireplace and pulled the hat down over her hair. When she turned to Ginny her face was ashen and her mouth trembling. Ginny got up quickly and led her to the sofa.

'You're exerting yourself too much. I didn't think . . .'

'It's because of lifting my arms. They suddenly seemed like a ton weight.'

'Put your feet up and I'll tuck you in with this rug. Now rest quietly and I'll put the hats away.' She lifted them and stowed them in the nest of tissue paper inside the box. She should have remembered: this girl was ill. And wasn't it the case that her energy went towards the end of the day? She looked down at her, and as she did, Beth opened her eyes. She was still white and drawn.

'I'm getting better, you know. I'm determined to get better. This is nothing. Excitement at seeing you, perhaps. We've been to see a neurologist and he's put me on to new drugs. He said if he'd seen me earlier he might have been able to operate to remove my . . . thymus, I think it was called, which could have cured me. If only I'd been married to Iain then!' She sighed. 'Nothing's too great an expense for him, absolutely nothing . . . it makes me wonder . . .' Her voice trailed away.

'I'm going to leave you now, Beth.' Ginny got up. 'I'll tell your housekeeper on the way out that you're resting, and she'll come in and see you're all right.'

'Come again, Ginny.'

'Yes,' she said, 'I will.' And, smiling, 'And maybe you'll have more hats to show me.'

'It's daft to buy hats. When will I ever wear them?' Her eyes were closed again. There was no expression on her face except an infinite weariness.

* * *

She called again just before she went to Ireland. She had had an uncomfortable feeling that her last visit hadn't done Beth any good, but on the other hand, apart from the pity she felt and which she despised, she was curious. What had drawn Iain to Beth McDonald even before she was ill? She might as well ask herself the same question about Magnus Muir, Craig Trumbull, and now Rollo. Chance meetings, common interests, and, in her own case, the pleasure of being sought after. Beth and Iain had played golf together . . . oh, why not accept that he fell in love with her and leave it at that.

It was her afternoon off, a calm, late September day, and she decided she would leave her motor car in the garage, take the train, and stroll up the Glasgow streets towards that magnet, Jonty's new shop.

She felt happy enough because that was her nature. You got used to an ache in your heart, a void which only Iain could have filled.

Rollo would soon be here and he was always fun. Or he had been during the last year or two when he had been making fairly frequent business trips to the Glasgow office. Her father now employed him in an advisory capacity and had sent him over from time to time to give the Glasgow partners the benefit of his advice in investment affairs.

Everyone had been guarded in their comments about that. Of course he was very different with his charm and insouciance from the average staid Glaswegian. Dan Johnson was more than likely to regard him as some bright foreign bird which had landed on his patch, Ernest didn't like ebullience in general, Aunt Maevy couldn't be won over in a hundred years by any form of blandishment, and Lizzie . . . well, she was the greatest surprise.

Generally she liked men to admire her, and Rollo made no secret of his admiration, but she seemed somehow wary of him. Ernest might have prejudiced her. She knew, or imagined, that there were no secrets between them. Lizzie shared everything with Ernest. He wouldn't lag far behind. Any man who on the surface was as reserved as he was, must have an outlet somewhere, and what better than the marriage bed?

She gathered that her father wanted Rollo to be accepted into the firm as a partner, but somehow the Glasgow lot had got together and suggested a three months' trial. It seemed churlish, or so Rollo wrote.

> I'm Patrick's blue-eyed boy here. What are they so cagey about? Even Robert doesn't welcome me with open arms at Springhill. Time was when the Van Dams were accepted anywhere. For two pins I'd tell your father to get on without me, but the old bloke seems to have grown quite fond. He knows I can do McGraths quite a few good turns on the Stock Exchange, and I don't like to let him down. So I've told him I'll go to Glasgow to please him for three months, but nothing in the world would persuade me to live in that dour place, even if they wanted it.

And I want you to promise that you'll come back with me as Mrs Rollo Van Dam. I don't care where we tie the knot but you and I are meant to live in New York. It's our kind of place, fast-moving, fast-living. We'll have a whale of a time together, a nice little apartment overlooking Central Park and a country house on the south shore of Long Island. I don't want to go up the Hudson Valley yet. There's a positive nest of McGraths there, and as for Mama, well, she won't live for ever and then I'll have to move back . . . we'll see.

She reached Jonty's shop and found it completed. The scaffolding had gone, the signwriters had finished. 'Interiors' it said in gilt lettering above the door. The curtains behind the display windows were velvet, a soft dove grey. It looked right. *Distingué*. There were two white easels ready to receive Jonty's choice of pictures, and an arrangement of flowers in a white vase.

Everything was turning out well for her boy, Auctioneer and Valuator, Fine Art Dealer, soon perhaps to be husband of Delia Wallace of Albany, New York State. *Her* future could be just as settled if she decided to marry Rollo. Would she be on the shelf if she didn't? That remark of Nan Porter's must have rankled.

Beth opened the door herself when she rang the bell. 'Ginny! Where have you been? I didn't like to write. I thought I'd put you off the last time. Come away in!' There was a new vitality about her. She was wearing an obviously new outfit, a pale *eau-de-Nil* dress with fur trimming at the neck, the nutria collar matching the chestnut shade of her hair which surely had been hennaed, and was, as usual, immaculate.

'I've been busy, I'm sorry. You look blooming, Beth. Have you come into a fortune, or something?'

'As good as. Come in and sit down, and you can share my good news.' Mrs Simpson was hovering in the hall, hands crossed at her waist, chin tucked into her chest like a bird. 'Some tea for Miss McGrath, please.' There was a new note of command. The woman scuttled away.

'Did you walk? I didn't see your car.'

'I came by train. I walked from the station.' They were in the drawing-room, and Beth took her hand, making her sit down beside her on the sofa. 'I enjoy it on a day like this. I've had my car taken to Crannoch. Something's gone wrong with the steering.'

'Maybe Iain will teach me to drive now . . . oh, Ginny, I've got such good news. I can't wait to tell you. The doctor, this neurologist I told you about, came yesterday, and he says there's no reason why this remission shouldn't last indefinitely. "You must have a good husband looking after you, Mrs Pearson," he said, and that's true enough.'

'That's wonderful news.' She tried to inject enthusiasm into her voice. Of course she was glad for Iain's wife. How else could she possibly feel? The heaviness in her heart was because it seemed like the end of a chapter. Beth and Iain were going to live happily ever after. All she could do now was live happily ever after with Rollo. She had never wanted Beth *not* to recover, surely? That was too horrible to allow into her mind even for an instant. 'All hope has fled, my heart is dead . . .' Where had those words come from? Jonty said sometimes he wondered the same thing. 'And Iain must be delighted,' she said, 'just delighted!' She repeated the word to convince herself.

'Yes, he is. This is his present to me. This dress. He got that couturiers at Charing Cross to bring it up to me and fit it, but he chose it himself.' It was made of the finest marocain, and the softness of the squirrel collar was becoming against Beth's face.

Desolation swept over her, making the pleasant room seem like an airless prison. This was the end. Beth was fully recovered, the end, the end. The word seemed to reverberate in her head. She got up, speaking hurriedly, 'Beth, I'm afraid I can't wait. I've just remembered, I must get an early train back. I have to get to Crannoch before six to pick up my car. I shouldn't have come at all . . . but I'm glad I did.'

'Oh, but Mrs Simpson's bringing in the tea!'

'I'm so sorry. It was silly to come at all, but if I hadn't I shouldn't have known . . . the aunts will be delighted when I tell them your good news. They take such an interest in Iain. And Lizzie, and Ernest. They've all felt so sorry for Iain, I mean, you . . . they think he's been so brave, *that* brave, they say . . .'

'Think . . . Iain?' Her mouth was half-open, the teeth looked moist as well as her lips.

'Did I say Iain? You, of course. You've never complained even with all you've had to put up with.'

'I've had very little to complain of since I married. Strangely enough, there was an immediate improvement. But I'm the least surprised of everyone. I *knew* I was getting better, you see. I . . .' she laughed, 'I *bullied* Iain into marrying me because I thought I was dying, but then I found I was getting better . . .' There was the sound of a door shutting. 'Oh, that must be him.'

He was in the room and she felt faint. She couldn't believe that she would react like this. Her head swam, and then she steadied, was able to speak normally. 'Iain! I have to come to your own house to see you. Beth's just been telling me the great news.'

'Yes, we're pleased.' His smile lit up his dark face. Each time she saw him he appeared to be thinner. 'Of course we don't want to count our chickens . . .'

'You'll never get Iain to dance the Highland Fling about anything,' Beth laughed. 'I thought you knew him.'

'No, I don't,' she said, her eyes on him, 'I don't know him at all, really.' She felt the swaying sensation again. This was terrible. She made a great effort of will. 'I was just saying I had to go. I've to pick up my car at Crannoch. I must catch the five-forty.'

He took out his watch and glanced at it. 'You'll never do it. I'll take you.'

'Why not run Ginny back to the Hydro?' Beth said. She looked triumphant, her head was held high, there was a flush on her cheeks. 'Yes, you do that, Iain, and Mrs Simpson and I will get dinner ready. We're having a special one. It's a secret. Pity you have to rush back, Ginny, or you could have joined us.'

'As if I would? No, there's absolutely no need, Iain. I'll pick up a taxi at Charing Cross.'

'He'll take you.' It was a new managing Beth who spoke. Her mouth was half-open in laughter, her lips red, making her teeth seem very white. She stood like that while Ginny put on her coat which Iain held for her.

They hardly spoke while he guided the car through the busy streets of the city, mere comments about the traffic at this time of night, about the preponderance of motor cars now, how some way of controlling the chaos must be found, policemen at the crossings, some kind of system of lights, perhaps. When they were clear of the city and the small town of Rutherglen, and were speeding through Cambuslang, she spoke.

'You must be absolutely delighted about Beth's good news.' It was a mistake. She had said it before.

'Anyone would.' His eyes were on the road. 'Remissions do occur in Myasthenia Gravis, of course, but this along with the new drugs the neurologist is giving her is a hopeful clinical picture. I'm quoting him.'

'So she could lead an almost normal life?'

'That's it.' He should bang the steering wheel, *do* something.

'She credits you with a large part of her recovery.'

He shrugged. 'Anyone would have done the same. What's that thing about "for better or for worse"?' What was concealed behind that calm face?

She looked at the long rows of tenements lining the streets, the women gathered at the close mouths, the children running about, the groups of collarless, unshaven men round the public houses on the corners. They seemed defeated in their attitudes, as if huddled together for warmth or company.

She should look away from herself, see what so many people were having to contend with, hunger, hopelessness. The Depression. So much for the 'Great' War . . .

'No one gets what they want,' she said.

'What do you mean?'

She dissembled. 'Those men out there without work, without hope, Ellie, my cousin, who lost her lover in the War, Beth . . . that was a cruel blow for her, her illness, out of the blue.'

'Yes, that's why I . . . well you know why.' He stopped short. 'But she's determined. She believes in mind over matter, and it's paid off.' He turned his head. 'Yes, look at those men. Very young, or old. The in-between ones were slaughtered . . . she wants to have children.'

She heard her voice. 'Is that possible?'

'Who knows? That's another problem. If the child, always supposing she was able to have one, was a girl, she could be a carrier. No one in their senses would want to perpetuate . . . lay up such a store of misery for someone else. You haven't seen her at her worst times. No, once you did . . . Let's change the subject, Ginny. How's the Hydro going?' Oh, he was deep and dark.

'The best season yet. Hardly any teething problems now, not even the drains.' She laughed, and she saw the smile curving his mouth, reflected in his eyes.

'I remember meeting you in Lizzie's Palm Court. I'd been looking at the drains for her, and when you were introduced you held out your hand *very* gingerly!' His laughter was quick and joyous.

'I was teasing you. You looked so serious. And you questioned me like a teacher.' She laughed too.

'I was nervous. I was overcome by your beauty.'

'That'll be the day,' she said cheekily.

'No, it's true. It still is. I don't think I'd met many American girls and you struck me as a creature from another planet.'

'It was the Yankee accent.'

'No.' He shook his head. 'It wasn't that.' He drove for a second or two without speaking, then, 'I suppose you'll be becoming Mrs Van Dam soon?'

'Who on earth told you that?'

'I notice you aren't denying it. Mr Van Dam isn't so reticent. I took him for lunch once on Mrs McNab's orders, or should I say, request?' He grinned, looking boyish for a second.

'"Orders" are right for Aunt Maevy. Was it to weigh him up?'

'Don't put words into my mouth.'

Here was something she could get angry about, release her pent-up frustration. 'I must say, at times you Scots are the most inward-looking, smug, clannish lot I've ever come across! And the McGraths are even worse than that. I wonder how on earth they ever accepted you into the firm! But, of course, you're a true-blue Scotsman with his own kilt and a buttoned-up mouth and you're good with drains! But Rollo, an American—never mind if his ancestors are far higher up the social scale than the McGraths—is looked on with suspicion. "Watch him! He's too handsome, too charming, he speaks with a Yankee accent!" At least he *speaks*. "*And* he thinks he's an authority on money affairs, *and* Patrick has been seduced by him, poor soul. He must be getting senile!" I'll tell you something, I don't think Rollo would *want* to be a partner in McGraths if you gave him a million dollars!'

'Well, well,' he said calmly, 'that's the cat out of the bag. I didn't know you felt so fiercely about him.'

'So I should, since I'm probably going to marry him.'

'You can't, Ginny.'

'What do you mean, I can't. *You* married. Everyone marries. I want to marry, have children before it's too late. Even your Beth does. What's wrong with that?'

'Nothing. Absolutely nothing.'

They were in the country now, despoiled by the bings, the slag heaps, but with green fields in between, with cows munching contentedly. They had moved with the times. 'What's wrong with that?' she repeated, still fierce. Her heart ached sickeningly.

'Nothing. You're free. Of course you can do anything you like.'

'Well, then?' she said, still fierce, still miserable, 'Say what you think for once!'

His voice was low. 'I never really gave up hope. I thought your children would be mine.'

'Am I hearing you properly?' She put her hands over her ears. 'No, I don't want to . . . !' She wanted to wail, to startle him with her wailing. 'Oh, you're a devil! What's the point in saying that now? It's too late! You have a . . . prior commitment. Beth wouldn't like to be called that. You shouldn't have said those things, Iain, about Rollo, about . . . *our* children. It's too late, you know, it's too late . . .'

He didn't answer. His foot jabbed at the accelerator. He raced the last few miles, turning into the road with its grey walls containing the Crawford Estate, taking the drive to the turreted Crawford mansion which was now the Hydro scarcely slackening his speed.

When he stopped at the steps he turned to her. 'You must forget what I said. You have this effect on me. I suddenly have a need to be completely honest with you. I ought to have learned by this time that complete honesty is sheer self-indulgence. I live a life of subterfuge. Beth accepts my silences. She thinks I'm overworked, rails against McGraths in a wifely sort of way. Her pleasure is in the married state. She seems happy with that. I hide my guilt . . .' his voice dropped, 'and my love for you.'

There was an afternoon silence on the Hydro. The beds of flame-coloured dahlias seemed to burn in it with their brilliance. The roof of Iain's motor car was closed, enclosing them in the dark tent. They looked at each other and came together, only with their mouths. Their arms remained at their sides.

Such a sadness, she thought, feeling love engulf every part of her, such a joy there could have been.

She straightened at last, touched his mouth. 'We shouldn't have done that. Never mind. You may kiss the bride.'

His face was grim enough. She hoped he would smile for his wife.

13

There comes a time in every girl's life, Ginny thought, when the only thing to do is to clear out, and then, smiling at herself, Is it a philosopher you're becoming in your old age? She was having a chat with herself on the train going from Dublin to Boyle.

She might as well get into the way of the Irish tongue which she had been hearing on every side since she had crossed on the boat from Stranraer. Goodness knows, she had had to adapt to the Glasgow one and nothing could be more difficult than *that*.

And Ellie had sung all their praises so often, the delightful girls (girls being a relative term since they were all nudging forty) . . . Clare, spirited and red-haired, 'like you, Ginny', and married to Aidan of the dashing blond moustache; Dymphna, the lawyer, now back in practice with her husband, Denis, having produced a little girl called Nora; and dark-eyed, dark-haired Moira, the eldest, who had a shy husband, Bryan Vaughan, who wore rimless glasses and was the father of Kevin and Rosaleen. With Clare's three, Michael, Aubrey and Fiona, that was six children. Everybody had children.

But best of all were Aunt Honor and Uncle Terence, Ellie had said, who seemed somehow to have kept Grandmother Maeve alive in that old house, Woodlea, where the bedroom she had used still had her lemony lily smell, her essence . . . 'I hope they put you in it too.'

She looked out on the strange landscape which Ellie had described. 'It's a different green from that around Sholton, fresher, more deeply green, and there are more open spaces between the little white cottages which seem like little hamlets of sheep. The big houses are secretive behind their long drives, like Woodlea. Only occasionally I would see a governess cart driving out with the lady of the manor sitting straight up behind the horse. The landed gentry all seem to have straight backs like Grandmother. Of course there will be motor cars now.'

It looked like a poor country, worse than Scotland. There the women scrubbed and 'pingled' to keep their children and their houses neat and clean. In the little villages which were close to the railway line they didn't seem to make much effort. Most of the children she saw running about were in rags, and the yards of the farms were untidy, with dung heaps close to the back door, on which scraggy hens pecked.

'Ah, but Boyle's a fine place, Ginny,' Ellie had said. 'Grandmother's best memory was of making a visit there with Uncle Terence and they stayed in a grand hotel where she said you could have fished for trout from the windows if you wanted. That was when Uncle Terence met and fell in love with Aunt Honor. The three girls belonged to a previous unhappy marriage, and when Uncle Terence added Robert and Terence from his first one, they had a fine, ready-made family . . .'

Yes, it had been the right time to clear out from Sholton, if only for a week, to get her thoughts straight. It had been an exhausting season at the Hydro, and she was tired out. No, that was an excuse, an evasion of the truth. She rarely got tired, she thrived on hard work, on the business of the Hydro, on making the guests feel happy.

Their pleasure was always hers. Nothing made her happier than to see the Hydro thrumming with activity, to hear the little trio playing in the Palm Court (Miss Finney of the wide black sleeves, Mr Jack and Mr John of the tight black trousers). She enjoyed seeing the young people rushing through the hall with their tennis racquets, their parents with golf-clubs, the old men jollying each other as they climbed the tower stairs to enjoy a cigar together; the queries from the staff, from the guests, the feeling of being the holder of strings, like Mr Allan who came to give the children a Punch and Judy show on wet days. And best of all she loved the strains of the orchestra from the Saturday evening Dinner and Dance, 'It had to be You,' 'I'll be loving you, Always . . .'

Always. Put that thought away. You were thinking of the Hydro, remember? Of being tired out?

But you knew that was an excuse. You knew it had become an untenable situation since that night when you had kissed . . . Oh, he could talk of what might have been, but he knew where his duty lay, and nothing in his temperament would allow him to forget that. How would you feel if Beth gave birth to a child which he had said should have been yours?

The solution lay in front of her, so clear-cut, so logical, that its very logicality made it difficult to accept: to marry Rollo and go back to New York with him. After her outburst in Iain's car, hadn't she said she would probably marry Rollo? She couldn't go back on that now and have him think she was still hanging on, waiting for him.

Beth was better, ready to have his child. There was only one sensible thing for her to do: stick to her guns. That way she would please her father and assuage that deep sense of guilt of not having been a good daughter. And there was also that strong female desire to be taken into account. 'You aren't like Belle Geddes,' Ellie had pointed out.

All the circumstances were forcing her towards it. Perhaps as Rollo's wife, with children of her own, she would be able to forget Iain. Ellie had done it with her lost lover.

But, Lizzie? Wouldn't she let down Lizzie? That wasn't a very good argument. Lizzie would be practical as always. She would say if asked that she mustn't let the Hydro stand in her way. Would she still say it, even if she and Ernest didn't care for Rollo?

The McGraths didn't interfere. They let you go to hell or heaven in your own way. Ellie had once said that her mother and grandmother seemed to her to carry this to excess, but as she grew older she had realised it was the only sensible way to behave.

She looked at her watch. She had missed the name of the last station, but it was about the time she was due to arrive at Boyle. Maybe the soft air and the softer talk and the ghost of Grandmother would put her mind at rest, because sure and begorrah, or whatever they said in this green land, she was sorely in need of peace.

She got up to gather her cases together and a young man jumped up too, doffing a hat with a very deep crown. 'You'll be after needing some help with those heavy things,' he said, swinging them down easily with one hand and ranging them neatly on the floor.

'I'm very indebted to you to be sure,' she said, choosing a phrase from some nineteenth-century novel she had once read as the least inappropriate to the occasion.

They were all there, or if they weren't, it looked like it. Uncle Terence and Aunt Honor certainly, she dashing in a black cloak with her hair flying over it and looking like the prototype of the Great Irish Author; Giselle, looking like nothing else than the prototype of the True Parisienne; two beautiful cousins with two little girls of about seven, dressed to kill in white frilled dresses and straw hats. One of them, the red-haired one, had a flag in her hand which she was waving tantalisingly out of reach of the other who was jumping up and trying vainly to catch it. Ginny stepped into Aunt Honor's arms and was lost in the hair for a second.

'Ginny! And not before time! Now, don't let this quair lot frighten you.' You, Ginny thought, smiling, are perhaps the most *outré* of them all. 'My, what a beauty you are! The most like your mother, Terence, wouldn't you say?' She looked up at her portly, smiling husband who reminded Ginny of Grandfather Terence, her mother's father, who had lived and died at Springhill where Edie and Robert now lived—the same grizzled redness of hair, the same florid cheeks, the same jolly manner.

'Wait till I give the lass a kiss!' She was enveloped in a warm hug smelling faintly of stables and cigar and maybe a touch of poteen. 'Yes, I think you've got it there, my love!' he said, holding Ginny at arm's length. 'Lizzie's hair is darker. But here now, what about our Clare? You're the mirror image of each other.' He pushed one of the young women towards her, red-haired and jolly also, and not having to be pushed at all.

'Ach, pay no attention to him, Ginny,' she said, giving her a resounding kiss, 'and you ten years younger than me and looking as fresh as a marigold. He sees his mother in everybody who comes around with our colour of hair. Sure and he's sometimes picking them out at the fair at the top of Bridge Street and saying, "Excuse me, miss, but do you know you have a great likeness to my dear mother . . . ?"' They all laughed.

'Did you ever hear such blethering?' The other young woman had come forward and embraced Ginny, dark-haired, dark-eyed like her mother. 'I'm Moira, the eldest, as if it didn't show. Dymphna's not here. She's a working girl like yourself. She went back with Denis to their office after she'd had Nora.'

'Dymphna and Denis are both lawyers,' Clare said. 'Very useful when we all want to divorce our husbands.'

'Is that likely?' She was going to like it here.

'Well, maybe it is with Clare,' her sister said, 'her Aidan's a very dashing fellow, a great favourite with all the ladies around here.'

'Away with you!' Clare laughed. 'And is it likely with three children hanging on to his coat-tails, not to mention me with the rolling-pin?'

Ginny met Giselle's eyes. She looked bemused. 'Fancy meeting you here, Giselle!' They embraced, French fashion.

'But you knew, did you not?'

'I did. Anyhow, I'm glad. I can see I'm going to need you. I don't think I can hold my own against those smart cousins.' She laughed.

'Oh, it is easy! They are so lovable.' Giselle looked as if she had brought Paris with her on to this country station, *soignée* even in tweeds and low-heeled shoes.

Clare said, 'Now, here's my Fiona, dying to make her speech to you.' She pushed forward the red-haired child.

'I'm thinking this is very silly.' She glared at her mother. 'So is the flag but it's all *her* idea. She says I have to say, "Welcome to Boyle and all your Irish relations!" Don't *you* think it's silly, Aunt Ginny? When I told Michael and Aubrey they just rolled on the floor laughing and said they were glad they were at school and wouldn't be made fools of.'

'Your mother is teaching you to have a sense of humour, love,' her grandmother said. 'Don't take it so seriously. Give Ginny a big kiss. That will do instead. And you too, Rosaleen.' The dark-haired girl came forward shyly. 'Moira's younger one,' Honor added.

'It was a very nice welcome anyhow,' Ginny said.

'Now that all that palaver's over—' Terence gathered them all together—'we'll get into the motor.'

A porter lifted Ginny's cases, she followed with Fiona and Rosaleen on either hand, Giselle walked with her father-in-law, Aunt Honor with her two daughters, all chattering like starlings. It occurred to Ginny to wonder what she and Sarah would have thought if their mother had appeared with her hair flying like a witch, not to mention a cloak, but Clare and Moira seemed well content with theirs.

'I think we'll all get in quite easily,' said Terence, looking back at them.

'We're just seeing you off, Father,' Moira said. 'We can't go back with you, can we, Clare?'

'No, we have the boys' dinners to see to, but you'll come and see us soon, won't you, Ginny?'

'I'd like to.'

'All come tomorrow to our place,' Moira said.

'But I wanted her first!' Clare's voice was a wail.

'Well, make it the following night, cushla.' Now it was Aunt Honor's husky voice. Giselle turned and exchanged glances with Ginny. 'That will give me two nights when I haven't to think what's in the kitchen.' Aunt Honor addressed no one in particular. 'My, how I miss ould Edna! Bridie isn't a light hand at all. And do you remember when Dymphna was at home how it was off with the business skirt and on with that apron? I miss Dymphna for that. If only I'd learned to cook as well as she did.'

'Well, you can't be a famous lady, author and cook roast pork and spuds as well,' Terence boomed.

'Now isn't your father a rare one for the fine words!'

'Step-father!' Clare sang out.

'And a sight better than Mr Dermot O'Rourke Daly, from all accounts.' This was Moira.

'God rest his soul!' Honor looked sober at the mention of her first husband. 'But to get back to plans: I want all you girls over at Woodlea tonight with those men of yours, and bring any of their pals along if you like, to amuse Ginny. I've done the shopping this morning and I'm hoping Bridie will supply the inspiration.'

'We'll be there,' Clare said. 'A word from you is as good as a command. Come on, Fiona, Rosaleen. You aren't going back with Grandma and Grandpa. Say good-bye nicely to your new Aunty. You'll be tired out with our gabbing, Ginny—Giselle's used to it now—so you be off to Woodlea and don't let them kill you with kindness.'

'*C'est vrai*, Clare,' Giselle said. 'I must get back to Paris soon or I will be a bad advertisement for Capel et Cie.' She blew out her cheeks, laughing.

When they had been waved off in the old-fashioned Daimler, literally—Rosaleen had the flag now—Ginny turned to Giselle. 'How is Terence? I haven't had time to ask you.'

'*Comme ci comme ça*. Excuse me, Ginny. I speak French too much here because I don't understand their language.'

'As long as you don't with me. Lizzie's the French scholar. But, he's been better?'

'Yes . . . he likes coming here. It relaxes him. And he paints the wonder horse, you know. How do you say it's name again, *beau-père*?' She raised her voice.

'The Sholtie Flyer. You're right there. It *is* a wonder horse. At her peak. I'm going to enter her at the Curragh next year. Maybe Epsom. She's built for speed.'

'Why not Longchamps or Chantilly?' Giselle asked.

'Ah, sure, the world's her oyster!'

'Don't start him on horses, for God's sake!' implored Aunt Honor. 'I'd be noticed more if I had four legs and a tail, and that's the truth.'

Under cover of the laughter Ginny said to Giselle, 'I'm glad about Terence. Maybe you should live in Ireland altogether?'

'Ah, no. You forget my job. We can't live without it. Not yet at least.'

'Now, this is Bridge Street. Someone was talking about it,' Aunt Honor said from the front. 'There's a fine market here at the top round the tower . . .'

'That's the Freeman's Inn,' Terence bent his head. 'My mother and I stayed there when we came visiting and a grand time we had. And her smiling at me over the candles on the dinner table like a young thing.' His voice was tender. 'And then we found this lass beside me in residence at Woodlea. Her first husband had inherited it and then died on her. You could say I came along at the right time.'

'That I won't deny,' Honor said. Ginny saw her lay her head on his shoulder for a moment. There was love between them all right. She felt lonely.

'Not that there hasn't been plenty of competition.' Terence laughed richly. 'And now a French beauty and an American beauty in the back of the old motor! We'll be the talk of the town.'

'And aren't we known as a good-looking lot, Terence, and quair with it, too. That's why I wear this great cloak when I set out to the station or the shops. The folks would be disappointed if I didn't.'

Ginny laughed. 'Maybe we should bow like Royalty, Uncle Terence.' She was going to enjoy herself here. It was a good place for broken hearts. And now that they were out of the town the countryside had a soft, sad beauty.

'Do you see the sun dying on the Curlew Mountains?' Honor said.

14

Ginny was sitting in the yard watching Terence at his easel. He was painting the Sholtie Flyer. Giselle had taken over the kitchen for the morning with the aid of Bridie, so that Honor could get on with her book. Terence senior had gone to Boyle to do the shopping. She had noticed that Aunt Honor had a way of organising her little world so that she was undisturbed, but once she had finished her 'stint' as she called it, she put all her energy into introducing Ginny to the neighbourhood.

They had gone to see the Cistercian Abbey at Boyle 'which had been plundered by that devil, Maurice Fitzgerald'—Honor had a habit of speaking about historical figures as if you were likely to meet them coming down Bridge Street on market day—and to Lough Key with its beautiful wooded islands, 'once the property of the MacDermotts, princes of Moylurg.'

'So you have princes here too, as well as in England?'

'England, she says? Them upstarts!' Aunt Honor gave a new slant to history.

Strandhill on Sligo Bay, with its kelp smell, was a place of special memories. 'It was here I knew Terence was for me, before *he* did. Such a sad boyo he was when he came visiting with his mother after his wife's suicide. But, oh that mother of his with her proud bearing and those blazing blue eyes. I remember her in her violet linen gown when we went on that picnic to Strandhill. It had a pleated bodice and her cream parasol exactly matched her cream buckskin shoes. Oh, the elegant ankle of her! A woman to put the life back in a man and she surely did that for Terence—though I think I helped.'

They had visited Dymphna's, Moira's and Clare's houses and met their husbands. Other young couples had been invited too, and any unattached males they could muster, although she would rather they hadn't. Sometimes Giselle and Terence came. She never ceased to admire the loving care Giselle showed him. As she explained it, 'I have to leave him each day to go to work when we're in Paris. He's good. He collects the children from school, and if he is not well, I get off early. He does everything he can to make our little household run comfortably, and no one is sorrier than he when he is not able to do his share. So when we are in Ireland I take the chance to be with him all the time.'

'Who is taking care of the children just now?' Ginny asked her.

'They stay with Maman. I cannot ask Madeleine now. She feels I am implicated in the affair with Jontee. Perhaps I am. After all I introduced them.'

'Don't blame yourself,' Ginny said to her. 'So long as you haven't lost a friend.'

'Not if I can find her a husband.' Her worry about Terence hadn't taken away her sense of humour.

She was delighted to hear about Delia, and curious. 'You have met her, Ginny?'

'No, she hasn't been to Scotland, but she has visited at Wanapeake. Sarah said in her letter that she seems quite a character.'

'What is that, a character?'

'An individual, not run-of-the-mill.'

'Ah, *bon*! Jontee is a character too. That was the problem with Madeleine. She is like a chameleon. Too feminine. A woman must, of course, be feminine but a little aggressive also. Men must realise that women have minds of their own. Perhaps I write to Jontee and say I am willing to make the wedding dress for this character.'

'Or perhaps you would make one for me?'

'Oh, Ginny!' She clasped her hands. 'Is this true? Who is he?'

'An American, Rollo Van Dam. He lives in Wanapeake.'

'When will the wedding be?'

'I don't know. I still have to tell him that I'm going to marry him.'

'Was the decision difficult?'

She nodded. 'I had to get rid of someone else first.'

'Was that difficult as well?'

'No, it was only in my mind. Don't you think you should be getting on with that wonderful soufflé you've promised us?' She still couldn't bear to talk about Iain.

* * *

'She's a beautiful horse, Terence,' she said. 'I can see why you like painting her.'

He didn't raise his head. 'Yes, horses are very satisfying to the eye. Father's very proud of this one. He has great plans for her. Maybe the Grand National.'

'That's ambitious. I bet we all make our fortunes.'

'Money isn't everything.'

She looked at his thin face. His eyes were permanently sunken now—either he didn't sleep or he was constantly struggling with some inward malaise. How cruelly random was mental illness, she thought. Even her constant hidden unhappiness about Iain couldn't begin to approximate to how Terence felt when he became depressed. And he was jockey-thin. His painting was his life-line. 'Here's your father! He'll tell us all about it.' She patted the bench beside her. 'Sit down, Uncle, and join the Admiration Society. Terence says you might be taking the Sholtie Flyer to England?'

'Well, I've written to the National Hunt.' He sat down, rubbing his hands. 'Nippy, this morning. You young things don't feel it. Yes, she's a great little chaser.'

'Have you got a jockey?'

'I'm negotiating at the moment. They book themselves well ahead if they're freelancing. I know the right man: it's just a matter of him being willing.'

'You want someone of the same type as Grandfather McGrath,' Terence said.

'Sure and I'll do it for you, Mr McGrath, for a consideration.' The boy holding the horse laughed.

'And I believe you would, Paddy, but this is a very special horse. You're right, Terence, my father had the hands for it. Gentle. When I think of that father-in-law of his, though he wasn't then and would have whipped him twice as hard if he'd seen into the future!' He drew a breath. 'Major Muldoon, my dear mother's father! Laid into him for paying attention to her! Locked him up, if you please! So they eloped. I always remember the name of the stable boy who let him out: Sean. When you think of it, if it hadn't been for Sean, maybe none of us would be here today—now, there's a thought!'

'Now, that's a wonderful story,' Paddy said, his round eyes bulging. 'There's a Sean McBride over at Balinafad, who runs a stable. Maybe it's the same man.'

'If it is he'd be about ninety. No, it's better left a mystery. My dear wife will turn it into folklore when she gets round to it. Hold her still, boyo. She's getting restless.'

'Sure it's because she's tired posing. It's past her time for her gallop.'

'Do you tell me that? Well, she's having her painting done.' He looked doubtfully at Terence.

'I've finished for the time being, Father.' He put his brush down and stretched his arms. 'We both need a rest, though I'm not going to gallop round a field.' He began to wipe his brushes with a rag, then whirled them in the jar of turpentine beside him. 'Yes, she's a horse and a half, that, Dad, her bone structure, and that small round head . . .'

His father was standing behind him, appraising the painting. 'You've got her. Yes, it's the Arab in her. Oh, she's a lucky horse, that, you can see it in her eyes. Off you go with her, Paddy.'

They sat in the yard with the long bars of sunlight splaying over the cobbles. Terence was quiet, but then he rarely talked much except sometimes at dinner when the wine seemed to loosen his tongue and a kind of febrile gaiety took its place.

They listened while his father reminisced about the old days in Scotland, about his brother Patrick, and what a worker he was. 'He couldn't get rid of the cart-horses fast enough. Wanted us with motors in the business. That's why he went to America. The pace suited him better. But, still,' His voice was softer, 'he'd had a lot to contend with. You won't remember your sister, Mary, who died, Ginny?'

'No, she died before I was born.'

'It bowled them over, him and your mother, and yet I had a young brother, John, drowned in the Sholtie, and I don't remember Mother except full of life.'

'Maybe she had more than usual to start with,' Terence said. 'It's a random endowment, cheerfulness in the face of adversity.'

'It depends on the amount of adversity.' His father's voice was firm. 'Nothing could beat what you and others like you had to go through in that terrible War, son, don't forget that.'

Terence shrugged. A veil of weariness seemed to fall over his face—more than that, Ginny thought, defeat. 'Ginny's getting married. Did you know?'

Her uncle opened his eyes. 'Now, that's the stuff to give the troops. A Scotsman, I hope, or failing that, someone from the Emerald Isle?'

'No, I'm sorry.' She laughed. 'From Wanapeake. A neighbour, and quite a catch, I'm told.'

'As long as he hasn't told you that himself! I couldn't be happier if you were my own daughter.' He patted her hand, 'When is the . . . ?'

'Here's Paddy coming running across the fields!' Terence, with his painter's eye, had seen the figure first. 'He's waving, and stumbling . . .'

'God in heaven! What's wrong?' Her uncle was first on his feet, his face contorted, purple-red, and Ginny got up quickly to stand beside him. 'If he's done anything to that horse I'll break his bloody neck . . .'

'Hold on, Father,' Terence said, 'it's probably nothing.'

The three of them started to run towards the boy. It *wasn't* nothing, Ginny thought; the boy was sobbing, slowing down as they drew near him. 'Oh, sor,' his hands were outstretched, 'Oh, sor . . . it wasn't my fault . . .'

Her uncle was the first to reach him, she and Terence at his heels. He was shaking him fiercely by the shoulders. She saw Paddy's head go back and forward like a stuffed doll. There was snot running from his nose into his mouth. 'What is it? Tell me, tell me . . . !'

Terence grabbed his father by the jacket and dragged him off the boy. The thought occurred to her that it was the first spontaneous movement she had seen him make since she had come here. 'Let him speak! You aren't doing any good . . .'

'Tell Mr McGrath,' Ginny said. She took a handkerchief from her pocket and gave it to the boy. 'Tell him, Paddy. It's all right.'

He blubbered, wiped his face, stuffed the handkerchief in his own pocket. 'It wasn't even a fence, Mr McGrath, so you can't blame me—or the horse. It must have been a rabbit hole. The grass had grown right over it, that was the trouble. There we were, galloping along as nice as you like, her foot caught in it . . . and . . . and she keeled over, throwing me. I think I hurt myself.' He waited for sympathy, looking from one to the other. 'Well, maybe not much, but it was the way she keeled over, sor, landing funny-like and her neck twisted. She's lying there . . . squealing . . .' He stopped, looking fearfully at his master.

Her uncle's face had drained of all colour now. He seemed to stagger. 'Terrible . . . terrible . . .' His hand went up to his eyes.

'You run and get the vet, Ginny,' Terence said. 'You're better at driving. I'll go with Father and wait. You'll have to show us, Paddy.'

'Where's the vet's house, Uncle Terence?' How shrunken he looked for a big man.

'What . . . ?' He looked up, dazed, then seemed to take hold of himself. 'On Church Hill, in Boyle. There's a monkey puzzle tree at the front. Anybody will tell you.'

'Sure, Miss, he's famous,' Paddy said.

'When I've found him, where do I make for?'

'Drive out o' Boyle first. Stop at the white cottages a mile before you come to our gates. There's a baker's in the middle—you can't miss it—then if you cut across the fields behind, you'll see us . . .' His voice faltered, the little spurt of normality gone, 'Maybe she'll be all right by that time, eh, sor?' His round face was pleading.

She didn't hear her uncle's reply. She was away, swift-footed, to the shed where the old Daimler was kept. She wouldn't tell anyone in the house yet, or even the other stable lads. Maybe it would be a false alarm. She didn't think so.

She had difficulty in steering the large car to begin with. It needed a good overhauling, and everything seemed to rattle, but she treated it roughly nevertheless, in her hurry, crashing the gears, standing on the accelerator as she drove up and down the winding sick-making road towards Boyle. She passed the cottages and saw the baker's sign, 'Thomas O'Flaherty, Hot Pies a Speciality'. She would know where to stop on the way back. More by good judgement than luck, or perhaps by looking for the church tower and steering as straight as possible towards it, she found the vet's house, ivy-covered, with its araucaria stretching out its branches as if to hide it, its gate swinging awry. Someone could make a fortune in Ireland if they would go round mending all the swinging gates which were awry.

She was lucky. Mr McGonagal was at his dinner, his wife told her, but she ushered her into the dining-room when she heard Ginny's story. 'Oh, my God, Devlin! Mr McGrath's winner! He'll be beside himself! Here, now, put down that knife and fork, will you, and listen to this young lady! It's Mr McGrath's mare, the one that's going to win all them races . . .'

He was a short man, bandy-legged. He might well have been the jockey Uncle Terence was looking for, and then she remembered that there might not be the need for any jockey . . . He sat forward as Ginny drove as if he were saddled and making for the winning post, and when she stopped at the group of white cottages, he was out and running across the field with his canvas bag over his shoulder as if the hounds were after him.

Some people had come out of the houses, curious, their mouths half-open. 'Is it an accident, then, Miss?' a woman asked her.

'Yes. Is there a way down for the car?'

'Sure there is, but Mr McGonagal wouldn't wait for that refinement, sure enough. Push open the gate for the lady,' she said grandly to a youth beside her, 'she wants to take the motor down to the accident.' He ran to do her bidding, and as Ginny drove down the rutted track, she was aware that there was a little group of people following her, as if they were pretending to be out for a walk.

She couldn't bring herself to get out of the car when she saw the horse on the ground. There was a high, keening noise coming from it. She wanted to put her head in her hands to shut out the sound.

She saw Mr McGonagal bend down and begin to feel the horse.

When he touched its neck it gave a human squeal and its head rolled in Ginny's direction. She would never forget its eyes, great protruding balls of agony, the thick fringe of the lashes. She turned away and saw the little group of people were standing respectfully at the side of the car, like a wake.

Together they watched Mr McGonagal get up off his knees, whack her uncle on the shoulder and shake his head, then speak to Terence who nodded, and went to stand beside his father. She hadn't thought of there being a rifle in the canvas bag. She supposed any self-respecting vet never travelled without one.

She saw him take it out, raise it to his shoulder, aim, and fire. The noise went ricocheting round the fields and bounced back from the dark clump of trees beyond them.

Paddy had slid down to his knees, as if in prayer. Terence had his arm round his father's shoulders. One of the men in the little crowd of spectators spoke. He was covered with flour, his face ghost-like, a professional mourner.

'Now, that's a tragedy. His best horse, too. A winner. What was it called?'

Someone said. 'The Sholtie Flyer.'

'Queer-like name. Maybe a bit too fancy.'

She sat stiffly, waiting for the vet to come to the car. She would have to drive him back for his dinner.

15

Rollo was at the Central Station to meet her, which she thought was significant. Life was going to be very different from now on with him in Scotland.

She wouldn't have been human if she hadn't felt a flutter in her heart. He was so handsome. His smile was so loving. It was a pity her tremulousness didn't dull the sense of inevitability at the sight of him. But her mind was fixed. If she couldn't please herself by marrying Iain, at least she could please her parents by marrying Rollo. And there had to be an end to lying sleepless in bed at nights. There was such a thing as self-respect.

Her mind went back to the time when she had travelled back from America with Aunt Kate. Then, she had thought, her place was where her heart lay with Lizzie and Ernest and their family. And Iain. She had still been hopeful, but not any more.

'Welcome back, sweetie! Been counting the days.' She saw a few admiring glances as he greeted her, sweeping her into his arms, entirely unselfconscious. His voice was very Yankee after the Irish she'd been listening to.

'Rollo, how nice of you to meet me!' She wasn't unselfconscious. She knew the insatiable curiosity of the Scots by this time, caught the eye of a douce housewife and smiled beneficently on her. He certainly stood out with his slim height, his pencil moustache above the smiling mouth, his light American suit—most of all his debonair air. 'Have you come from York Street?' she asked.

'Yes.' His raised hand seemed to cause a porter to materialise out of thin air. 'Follow us, please.' He put his arm round her waist as they walked in front of the man with her cases. 'We were in the middle of a board meeting but I said, "Excuse me chaps and lady—?" quite a lady, Mrs McNab, isn't she?—" but I have to meet our beautiful Ginny due back from Ireland."'

'Aunt Maevy wouldn't like that. She's a stickler for discipline.'

'No worse than Ernest. And Jonty's beginning to take a lead from him. Ernest's changed since the Wanapeake days, quite dry, sometimes. I get the distinct impression that they don't approve of me.'

'Oh, I'm sure you've got it wrong.' She stopped. 'Look, Rollo, I'll get a train very easily from here and you can get back to your board meeting.'

'Not a bit of it, dear one. Some homecoming *that* would be. I'm going to take you into the Central Hotel right here—' he had stopped at the entrance door leading from the station—'and give you a good shot of whisky or whatever you fancy after that miserable journey you had. Tossed about on the briny ocean, weren't you?'

'No, really . . .'

'Now, you must do what Uncle Rollo tells you.' He put her in front of him and propelled her through the revolving door, leaving the porter to follow with her cases. He guided her to a seat in the lounge and paid off the man. A waiter appeared almost immediately.

'Yes, Mr Van Dam?' He obviously knew him.

'Two doubles, Bill. Is that all right for you, Ginny?'

'Well . . .' she couldn't think of a good alternative. Never mind, she consoled herself, she could toy with it, and a sip or two would get rid of that queasiness in her stomach after the sea crossing. She wasn't a good sailor. 'The waiter appeared to know you, Rollo.'

'Yes, I'm staying here. Ernest suggested a room at the Hydro, but I turned that down, even if it meant the chance to see more of you. I can be at the office from here in five minutes, and I'm ready to go out on the town at night, such as it is.' He took her hands across the table, 'Do you still love me, Ginny?'

'Who said I did?' And yet it was difficult to resist his charm. Rollo was the sort of person who was hard to remember in detail, and yet when you saw him again you were almost bowled over by that particular kind of attraction he had. She had to admit it was sexual. Her body felt titillated by his presence.

'It's in your beautiful blue eyes. They're eating me up.' He laughed at her, 'I'll let you off tonight, but after that I'm going to be very demanding. You may remember I asked you a certain question in my letters. I'll want an answer *tout de suite*.'

'We'll see.' She smiled with her eyes as she sipped her whisky. Silent flirtation. Her tension disappeared. This was very nice. A smart hotel where Rollo was known (he always seemed to be known in hotels and roadhouses), and, really, he was very good to look at, insouciant.

'A very sad thing happened when I was in Ireland,' she said.

'Uncle Terence's favourite racehorse had a fall and broke its neck. It had to be shot.'

'Oh, my God, that's terrible.' His concern seemed genuine. 'I thought of polo ponies once, but the trouble of transporting them all over the place turned me off the idea.'

'I suppose it costs an awful lot to train them too. My uncle has two or three stable boys. He came out of the firm years ago, you know. I've never known whether he's rich or not.'

'What do you say if I send him a little money present just to show my sympathy? I could make it up in ten minutes on the Exchange. Would that please you?' He smiled engagingly.

She was appalled. 'I don't think it would be a . . . sensitive thing to do, Rollo. You know the McGraths. They're very proud. He might think . . .' she nearly said, 'you were being ingratiating.' She was glad she hadn't. His face had clouded.

'Well, I'm sorry I'm not "sensitive" enough for you, as you put it. Forget it.'

'Now I've annoyed you.' She wasn't going to crawl. 'I could ask Ernest.'

'No, don't ask Ernest, of all people. And your Aunt Maevy would have a fit if we took anything out of the kitty.'

'But you weren't thinking of that? It was a personal offer, wasn't it?'

'Expenses cover a multitude of sins, dear heart. Let's drop the subject. Will you come into town this evening and let me give you dinner here? I want to have a long talk about us . . .' his smile was charming, boyish, 'I can't wait. *And* we won't mention either horses or McGraths.'

'You did really mean a personal gift, though, didn't you?'

'Of course I did, little silly. I was just joking. You're getting as strait-laced as the others in the office. One thing, Ginny, whatever they do or say, I've decided to go back home after three months. I feel your father is much more sympathetic towards me than the crowd here. I've only been here a week and I honestly don't think I could stand it permanently.'

She sipped her whisky, listening to him. There was something in what he said. They were clannish here, and critical. They thought *their* way was always right. That was why Father had gone to America in the first place. He had once said to her that they wouldn't move with the times.

'I like Jonty—' Rollo was still talking—'but he's not all McGrath, is he? There's a lot of the Crawford side in him. But he's already dug in with his office and his showroom in Sauchiehall Street. His fiancée is coming at Christmas, I believe, and they are going to look for a place of their own farther out than Sholton. He's artistic, but he has a good business head as well. Yes, he's a good egg, but the others . . .'

'Jonty was always my favourite,' she felt deliciously hazy, 'my boy. But he won't be my boy any longer, now that he has Delia. Sad . . .'

'Well, why don't you have me?' He took her hands again. He was really incredibly handsome. 'You could come back with me and we could look for a decent house on Long Island. A lot of my pals on Wall Street live there . . .'

Everyone was settling into nests, houses, whatever you liked to call them—even Iain in his comfortable flat with Beth, now cured. If she stayed at the Hydro she would only become older and harder, and barren . . . Hadn't Belle once said something about a barren body and a barren soul?

But over and above that there was his incredible attraction. His hazel eyes were dancing, yet loving, and she thought of the life she would have with him, its fun and gaiety, altogether different from dour Scotland with its drizzling dampness and its dour men, like Iain.

She had given it a good try, but she was American at heart. Her life and Rollo's in a pleasant house on Long Island would be happy. She saw green lawns, the ocean, a nursemaid with flying streamers to her cap, heard the laughter of children. Everyone was married, even her beloved boy was on the brink of it. The time had come.

'All right,' she said, smiling, 'I'll marry you.' It was a strange feeling. The decision took a weight from her heart, and yet it left it . . . empty.

16

Maevy was putting her folders into her briefcase at the board room table in York Street. Jonty and Ernest had stayed behind the rest. 'Well,' she said, 'that seemed to go all right.'

'I enjoyed it anyhow.' Jonty looked dapper and young in his formal attire of black jacket and striped trousers which he wore for his shop.

'They took to you all right.' She looked fondly at him.

'Just as they do in Sauchiehall Street. It's that Crawford elegance.' Ernest was wry, as usual.

'Don't, Ernest,' he grimaced. 'You'll make me blush.' He had felt pleased with his appearance, nevertheless, when he had surveyed himself in the mirror in his attic suite on top of the stable block. 'A far cry from khaki.'

'We don't want that to happen again,' Maevy said, 'although we're still paying for it with unemployment and lack of housing . . . and lack of young men. We'll see what the Labour Government will do for us.' She sighed. 'Quite a milestone today with those new petrol vehicles, Ernest, all the same.'

'The pneumatic tyred delivery? You're in at the beginning, Jonty. They're the first we've had.'

'I was impressed by that back-loads system—' he wanted to appear *au fait*—'you know, to cut out the fly-by-night operators who use ex-Army lorries.' In fact he had a sneaking sympathy for them, had felt uncomfortable when it was discussed. There, but for the grace of God . . .

'That's Dan's idea. He always watches the pennies. If you carefully monitor the outward journeys from Head Office, you can keep an eye on the return trips.'

'It's Iain who does the fighting for us. If the railway companies had had their way we should have been doing only local removing.' Maevy was justly proud of that side of the business, having been instrumental in buying the large repositories in the East End which had proved such a godsend. 'There's no money in that. He's fought tooth and nail for us to get the longer trips.'

'What limit did they set?' Jonty asked. Because he was basically not interested in the business he worked harder at it.

'Fifty miles,' Ernest said, 'but that's no good to us when with our vehicles we can go all the way to the ports for shipment to Europe or even America. Besides, customers prefer the superior speed and door-to-door element. He's like a terrier, Iain.' He looked at Maevy. 'I think he's the right successor as chairman when I pack up.'

She bridled. 'It will be the first person who wasn't related to the McGraths, then. What about Jonty?'

'I'll be sixty-five in ten years' time. Jonty will only be thirty-four. We'll see.' He smiled at his step-son. 'You made a pretty good showing today. If you go on like that . . .'

'Because of Ginny leaving with Rollo, Mother has suggested I take over the Hydro. Maybe she just wants me to swan around in this gear for effect.' He grinned. 'I wouldn't mind having a go at the management side. I don't intend to be a shopwalker at Sauchiehall Street. I want to be behind the scenes most of the time, going to auction sales and so on. I wouldn't mind helping her out to begin with. It would be fun.'

'Did Jack Richardson sort out that expense account of Rollo's, by the way?' Maevy said. Ernest looked at Jonty doubtfully. 'Oh, don't mind Jonty! He's in the firm now. He's entitled to know what's going on.'

He felt uncomfortable. It wasn't difficult to see that Rollo wasn't a great favourite with the board although he was a great success in the office, especially with the girls on the typing staff. 'Don't tell me if you don't want to.' He felt his chin go up.

Ernest made a brushing movement with his hand. 'Rollo's expenses are damned high. Then we learn that he'd sent some money to your Uncle Terence in Ireland because his horse had to be shot.' He must have seen Jonty's looks. 'Nothing much wrong with that, although I don't think there was any need for it. But he put it down to expenses.'

He felt a twinge of compassion for Rollo. They were all against him here. And yet perhaps there was more than he knew about. They weren't unfair. He said, knowing he was using his 'lord of the manor' voice as Ginny called it, 'Are you sure you all haven't got your knife into him? Nothing he does seem to please you.'

He saw Maevy and Ernest exchange glances. 'Nothing he does is *right*,' she said, 'you might as well know.'

'But you haven't given him a chance. Three months!'

'It was he who elected to go,' Ernest said. 'Things came to light just after he arrived. He's been using the firm's money to invest with. Patrick okayed it and Dan Johnson had to accept it. But he's lost us a few thousand already. Of course he says it's long term, that we'll get it back and more . . .'

'But isn't it a good idea to use your working capital? I'm no trader like Rollo, but that's what firms do, isn't it?'

'Not if they've left too little in the kitty to buy all the necessary equipment which progress makes necessary,' Maevy said sharply. 'That's what keeps McGraths in the front. You saw the list of new vehicles the Works Manager presented at the meeting—new refrigerator lorries, transporters of bulk liquids, vehicles for vegetable oils, of special steel with temperature control . . .'

'Yes,' he spoke sharply too, 'I read it, Aunt Maevy, the low-loading platform trailers, the electric cranes . . .' He saw her hurt face. 'I'm really an ignoramus when it comes to all that.' He smiled at her, 'Now, if you were talking of the latest books, Galsworthy, Mottram, and James Joyce . . . perhaps I shouldn't mention him.'

'I've read *Ulysses*,' she said calmly. 'I've read a great deal in bed since Charlie died, and listened to music, gone to concerts. I wouldn't miss Sir Thomas for the world. Oh, I do lift my head sometimes beyond McGraths!' *Her* chin went up.

'What a cultural gathering this has suddenly become.' Ernest was always a smoother of troubled waters. 'Shall we discuss Einstein's theory of relativity instead of low-loaders?'

'I'm all for Sir Edwin Lutyens and his new Cenotaph myself,' Jonty laughed.

'And what about crosswords? Now, there's something really new! Lizzie and I have begun to do them. And talking about Lizzie, you and I had better make tracks for home. You know how she likes her evening sherry with us. Why not join us, Maevy?'

'No, thanks. Isobel has invited Belle Geddes for dinner. We're going to have a nice hen party and talk about all of you.'

Oh, they were close-knit, Jonty thought, as he walked with Ernest to their motor parked behind the office building. Rollo is an outsider. They'll never treat him as anything else. And yet, why had they accepted Iain Pearson so willingly?

'Ernest,' he said, when they were driving along Argyle Street, 'it occurred to me, Rollo's not settled here for one reason or another, I accept that, but Iain Pearson appears to do no wrong as far as all of you are concerned. It isn't just that he's a Scotsman, is it?'

Ernest waited till he had negotiated a difficult bit of traffic. 'You've put your finger on an interesting point. It's quite simple. Some people are trustworthy. Others aren't. It's something you know instinctively when you've been in business for a long time.

And if on top of that they have a fine brain, like Iain—well, enough said.'

'But Uncle Patrick thinks the world of Rollo, and he's been in business longer than you. Rollo's from a well-known family in Westchester. There's nothing in his record which can be . . .'

'Uncle Patrick has a mote in his eye. He's been surrounded by women since Gaylord died. You know how little he talks. But that doesn't mean he hasn't secretly longed for a son, *his* son. And Ginny prides herself on going her own way, leaving Sarah to be the dutiful daughter, but in the end she's doing the same thing as Sarah, she's pleasing her father by marrying Rollo.'

Jonty sat silent, turning the conversation over in his mind. Was Ernest right? He would hate like hell to see Ginny launch herself into an unhappy marriage just to please her father . . . 'She was in love with Iain Pearson,' he said.

Ernest drove skilfully for a few minutes. You had to watch out for children in the Gallowgate. They weren't used to motor cars. 'That's an additional complication,' he said at last. 'But Rollo's the winner. He at least isn't married to anyone else.'

He nodded, scanning the street with Ernest. How lucky he was with Delia, both unencumbered, a clear path ahead of them. He had even, one evening with her in Florence, told her about Madeleine, called it a 'friendship' certainly, and she had taken it quite well. 'You were missing your mother,' she'd said, and then, 'I wouldn't want to be your mother to you, just your wife.'

17

'If you're going to have a quiet wedding, I'm going to give you a reception in the Hydro,' Lizzie said.

'There's no need, honestly. It's just . . .' Ginny looked at her cousin, 'we both feel we can't face a big affair back home. Rollo has heaps of relatives he's no time for, and I feel it's too much for Mother, and there's Sarah . . .' She felt it would be tactless somehow to flaunt herself in white in front of her sister. Even more importantly, now that she had decided to marry Rollo she wanted the deed done quickly. Family weddings took ages to arrange.

'Well, that's up to you both, of course. But Ernest and I can't let you go without some appreciation for all you've done for us, even if you hadn't been getting married.'

It was a week before Christmas. They had seen Peter Kennedy, the Sholton minister, and he would marry them wherever they wanted. She had bought a simple short cream dress, with a cream hat veiled in bronze to match her high-heeled shoes. The three months since she had returned from Ireland had flown in one way, dragged in another.

She had been fêted and taken out a great deal by Rollo who had the capacity for finding out the 'best' places to be seen at in whichever town he found himself. The Central Hotel had been a frequent meeting-place, Rogano's another. He knew hotels within driving distance of Glasgow, at Drymen, the Hydro at Skelmorlie, the farther afield one at Crieff in Perthshire.

When she teased him about liking sophisticated backgrounds, he denied it. 'Look how happy we were when we went to Melrose that weekend, the lovely walks we had.' It was she who had suggested the walks.

'But you have to have a sophisticated life in the background.'

'Why live like pigs? I need a civilised setting. I've been brought up to it. So have you. You wouldn't like a hole-in-the-corner place after running the Hydro, would you?'

She didn't know what she would like any longer. She had

stepped on a wheel which was whirling her towards marriage with Rollo, running a house with servants on Long Island, visiting her mother from time to time—'the old lady had to be kept sweet', as he put it; the bonus would be seeing Ellie and Edie and her own family, and perhaps having children. Besides, Rollo would make her happy. He could even now make her tremble when he caressed her. And as for the general McGrath opinion of him, she would ignore that, although in fairness to them it had never been stated. But they were a close lot . . .

Once, when he called at the Hydro, his visit coincided with Iain's, and she had watched them together, both of equal height, Rollo effusive, Iain quietly smiling.

'They've let you out from the dragon house?' Rollo joked. Iain raised his eyebrow. 'York Street, old chap. The fortress.'

'Oh, it's not as bad as that. I was on the point of asking Ginny if you'd both come to our house for dinner one night. Beth was so pleased to hear about your engagement.'

'Absolutely delighted. We'd love to, wouldn't we, Ginny?'

'Yes, of course. How is she, Iain?'

'Fine, beginning to enjoy life.'

They had gone a week later to the flat off Woodlands Road and had been warmly welcomed by both Beth and Iain. She had looked well, but still had the slightly febrile air which seemed to be part of her personality. She was demonstrative with Iain, sprinkling her conversation with endearments. Iain was caring but more detached. Once, when Rollo was amusing Beth with tales of New York, Ginny's eyes met Iain's, and she thought she surprised a look of sadness in his which struck an echo in her own heart. Bleakness at her future with Rollo flooded her and she got up, excusing herself.

In the bathroom she rinsed her face in cold water, patting it dry while she looked at herself in the mirror. 'Go through with it,' she told the white-faced girl there, 'Don't spoil Beth's happiness, or his, by a single word or glance. He made a choice, now so have you. Think of Ellie. It turned out all right for her. It will be all right for you . . .'

So she had accepted Lizzie's offer, and thanked her, and yet their old easy familiarity was lost. Lizzie is trying too hard not to say anything against Rollo, she decided.

The week before the wedding Jonty came to see her, dressed in his 'shopwalker's outfit' as she called it. He hugged her and it was like old times. 'I feel a bit of a clown, actually. It's better when I'm at the Union Street office.'

'You look very handsome. One look at you and those rich West

End matrons will buy whatever you put in front of them.' She thought wistfully of the young khaki soldier who wrote poems.

'It's going very well but I only go in now by appointment. The auctioneering and valuating thing suits me better. I'm a tactile sort of person. I like to touch beautiful things, assess them. Who said all art was selection?'

'You must miss Delia, then,' she said, laughing.

'Like anything. The thing is, she isn't a raving beauty like you or Mother, so she's only beautiful to me. And that makes her very special.'

'All art is selection, you said. When will you be married?'

'June. We've decided not to rush. She's coming here at Christmas so you'll meet her then, and we're meeting in Paris in April because Giselle's making her wedding gown and I'm going to see the Paris *Exposition des Arts Décoratifs*, "Art Déco", it's called. It's the latest thing, and I must keep up with the trend. I'm hoping, just hoping, to buy one or two pieces by Lalique.'

'What an interesting life you lead! Where are you going to live, Jonty?' She preferred talking about his future rather than her own.

'When Delia's here we're going to see a house I've had my eye on for some time by the river. Ferniegair, it's called. It's right, but shabby. An old couple live there just now, and I have first offer when they move. I'll enjoy getting it refurbished for Delia.'

'Will you be married here?'

'No, at Albany. You'll be a staid old married lady then, and you and Rollo must come to our wedding.'

She said, feeling wistful, 'You're happy, Jonty?'

'So happy.' He came and sat beside her and put his arm round her, her own lovable boy. 'Why are you so sad, Ginny? Ladies about to be married ought not to be sad.'

'Who said I was sad?'

'Bristly Ginny! You've looked sad ever since you came back from Ireland.'

'I hate to leave you all. And the Hydro. It will flop without me.' She tried to joke.

'I'm taking it over until Mother finds someone else, so it won't flop, and there are the aunts.'

'I'm sad to leave the aunts, and Ernest, and Lizzie, and Annabel, and Kit, and you.' She began to weep and he put her head on his shoulder, stroking it.

'Have a good cry.' He produced a handkerchief. 'Use this or you'll spoil my nice suit, and then those West End matrons will turn up their noses and go elsewhere.'

She wept for a long time, and her sorrow seemed to flow out

in the tears, her deep longing for Iain, her love for this family with whom she had spent so much time, her love for Jonty. 'My boy,' she said, 'did you know that's what I've always called you, to myself? I'll have to stop that now that Delia's on the scene.'

'You'll always have a bit of me Delia won't touch.' He stroked her head, smoothing her hair. 'You don't have to go through with it, you know.'

'With what?' She stiffened.

'Getting married to Rollo. You can still break it off.'

'What are you talking about, you silly boy! Of *course* I'm going through with it. We're *eminently* suited.' She remembered an American phrase, 'We'll grow into each other.' She sat up, mopping her eyes. 'You don't like him either.'

'If you only knew it, I'm his champion. But he's a dyed-in-the-wool New Yorker. You know what I mean by that. Sometimes I don't think Ernest and Aunt Maevy and Dan Johnson and all the rest of them take it into consideration. In many ways he's like a strange, foreign bird. He doesn't . . . fit in here, but that's not his fault.'

I did, she thought. 'Priscilla Vogel once said he was like an American robin.'

'I don't know it.'

'A big, bold bird . . .'

'Ah . . .' They looked at each other, not speaking, then he leaned forward and kissed her. It was unusual for him. Generally it was a hug. 'If I'm your boy, you're my Wanapeake girl. Nothing will get you down. I know you, Ginny. You'll make a go of it.'

'Sure,' she said, 'I'll make a go of it.' She smiled at him, was glad he hadn't mentioned Iain, nor made any criticism of Rollo. 'And don't forget, I'm going home.'

* * *

They were married, not in the church, but in the Palm Court of the Hydro which was closed that day to visitors.

She stood in the midst of the palm trees and the glossy-leaved camellias and what Lizzie called 'exotica', and became Mrs Roland Van Dam the Third, in a short cream ribbed silk dress and a cream cloche hat swathed with bronze veiling which matched her shoes.

And Annabel, a shy thin girl of eighteen in a golden-brown velvet dress, attended her and held her bouquet of forced bronze-coloured roses; Annabel who, although shy, had refused her father's offer to send her to a Paris finishing school and elected to go to Glasgow University instead, to study English literature.

Lizzie, with tears in her eyes, kissed her, taking off the spectacles with the jewel-encrusted chain, and her scent was the same as the faint scent in the room at Woodlea, a lemony lily smell. Grandmother, from all accounts, had faced up to all manner of things. She would do the same. She didn't say any of this to Lizzie, but instead, smiling, composed, 'I thought you would have provided some holy water from the fountain, Lizzie.' Her cousin hugged her and said, 'Oh, Ginny, we'll miss you.'

Iain and Beth did not come. Everyone was slightly surprised at that, because Dan Johnson said he had been in the office that day. They all hoped Beth was all right, because she seemed to be blooming these days. But the aunts were there, 'the Siamese triplets' Jonty had once called them, smiling, loving, a composite living embodiment of the McGraths.

Her parents weren't there. Not through any disapproval—her father had written a warm letter with a large cheque—but because the weather was inclement at this time of year and they would see both of them very soon. Sarah said the same.

Delia Wallace had come, and she was as Jonty had described her, prim as a Puritan miss until you looked in her eyes. That was where her beauty lay, of character, and in her corn-coloured hair which was unfashionably long but done up in a heavy golden plait with a little posy of flowers behind one ear. When she saw her with Jonty she knew she and Rollo never looked like that. But, then, they were much older.

Rollo charmed everybody, including the waitresses who helped to serve them from the groaning table Lizzie had arranged, and he made a witty reply to Ernest's speech, saying that he was a modern Columbus come to Scotland to take back what belonged to them, their most precious jewel who was even named after one of their own states, which in turn had been named after the Virgin Queen. He intended to remedy that. The men there roared with laughter, but she saw Ernest, who was fastidious, look away.

They stayed the first night at the Central Hotel since they would be sailing the following morning. She got mildly drunk at dinner and there was no embarrassment, and she was able to enjoy losing that virginity he had joked about. He was incredibly handsome, and he seemed to suffer no embarrassment either as he stripped naked and leaped into bed beside her. Indeed, he seemed to revel in his nakedness. The proximity of warm skin was potent, she found.

And she discovered a strange thing: he was more passionate in his talk than in his execution. He was debonair and playful up to his own swift, satisfactory orgasm, and hers. But she had said she wanted to have children, and he had no objection because the Van Dam line had to be carried on after all, and they both quite liked the thought of that Long Island house with its servants and the laughter of children and the sound of their running feet. No Long Island mansion was complete without them.

She knew that night she had conceived. So, that's something, she said to herself, as she settled to sleep with Rollo's little playful kisses covering her face—moth-like, not at all like a bold American robin.

18

Delia's mother had insisted on accompanying her to Paris, but fortunately she had an old friend whose husband was in the American Consulate, and although Mrs Wallace and her daughter stayed in a discreet hotel in the fifth *arrondissement*, she was modern enough to allow Delia to meet Jonty without acting as her chaperone.

Quite a significant part of Delia's character came from Bertha Wallace, and having met Jonty and come to the rapid conclusion that he was a young man of parts, she was content to spend time with her old friend, Sadie Gomm, and leave Delia in Jonty's care. She had the satisfaction bordering on a quiet elation which every mother feels when she sees her daughter has made a wise choice.

They were on their way in a cab to meet Giselle and Terence at their apartment in Passy, and Delia was ecstatically happy to be with Jonty again. Evidently he felt the same, because he pulled her into his arms and kissed her as they swung along by the Seine, saying, smilingly, as he released her, 'How disappointing! You didn't squeal and say "Don't!"'

'I should only have squealed if you hadn't. Paris in April! It's absolutely wonderful and I'm the happiest girl alive. Do you think they'll like me?'

'You know perfectly well they will. You're just being provocative.'

She smiled at him from under the brim of her large hat. It was so satisfying to know that he understood her as well as loved her. 'I've read too many novels. I know exactly how a young affianced lady generally behaves. But if you don't like it I'll drop the whole thing.'

'Be yourself, my dearest darling.'

'Well, I am a little apprehensive, then—not whether they'll like me as a person, because I can't do anything about that, but whether your cousin will think me suitable to wear one of the creations of Capel et Cie.'

'Goose!'

'That's just it. Will she be able to make a swan out of a goose?'
'All girls are beautiful on their wedding day, regardless of what they wear.' And, rather tactlessly, she thought, 'You should have seen Ginny, my young aunt, and she didn't even wear a wedding dress.'
'Ah, but she's a beauty to start with.'
'Yes, she is.' He looked pensive. 'I hope she's happy.'
She would be magnanimous, although he shouldn't have agreed with her so readily. 'I hope so too. Have you heard from her?'
'Yes, she's having a baby. But she says she'll manage to come to our wedding by hook or by crook. I'm so glad.'
'So am I.' He had a large heart. She leaned against him and put her head on his shoulder, removing the obtrusive hat first.

* * *

Giselle took a long, smiling look when she had been introduced. 'Yes,' she said, 'I see it already. Sculptured. You're not a fluffy type, thank goodness. I'm not much good at frills. And your hair. *Parfait*. We can sculpt it as well.'
'So there you are, Delia darling,' Jonty said. 'All your worries are over.' And to Giselle, 'This silly girl actually thought she wouldn't be good enough.'
She turned her hands out in French disbelief. '*Mon Dieu!* Three fittings. The first one tomorrow morning.'
'Isn't she efficient?' Jonty said.
Delia thought she looked tired. The beautiful eyes were dark-ringed and her neck was angular as if she had lost some flesh. Jonty had told her of Terence's illness.
'Where's Terence?' he said, as if his mind was going along the same lines.
'He's resting. It is not one of his good days, Jontee.' She spoke with a calm acceptance. 'But I hope you'll see him before you go back to Scotland. Now, come and sit beside me, Delia,' she put her arm round the girl, 'and we'll get to know each other. You must tell me your tastes. It all goes into the dress.'
'Jonty first, and Italian Art second,' she said. 'They both go together.' She smiled with love at him. 'We met in Florence. Oh, I haven't had time to tell you, Jonty. I'm working with a picture restorer in Albany.'
'See how she tries to prepare herself to be a suitable wife for me, Giselle.'
'Medici,' Giselle said, 'wide sleeves and a square neck. Pointed

slippers, hair in a coronet, the plaits threaded with a narrow velvet ribbon, coral-coloured to match the tone of your skin, coral pink rosebuds for a small nosegay. I don't want the lines of my dress to be obscured by a cornucopia. Keep your eyes open at the *Exposition*, won't you, Jonty. You might pick up some good ideas for me.'

'Oh, did your mother tell you we were going? We called to introduce Delia to her.'

'*Naturellement*. My mother uses the telephone like a jungle drum. You'll enjoy it, in fact it is essential for you to see it, and you too, Delia. Your dress will follow the same theme, all the clutter of the *Belle Époque* removed, and now the simple geometrical shapes, the clean outlines. Paul Poiret goes too far as usual. He's showing his gowns on three barges on the Seine, can you imagine? Too lavish. But do go to the *Pavilion d'Élégance*. All the best couturiers are there—Chanel, Patou and Lanvin. Raoul Dufy's showing—' she looked sad for a moment. 'Terence hasn't been able to go to see his work.'

'I'm so sorry,' Jonty said. 'Do you think he'll be going to Ireland for a holiday? It seems to suit him.'

She shook her head. 'No, if anywhere, it will be to Condé, to Dr Reynaud. His father has enough worries.'

'I never think of him as having worries. Is it serious?'

'I think so. It's because of . . . Ginny's husband.' She looked at Delia. Delia looked at Jonty.

'She's one of us, Giselle. We have no secrets from each other. She knows about all our family skeletons.'

'And Jonty knows all about mine.' Delia half rose. 'But I'll . . .'

Giselle held up her hand. 'You belong with us now. *Ça suffit*. Apparently he and . . . What is his name, the husband?'

'Rollo.'

'Ah, yes. Rollo and Terence's father became quite friendly. This Rollo had sent him a present of some money when his poor horse had to be shot, and although he returned it, it began a correspondence between them.' Delia remembered that when Jonty had told her of this in a letter she had thought that the gift sounded like a sprat to catch a whale. 'Rollo . . .' Giselle smiled at them, shrugging her shoulders at the apparent strangeness of the name, 'he seems to have suggested that Terence's father should send him a regular sum for investment and he would become rich.' She shook her head. 'That has not happened. He has become poor instead.'

'That's terrible.' Jonty frowned. 'I'm beginning to think Ernest and Aunt Maevy—well, never mind.'

Giselle looked at him. 'We think he was tempted because he has had very large goings out recently.'

'Outlays?' Delia suggested.

'*C'est ça.*' Giselle's look congratulated her. 'He has had the stables extended and rebuilt, bought new . . . stock, horses, and so on and so on. Ah, everyone has their dream.'

'I don't like it.' Delia saw the unease in Jonty's face. Also that he wasn't going to commit himself further.

'I had hoped to see Clovis and Jaime, Giselle,' she said. 'Are they out?'

'No, they're in bed. They make much noise and Terence is upset by it. So I give them a special tray of . . . titbits, yes? And tuck them in. Do not feel sorry for them. They have learned when they must be quiet for the sake of their father.'

What problems there were in families, Delia thought, especially if they were widespread like the McGraths. She was an only child and her father and mother had been the same. 'Very unprolific on both sides,' Bertha Wallace had said. She had always been undemanding as far as Delia was concerned, possibly because she was always busy with her own affairs. Her father was a quiet solicitor who took a back seat to his wife and daughter. She didn't remember any great family problem when she was growing up.

Still, she thought now, philosophically, it looks as if I'm going to have plenty at second-hand when I marry into the McGraths. The fact that she would be Lady Crawford hadn't dawned on her yet, or only occasionally.

In the cab going home Jonty kissed her again, more passionately this time since it was dark.

'Father always says that money transactions between members of a family are a mistake,' she said when she came up for air, 'I don't know how he's any judge since he hasn't had any as far as I know, but then he may have seen plenty of them with his clients.'

'Why the generalisation?' Jonty said, eating her up with his eyes and wishing they were married. Delia wasn't Madeleine. He would have to wait.

'You know. Apropos Terence's father and Ginny's husband. I thought all the McGraths were as rich as Croesus?'

'Well, there's plenty of money in the firm but it's always being ploughed back. Oh, we aren't paupers, far from it, and as I'm a Crawford you'll be kept in the style to which you are accustomed,' he grinned at her, 'but my grandfather—don't forget that's what he is—came out of the firm voluntarily after his first wife died and went to Ireland to breed horses—they're in the McGrath blood, or at least his—so he's been living on unearned income for a long time.'

'I see that,' she said.

'That's why he must have been tempted when Rollo offered him a chance to make some quick money. Anything to do with horses eats it up. I had a friend at Eton, Craven, and they kept polo ponies. He said it cost his father a packet.'

'But I thought his wife was a famous author?'

'She's well known, but I don't think the kind of books she writes, non-fiction, are runaway best-sellers. And there might have been a lot of expenses, three girls to educate and his two boys. Girls' weddings cost the earth, I'm told.'

'Yes, my father is beginning to sigh every time he signs a cheque.' She smiled at him.

'It's worth it to get you off their hands.'

'It was she who did the kissing this time, or at least instigated it. 'Do you know, Lord Crawford,' she said, 'I think I'm going to like living with you,' and after more kissing, which was prolonged, 'I bet your poor grandfather's money has been swallowed up on the New York Stock Exchange by this time. Father says the market is very nervous just now and that you have to keep an eye on it.'

'What I'm wondering,' Jonty said, moist-eyed with love, 'is if we should have been keeping an eye on Rollo.'

19

It seemed no time from their own wedding until they were at Delia's and Jonty's, in Albany in June. Ginny wasn't able to wear her own short cream dress because, being six-months pregnant, the occasion demanded something more unobtrusive.

In spite of that it was a lovely celebration. She liked Delia's parents, seemingly a well-matched couple and able to take their only child's wedding in their stride, and best of all, the opinion she had formed last Christmas of Delia was confirmed. She appeared to have something more than youthful prettiness—character and personality. Jonty had been right.

'It's no good, Ginny,' she said, greeting her, 'I've tried and tried but I can't compete with you. Jonty has put you on a pedestal.'

'No, no,' she said, smiling, 'I just stood in while he was waiting for you to come along. Now I bow out gracefully, not that it's possible at the moment.' She made a downward sweep of her hand towards her swollen stomach.'

'Yes, Jonty told me. But it only makes you more beautiful than ever, and I'm not in the least bit jealous. Isn't that good?'

She was so happy to see Ellie and Kieran, Robert and Edie, her mother, father and Sarah. In a way, in that grand house on Long Island, she felt more cut off from them all than she had in Scotland.

And Lizzie, Ernest and Annabel were there. Kit had been left in charge of the aunts who had decided to stay at home to keep an eye on him and the Hydro. She hugged Annabel, tears coming into her eyes. 'My, what a grown-up young lady! And elegant!' Rollo was at her side. 'Don't you think so, Rollo?'

'Beats the bride in looks, I'd say,' he said, embracing Annabel almost too readily. 'And Lizzie and Ernest! The proud parents.' Ginny noticed his greeting of Lizzie was more formal, his handshake with Ernest not over-enthusiastic. Or was it the other way round?

'Nothing would have kept us away today,' Lizzie said, 'even if the Atlantic Ocean were twice as broad.' What a beauty still, Ginny thought, kissing her, forty-seven now and still with her luscious skin and hair and those beautiful eyes, now with new and even more flattering spectacles which swung more on their jewelled chain than rested on her nose. The little affection of putting them on and off had become part of her personality, another enchantment.

Rollo took Annabel off to meet some other people, his arm round her waist. Lizzie made no comment. 'Are you happy, darling?' and not waiting for a reply, 'Isn't it the *end* with a great bump at the front! I can't tell you! The relief of getting rid of it is tremendous! But, oh, Ginny, the glow of satisfaction when you see the little thing for the first time! You'll be in the seventh heaven. You and Rollo,' she added. She was wise, Lizzie. Rollo was family now.

Lizzie was whisked away by Mrs Wallace and Ginny moved to Robert and Edie, who were talking to Kieran and Ellie. The McGraths glowed, the Murray-Hyslops were graver but had 'grown into each other', except that Ellie would never really be possessed by anyone after Joe. But being Ellie, as in her career, as in everything she tackled including marriage, she would make a success of it.

'You're going to know such joy when the baby comes,' she said. 'James made up for everything. And now with Betsy Ann my life has been made complete.' Her eyes were saying more.

Her mother was frillier than the bride, but aged, her father drawn and a bad colour, but he was effusive with Rollo who had joined her again.

'I introduced Annabel to Sam and Ben. What a little charmer she is with those dark eyes!'

'How are you, my boy?' her father said. 'We don't see enough of you and Ginny now that you're in that fine house on Long Island.'

'We're tip-top, Patrick.' He never addressed him as father-in-law. 'I do try to get in to your office from time to time, but I'm pretty tied up in Wall Street.'

'Of course, of course. I wish I had learned to play the market instead of earning money the hard way.'

'He shouldn't be going up so often to New York,' her mother said, 'I keep telling him but he won't listen.'

'Aren't you thinking of retiring yet, Father?' Ginny asked him. Each time she saw him he looked older, more frail.

'No, no,' he shook his head impatiently. 'I've a few new plans which Rollo is helping me with. And there's the Travel Section. Sam and Ben are the bosses there, but they've got plans too, expensive ones since they're young and go-ahead, and the extra money has to come from somewhere.'

'Don't you bother about that, Patrick,' Rollo said. 'I know where the crock of gold is.'

'I don't know where I should have been without Rollo,' her father said. Ginny met Sarah's eyes, and she saw uneasiness in them. She too? But Father was astute and cautious, always had been. Or was it that Ernest had been right when he said Rollo had taken Gaylord's place? Her heart was heavy as she looked at Rollo's smiling face. She must trust her husband, cleave to him.

Jonty came and sat beside her at the reception after the wedding. 'Wasn't she lovely, Ginny? And look at her now, my wife!' She followed his eyes to where Delia was talking to a group of people. The gown was worthy of Capel et Cie. She looked radiantly happy, and not at all bridelike. She was laughing heartily, her head thrown back. 'She said she was sure she would trip over the train going up the aisle and it was only the thought of Giselle's disappointment which kept her from doing it.'

'You both look so happy. Oh, I'm glad for you! So much in store for you both.'

'So much in store for you and Rollo,' he said. 'Have you chosen a name yet for your bundle?'

'Yes, Jonathan Roland. I'll call him Jonro.'

'You're so sure it will be a boy?'

'Yes. Oh, Jonty.' She looked at him with love. 'All those times we confided in each other, and now you have the best girl in the world. You'll have fun. It's in her eyes.' And then, because her emotions were near the surface, 'Rollo is full of gaiety, but we don't have *fun*. Isn't that strange?'

'He's far more sophisticated than I am. I'm a simple soul.'

'You have simplicity of soul, which is very different.' The words came impulsively, 'Do you like Rollo?'

'He's very . . . likeable. Such style. It's he who should have a title, not me.'

'You can't see yourself. Oh, he's proud of his lineage. So is his mother. I think that's why he was quite pleased to have a baby to share in it.'

'Jonro Van Dam should sound very nice when he goes to Groton.' He got up. 'I must make my rounds, Ginny darling. Strict instructions from Mother. I saw you sitting alone. Where's Rollo?' They searched the room with their eyes and possibly saw him at the same time with the pretty bridesmaid. 'You're my dearest, youngest aunt,' he said, looking down at her.

'And you're my boy.' She laughed so that it shouldn't sound too sentimental.

Mr and Mrs Wallace were generous in their hospitality. The champagne flowed and Rollo had a good share of it. He became the centre of interest with the pretty bridesmaid who seemed to like the experience. They danced together because, as he had said to Ginny earlier, 'You aren't up to it, old thing.'

She wasn't left alone. She talked and laughed with her cousins, with guests to whom she was introduced, saw them one by one take their leave. Rollo was still whirling round the room with his coat tails flying, his chestnut hair silkily waved, very handsome, very suave. She saw the pretty bridesmaid being gathered up by a stern father and mother and took the opportunity to cross the room to him.

'We should be going too, Rollo. It's an hour since we saw off Jonty and Delia. I don't want to be the last.'

He took in the room with his social smile. 'Don't want to miss anything . . .' She knew by the flush on his cheekbones that he was slightly drunk.

'There's nothing to miss. It's over. Let's go. I've said good-bye to everyone. I couldn't catch your eye because you were dancing.'

'Great little girl, that! Marianne something-or-other. Knocked all the others into a cocked hat, didn't you think? Except my own sweetie.' She softened. Pregnant ladies could do with reassurance.

'I never make comparisons.' She smiled. 'Come on, *please*.'

They made their way to Mr and Mrs Wallace. They looked tired, but Bertha Wallace brightened when she saw Ginny. 'I've been so glad to meet you, Mrs Van Dam. When the baby arrives you must come and visit with us in Albany. I know Delia and Jonty regard you as their greatest friend, as well as relation.'

'I hope I'm included,' Rollo said.

'Of course, Mr Van Dam.' If she intended a slight, Rollo was past noticing it, Ginny thought.

She knew he was in a bad mood when they got into the car. She expected it. He was always touchy when he had been drinking, imagining slights where none were intended. The car wheels went over the edge of the driveway of the hotel, ploughing through a bed of roses. 'For goodness sake, Rollo,' she said, 'mind what you're doing!'

'It's a crazy bend, but—*I* know. You're going to say I'm drunk.' He pouted.

'I wasn't, as a matter of fact, but now that you mention it . . .' She tried to speak lightly.

'You're jealous,' he said, 'that's what it is. You told me on the way here that you wouldn't be able to dance, and then you shoot black looks at me when I'm trying to make myself sociable.'

It was unfair but she fell into the trap. 'If making yourself sociable means flirting ostentatiously with one of the bridesmaids, all right, have it your own way. I don't mind, it gave me a chance to speak to people, but goodness knows what my family thought of you.' That was a mistake. She saw his face darken, the mouth grow tight. She could have eaten her words, but couldn't bring herself to apologise. She waited, but he was silent, concentrating on the traffic, and she did the same. When they were free of the town she sat back, relieved. But it was short-lived.

'You and your precious family!' The words erupted from him. 'I hear of nothing else. I'm a Van Dam! The McGraths can't hold a candle to us, even if your precious Jonty *has* a title.'

'What a childish thing to say!'

'Well, I'm right, aren't I?'

'Of course you're right. Who's disagreeing? My family started as common carters, my grandfather went down a mine and so did my father and Uncle Terence, for that matter.'

'Well, there you are, then!' He was triumphant. 'And to think that upstart, Ernest, wrote a stinking letter to me and said he'd be obliged if I didn't have any more financial transactions with that . . . that old Irish toper!'

'You're ridiculous.' She had to laugh. 'Uncle Terence isn't even Irish, far less anything else.'

'Well, he acts Irish and he has an Irish wife.'

'What kind of financial transactions were you having with Uncle Terence?' She suddenly felt fearful.

'He wanted a flutter on the Stock Exchange, so I obliged.'

'Did he lose much?' She knew he wouldn't have gained, or there would have been no need for Ernest to write.

'It's the swings and roundabouts. You know that. He'll get it all back in due course and more. I was only trying to do him a good turn.'

She sat silently as he drove far too fast towards New York. How lovely the Westchester countryside was. No wonder some of the richest people in the country chose to have their estates here. Those manicured lawns rolling under the gracious trees . . . but did the landscape look rather tamed? Her thoughts swivelled again to Rollo. As long as he hadn't appropriated Uncle Terence's money . . .

But he wouldn't do that, surely? He had said himself he was only trying to do him a good turn. She was still in the dark about that gift he had said he would give her uncle when the Sholtie Flyer had broken its neck. Had Uncle Terence accepted it?

Who are you going to believe in? she asked herself, the McGraths or your husband? She looked at his profile and the downard turn of his mouth. This was the man she had chosen to marry, the father of her coming child. 'Poor Rollo,' she said, laughing, 'I love you, if nobody else does.'

He wasn't going to be teased. 'It's a bad business when you try to do a good turn for a relation of your wife's and the whole family turns against you . . . and them only common carters.'

'Oh, Rollo!' She bit her lip to prevent herself from laughing again.

She sat silently as he tore up the river towards New York, held her breath and controlled her sickness when he went through the city streets with lurching turns at street corners, relaxed when they were through Queens and driving towards Long Beach.

It was a beautiful evening. The sky expanded as the buildings fell back from it, held its cerulean blueness for a time then faded into mauve, deepened to purple and was streaked with fiery orange as the sun set.

When they got home she would walk down to their beach and sit and look at the ocean. It was much better than going into the house with him to be the butt of his bad humour. He always got quarrelsome when he had drunk too much and went straight to the bottle when he arrived. The moonlight on the ocean would calm her. She would think of the baby, and Delia and Jonty's happiness, and how lovely it had been to see all the family. She would try not to think of Iain.

Coming near Southampton, the mist came down. It was different from the sooty fog she remembered in Glasgow when sometimes, shopping for Lizzie, she would be caught in it. Her memory was of its yellowness, the sudden silence which seemed to fall on the busy streets, the ghostly quality of the passers-by. But here it was a grey-white mist which rolled in from the ocean like a huge blanket being unfurled over them.

'Go slowly, Rollo,' she said, 'it's getting worse.'

He laughed. 'I know every inch of the way. That's the advantage of travelling to New York every day. I could do this trip with my eyes shut.'

'That's what this is like. Rollo!' She felt something rattle along the side of the car.

'Just a branch, sweetie. It'll clear away as soon as we get to the top of this hill. Come on, you!' He whacked the steering wheel, 'get some speed up!' She heard the crash of gears, and then, the engine responding quickly, the car took a leap forward. 'Christ!' He fought with the wheel, wrenching it from one side to the other, there was a bump and a tearing, ripping sound, and she was thrown back violently, then to the side, striking her head on the struts of the hood. She realised they were sitting sideways on to the road, the car's bonnet buried in a dark clump of bushes.

'You fool, oh, you fool!' She was furious with anger, a primeval ugly anger, strange to her. 'You might have damaged the baby! What are you playing at? You won't damn well listen!' She looked at him. His head was bent over the wheel, she could make out a black trickle of blood running from a cut on his forehead. The anger seeped out of her. 'Rollo! Are you all right?'

'All right.' His voice was weak. 'Just a knock on the head. I'll be fine in a minute.'

'This is terrible!' She felt like wringing her hands. 'What should we do? Rollo! We're blocking the road.' Her head was dizzy but she made herself think, 'We could cause an accident . . .'

'Doesn't matter as long as you're all right. Just sit quietly for a minute. Don't speak . . .'

She helped him to rest his head on the padded back of the seat. Her head was clearer now, but the fear was still there. The baby. What about the baby? 'I'm going to listen,' she said, 'and if I hear any traffic coming I'll blow the horn hard, to warn them.'

'Good for you, Ginny. Capable. You take charge.' He didn't raise his head. 'Be as right as rain in two ticks.' He groaned.

'I don't know if I can say the same.' Her anger flooded back. 'I'm worried sick about the baby.'

'Do you feel anything?' His voice was slurred.

'Only a dragging sensation. No . . .' she wanted to say 'blood', couldn't form the word in case the fear became fact. She heard in the distance the steady thrumming of an engine, then the sound increased as the motor began to climb the hill. She pressed the bulb of the horn, pressed it again fiercely, and it seemed louder in the fog, a raucous, blaring, ill-natured sound. No one could disregard it.

The engine she had heard seemed to splutter quite near, and she saw the bulk of a motor car in front of them as the sound died. She heard voices, the slamming of doors and two men emerged from the fog. 'Here, what the devil is this?' The voice had a fat sound; the owner, she saw, *was* fat, dressed in some kind of light sports clothes.

'Could you help us?' she said. 'My husband lost his sense of direction. We crashed into the hedge, I think.'

'Are either of you hurt?' The other man, wearing a pale cloth cap and a tweed jacket, sounded more businesslike.

'We're all right, chaps.' Rollo's voice was stronger but he didn't move. 'Little wifie here is having a panic.'

'What about you?' the man said, turning to Ginny.

'Shaken, that's all, I think.'

'Do you live near here?'

'Yes,' she told him, 'just five miles farther on.'

'What to do, Bobby?' It was the fat man again. And turning in their direction, 'We're going for a spot of deep-sea fishing at Montauk, planned it for months.' He sounded disconsolate.

'Let's see.' The man called Bobby pondered under the peak of his cap, 'Tell you what, you drive those people home in their car and telephone the police from their house. And the doctor. I'll tuck this motor of ours out of the way . . .'

'No, no!' Rollo shook his head. 'Better if the three of us try to straighten up my car . . .'

Ginny interrupted. 'We haven't found out if it will start or not. Move over, Rollo, I'll try.' She was afraid the two men would discover that he was tipsy. She got out shakily and climbed into the driver's seat, grasping the wheel thankfully. When she pressed the ignition the car started without protest. She reversed it slowly out of the hedge while the two men directed, and straightened up.

'Well done!' The man called Bobby was at her side. 'How do you feel?'

'Well enough to drive home.'

'Sure?'

'We'll be all right.'

'Wouldn't you like one of us to come with you?'

'No, thanks. I know the road well. I'll get on in case someone else comes along. Many thanks.'

'Many thanks.' Rollo waved a hand. 'See you again. Good fishing.'

She felt sick as she drove. Rollo had sat up straight now, voluble because of his guilt. 'That damned fog! Destroys all sense of direction. One minute I was . . . next minute . . . Damned decent chaps. Should have asked them for their address . . .'

She let him gabble on, intent on following the road and not being physically sick. A fine trembling throughout her entire body was making her hands shake, but there was no awareness of . . . blood. She would know immediately by the wetness. It was imperative that she keep this baby.

When she reached their drive she drove even more carefully

because now she was having waves of dizziness. She stopped at the door and got out, only able to take care of herself. She knew Rollo followed her, still talking.

Their butler, Robbins, opened the door. Rollo's voice was cheerful. 'Had a little accident on the way home. Very devil of a fog . . .' She saw the alarm on Robbins' face, saw his eyes go from one to the other.

'Would you ask Mrs Robbins . . . ?' Another wave of dizziness made her stagger towards the tall-backed sofa. She didn't reach it. Everything went black.

20

Fosters,
Southampton,
Long Island,
June, 1929

Dear Iain,

I had your sad letter telling me about Beth's death a week ago.

I didn't want to write the ordinary letter of condolence. I felt you deserved more, but I had to wait for a little until I knew what I wanted to say, or should say, apart from expressing my deepest sorrow for your loss, and for me, the passing of a dear friend.

When you told me Beth's words, 'Tell Ginny that I tried to make you happy,' I wept, at first bitterly, shamefully, and then my mood changed and I was able to mourn the passing of a fine, brave and generous spirit.

I had got to know her in the letters we exchanged. Ostensibly they were 'keeping in touch' letters, she telling me of Glasgow, I of my life here, but there was an undercurrent, a deeper level, and we became close friends.

Because of that friendship I want to be as honest with you as you were with me in your letter. Who knows whether you did the 'right' thing in marrying her when you loved me, when I loved you? What is 'right'? What I do know is that you made her happy, which is the important thing, have no doubt about that. The rest follows—her wish for a child and, unhappily, her death. You couldn't foresee her inability to carry a child, the miscarriage, the blood poisoning. Think instead of the happiness you gave her when she knew she had conceived.

I can sympathise so deeply with Beth in her wish to have a child and to give you one, and your despair when she died. You mustn't blame yourself. That was to be her gift to you, and in a way I wonder if she knew it was going to be her supreme gift. One thing I do know: she was idyllically happy in her last letter to me, and never once did she complain of fear or pain, although she wrote from her bed. 'Just resting up', she said.

I can begin to feel her pain and sorrow in that last week of her life because I too once suffered a small part of this anguish. After Delia and Jonty's wedding in Albany we had a motor accident on the way home, and for a time I thought I had lost my first child. But I hadn't a chronic illness to contend with and all was well. I didn't deserve such luck. *She* did. She makes me feel humble, and I shall never forget her. And you made her happy, Iain. Cling to that.

I have come a long way from the brash Ginny of my Scottish days in the Hydro. I have 'quietened down', as mother says. They no longer say, 'Trust Ginny!' I am a predictable young matron with two children. Jonro is now three and a half, Susan—Suki we call her—is two. They are my love and my consolation.

Life goes on. Since this is an entirely honest letter, I can tell you that my life with Rollo hasn't been happy for some time. I went into this marriage stubbornly, determined to make the best of it since I couldn't have you, the man I loved. It was a now-or-never marriage, a nesting-instinct marriage. I knew it would please my parents. I had been a problem to them when I was young and I wanted to remedy that. Rollo was the son my father had lost.

These were the wrong reasons, and I blame myself to a large extent that Rollo became a philanderer. I failed him. I wasn't giving him the respect and love which were due to him. Had I been jealous, it would have been better. All I did was fulfil the role of wife and mother and put up a 'Van Dam front', and that wasn't good enough. I know that now.

So, here I am, *entre les deux guerres*, as T. S. Eliot says—I read a lot now—and I have time to think also in this great white house on the Atlantic Ocean. That must be a new Ginny to you. I think of all kinds of things, mostly of the past, and I think sometimes of the dichotomy in the temperament of most of the McGrath women.

Along with a necessity to go out into the world—look at Aunt Maevy, Ellie, Lizzie, and of course the original Maeve McGrath—there is this protective, fierce love they have for their children. Once they are able to fend for themselves we give them complete autonomy, but until then they're in our care. Think of Jonty and Ellie, the freedom they were given to shape their lives.

Many people wouldn't mind changing places with me, I know, a smart young married woman in what is one of the most delectable regions near New York, amongst other women similarly placed, although strangely enough, it hasn't the same appeal for me as the Hudson Valley—maybe not strangely, since that is my home.

But I love the ocean. It calms my spirit and widens my perspective. It is my release. We have our own beach at the foot of our lawn, and it has become my private place when I want to be alone. That isn't difficult. I have a good nursemaid and I see very little of Rollo.

He has never taken me into his confidence in money matters, and at the beginning this hurt me because I thought I had run the Hydro fairly efficiently. But I can read, and the *Wall Street Journal* is always around. What is going on, Iain? What about that man, Clarence Hatry? Has he anything to do with this gathering panic to buy, buy, buy?

There's something strange happening, surely. It doesn't *feel* right, the boom seems to be without substance, like a phantom, like a bubble about to burst. Do you remember the Spanish flu which decimated the American forces in 1918? Kieran McGrath caught it and nearly died. This feels the same.

I was at the Plaza Hotel with Rollo yesterday—we go there since the Waldorf is no more—and you would have had to be pretty insensitive not to feel this *excitement* in the air. I had seen it in Rollo as we drove up to New York, his frenetic gaiety, the cocktails before we left, his insistence that I look 'good' (he even chose the dress and hat I should wear). Does this make me sound spineless, not like the old Ginny? Well, I guess I've learned to save my ammunition for the things that matter.

In the oak dining-room there wasn't a seat to be had—we had a reserved table along with some Wall Street friends—and everyone seemed to be celebrating something or other. All the talk was of the money they had made. One of them was staying in the hotel for the weekend with a girl not his wife—because he had cleared half a million that morning! The champagne was flowing. Yes, I know Prohibition is still here, but money buys anything.

I could spot all the famous dealers at other tables. Rollo didn't have to point them out to me. John J. Raskob with a party—he's responsible for the disappearance of the Waldorf; Charles Mitchell, with a thin little man whom Rollo said was Mr Durant. You'll probably know of him because of road transport. He rarely goes out in public and Rollo says he doesn't seem to get any pleasure out of his millions—no drink, picks at his food.

What I had noticed was that as the noise and the laughter increased and the orchestra played louder in competition, Rollo's mortification grew. I knew all the signs, too much drink, too loud laughter, name-dropping. I knew he wasn't sharing in the good fortune of the others, and that I'd have to bear the brunt of his temper on the way home, although he wouldn't tell me why.

'No need to worry about the Anaconda shares,' he announced, waving his hands, 'the boom will go on.' I knew then that was where his money had gone this time. Our friends were celebrating their *rail* deals, which didn't help. 'Copper will bottom out without a doubt,' he assured them gaily. Usually he commands respect, after all, he's persuasive and charming—I should know—but for the first time I noticed them exchanging glances. They no longer believed him, or in him, and even worse, as he drank more and more, I knew that he knew this. I pitied him, and that's a bad thing in marriage.

I can't fathom how it's done, I mean, the upkeep. I secretly worry. We have a large staff, a large house, money is spent lavishly on entertaining, and yet on the other hand I know that Uncle Terence has completely lost confidence in him since he lost most of his money. He had to retrench drastically in the stables, and he's only got his own horse now and a young filly which he's kept because he says it has 'something'.

He wrote about this horse to me—'roan-coloured, a fine spirit, mischievous but not malicious. She has a great heart like my mother (he and Grandmother were devoted to each other), and she'll have the same grace and style. I can't afford a jockey now, but Paddy can do anything with her. And she's a fighter, like Mother. She'll give 105 per cent if it kills her, not 95 per cent like most. I've named her the Sholtie Flyer, Mark Two. She'll come home one of those days and make all our fortunes, mark my words.' Dear Uncle Terence, he has the same spirit.

Rollo takes no share of blame in his misfortune although it was he who introduced him to gambling on the Stock Exchange around the time when the first Sholtie Flyer died. 'I only did what your Uncle Terence wanted,' he said once to me.

Father is the puzzle. He adores Rollo. It's as if all his shrewdness evaporates when he's with him, almost as if he's under his spell, and Mother, of course, follows in his footsteps. I believe if he jumped off a cliff she would follow suit. I have no way of knowing what you think of him in the firm but I don't feel happy about his transactions here. No, that isn't strong enough. I'm filled with a dull kind of fear. This sounds unloyal to my husband, but my first loyalty is to my family.

Rumours are rampant here amongst women friends when they meet at swimming parties, childrens' parties, afternoon tea parties, at which the men are never present. Their wives pick up gleanings at the dinner table or from their staffs, and retail them to each other, because it isn't the first chauffeur who's said he is giving up his job to live on his money. I think they pick up tips when they're driving their owners about, and they say that some of the shoe-shine boys in Wall Street have given up business!

I've long since given up trying to get any information from Rollo. 'You've no complaints,' he says, and then he buys a new motor car or invites people for a weekend and tells me to spare no expense. Crates of champagne arrive. Delicacies from New York although we have a cook. Sometimes I wonder why someone like me has allowed herself to become a mere decorative adjunct, and then I realise it's because I haven't cared enough to be anything else, and I hate myself. And then there's the children. Always the children. It's like living in a dream world I've made for myself. I've barricaded myself from the real one. It's the only way for me to live. If I allowed myself to really *think*, I'd go mad.

I saw in Scotland how women came into their own during the War. I was one of them. It was a happy time, so happy, looking back, although my work in Lizzie's hospital couldn't be compared with those women who rushed into munitions factories or special people like Ellie. What went wrong, I wonder? When the War was over, were the men afraid of competition, or was it the old fear of the labour market being flooded? Or was it that everyone wanted it to be just the same as it had been and didn't realise one can never go back? It's an uneasy time. Sometimes I feel we're all holding our breath . . .

How solemn I'm becoming, not at all like 'our Ginny'! I remember visiting Magnus Muir, an old suitor of mine, at their 'family seat'—Jonty and I used to laugh at pompous expressions like that —and how skittish I was with the two brothers! And about Lady Muir's woollen drawers! That was a joke beween Jonty and me. I always felt the world was mine, and that ahead of me was a great, wonderful future.

But you've to make do with what you have. Ellie has taught me that. She and Kieran have made a wonderful success of their marriage. They are loved and respected everywhere. And perhaps Jonty is the greatest success of us all because he got his trials over early when he went off to the War, and then he met and married his one true love, Delia.

How I wish I could visit them in their house up the river from Sholton, Ferniegair. How Scottish that sounds! And see their little daughter, Maeve. Grandmother Maeve became Lady Crawford, this new little girl of Jonty and Delia's is Maeve Crawford. It's as if we have come full circle in the history of the McGrath family. And for many of us it is the end . . .

Am I going on too long? About cabbages and kings? It's as if you were sitting across this table from me, a bleached plank one, on my beach. The sun is shining, the seagulls are dipping over the water. And by writing I can see you and keep you and never let you go . . . I think of you so often, Iain. You are always in my heart.

I hope you'll be happy in time in that pleasant flat of yours and find solace in it, because it was there you made Beth happy.

With my love,
Ginny.

21

Iain sat in the board room of McGraths, listening to Ernest's eulogy. He didn't look sixty, any more than Maevy looked sixty-seven, but he could understand her wanting to be at home after working so long in the firm. 'I want to spend more time with my sisters,' she had said, 'while we have each other. Then there will be no regrets.'

Ernest, of course, wasn't retiring. His work with Globe Express Deliveries took him more and more to London, and he and Lizzie had a coterie of new friends there, now that they had acquired a flat in Mayfair. That would suit Lizzie fine, and she had said she wanted Annabel to get a taste of cosmopolitan life since she had elected to go to Glasgow University and not to a finishing school in Paris as she had planned . . .

'A new technology had to be mastered, and we had a good representative of the new breed in Iain Pearson, who has led the firm competently and confidently forward.

'But not only is he an excellent engineer, which we all knew, but he has proved to be a first-rate businessman. Through all his troubles, and he knows he has our deepest sympathy in his recent sad loss . . .' *Those great eyes in that white face, the trembling lips, 'Tell Ginny I tried to make you happy . . .'* he has never faltered, showing a constant dedication to his work, which, allied to his business acumen, has been responsible in no small way for our present success.

'Indeed, I would go further and say that had it not been for our steady financial position, thanks to Iain, we couldn't have weathered the storm when we discovered that Roland Van Dam had deprived the American branch of a vast sum of money, due to unwise speculation on Wall Street . . .' Feet moved under the table. Tempers were in check.

'The fact that he was using working capital to buy on the Exchange, so disastrously as it happened, might not have come to light so quickly had it not been for Patrick McGrath's illness. He confided in me when I made a quick trip over there, and I assured him that although the boat is rocky, we'll survive. The profits from the new young branch of the company, devoted to travel, have helped, thanks to Sam Murray-Hyslop and Ben Vogel.

'But I think you will all agree that it is necessary to prosecute. Embezzlement is a criminal offence, and we would be failing in our duty to our shareholders if we didn't recognise this. You can imagine how deeply this distresses the family, as Mr Van Dam is married to Patrick's daughter. I thought long and hard about all this before I reported the matter to our parent company, as you can well imagine. But to happier things . . .'

He had guessed there was something badly wrong from that letter Ginny had written, and had been glad that her father had told Ernest before he was obliged to do so himself. Such pity in his heart for her, as well as love! He thought of her on that beach she was so fond of, sitting alone, gazing at the sea. A girl like Ginny wasn't meant for sadness.

At night, when this love welled in him, he had had wild thoughts of writing and saying, 'Come away with your two children to Scotland. I'll take care of you,' but knew it was no use. There was that stubborn streak in all the McGraths. Always, during the course of our love, there have been difficult choices, he had thought.

He'd had his suspicions about Van Dam from the first day he had come into the Glasgow office, but had given him the benefit of the doubt more than once, because of Ginny . . . Ginny, he thought, sitting listening with one part of his mind to Ernest, will it come right one day for us, do you think?

'Iain's qualities emerged as his commercial responsibilities grew.' He paid attention to Ernest, smiling wryly at the praise. He had only done his job. 'His drive took us forward when most companies were falling by the wayside. And although he rapidly climbed the ladder, he never lost his most valuable asset, the common touch. He always enjoyed the confidence of the workers because he cared for them. Underneath that stern exterior,' Ernest smiled across the table at him, 'there is a tender heart. We saw that quality in his personal life as well, and we know how happy he made his wife, Beth, who suffered so long and so bravely . . .'

His eyes caught Jonty's and he saw the sympathy in them. He and Delia had often visited Beth and shown great kindness to her. The two women had been pregnant at the same time, and Delia's loving 'chivvying', in that pawky way of hers, had been worth a load of doleful sympathy which Beth was forced to bear after she lost the baby.

When he had gone to Ferniegair for dinner one night after her death, that rambling old house with the river nearby, and had seen that new scrap of humanity called Maeve, he had felt such a rush of love in himself, for everyone, for this young couple and their baby, for the McGraths, for Beth, for Ginny, for humanity. He knew his eyes had filled, and that Jonty had noticed. 'Things will turn out all right for you in time, Iain,' he had said. He hadn't meant *this* honour, but something far more . . . Ginny.

'And so,' Ernest was saying, 'it's with the greatest pleasure that I hereby propose that we appoint Iain Pearson as the new chairman of the McGrath Carting Company.'

He was glad of that applause when he got up to speak, not for what is signified, but that it had given him time to control himself.

'I thank you all from the bottom of my heart for the confidence you have shown in me. I hope it's not unjustified. Anyhow,' he said, smiling at Maevy, 'we'll see how the bools run . . .' There was laughter with the applause.

22

It was more than rumour, it was black, ugly fact. Yesterday she had left the children in the care of their nursemaid and gone to Wanapeake because of a letter she had received from Sarah.

'I think you should come and see Father. He is far from well. It might do him good to speak to you . . .' Rollo, she had thought. It's Rollo. He's killing my father now . . .

The little town had an air of apprehension, she thought, as the cab bore her from the station. The few shoppers seemed to have anxious faces. She imagined there was a silence hanging over it. The streets were quieter than usual.

'Big trouble up in the city,' the driver said to her as he drove up the hill towards Claremont. She was glad he didn't know her. 'All those get-rich-quick guys. Never dabble myself . . .' His face in the mirror was smug.

'You're wise,' she said.

Her mother met her at the door, and it was as if she betrayed all the apprehension of the city in her drawn features. She looked old and worn. Sarah wasn't there. She had been called out on an urgent case. One of her fallen women had tried to commit suicide, which didn't seem unreasonable. 'There will be more suicides if you ask me,' her mother said. Ginny missed the usual warmth in her embrace. 'Go on up first, Ginny,' she said, 'perhaps it'll cheer him up to see you. You were always his favourite.'

He was in bed, pale, drawn also. The Wall Street face, she thought, and wondered if she was becoming fanciful. 'Well, Father,' she said, kissing him, 'I'm sorry to see you laid up. I came as soon as I got Sarah's letter.'

'I'm ashamed,' he said. 'All the life's gone out of me. Dr Melvin says my heart's bad, but it's not that. It's the worry of it all.' His eyes were sunken as he looked at her. 'I don't feel I can go on.'

'That's not like you.' She knew she was being falsely cheerful, and decided at least to be honest. 'Is it to do with money, Father? The trouble in the city?' He sighed deeply and looked away from her.

'Father,' she said, 'I read the papers. I listen to the radio, I know there's trouble brewing on Wall Street. Rollo told me he was staying up in town tonight. I could see he was *distrait*, worried. He's been like that for some time . . .'

'It's too late. *He*'s too late to do anything now. Prices have been plummeting all day. God knows what tomorrow will bring.'

'It *is* Rollo behind your worries, isn't it? I've been torn for so long. Oh, Father, why did you ever listen to him?'

'*You* listened to him,' he said. 'You live out there on money which doesn't belong to him. I didn't say that to you!'

'Oh, don't!' She buried her head in her hands, feeling her heart contract with a sudden sharp pain. Truth hurts, she thought, truth hurts . . . 'I never knew what was going on, I swear. I know that isn't any excuse, but I was defeated long ago. I gave up trying to get him to discuss business, financial affairs. The rows were too bitter. They had to stop. I had to think of the children . . .' There was silence for a long time, and then she felt his hand on the back of her head.

'I shouldn't have said that. It was cruel of me. I encouraged you. I wanted to see you settled. Dry your eyes.'

She took her hands away, looked at him. 'I'm not crying. I got past that long ago. Father, I can't explain my attitude. I've been like ice inside. I couldn't allow myself to think.' *Except about Iain. You never banished him.*

'Don't blame yourself. You weren't involved. I saw the light too late. I shouldn't have trusted Rollo, but I did. It wasn't like me. I had to tell Ernest the truth when he was here.'

'But you *knew* Rollo was investing money for the firm, surely.'

'Yes, for some time. But I came to my senses after I'd had a letter from my brother in Ireland telling me the straits he was in. I told Rollo that our working capital was too far depleted, that it had to stop.'

'But it did, didn't it?' She looked at him, '*Didn't* it?'

'No. No, it didn't.' There was despair in his voice. 'Unbeknown to me he has been appropriating the firm's funds and gone on playing with it.'

She felt sick. 'You mean . . . *embezzling*?'

'Yes. I have to call it that. I don't think he sees it that way, give him his due. It took me a long time to realise that his judgement is faulty.'

'And Ernest knows?'

'Yes. I had to tell him of my suspicions, and he had the books checked right away. I know he's your husband, Ginny, but my loyalty to the firm comes first. Ernest understood that. You have to try and understand. It wasn't easy. But she too had voiced her suspicion to Iain. Where did one's priorities lie when it came to loyalty. Her father had been prepared to love Rollo, far less trust him.

'What will happen!'

'I don't know.' His voice was weary. 'It's in Ernest's hands. He'll take it to Globe Express. He's meticulous in matters of this kind. He plays by the book.'

'I can't believe what I'm hearing!' She heard her voice rise. 'I knew Rollo was unwise, but, *stealing*, that's what this is, *stealing* . . .'

'He'll have a different name for it. When I heard this morning of all those firms we had money in, going down one by one—Tel and Tel, General Electric, Westinghouse—those firms he continued to put money into, I felt . . . finished. As if my life, my useful life, was over.'

'Don't say that. Please.' She put her hand on his, 'Does Mother know?'

'She does now. It's the first time in all our life together that I've kept anything from her, and how I wish I hadn't. She has a shrewd mind. She wouldn't have been as blinded as I was. She loves this house. We've made it our home. It'll have to go.' He lay back on the pillow, his eyes closed in his sunken face. His hair seemed to have thinned and lay close to his skull, like that of an old man. Both her parents were old, she realised.

Rage burned in her against Rollo, a brief, burning rage to be immediately dowsed in shame. She had lived, was living in a house larger than Claremont, which ate money, in a deliberate kind of dream world because it was her only method of survival. She had felt it necessary to construct some kind of stable environment for Jonro and Suki, felt it necessary to make the best of a bad job with Rollo for their sake. She should have given up thinking of what might have been and tried instead to be a true wife to him.

She sat in despair, her eyes on her father's worn face. Where was that pompous but reliable man whom she had always admired but sometimes resented? How had he become such an easy dupe of Rollo's? But why hadn't she warned him of her suspicions, too? There had been an absence of trust, between herself and her father, between herself and Rollo. She was the greater culprit. Her father's love for her had made him reluctant to criticise her husband. She had had no love for Rollo for a long time but had kept quiet.

She was sitting in speechless misery when her mother opened the door. She came immediately to the bedside and stroked her husband's hand, and there was such love in the gesture that Ginny turned away. 'Come and have some lunch,' she said, 'We'll let him rest.'

In the hall her agitation was so great that she stopped, putting her hand on her mother's arm. 'I can just get the two o'clock train home if you'll have a cab called for me. I'm very worried. I feel so responsible for Father being ill.' She burst into tears, and Maria took her in her arms.

'No one is responsible, except your husband, but even he can't be blamed entirely. Patrick is an experienced businessman, he of all people should have known. Rollo charmed him, as he charmed you.'

'But you must have *seen*,' she said, sobbing. 'Why didn't you say?' When did *you* last ask for advice, she thought.

'I never thought he was right for you.' Her mother's voice was calm. 'But I've always followed your father in his decisions, always will, to the end.' She released Ginny, and her voice had the briskness of someone who had been given a new lease of life by misfortune. 'Come and have a bit of lunch with me and you can catch the next train. Your sister would be hurt if you didn't see her, and so should I if you dashed away. Our Ginny . . .' She smiled.

'Am I still?' She smiled, wiping her eyes, the tears flooding into them again, having to wipe again . . .

* * *

She slept fitfully that night, and from early morning she was up and dressed. She breakfasted with the children, shopped, but when she returned she went into the drawing-room with orders that she wasn't to be disturbed. She turned on the radio and sat down, determined to be calm.

There was panic on Wall Street without a doubt, although that was a word the announcer was careful not to use. Apparently there were all kinds of manoeuvres behind the closed doors of the great financiers—the announcer called them 'plans'. President Hoover was 'going to act'. Meanwhile, crowds of frightened investors and curious onlookers were gathering on Wall Street.

Where was Rollo in all this? He hadn't telephoned. Had *he* a plan to recoup the money he had stolen from McGraths? Or had he run out of plans? Where had he spent the night? Had he catnapped in the office? He had always been good at that. Here, sometimes, she would come down in the morning and find him asleep in this room. Papers would be strewn around him. He would gather them up, go upstairs and shower and shave and go off again, as fresh as paint.

Now the radio voice was saying that the crowd had grown to several hundreds, small investors demanding to know if their money was safe. There was a long line of distraught-looking people standing at the doors of the Bank of America . . .

'There is a hush, more dramatic than the clamour, as if this is the moment, the big moment. Police wagons have arrived and policemen are spilling out of them to take up positions at what they consider to be strategic points.' The voice quickened, drama was in the air . . .

'Here it is, like an army going into battle. Cots are being carried in for the thousands of workers in the brokerage houses who can't leave their posts, containers of coffee and food. Every hotel room in the vicinity is booked, perhaps to be relet.' There are always people ready to make a quick buck—the phrase came into Ginny's mind. It was one she had heard Rollo use. 'Ten o'clock. The fateful hour. Now the Stock Exchange is open.'

Macy, the parlour maid, came in with a tray on which was a coffee pot, cup and saucer and a plate of biscuits. 'You didn't eat a thing at breakfast, madam, Cook says. She's made your favourite cookies.'

'That's kind of her. Put it there, thank you.'

The woman placed the tray on a small table beside Ginny and then stood. 'It's buzzing with talk in the kitchen, madam.' Her eyes were bright in her swarthy face. 'The grocer boy's just been and he says that everybody's going mad in the city . . .'

'Thank you, Macy,' she said again. 'Will you tell Cook to make dinner late tonight? Nine o'clock.'

'Yes, madam.' She thought Macy sniffed before she went out. They always knew in the kitchen what was going on, and some of them might well have been playing the market. Maybe, the knife was in her heart again, they're worried about their jobs. Father had said Claremont would have to go. So might their house.

Now the reporters would have to telephone their news from the visitors' gallery. She couldn't bear to sit here waiting. She got up, leaving her coffee untouched, and went out into the garden. It looked grey and uninviting, like the day, but there were some dahlias flowering bravely in the beds, and the ocean was a broad strip of molten metal at the foot of the lawn. In the distance she could hear the voices of the children playing in the sand-pit, and nearer, the snip-snip of the gardener's clippers as he trimmed the laurels.

It was beautiful, certainly, in its broad spaciousness, its landscaping had cost a small fortune in itself; but it was soulless because there was no love between Rollo and herself. The only thing she would miss if they left would be the ocean, and that didn't belong to the house. It was the property of everyone. She turned and saw Macy coming towards her across the lawn, her cap ribbons flying, her apron fluttering like a flag. 'The telephone for you, madam!' She waved her arm. She looked cross at having to venture out in the cold.

'Thank you, Macy.' She ran past the woman, her heels sinking into the damp turf, impeding her, and up the stone steps into the hall. She lifted the receiver. 'Hello?' It would be Rollo. What state would he be in?

'Ginny?' The voice at the other end was a woman's. 'It's Marsha.' Marsha Phillips was her nearest neighbour. 'Were you listening to the radio?'

'No, I couldn't bear it.' Clyde, her husband, was in Morgans, and they dealt mostly in bonds. *They* would be all right.

'You missed a surprise! The market took up immediately the Exchange opened. Prices are firm! Trading is big and brisk, they say.' Big and brisk described Marsha Phillips, too. 'Isn't that marvellous?' Her voice was honeyed. 'I knew you would be anxious, dear.' How did she know that? Had she and Clyde talked about them, wondered where their money came from?

'Big and brisk?' She felt the lightness of her heart as the load lifted. 'Yes, it's wonderful! I should have stayed by the radio. Thanks for telephoning, Marsha. I might have missed it.'

She hung up and looked at her watch. Ten-twenty. She had just time to use the downstairs lavatory. Her insides were churning. She went, muttering to herself, 'What a relief, what a relief.' In less than five minutes she was back at her seat by the radio in time to hear the announcer's voice, puzzled, apologetic.

'After a brief flutter, the news is that the market has started to come down.' The old ache was back again, a heavy, dull soreness. It wasn't all right at all. She listened, rigid with fear, as he explained the difficulties, the general confusion, the difficulty of learning the exact details because of the slowness of the ticker. She had the impression that he was striving for impassivity, but losing.

'There is no doubt about it, after that brief period of hope, the market is collapsing.' She sat motionless in the big opulent room, feeling nothing as figures were quoted, percentages, and then the voice hit her senses again. 'Eleven o'clock and there are indubitable signs that panic has set in amongst the crowds on Wall Street and inside on the floor of the Exchange.'

She listened at one remove, it seemed, to a reporter's description of the sight which had met his eyes from the visitors' gallery. 'Floor brokers were being pinned against the trading counters by hysterical crowds.' 'Post Two seemed to be the epicentre.' 'If steel goes down it will carry everything else down with it . . .'

'It's like a scene out of Dante's inferno,' the announcer said, as if remembering his school books. 'A broker who has fainted has just been carried out. There are rumours about ruined men who have gone off their heads and jumped out of windows. It's pandemonium . . .'

She sat through it, numb, wondering if she would hear Rollo's name mentioned as yet another casualty; she lived and felt every minute of the scene until the visitors' gallery closed at half-past twelve and the reporters had left.

There had been one grain of hope, an announcement that there was to be a meeting in the offices of J. P. Morgan of the principal financiers and banks, to see what could be done. It was hoped that their concerted efforts might steady the market.

She had lunch with Jonro and Suki in the nursery, feeling marginally more cheerful. All was not lost. Perhaps Rollo might even recoup his losses and be able to repay McGraths and her father. Now you're thinking like him, she told herself. No amount of recouping would ever restore her father's health now, and it could well be too late as far as McGraths was concerned. Ernest, her father had said, played by the book. Prison. She said the word to herself, trying to imagine it—policemen arriving at the door, Rollo being taken away in a van.

'Could we go in the train with Nursie today, Momma?' Jonro asked.

She tried to look normal, even managing to smile at the girl. She too had a sick father whom she liked to visit. 'Are you sure they wouldn't be in the way, Myra?'

'No, madam, far from it. Pop loves to see them.'

'We love the train,' Suki said. She had hair like Rollo's, a glossy red-brown, and his bold good looks. 'More than Pop.'

'Hush, Suki. All right, but be sure and behave and do what Nursie tells you. And don't hang out of the train window.'

'They'll be safe with me, madam. It will give you some time to yourself. You'll want it today.' Of course they talked in the kitchen. Well, there would be no Nursies if the bottom fell out of the market and Rollo was incarcerated in Sing Sing. Her thoughts didn't make sense to her any more.

She was back in her seat beside the radio to hear the announcement: 'Mr Thomas Lamont, senior partner of Morgans, has made a reassuring statement followed by the Acting President's appearance on the floor.' He had gone straight to the post where steel was sold, and a multi-million dollar pool was being used to steady the market. Mr Richard Whitney—his name was said with bated breath, it seemed—was going from post to post spending it.

The market was saved, but not the fortunes, nor in some cases the lives of people who had rushed away in the middle of the panic and taken their own. Had Rollo been one of the lucky ones who had held back from selling too quickly? If he had, it would be a change for him. He must be the only person who hadn't recognised that he was devoid of any business acumen or flair.

At three o'clock she was still there, the radio turned on although she was hardly listening. It would be some time before the ticker would finish recording the day's gains and losses. Rollo would stay for that. She drank the now cold tea a silent Macy had left for her, unable to make a move, her mind full of the day's events.

It seemed the market had steadied, but the weight on her heart was heavier than ever. Reason told her Rollo wouldn't have come out well from the day's trading. There had been so many missed opportunities in the past, recriminations, wild attempts at recouping. It would be the same all over again, but much, much worse because this time he was using money which didn't belong to him . . . the Voice was there again.

'When the market closed, Mr Thomas Lamont of the House of Morgan led the Press upstairs to his private office and made the following statement: "There has been a little distress selling on the Stock Exchange . . . we have found that there are no houses in difficulty . . ."' There was no irony in the flat tones.

Laughter gathered in her throat, choking her. She put her hand to her mouth, wondering if she was hearing right. Surely that was one of the greatest understatements of all time. Abruptly she switched off the radio and stood up, feeling herself swaying on her feet.

She couldn't stand the house a moment longer. She went out of the room, picked up a coat in the hall and went outside. It was colder now and the wind had risen; not a day for sitting and watching the ocean, but she could walk.

The wind buffeted her as the news all day had buffeted her, the sea was angry as if it, too, was involved in the day's happenings, and occasionally a cloud of spume thrown up from the waves half-drenched her. She took a perverse pleasure in the cold and wetness. It suited her mood.

If Rollo was ruined, a least they had this place to sell—if it wasn't mortgaged to the hilt. Perhaps he could live with his mother in Wanapeake, and she could stay temporarily at Claremont with the children. Mrs Van Dam wouldn't want her, or them. She had never been subservient enough to the great lady of Wanapeake, nor good enough for 'her darling boy'.

Speculations were useless. She hunched her shoulders, stuck her hands deep in her pockets. She must wait until Rollo came home, and see what kind of state he was in. One look would tell her. And she mustn't think of Iain. She had to manage this thing on her own, and what would be the point of running away, to Scotland or anywhere ese? She told herself that she mustn't allow her anger at what Rollo had done to her father to make her vindictive. She was to blame, too, by her indifference.

She walked for a long time, her hair soaked by the rain, her skirts drenched, in a deep kind of misery. When she got back to the house there was no sign of Rollo or the children. Myra would be giving them tea at her house. She remembered that Rollo generally brought back the evening papers with him from the city. She changed quickly into dry clothes. She would drive down to the village and get them.

There was a queue of people at the drug store, some of whom she recognised—mostly servants in houses she was in the habit of visiting. Their curious looks made her realise she should have sent Robbins. She had to wait for half-an-hour before it was her turn. No one gave way to her. They were all equals now.

She couldn't wait until she got home. She stopped the car at the side of the road and quickly glanced through the paper. It had been impossible to avoid seeing the huge letters on the first page: WALL STREET CRASH! PANIC SUICIDE LEAPS! Inside she came across a less dramatic paragraph.

'Representatives of thirty-five of the largest wire houses in Wall Street issued a joint statement saying the market was fundamentally sound and technically in better condition than it had been for months. The worst is passed . . .' It didn't make sense. Well, she would soon know the worst, or the best.

She went straight upstairs when she got back and found the children being tucked up in bed by their nurse. She hugged them, thinking they were the only constants in a shaking world, listened to their excited decriptions of travelling on the train, then went downstairs to wait for Rollo.

23

It was after ten o'clock when he came into the room, pale, drawn, but his eyes were glittering. 'What a day!' He flung himself down on the sofa beside her. 'Have you listened in?'

'Yes,' she said, 'most of the day. Have you eaten?'

'No, just had a few drinks. I'm ravenous. Can you rustle me up something.'

'It's cold. I thought that would be better.'

'Anything. God, I'm tired!'

'You look it.' She touched his hand briefly, hesitantly. She thought she should have kissed him, but he hadn't made any move.

He stretched his legs in front of him, yawned loudly. 'I got no sleep last night, I can tell you. Let's go in, then. I told you I was famished.'

'I haven't eaten all day either. Rollo . . . ?' He pretended not to hear her. She followed him when he got up.

When she had given him a generous helping of smoked ham and salad, she said, 'How did it go? I've been worried sick.'

'You surprise me.' He waved his fork at her. He was wolfing his food. '*I* do the worrying in this house.'

'Don't be ridiculous, Rollo. There's panic! I haven't left the wireless all day.'

'I'm tired,' he said, 'can't you see I'm whacked? Leave it. What did you do yesterday?'

She looked at him. His head was down, he was pushing food into his mouth. 'I went to see Father. He's very ill. I didn't realise how ill he was.'

'Pass the decanter, honey.' He had gulped his first glass of wine in a matter of seconds. 'Your father's a worrier, always has been. That's his trouble. You have to take risks in the money game. I'll tell the world!' He waved his fork again.

'Not with other people's money!'

He stopped drinking, put down his glass. 'And what does that little wifely remark mean, may I ask?'

'Just that he told me everything!' She was suddenly furious. 'That you have helped yourself to some of the firm's money when it was stopped officially. He's ill with a heart condition as a result! I tell you, if you've lost that too, it will be the last straw for him.'

'You're going to blame me. Is that it? Let me tell *you*, you and your precious father just don't understand the money market. It's not what you think. You can't tell immediately, it's a chain . . .' She interrupted him.

'Some people can, judging by the suicides there have been today!'

'Ah!' He nodded, giving her a gleaming glance. 'Now we come to the nub of it. You want me to leap out of the top floor, is that it? Just to satisfy your guilt about your father, your concern about the McGraths? I seem to remember you telling me once about how your family never really understood you.'

She was ashamed, muttered, 'That was a long time ago. When we were first . . .' Her anger was punctured.

'I mean . . .' He pushed back his empty plate, white-faced. 'How would *you* feel? I get back home after a terrible two days up there, not knowing where to turn, and you tell me you're worried about your father! Not your husband, oh, dear me no!' He leaned back. 'Any dessert?'

She wasn't going to weep. She'd done enough of that. She cut a slice of apple pie, poured some cream over it. 'That's cold too, I'm sorry.' He shrugged, took it, not meeting her eyes. 'I'm worried,' she said, 'whether you believe it or not, about how you have been affected by today's happenings on Wall Street. Who wouldn't be? And I'm worried about my father and McGraths because I'm part of them too. I'm waiting for you to tell me.'

'Honestly, honey,' his eyes slid away from hers, 'I've told you before. You wouldn't understand . . .' His voice trailed away. The silence seemed to fill the room. She looked at his downbeat head. This was the Rollo who had charmed her a long time ago in Scotland, Mrs Van Dam's spoiled boy.

She said gently, 'I would if you told me. I'm not stupid. I've listened all day to the radio, I've understood what they're telling us, that thousands of people have lost everything, that now the financiers have put money in to try and hold it together, but too late for many. If I couldn't understand that I could sense the atmosphere even in this house. Marsha Phillips phoned me this morning to tell me it was going to be all right. That wasn't entirely altruistic. She was rather premature, as it happened. And you could cut the atmosphere in the kitchen with a knife. Macy stares at me when she comes in. I bet she's lost money.'

'They're spies,' he said, lifting his glass, waving the other arm in an extreme gesture—how well she knew this red-herring tactic —'spies, the whole bloody lot of them! Bite the hand that feeds them. That bloody chauffeur listens to me talking to other brokers. It isn't my fault if they've lost out.'

'The point is, have you?'

'There you go.' He pettishly pushed the plate away from him. 'Can't bear it cold. You take everything that's going, motor cars, run-abouts, servants, nursemaids, the lot, but you never give me credit for providing it, for anything in my work . . .'

'Because you left me out, Rollo. The only indicator I have now is my father and he's nearer death than life at this moment.' That was stupid, stupid, she thought, wincing as he banged the table with his fist.

'Oh, to hell with your bloody father! People like him want all the rewards but don't take any of the risks. He's not been born into the business world. You once told me what he was, a miner, or something . . . it's *all* about taking risks.' It was farcical now. Didn't miners take risks every day of their lives? 'I've spent most of my working life doing just that, mostly for other people, and then when I sweat blood trying to get them out of trouble when the market collapses, they say it's *their* money I'm using.'

'Well, isn't it?'

'It doesn't work like that!' He stared at her as he lifted the decanter and splashed some wine into his glass. She saw the red stain spread over the white damask. Would they be able to afford the laundry bill? 'There are tips, feelers, calculations, speculations. There are right times and wrong times. It's like having antennae. You buy when it's low. I've done that. That's why I was so late tonight, hanging on until the ticker had finished. I'm waiting for Jones to telephone me.' He looked at his watch. 'Any minute.'

She felt utter weariness. 'Would you like some fruit salad instead of the pie?'

'No, thanks. Made a bit of a pig of myself with the first course.' There was a glimmer of the charming spoiled boy. 'I've been on a liquid diet for the past two days. Only way to keep going . . .' The telephone bell rang loudly in the hall. He got up unsteadily and made for the door, bumping into Robbins who was opening it.

'For you, sir.'

'Bring it in here.' And when Robbins appeared with the apparatus and plugged it in, 'That will do. Shut the door behind you.' He spoke brusquely. The slight slam was out of character for Robbins. Was he ruined too?

He sat down heavily beside the telephone. 'Hello, Jones!' His voice was flamboyant. 'Got it straight now, eh? Shoot!' Silence. She watched his face, the lines round his mouth sag, the colour drain out of it, leaving it yellow because of his tan. The silence lengthened. He was making sounds and then the words burst from him, 'My God!' Then a slow, punctuated whisper, 'Oh . . . my . . . God . . .' He hung up. He put his elbows on the table and his head in his hands. She heard his sobs, a noisy, nasal kind of weeping, like a small boy who hadn't a handkerchief.

She got up, went to him and put her arm round his shoulders. 'Come upstairs, Rollo. They'll be in soon to clear . . . the servants.'

'Bugger the servants.' He moved his head.

'Come on. I'll help you.' She got him to stand, guided him out of the room as though he were blind, and helped him slowly upstairs, his arm around her now, still weeping. 'Don't worry.' Silly thing to say. She gave him a handkerchief. She heard the baize door to the kitchen swing. Robbins would be watching.

She got him to lie down on the bed and took off his shoes. 'Tell me what Jones said.' She covered him with the quilt. 'It'll help, I promise you.'

'Nothing will help.' He shook his head pettishly and turned away from her.

'We can make plans, decide about going into a smaller house, perhaps move back to Wanapeake. This place would fetch the earth if we sold it. Think what we've spent on it.'

He rolled round and looked at her. His eyes were wide and tearless now. 'You don't understand, do you? You've never understood how much this place means to me, our position, how we *look* to people. From the start you haven't been interested, God knows why. There's something there I can't get to the bottom of. If you had been having affairs I would have understood. You were always attractive to other men, I've watched you, but I can tell you here and now, you've been useless to me, for a long time.'

She stood looking down at him. There was no anger in her, just a sense of failure. He was right, of course. She had never been a good wife to him, not even good in bed. She could no longer remember whether that was before or after she knew he was having affairs. Her mistake had been in believing that you could make the best out of second best. Ellie had done it, but Ellie had had a career to bolster her up, and in any case, she was special.

'I'm sorry I failed you,' she said. 'So sorry.'

She went out of the room and into the nursery. The children were sleeping deeply. He should have added them to her list.

They *looked* good, completed a good-looking family in their gracious home on Long Island.

Their room was lit by a moon which she could see breaking through wild-looking clouds. Their dark bulk was edged with silver. She bent over each child in turn and lightly kissed them on the forehead. Jonro rolled over pettishly, a small Rollo in the gesture. Did they *both* resemble him? One of Suki's plaits stuck out from her head in a comical fashion.

She sat in the room for a long time wondering what to do. Should she make up a bed in the spare room and leave Rollo as he was? The marriage was over, had been for a long time. They were bad for each other, she was the wrong kind of person for him, as he was for her, but the children were an amalgam of them both.

He was an embezzler. He would be prosecuted. 'Ernest plays by the book,' her father had said. But she couldn't walk out on him. Perhaps he would be glad of her support even if she couldn't give him her love. And when his affairs were straightened out they might come to some agreement. She kept Iain out of her mind. Marsha Phillips was on her second marriage. 'You know what to avoid,' she had said, 'The first time you haven't the experience.' But *she* had known what she was doing. She wouldn't even think of the future. There was the present to deal with first.

She got up, feeling the load slip away from her. Loads were always the result of indecision. The broad landing was also flooded by moonlight from the tall window looking over the grounds at the back—the lawns, the flowerbeds, the walled garden, the orchard where the children's pony grazed. It looked too contrived, but it *looked* good. She would tell him that she would stand by him, support him in every way, fit into the pattern, at least. She owed him that.

Her hand was on their bedroom door when she heard the shot. It gonged in her ears, and she stood for a moment, petrified by the clamour in her head, before she made herself push it open and go in. The same moon was lighting the room.

Rollo was sprawled on his back, one arm flung over the side of the bed, a gun was lying black on the white fur rug where it had dropped. His legs were apart. She saw the stockinged feet, incongruous . . .

When she was propelled towards him, slowly, reluctantly, as if there was a hand on her back, and her eyes had travelled towards his face, she found that it simply didn't exist. It was a bumpy mess of blood. It had been blown to pieces. He must have put the gun in his mouth. There was no Rollo to say, 'Oh, Rollo!'

to. Her legs gave way and she found herself kneeling at the bedside, dealing with a compulsion to retch, to relieve her stomach somehow of the awful sickness. The peach satin quilt was black with blood. The feathers would be red . . .

She heard the voices, the rushing footsteps on the stairs. The voices became louder, and when she turned she saw Robbins and Macy in the doorway. The butler looked like a ghost. The shriek which came from Macy's mouth should have been hers.

24

They were all there, the McGrath family. There had been many gatherings of them over the years, from the time of Maeve and Kieran McGrath in the last century—weddings and funerals and christenings, the ebb and flow of life and death—but there had never before been one at a race course.

Terence's little filly, the Sholtie Flyer Mark Two, was now a sleek, fleet, roan-coloured three-year-old, who had distinguished herself in three countries and become a horse to be watched. Here at Chantilly, in the Île de France, she was entered for the Prix de Diane Stakes, which had first been run in 1843, eight years before Maeve and Kieren McGrath were married.

Indeed, Terence saw in his filly a strong resemblance to his mother: a great heart combined with an airiness of spirit and an elegance which particularly suited the French course; but whereas Paddy, her lad and jockey, loved her like a woman, more than he would ever love a woman, Terence's love was fatherly and proud, that of the Grand Caliph of the stables.

The invitations were sent out well in advance: Giselle and young Terence, her parents, Emily and Charles Barthe, even their two elusive sons, Marc and Olivier, who were ardent race-goers and recognised in the Sholtie Flyer, when they saw her in the enclosure, that certain something which denotes a winner.

Lizzie, Ernest, Jonty and Delia were there from Scotland. Annabel couldn't come as she was writing a thesis, and the three aunts had demurred gracefully. Their travelling days were over, they said. They would listen in on their newest toy, their bakelite wireless with its gold mesh inset and important knobs. Isobel was the champion twiddler.

Honor was there from Ireland with Terence, of course, and her three girls and their husbands. 'And whyever would we not?' Clare had said, 'and see that little Sholtie Flyer flying up to the winning post like a piece of thistledown over a bog!' Which wasn't very complimentary to Chantilly, that capital city of horses.

From America had come Edie and Robert, Ellie and Kieran.

Patrick had died a month after Rollo had shot himself, and Maria was too frail to travel. She was now living with Edie and Robert in her own old home, Springhill. Sarah, also had refused politely. She had set up home with her Fallen Women in an old house they were refurbishing on Wanapeake Point, and she felt she could not leave them, or her mother.

And Ginny. She was now installed in a small house in Wanapeake which her mother had bought for her. When she had demurred Maria had said that Claremont had fetched a good price, and she had to provide somewhere for Sarah when she gave up her good works. It would be there for her own use too if Edie and Robert grew tired of her, but meantime living at Springhill was bringing peace to her soul. She could sit on the lawn running down to the river and dream the days away . . .

A strange thing had happened to Ginny after she had found Rollo dead. There were nightmares, of course, when she saw and re-saw the mess which had once been his fair face, the chestnut hair dark with blood, but in the day-time her old self had reasserted itself.

She set about selling the long white house on the Ocean, getting rid of the servants, and going into Rollo's business affairs with all the acumen she had used to make the Hydro a success. There was very little left when it was all done—nothing but a refund for Jonro's first term at an expensive preparatory school on Long Island.

She would have had nowhere to go if her mother hadn't come to her rescue, and nothing to live on if Ellie hadn't found her a part-time job in the hospital where she worked. That way she kept her pride. McGraths had offered her an annuity, but she had refused it; Rollo had done enough damage there. She still knew she had no vocation like Ellie in dealing with the sick, but her mind and fingers were quick and efficient. She didn't disgrace herself.

The death of her father, coming on top of Rollo's, was a bitter blow, but it had given her the benison of a small legacy. Her ticket to France had come as a gift from Ernest. 'Since you won't let the firm help you, please accept this at least. Everybody wants you to be there. Don't disappoint them.' Everybody . . . ?

After that, the nightmares changed to dreaming of Iain. He had written regularly to her since Rollo's death, letters which revealed a new Iain, full of hope for the future. The last one came the week before she set off with the others in the liner from New York. 'I'm counting the days until I see you at Chantilly. The waiting's over . . .'

Terence was the lucky one, sure enough. The day of the Prix de Diane was perfect, warm and sunny. A handsome private coach, courtesy of McGraths, picked them up from their various hotels, and they were off, laughing and chattering, past the old Church of St Paul, past the Gare du Nord, along the rue La Chapelle, and past the church where Joan of Arc had spent the night before the great battle.

'St Denis,' Iain said, sitting beside her as naturally as she had ever imagined, 'all the kings of France were buried there.'

'You look so different, Iain.'

'So do you.'

'How different?'

'More beautiful, thinner, your eyes are bluer because there are dark shadows under them. I love you.'

'It's too soon to say that.'

'I've never stopped thinking it.'

The road was busy and the whole world was going to the races. Four people passed in an open tourer, the men holding on to their top hats, the ladies having had the sense to tie on their flowered confections with chiffon scarves. They were able to wave up gaily to the people in the coach, and the whole McGrath family waved back.

'Everybody's going to the races,' Ginny said.

'All the world and the McGrath family. I'm the only outsider.'

'But you had to be here. You're the Chairman. Ernest told me you organised everything, even the picnic baskets.' She turned her head, and it seemed all the McGraths were looking at her and Iain and smiling. They didn't think of him as an outsider.

'Hello, Lizzie!' She waved, overcome with happiness. 'Aunt Honor, hello!' And surely the blond head was that of Aidan O'Brien, Clare's husband. How handsome he was in that top hat tipped sideways on his fair hair. Rollo would have been handsome too, the dashing Rollo Van Dam. It was strange they had never gone to the races together. The atmosphere would have suited him. Perhaps he preferred to lose his money—and other people's—on the Stock Exchange.

'Was it terrible for you, the last days with Beth?' She turned back to Iain.

'Sad, not terrible. She was smiling when she died, although that might have been something to do with the shape of her mouth. She always seemed to smile, even when she was in pain.' *The snarling smile Ellie had told her about . . .* 'But not as sad as Rollo's end. You found him . . . shot?'

'Yes. He had no face.' She felt his hand go over hers. Neither had Gaylord after that other shooting. The coincidence only now struck her. Kieran must have told her, or Ellie, and it had stayed in her subconscious. 'It was no worse than the War, I suppose.' Jonty had had his nightmares too, she remembered. He had told her about them, and how he had got peace eventually by imagining his friend alive. She must think of Rollo in the same way, at the balls they had gone to together, dining in the Waldorf or the Plaza, his charm, his gaiety. He had been a performer. He liked to believe that people were thinking how handsome he was, how insouciant. They probably were. At home with no audience but her he had been different, especially during the last month before the Crash. She remembered him with his head in his hands, and she shuddered, leaning close to Iain.

'This is a happy day, a McGrath day,' he was saying. 'Look, we're in the country now, the Île de France, so French.'

'I didn't know you knew France.'

'There's a lot you don't know. He laughed out loud and she saw how handsome *he* was now that the pall of sadness had been lifted from him. There were laughter lines at the side of his eyes and round his mouth, his hair grew thick and peaked on his brow, the hands clasping his top hat were well shaped.

'I'm glad you have well-shaped hands,' she said.

'You should see my feet.' He grinned at her, and they both burst into laughter. Uncle Terence's rich voice came from the back.

'Share your joke wit' us, Ginny! We're all sitting here shaking in our shoes for that little horse of mine.'

She turned and smiled at him, at everybody who came within her range. 'We're just laughing because it's such a happy day. And your little horse is going to win. Sure enough!'

Aunt Honor, wrapped like a mummy in diaphanous Isadora Duncan chiffon, was easily identified by her dark Irish eyes and her brogue. 'Sure and he wouldn't have dragged us all this way if he didn't know the little lass was going to be up there at the front.'

Giselle and Terence were sitting quietly, close together, locked in their shared secret. They smiled when she waved. They looked happy. It must be a good time for him. And he had painted the original Sholtie Flyer, she remembered. How time passed. She remembered sitting with her uncle watching him, and then that nightmare drive to fetch the vet. But what about Paddy's and Uncle Terence's feelings on that awful day? Everybody had their nightmares. That was the truth of it.

They sat on the grass with the long, low, gracious building of the *Grandes Écuries* behind them, 'putting Woodlea in the shade',

Uncle Terence said, and ate smoked salmon, and duck with orange, and salad and patisseries, washed down with never-ending bottles of champagne. There were tables, of course, but Aunt Honor said it wasn't a 'right' picnic if you didn't sit on the grass, and to the devil with all those fine folk.

On the other side of the course they could see people milling about and having a good time and probably a better view of the mounted *Garde républicaine* trotting along, but the fanfare for the opening stirred everyone, especially the picnic party. They rose and strolled in couples to see the star performer, the Sholtie Flyer Mark Two, ready to go. She was smiling and prancing on her little feet and generally enjoying herself, but Paddy was a shivering wreck.

'That's good, boyo,' Uncle Terence said, whacking him on the back, 'sweat it all out of your system before you go. It will make you all the lighter!'

Ginny and Iain wandered about, saying wise things to each other about form, quoting from the card, *'Plutôt petite, mais assez bien faite,'* and *'précoce'*, and a *'bon stayer'*. Iain, she thought, was a cheerful and competent host, speaking to everyone, making sure they had everything they needed. He wore his top hat at an angle and he complimented the ladies on their outfits, and although they said they didn't believe a word of it, Ginny could see that they all liked it, especially Edie who, in strong silent Robert McGrath, hadn't a husband who went in for extravagant praise.

When the start of the race drew near, all the ladies went to make themselves comfortable while the men put on the bets and no doubt did the same thing. It gave Ginny the opportunity to speak to Lizzie, still beautiful in a white outfit with a zebra-striped hat and umbrella, and Delia of the corn-coloured hair and the humorous face, and the Irish girls who showed more of their knees than their faces, hidden under huge flower- and fruit-laden hats. Aunt Honor had trimmed them from her 'odd-bag', they said. Clare, in vivid Irish green and high tottering heels, was already wailing, 'My feet are killing me and us hardly started!'

Her mother proved her originality, and her oddity, by parting her diaphanous skirts and revealing two strong bare feet encased in thonged sandals. 'I've never liked me toes to be pinched,' she said, letting the skirts fall again like a theatre curtain.

And now they were in their seats again for the *Défilé de la Présentation des Pouliches*, and the Sholtie Flyer was dancing round in little circles and showing off like mad and smiling at the crowd, and Paddy was crouched over her like a little old man, looking neither to right or to left. Ginny saw Uncle Terence take off his top hat, wipe his forehead and put back the hat again, tilted backwards, the better to see, no doubt. Aunt Honor would have hold of his hand, she felt sure. Iain was certainly holding hers, naturally, lovingly, as if they had never been parted, as if they had never had to wait, as if they would never be parted again.

'Did you put it on for a place, or to win?' she asked.

'To win, of course.' He turned and they smiled at each other with their eyes.

'Isn't it lovely here, Iain, the most beautiful place on earth? Those beautiful stables, and the white tents, pavilions, and the green grass and the bright colours of the hats . . .'

'And the châteaux in the distance.'

'Little *and* big.'

'We'll come here and see them another time.'

'The food was lovely. Did you plan it?'

'No, Delia did. She drives down to the Hydro quite a lot from Ferniegair and helps Lizzie. They get on fine together.'

She felt a wistful envy. 'I miss that part of my life, like another world. Scotland, and the Hydro, and the family, Ernest and Lizzie, Jonty, Annabel and Kit, the three aunts . . .'

'You can have them back whenever you're ready.' He turned to her that new smiling face which had been there all the time behind the sadness. 'Whenever you're ready . . .' his voice was drowned by a great roar from the crowd: 'They're off!' He handed her his glasses.

There she was, running third already, head up, enjoying herself, Paddy crouched on her back like a leprechaun in his green coat and striped cap. Ginny lowerd her glasses for a second, overcome, then raised them again.

God in heaven! Now she was at the front, fairly pounding along —no, that was the wrong word, the stream of horses looked as if they had wheels under them . . . She said, glasses to her eyes, 'Iain, I hardly dare . . .'

'I know. Only twenty-one hundred metres, so quick, a flash of colour . . .'

'She's slipping back . . .'

'No, she's holding. She's teasing Paddy . . .' He was babbling. 'I'm like a boy let out of school, a man out of prison, she's holding, holding, the wee devil! Look at her . . . my tongue's been clogged . . . for ages . . . clogged with the things I've wanted to say . . . The release, God, the release of it . . . !' Luckily the French people around didn't understand, and the McGraths were too busy minding their own business.

The roar went up all round them, hardly human in sound, like the heavens cracking open, like a river bursting its banks. She was being crushed in his arms, glasses between them, she felt the closeness, the warmth of his body through her thin dress . . .

She heard the excited voices, the congratulations—'What did I tell you', 'My heart was in my mouth'—the laughter. Irish and Scottish and American voices, all the McGraths in a fantastic medley. If she married Iain, that would make him one too, in a kind of a way. That would make it complete.